MONKEY KING

Vol.
08

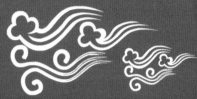

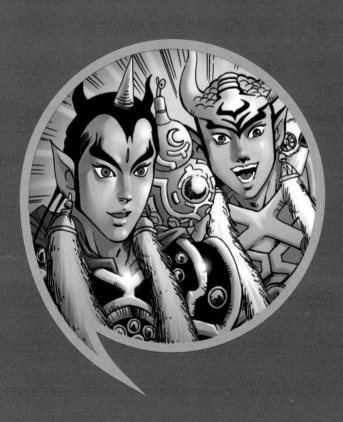

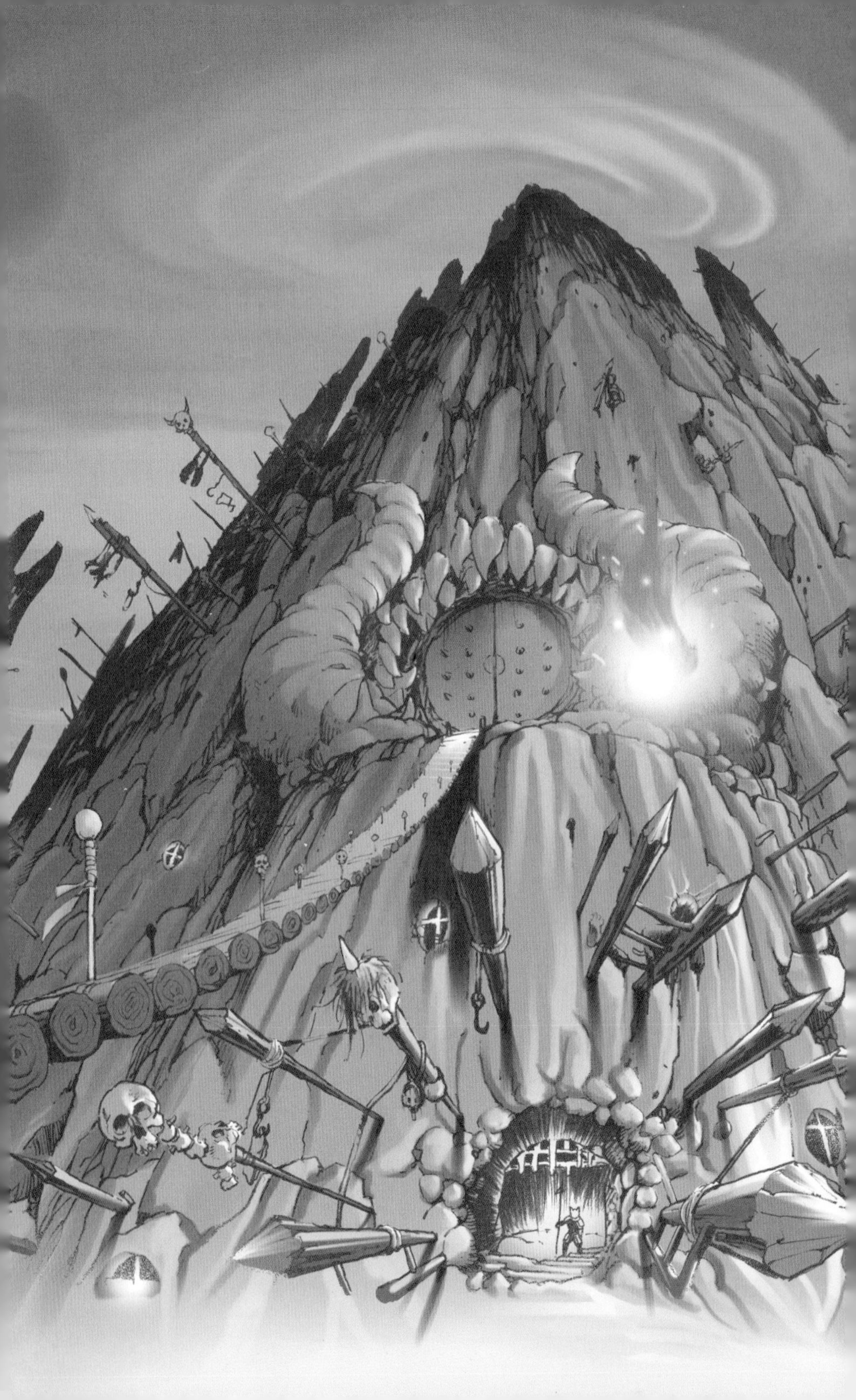

Treasures of the Mountain Kings

Created by WEI DONG CHEN

Wei Dong Chen, a highly acclaimed and beloved artist, and an influential leader in the "New Chinese Cartoon" trend, is the founder of Creator World in Tianjin, the largest comics studio in China. Recently the Chinese government entrusted him with the role of general manager of the Beijing Book Fair, and his reputation as a pillar of Chinese comics has brought him many students. He has published more than three hundred cartoons, which have been recognized for their strong literary value not only in Korea, but in Europe and Japan as well. Free spirited and energetic, Wei Dong Chen's positivist philosophy is reflected in the wisdom of his work. He is published serially in numerous publications while continuing to conceive projects that explore new dimensions of the form.

Illustrated by CHAO PENG

Chao Peng is considered one of Wei Dong Chen's greatest students, and is the director of cartoon at Creator World in Tianjin. One of the most highly regarded cartoonists in China today, Chao Peng's fantastic technique and expression of Chinese culture have won him the acclaim of cartoon lovers throughout China. His other works include "My Pet" and "Searching for the World of Self".

Original story
"The Journey to The West" by Wu, Cheng En

Editing & Designing
Sun Media, Design Hongs, David Teez, Jonathan Evans, YK Kim, HJ Lee, SH Lee, Qing Shao, Xiao Nan Li, Ke Hu

Characters

Volume 08

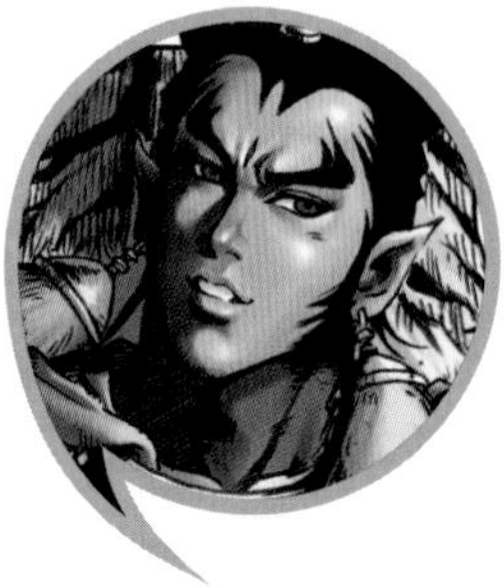

THE GOLDEN HORNED KING

The Golden Horned King was once the guardian of Tai Shang's golden furnace who became the ruler of Mount PingDing with his brother. He and his brother hatch a plan to capture San Zang, whose flesh they've been told will grant eternal life if eaten. The Golden Horned King wields a powerful sword that can create fire, as well as one of his kingdom's five precious treasures, a palm leaf that can fan the flames.

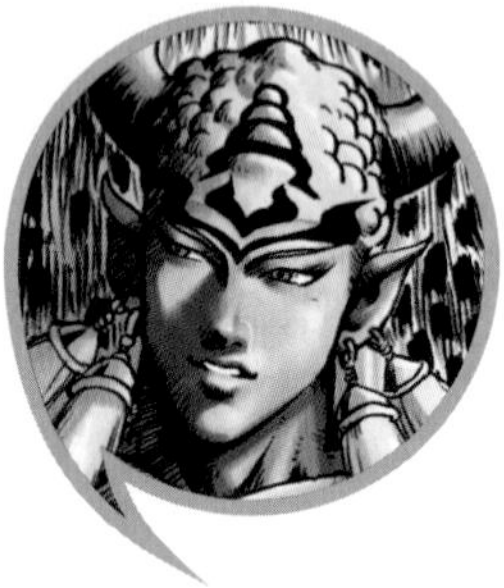

THE SILVER HORNED KING

Like his brother, the Silver Horned King was once the guardian of one of Tai Shang's heavenly furnaces. When he learns that San Zang is close to his kingdom, the silver king sets out with several soldiers to capture the monk. The Silver Horned King also wields one of the five precious treasures of the kingdom, the Seven-Star Sword, which is powerful enough to cut a mountain in half.

THE GUARDIAN OF DAYS

The Guardian of Days is one of four heavenly time keepers. In Journey to the West, the Guardian of days disguises himself as a person to warn San Zang and his disciples that they are about to enter into the kingdom of two monsters who are more powerful than any they have encountered so far. Sun Wu Kong sees through the deity's disguise, but heeds the warning nonetheless.

JINGXI AND LINGLI

JingXi and LingLi are two subjects of the horned kings who are dispatched to recover Sun Wu Kong from beneath the mountain under which he is buried. They are armed with two very powerful enchanted treasures: a pair of calabashes that can capture and melt a person who responds to his name being called. Neither JingXi nor LingLi realize that Wu Kong has been freed from beneath the mountain, and when they encounter Wu Kong, disguised as a Taoist guru, the monkey tricks them into trading their calabashes for the fake one he is carrying.

Characters

Volume 08

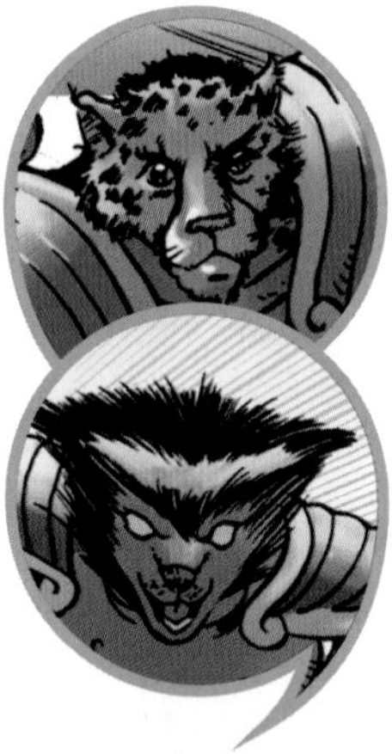

BASHAN AND YIHAI

BaShan and YiHai, two guards of Mount PingDing in the service of the gold and silver kings, are dispatched by the brothers to retrieve their mother, who has been invited to a special feast of pig's ears and monk flesh. As they depart on their mission, the pair are approached by Sun Wu Kong, disguised as another guard. Wu Kong defeats BaShan and YiHai to get to the kings' mother.

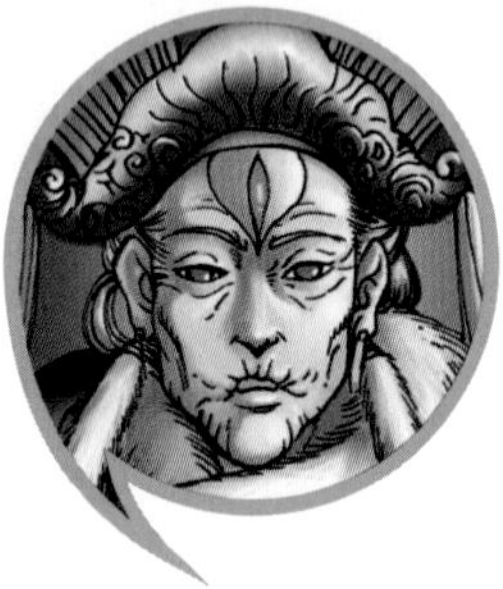

THE NINE-TAILED FOX GOBLIN

The Nine-Tailed Fox Goblin is the monster identity of the old woman who the brother kings call her their mother. She possesses the fifth and final enchanted weapon of the kingdom, a golden rope that can tie up any living creature or deity, even Sun Wu Kong.

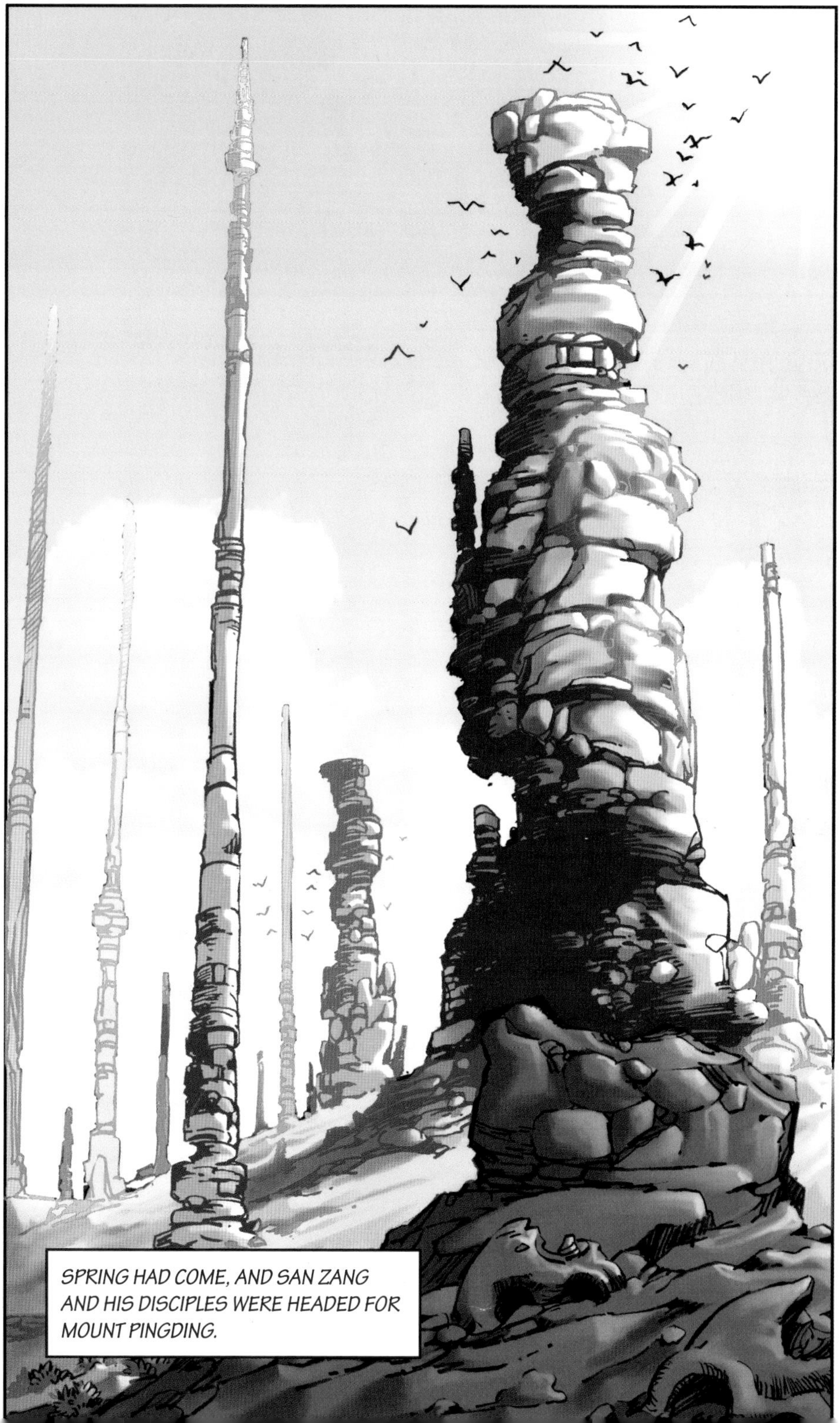
SPRING HAD COME, AND SAN ZANG AND HIS DISCIPLES WERE HEADED FOR MOUNT PINGDING.

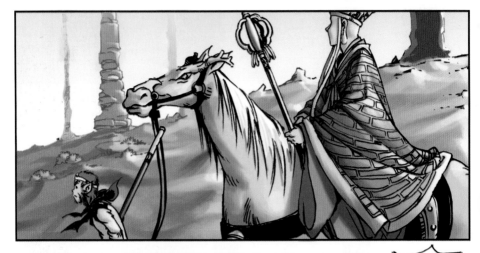

All right! I know you're hiding there. Show yourself!

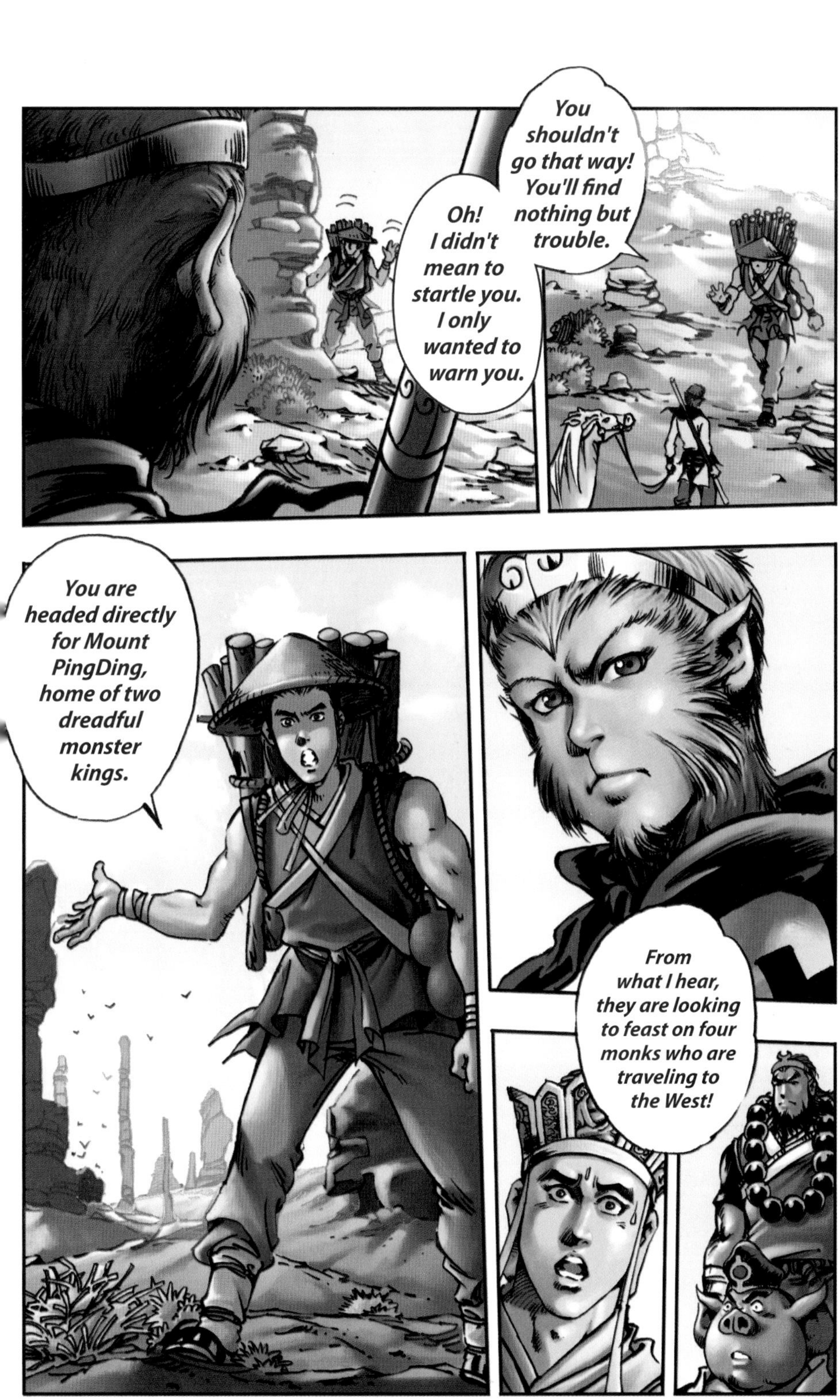
You shouldn't go that way! You'll find nothing but trouble.
Oh! I didn't mean to startle you. I only wanted to warn you.
You are headed directly for Mount PingDing, home of two dreadful monster kings.
From what I hear, they are looking to feast on four monks who are traveling to the West!

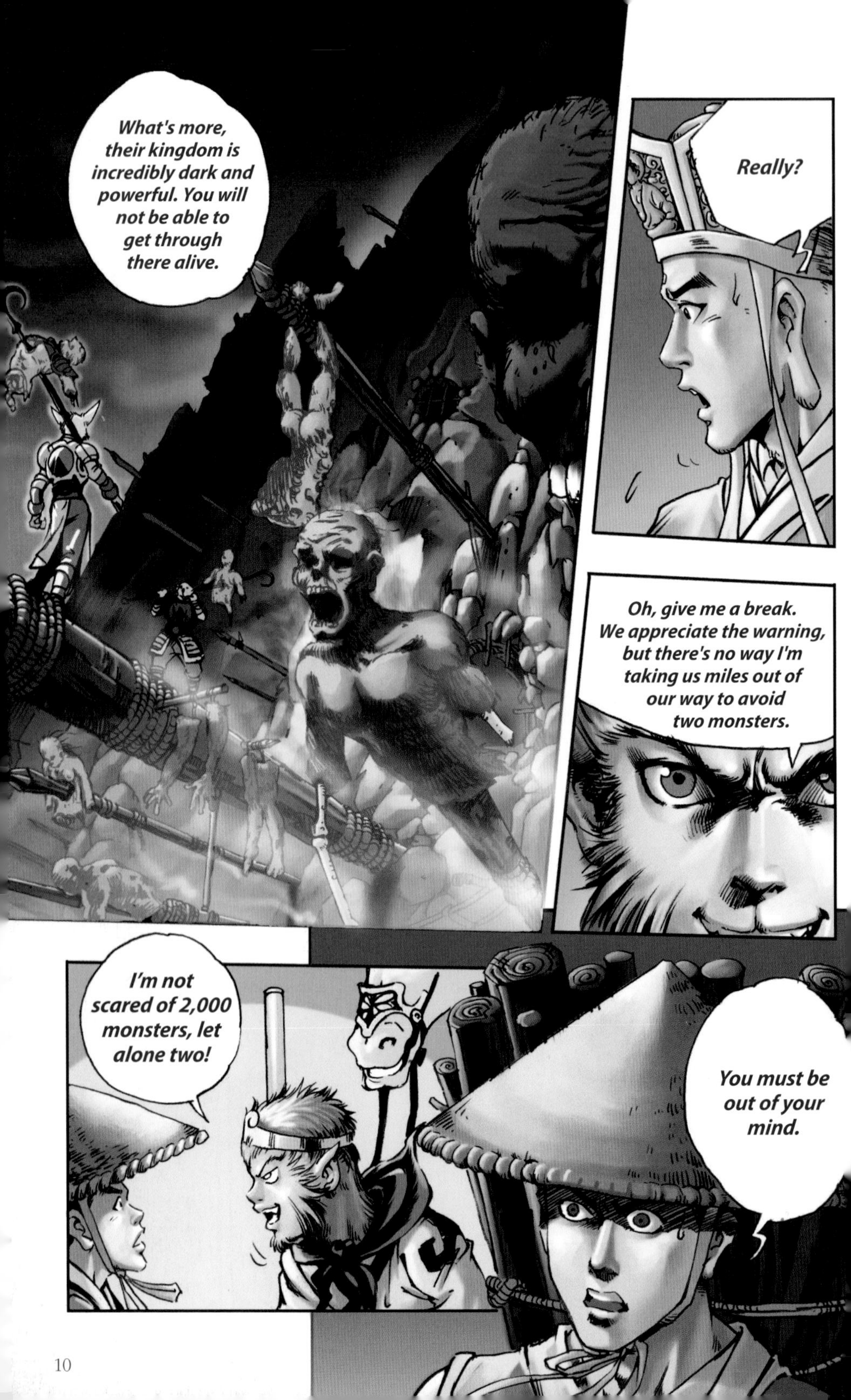
What's more, their kingdom is incredibly dark and powerful. You will not be able to get through there alive.
Really?
Oh, give me a break. We appreciate the warning, but there's no way I'm taking us miles out of our way to avoid two monsters.
I'm not scared of 2,000 monsters, let alone two!
You must be out of your mind.

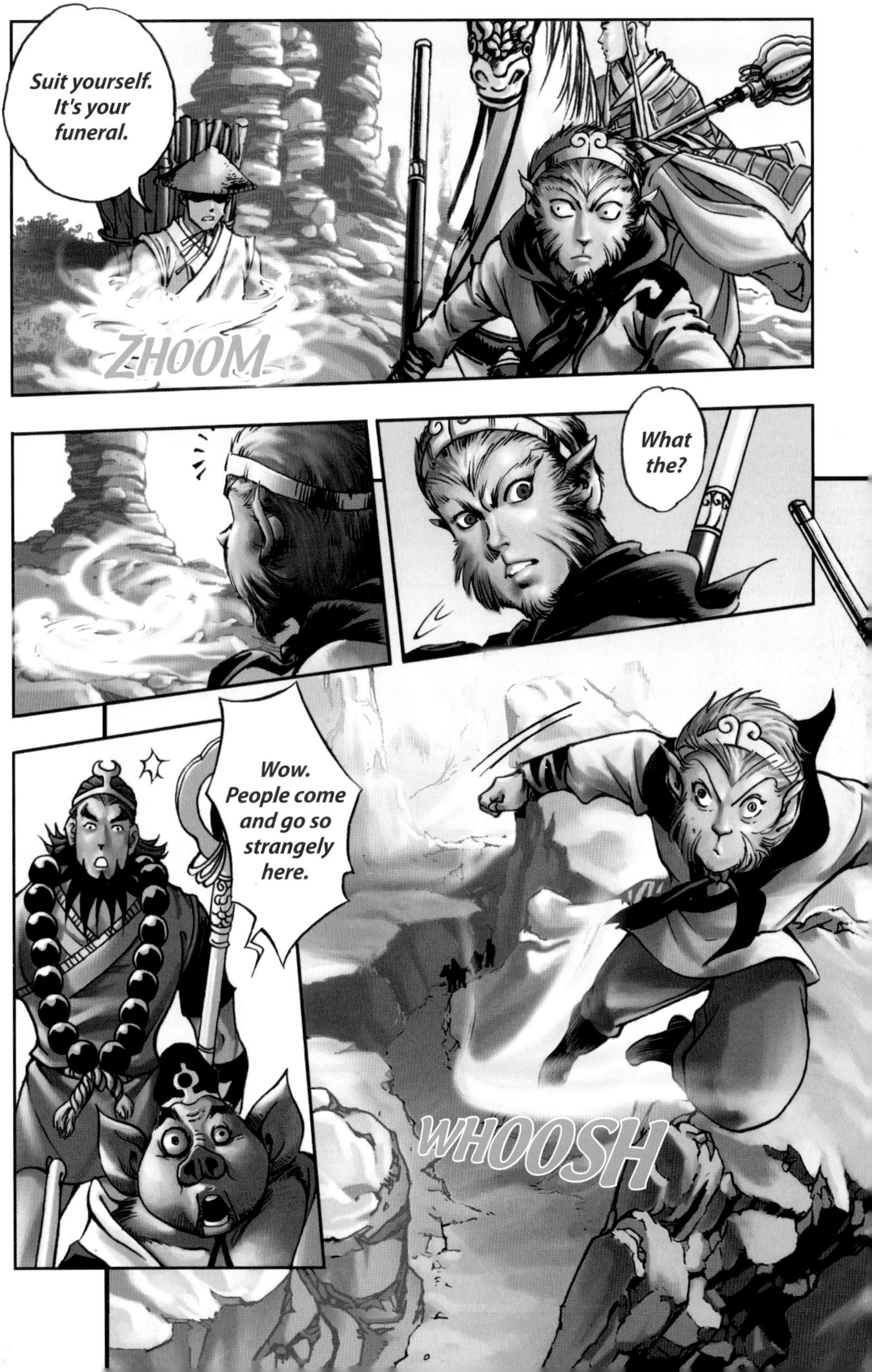
Suit yourself. It's your funeral.
ZHOOM
What the?
Wow. People come and go so strangely here.
WHOOSH

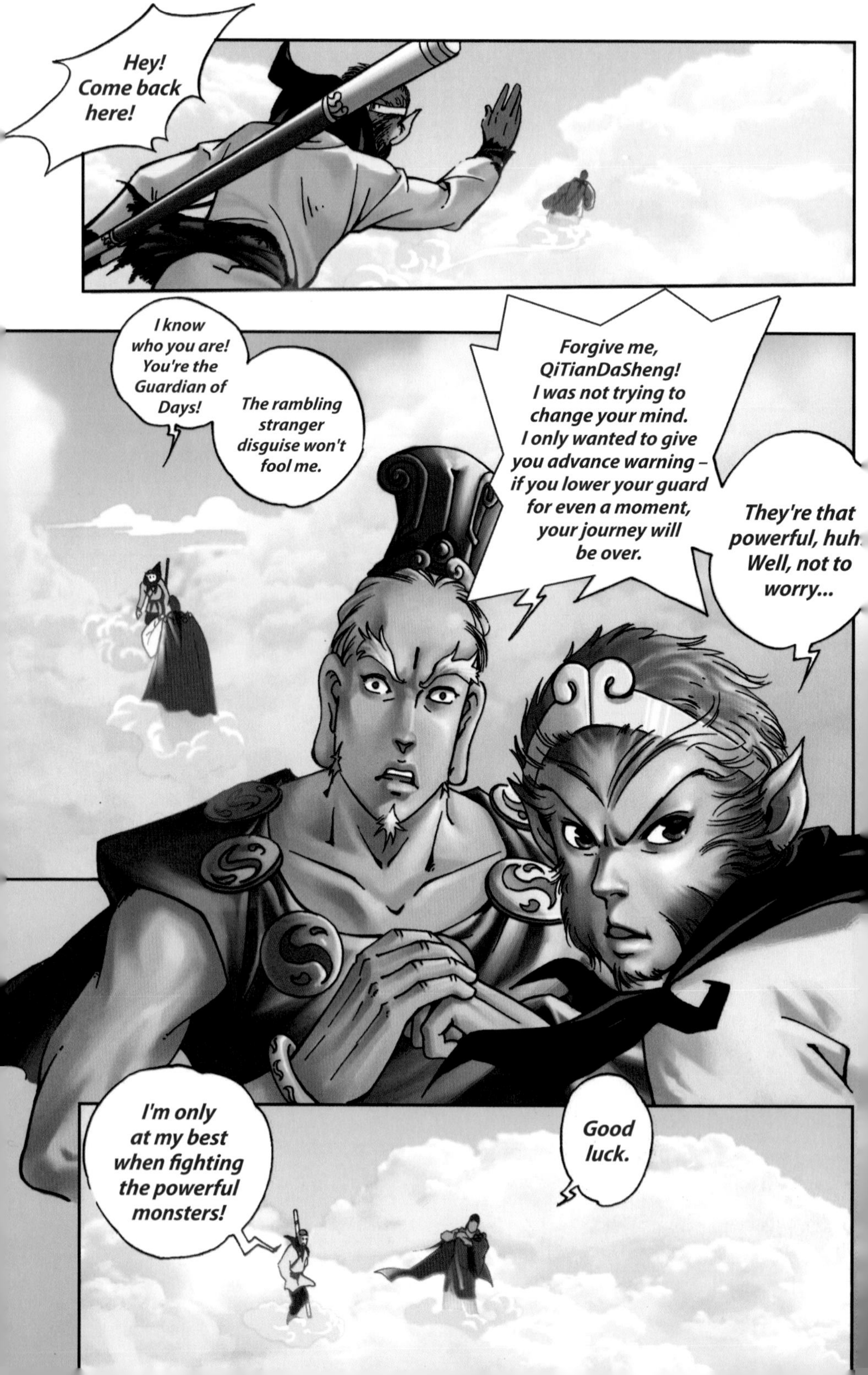

Hey! Come back here!
I know who you are! You're the Guardian of Days!
The rambling stranger disguise won't fool me.
Forgive me, QiTianDaSheng! I was not trying to change your mind. I only wanted to give you advance warning – if you lower your guard for even a moment, your journey will be over.
They're that powerful, huh. Well, not to worry...
I'm only at my best when fighting the powerful monsters!
Good luck.

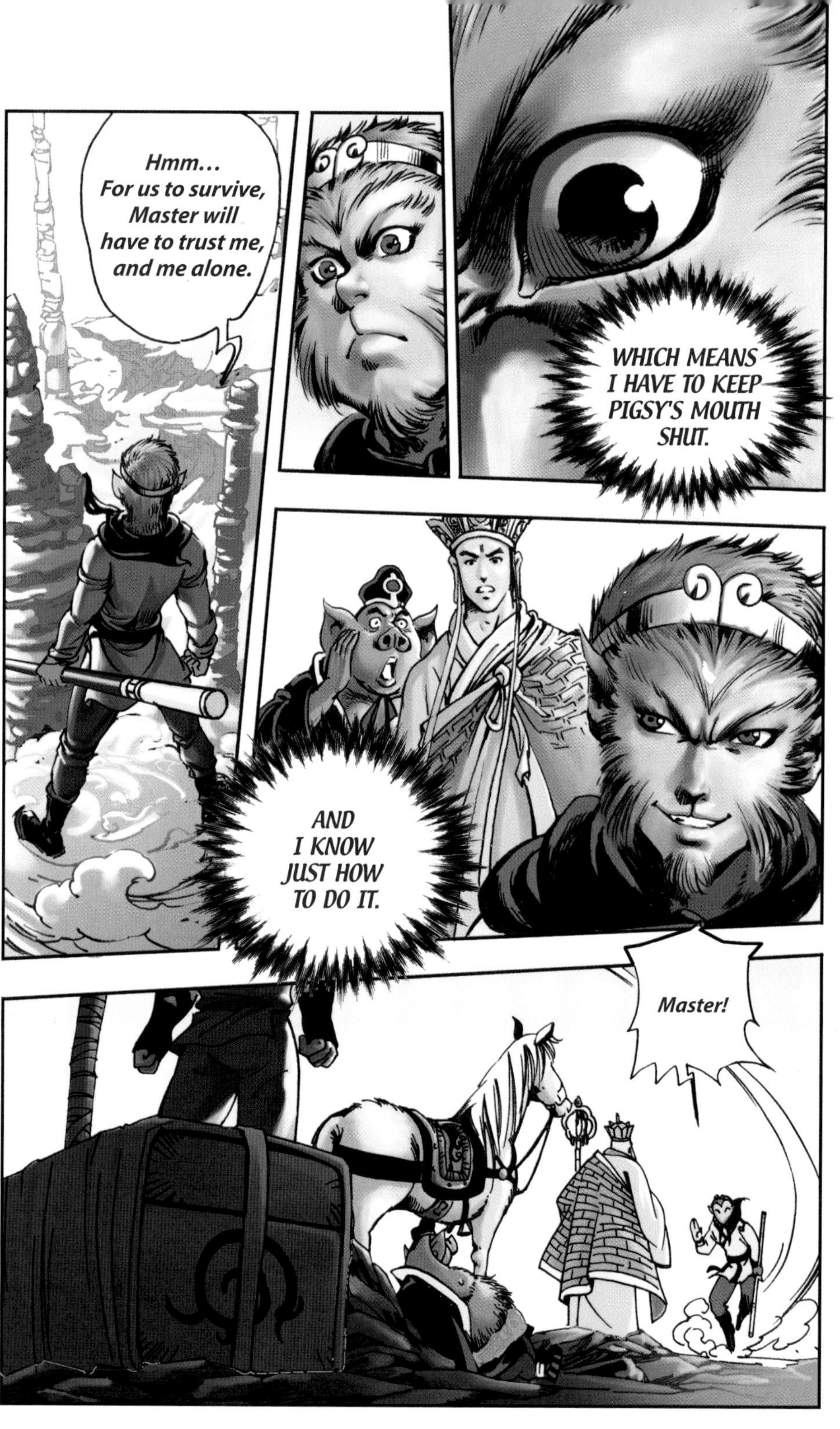
Hmm...
For us to survive, Master will have to trust me, and me alone.
WHICH MEANS I HAVE TO KEEP PIGSY'S MOUTH SHUT.
AND I KNOW JUST HOW TO DO IT.
Master!

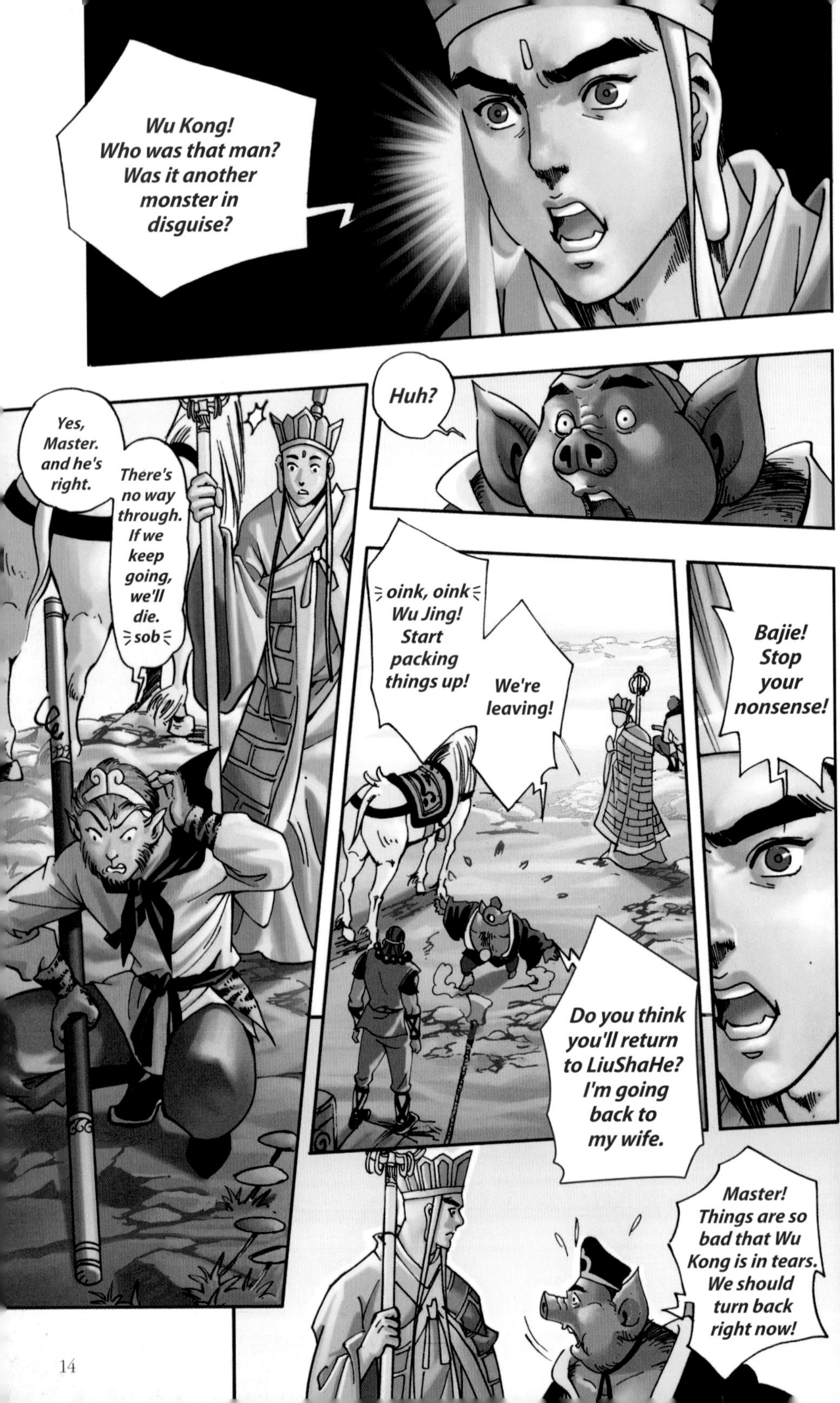

Wu Kong! Who was that man? Was it another monster in disguise?
Yes, Master. and he's right.
There's no way through. If we keep going, we'll die. ⋛sob⋚
Huh?
⋛oink, oink⋚ Wu Jing! Start packing things up!
We're leaving!
Bajie! Stop your nonsense!
Do you think you'll return to LiuShaHe? I'm going back to my wife.
Master! Things are so bad that Wu Kong is in tears. We should turn back right now!

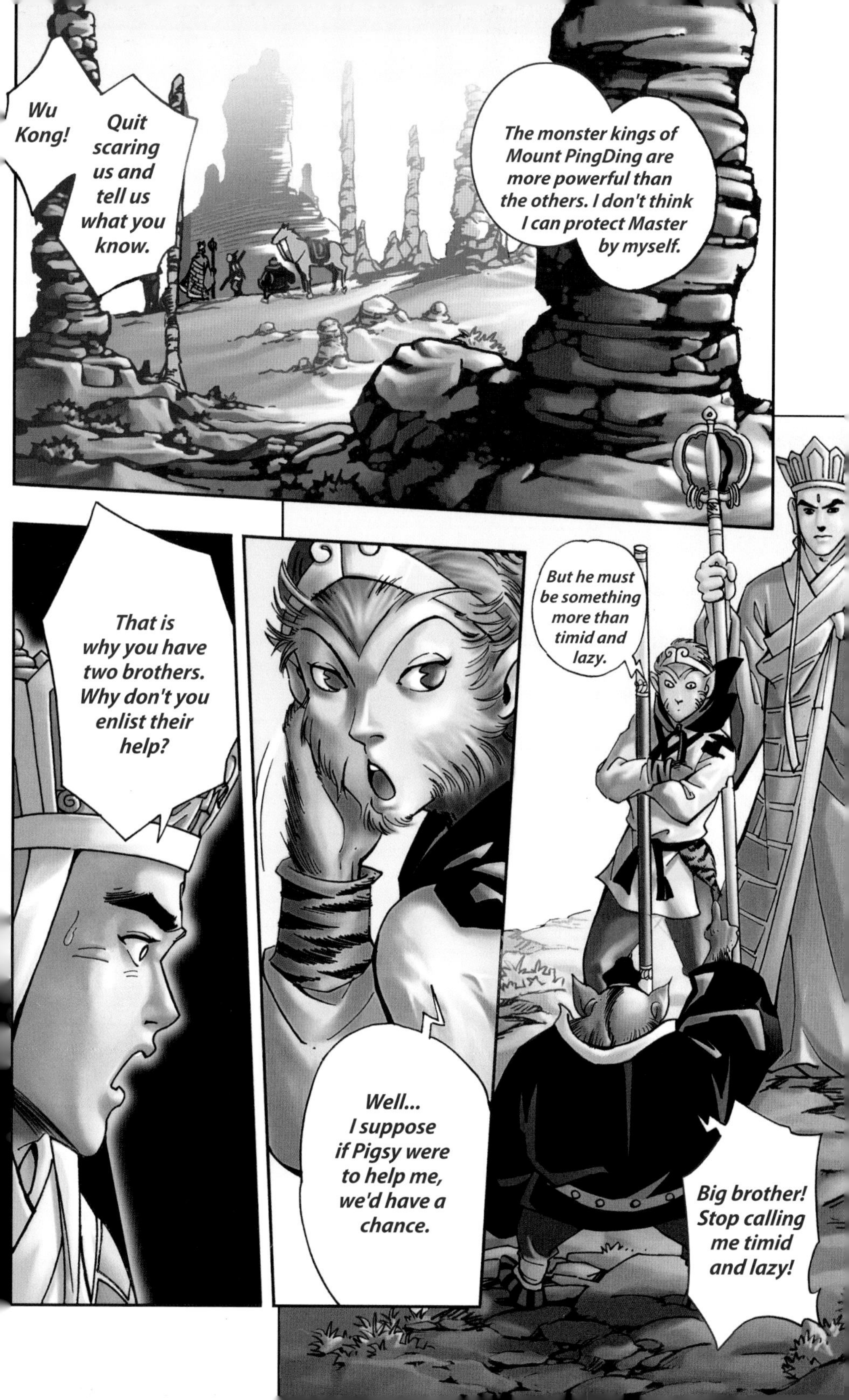
Wu Kong!
Quit scaring us and tell us what you know.
The monster kings of Mount PingDing are more powerful than the others. I don't think I can protect Master by myself.
That is why you have two brothers. Why don't you enlist their help?
Well... I suppose if Pigsy were to help me, we'd have a chance.
But he must be something more than timid and lazy.
Big brother! Stop calling me timid and lazy!

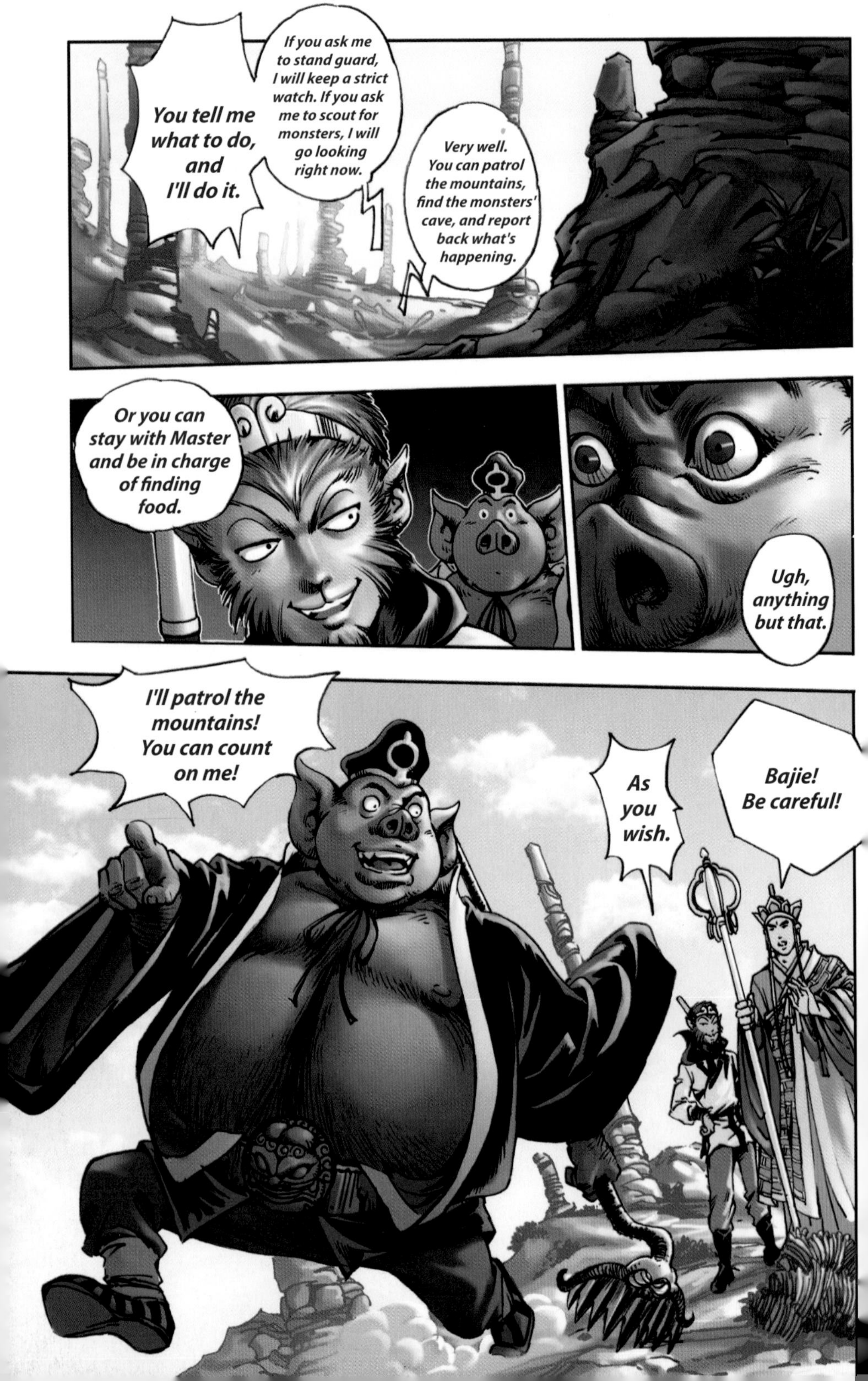
You tell me what to do, and I'll do it.
If you ask me to stand guard, I will keep a strict watch. If you ask me to scout for monsters, I will go looking right now.
Very well. You can patrol the mountains, find the monsters' cave, and report back what's happening.
Or you can stay with Master and be in charge of finding food.
Ugh, anything but that.
I'll patrol the mountains! You can count on me!
As you wish.
Bajie! Be careful!

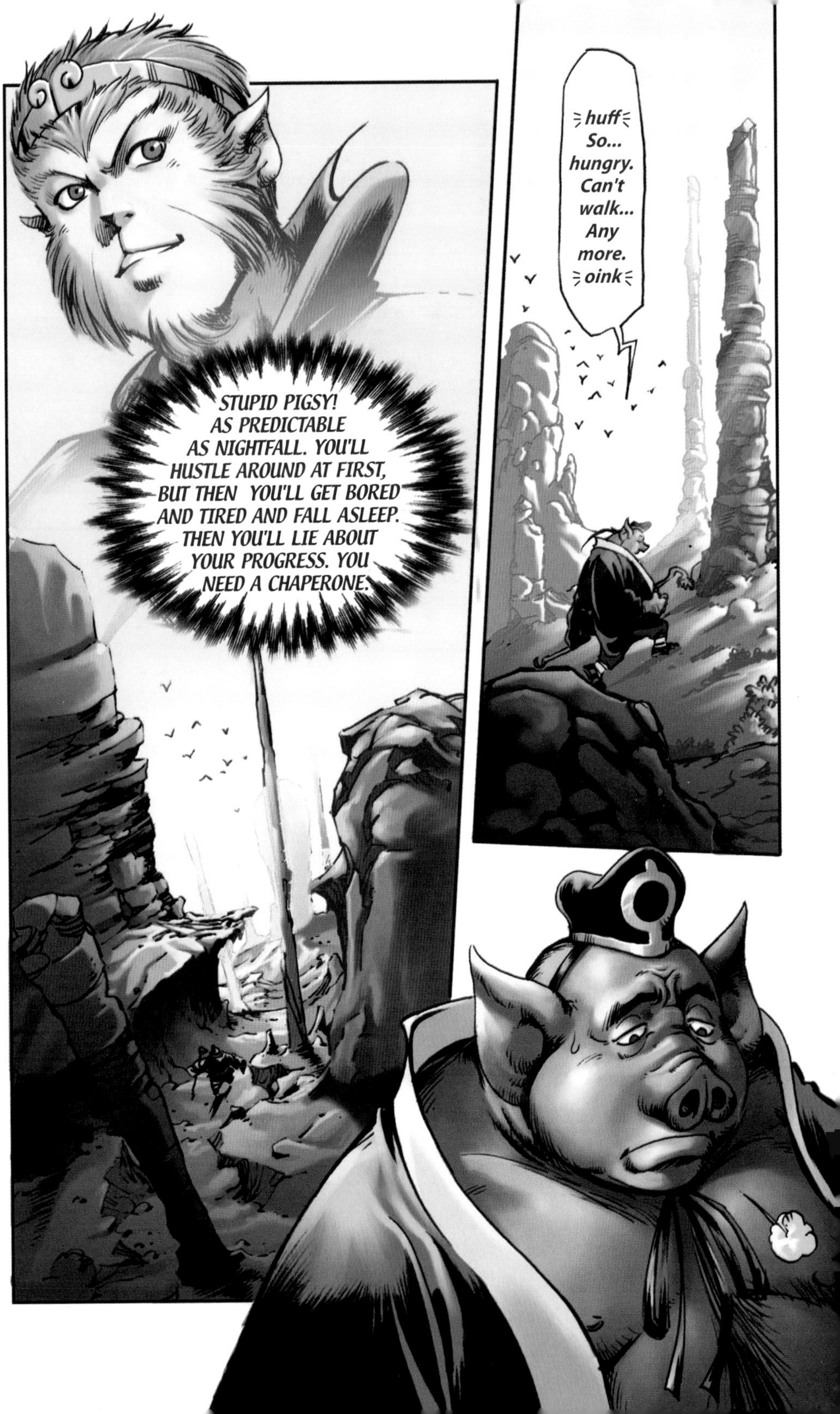
STUPID PIGSY! AS PREDICTABLE AS NIGHTFALL. YOU'LL HUSTLE AROUND AT FIRST, BUT THEN YOU'LL GET BORED AND TIRED AND FALL ASLEEP. THEN YOU'LL LIE ABOUT YOUR PROGRESS. YOU NEED A CHAPERONE.
huff So... hungry. Can't walk... Any more. oink

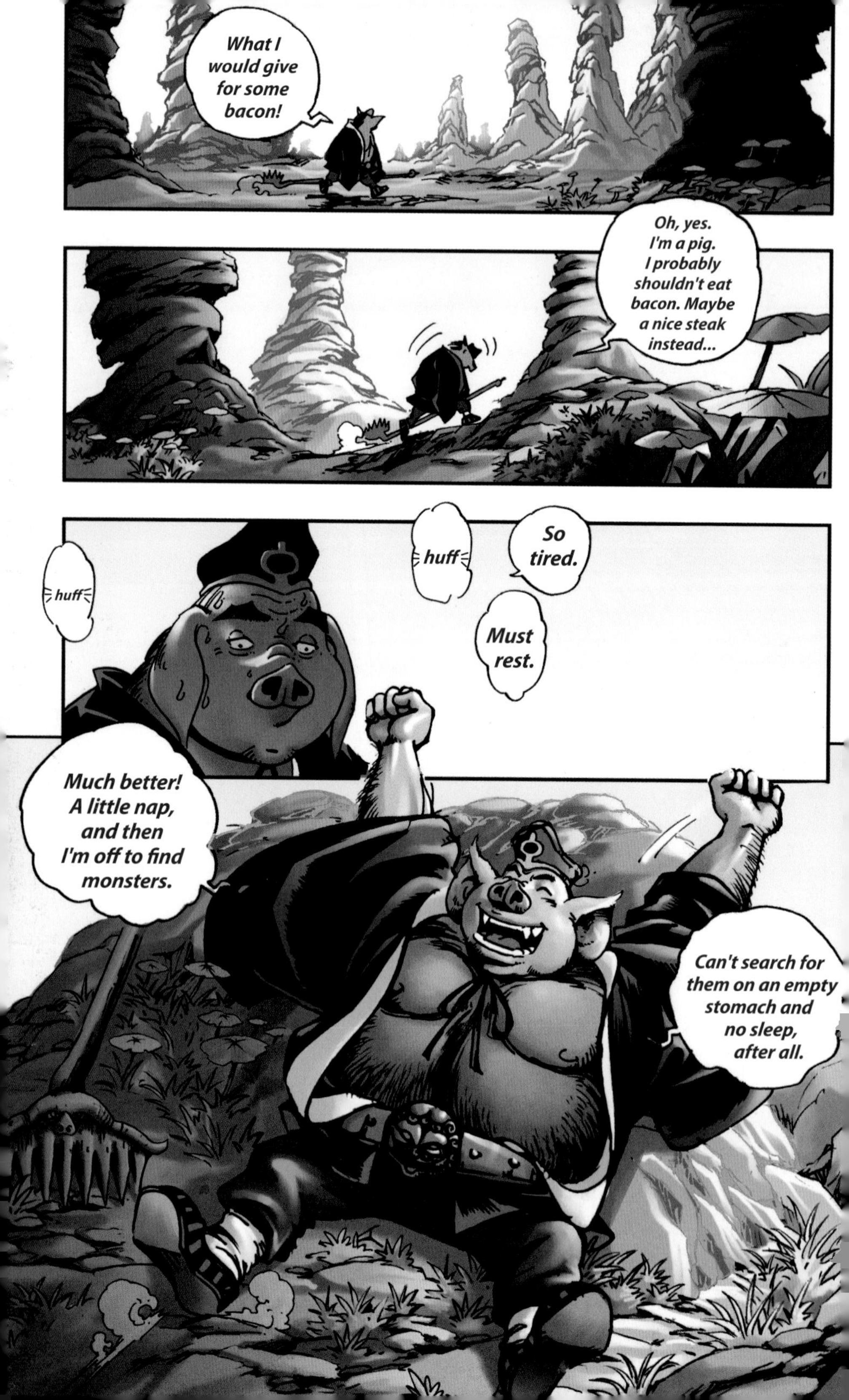
What I would give for some bacon!
Oh, yes. I'm a pig. I probably shouldn't eat bacon. Maybe a nice steak instead...
huff
huff
So tired.
Must rest.
Much better! A little nap, and then I'm off to find monsters.
Can't search for them on an empty stomach and no sleep, after all.

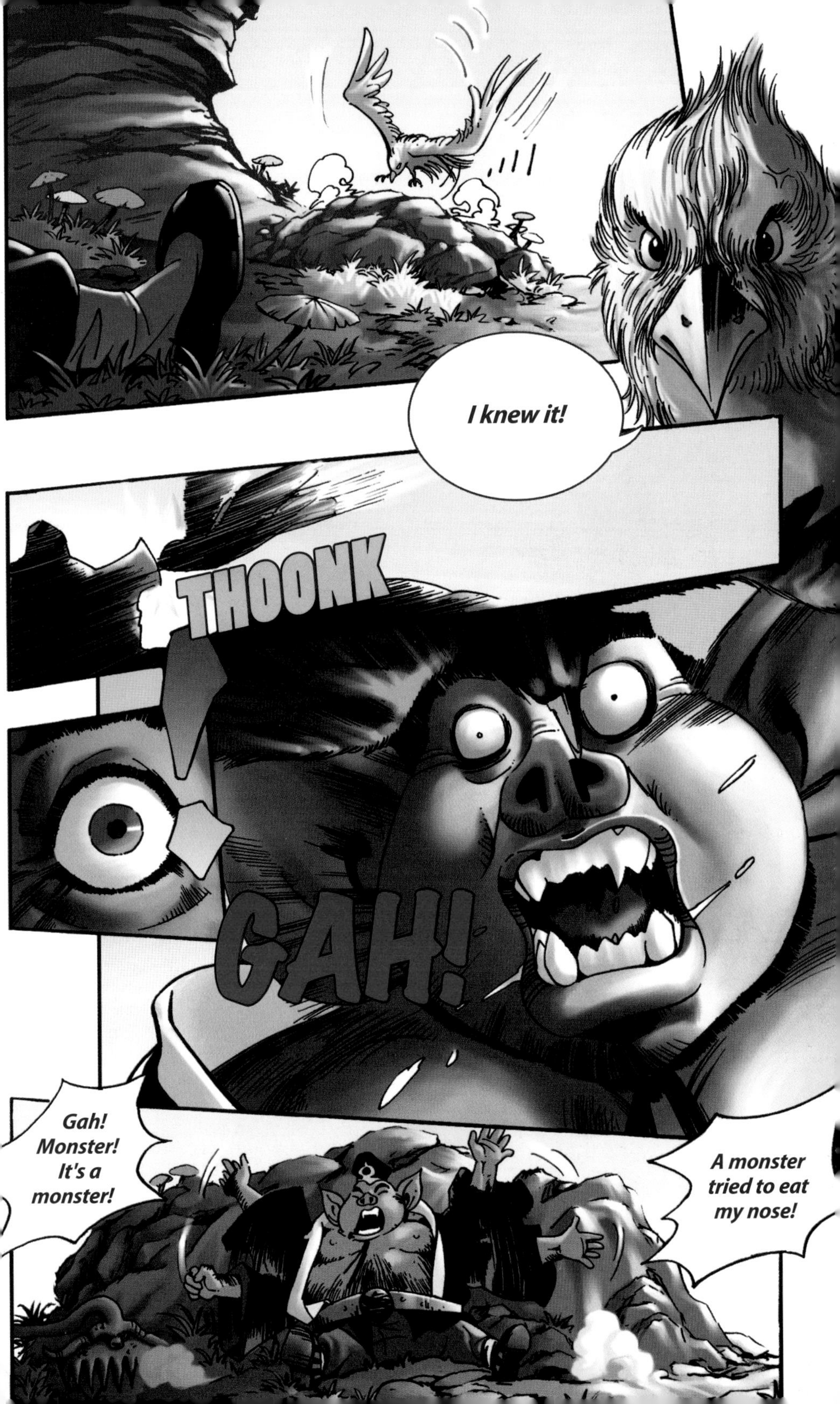
I knew it!
THOONK
GAH!
Gah! Monster! It's a monster!
A monster tried to eat my nose!

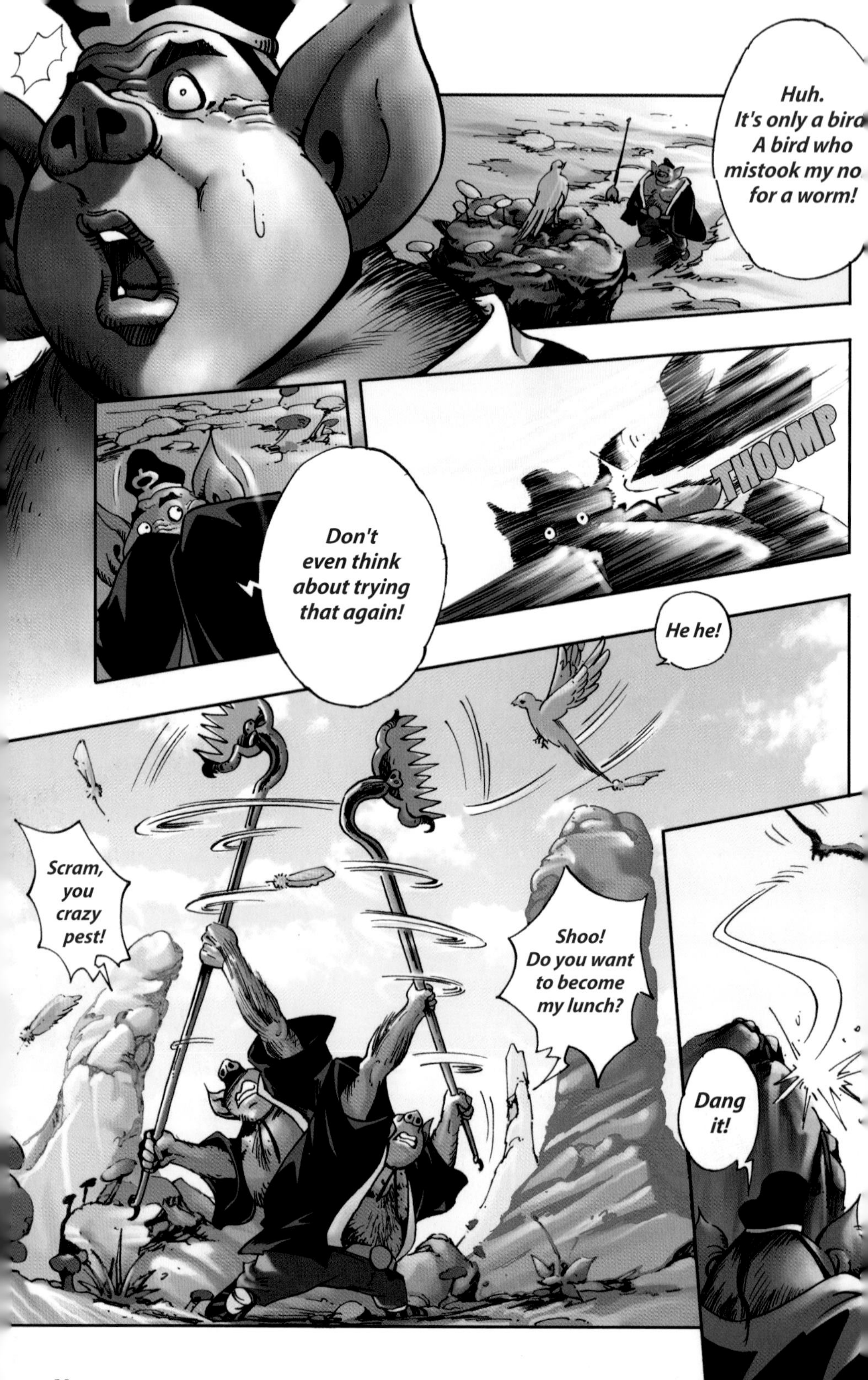
Huh. It's only a bir A bird who mistook my no for a worm!
THOOMP
Don't even think about trying that again!
He he!
Scram, you crazy pest!
Shoo! Do you want to become my lunch?
Dang it!

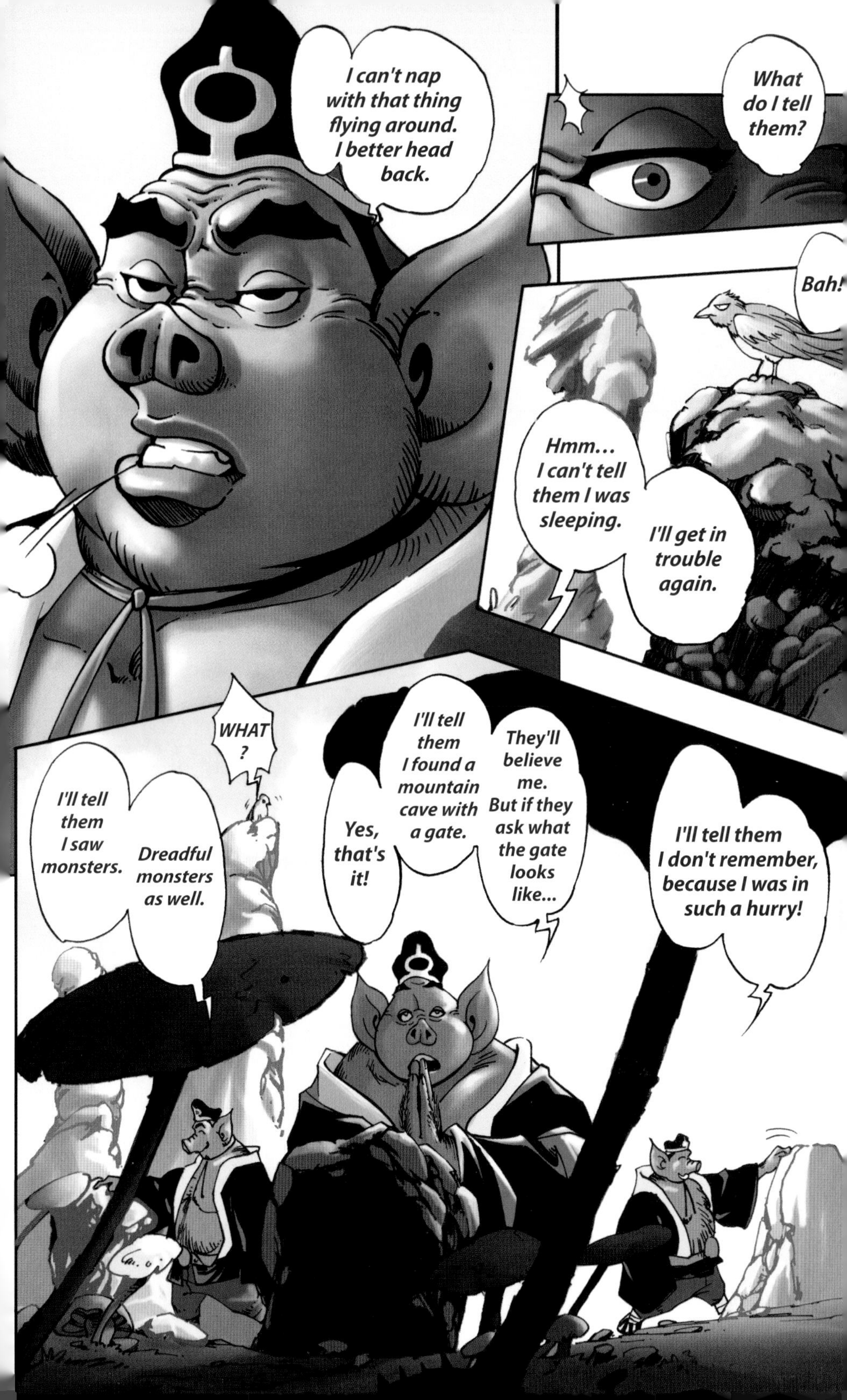
I can't nap with that thing flying around. I better head back.
What do I tell them?
Bah!
Hmm… I can't tell them I was sleeping.
I'll get in trouble again.
WHAT ?
I'll tell them I saw monsters.
Dreadful monsters as well.
Yes, that's it!
I'll tell them I found a mountain cave with a gate.
They'll believe me. But if they ask what the gate looks like...
I'll tell them I don't remember, because I was in such a hurry!

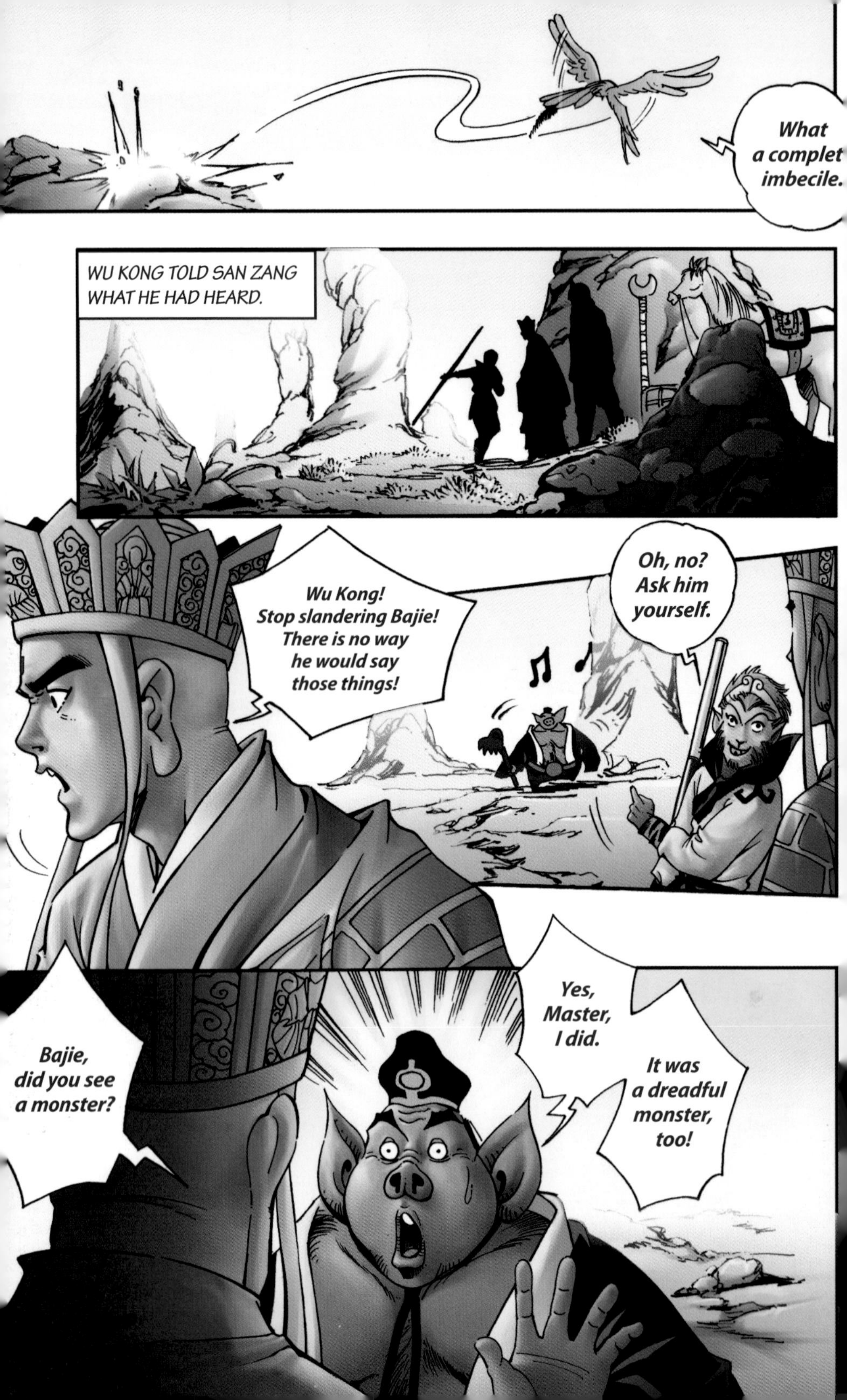
What a complet imbecile.
WU KONG TOLD SAN ZANG WHAT HE HAD HEARD.
Wu Kong! Stop slandering Bajie! There is no way he would say those things!
Oh, no? Ask him yourself.
Bajie, did you see a monster?
Yes, Master, I did.
It was a dreadful monster, too!

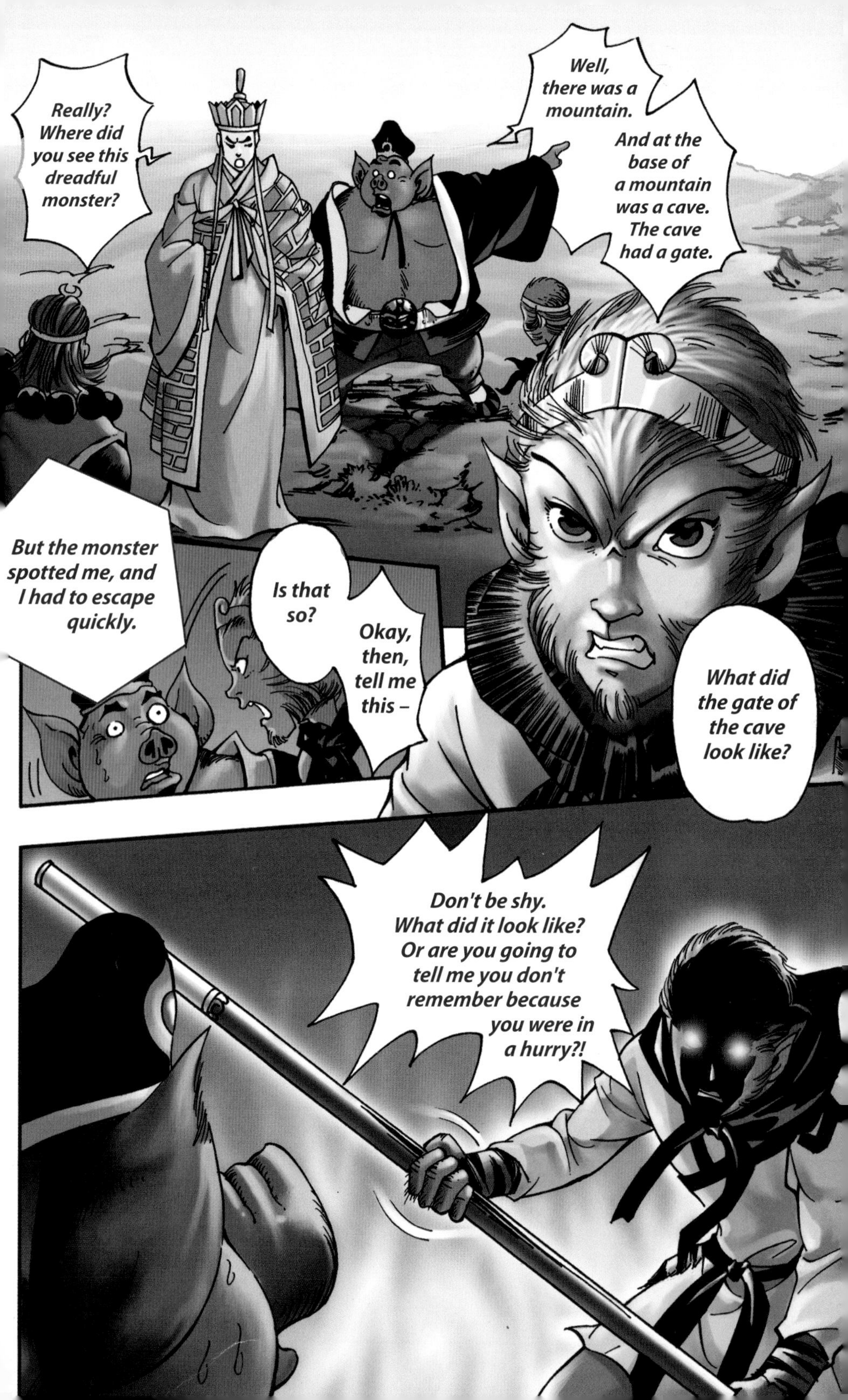
Really? Where did you see this dreadful monster?
Well, there was a mountain.
And at the base of a mountain was a cave. The cave had a gate.
But the monster spotted me, and I had to escape quickly.
Is that so?
Okay, then, tell me this –
What did the gate of the cave look like?
Don't be shy. What did it look like? Or are you going to tell me you don't remember because you were in a hurry?!

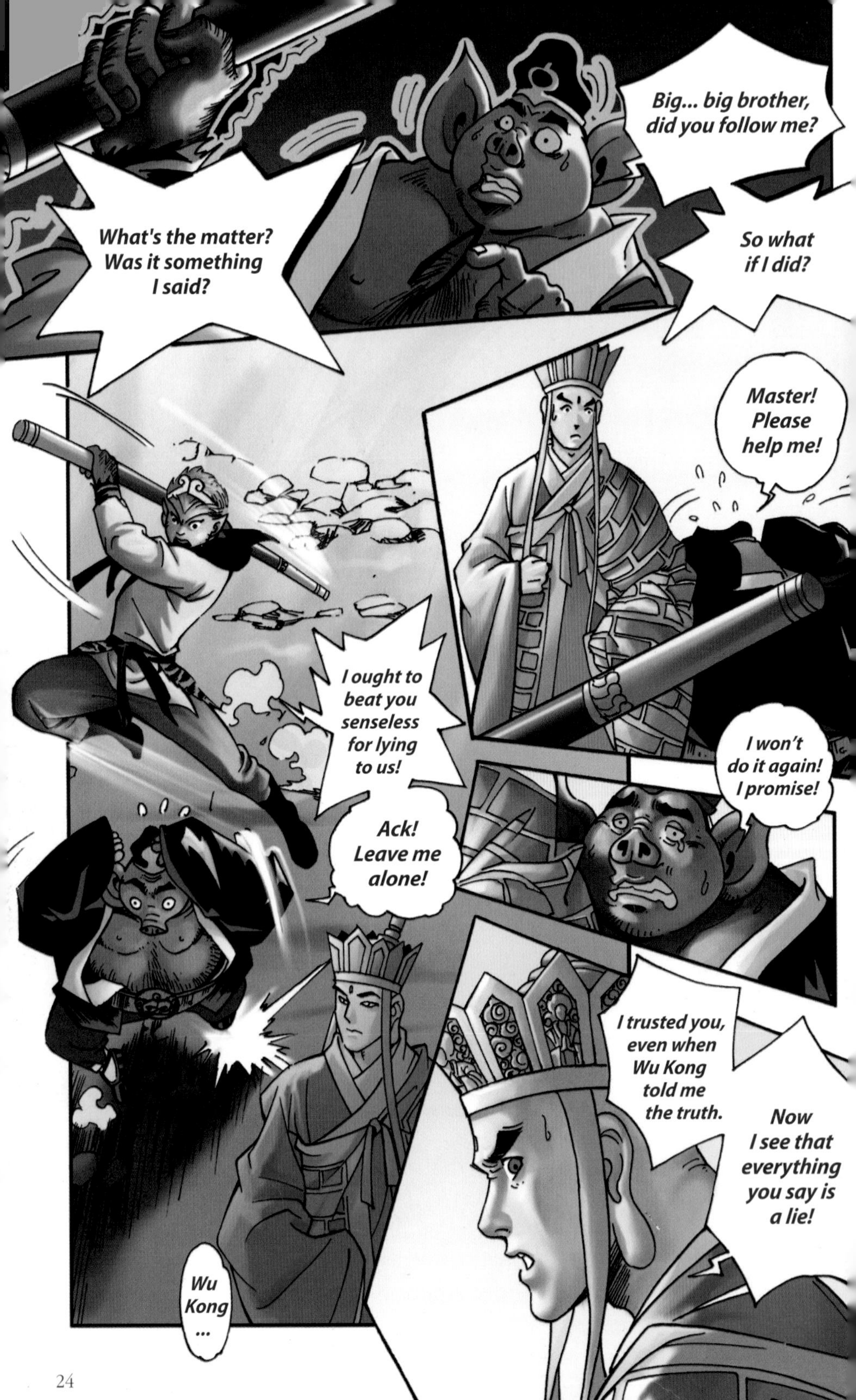
Big... big brother, did you follow me?
What's the matter? Was it something I said?
So what if I did?
Master! Please help me!
I ought to beat you senseless for lying to us!
Ack! Leave me alone!
I won't do it again! I promise!
I trusted you, even when Wu Kong told me the truth.
Now I see that everything you say is a lie!
Wu Kong ...

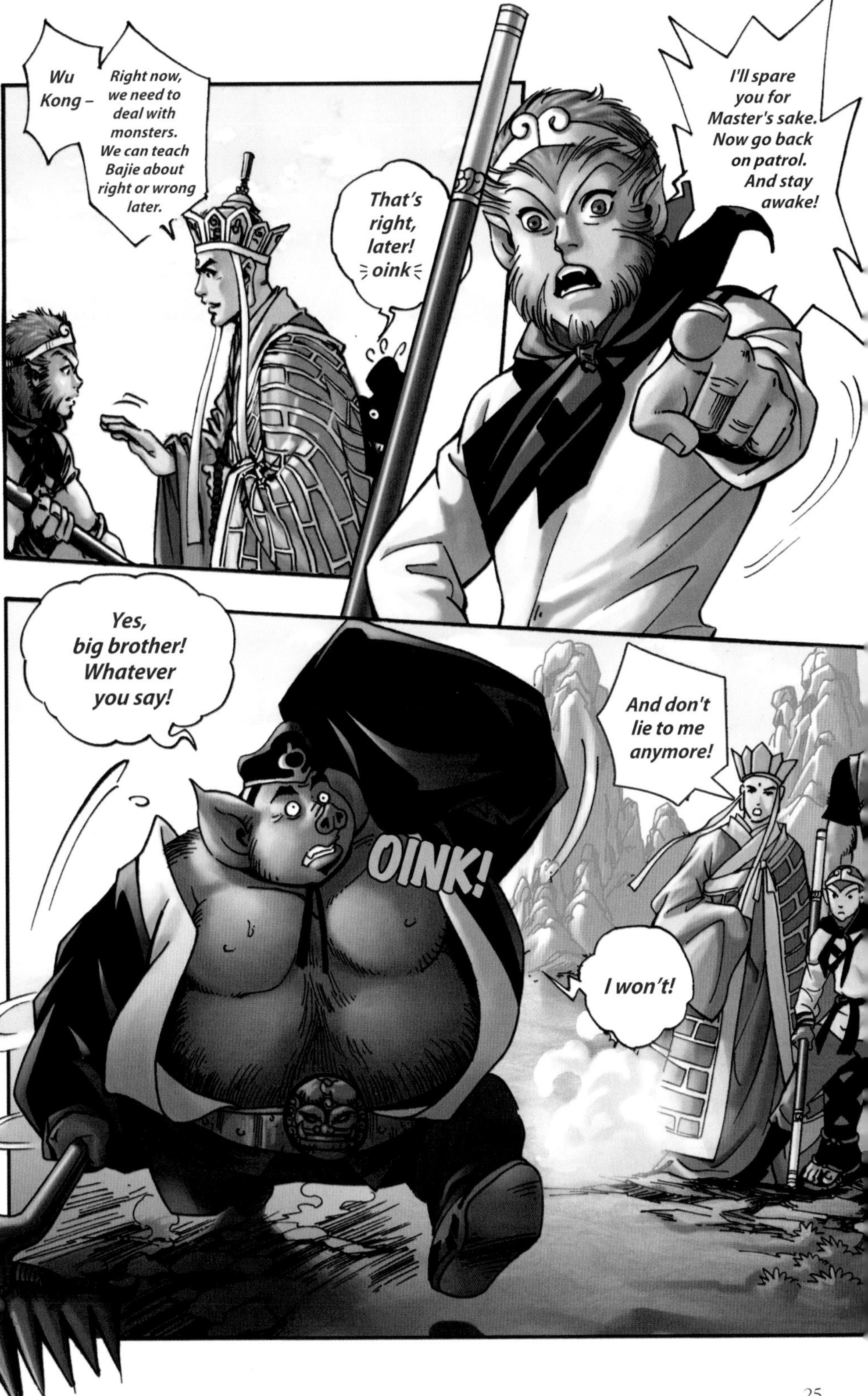
Wu Kong –
Right now, we need to deal with monsters. We can teach Bajie about right or wrong later.
That's right, later! oink
I'll spare you for Master's sake. Now go back on patrol. And stay awake!
Yes, big brother! Whatever you say!
OINK!
And don't lie to me anymore!
I won't!

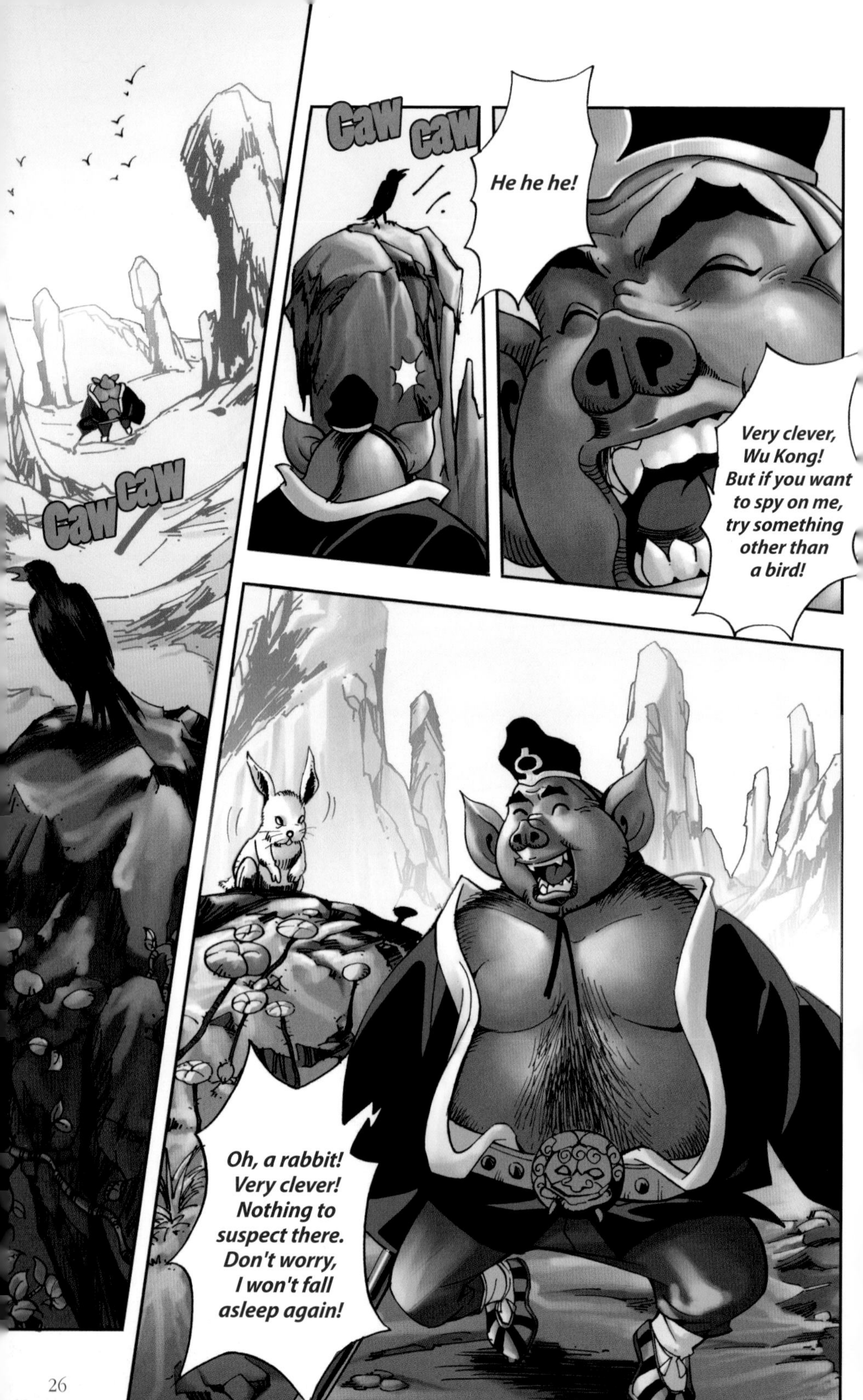
Caw caw
Caw caw
He he he!
Very clever, Wu Kong! But if you want to spy on me, try something other than a bird!
Oh, a rabbit! Very clever! Nothing to suspect there. Don't worry, I won't fall asleep again!

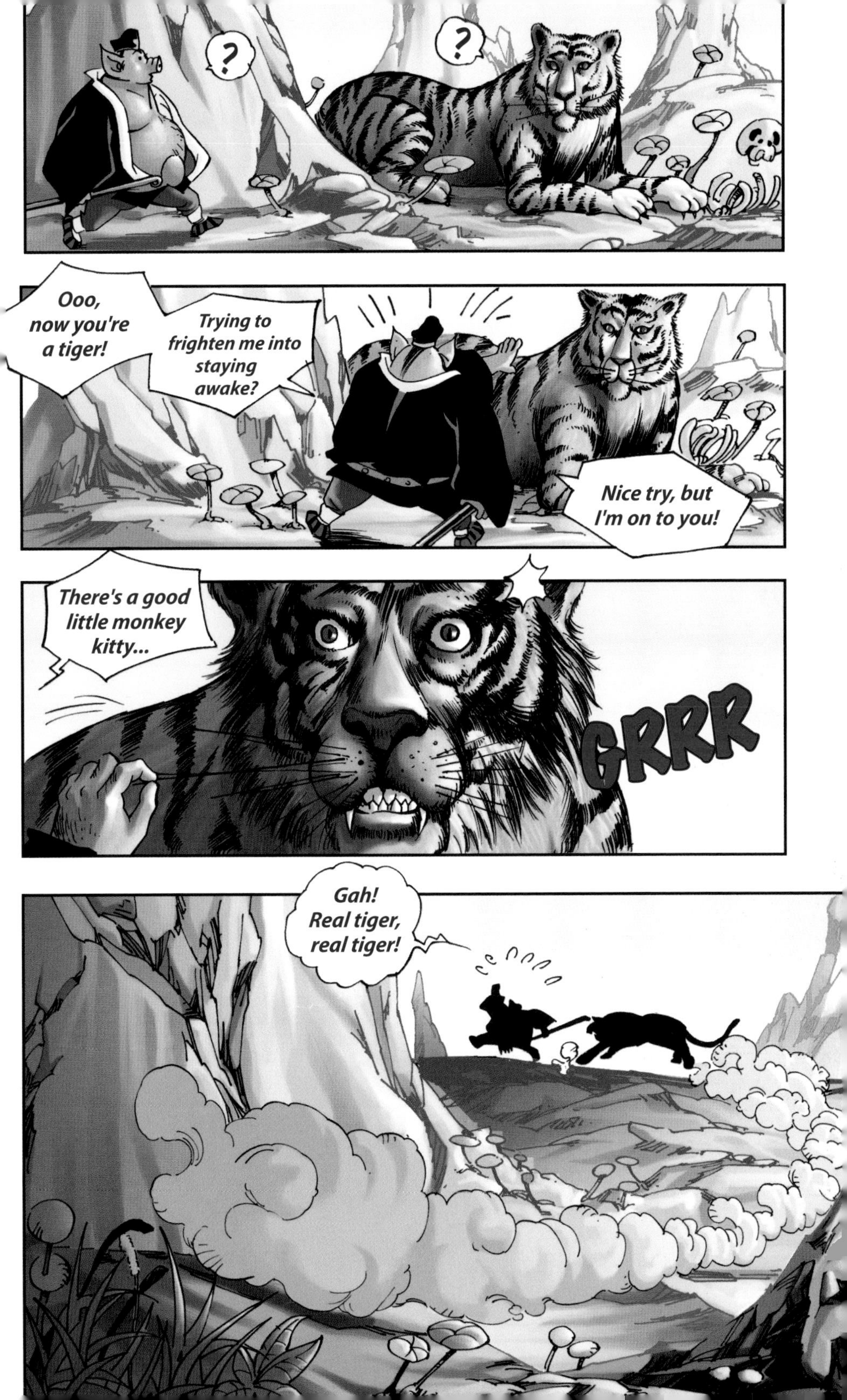
?
?
Ooo, now you're a tiger!
Trying to frighten me into staying awake?
Nice try, but I'm on to you!
There's a good little monkey kitty...
GRRR
Gah! Real tiger, real tiger!

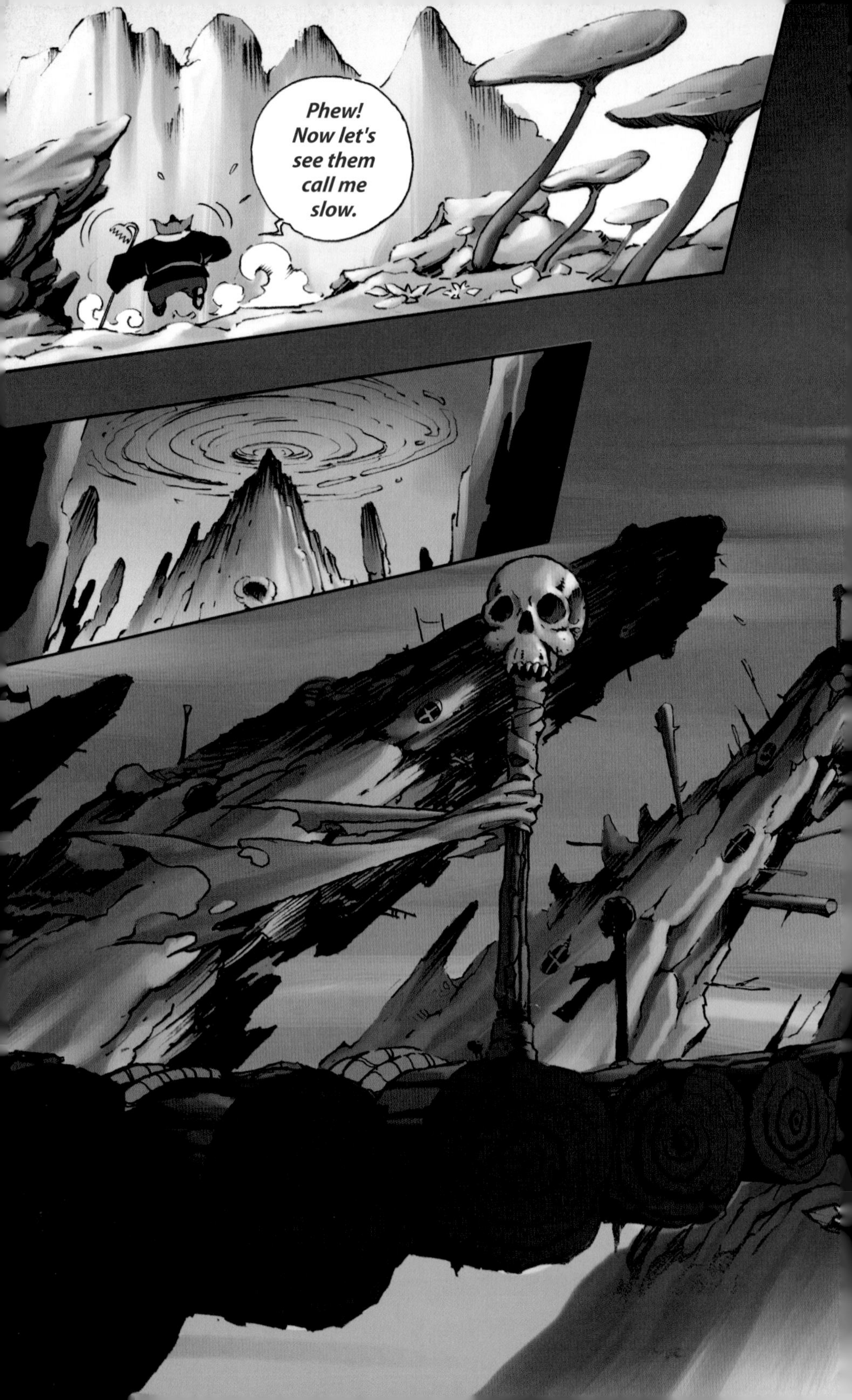
Phew! Now let's see them call me slow.

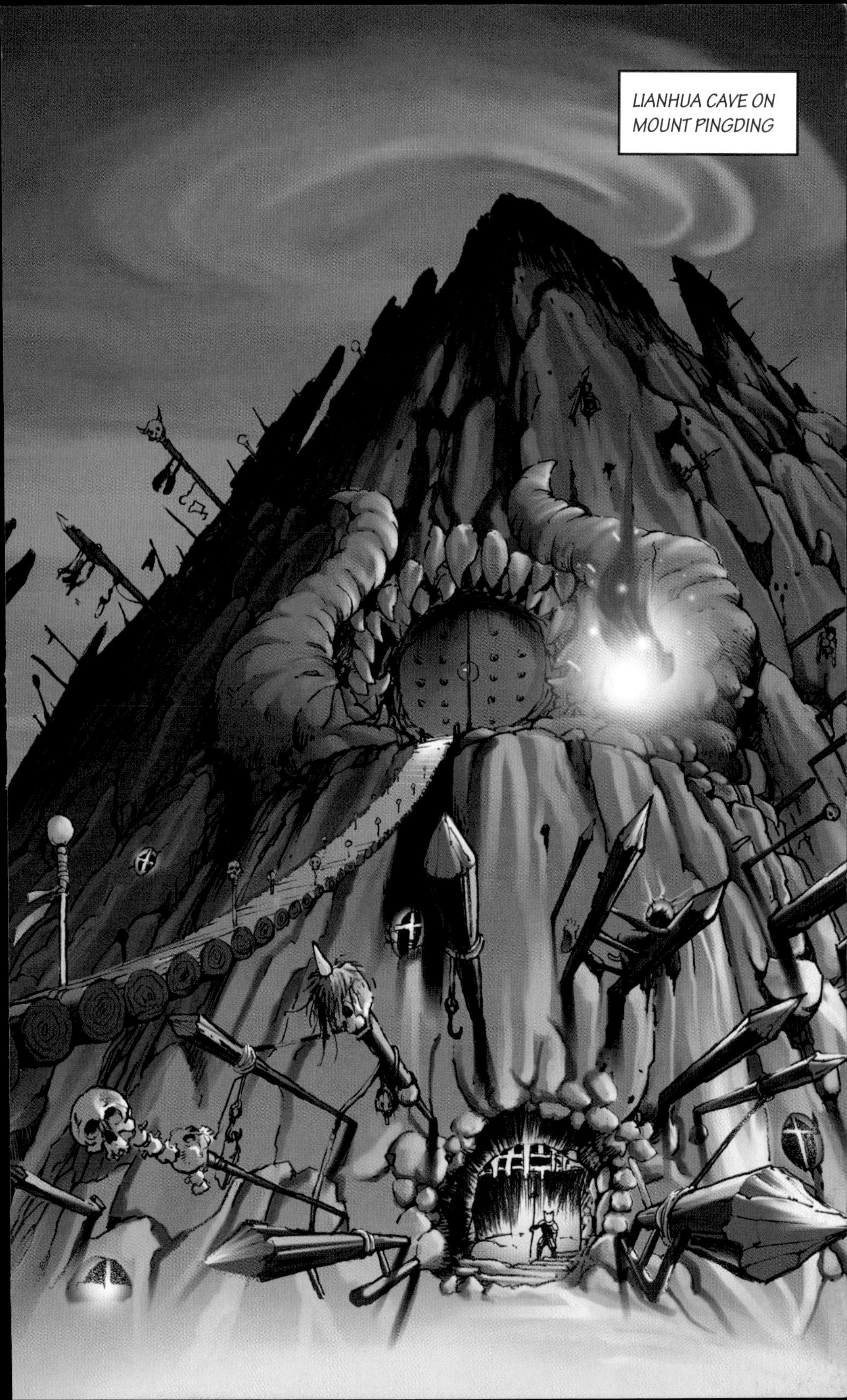
LIANHUA CAVE ON
MOUNT PINGDING

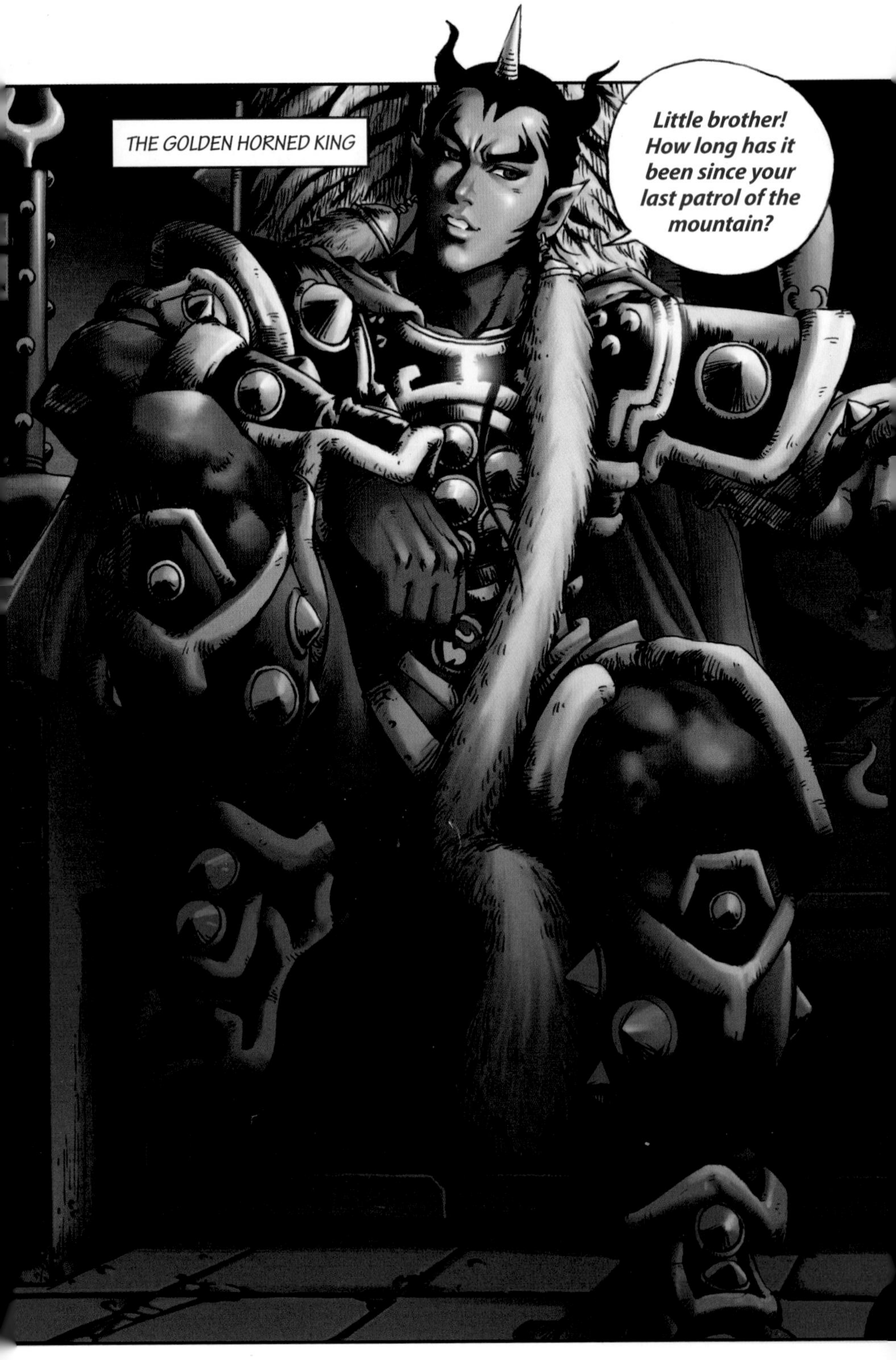
THE GOLDEN HORNED KING
Little brother! How long has it been since your last patrol of the mountain?

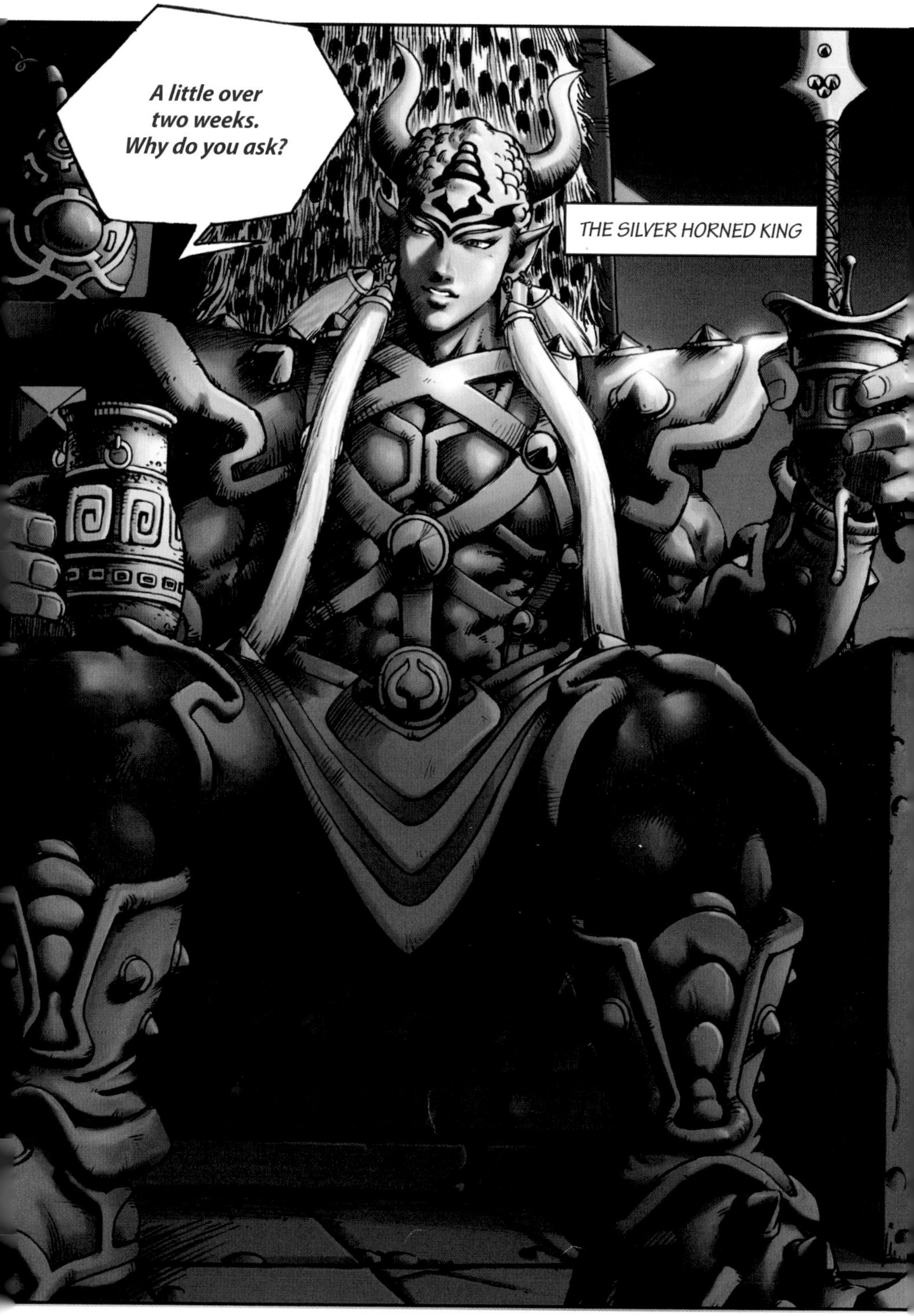
A little over two weeks. Why do you ask?
THE SILVER HORNED KING

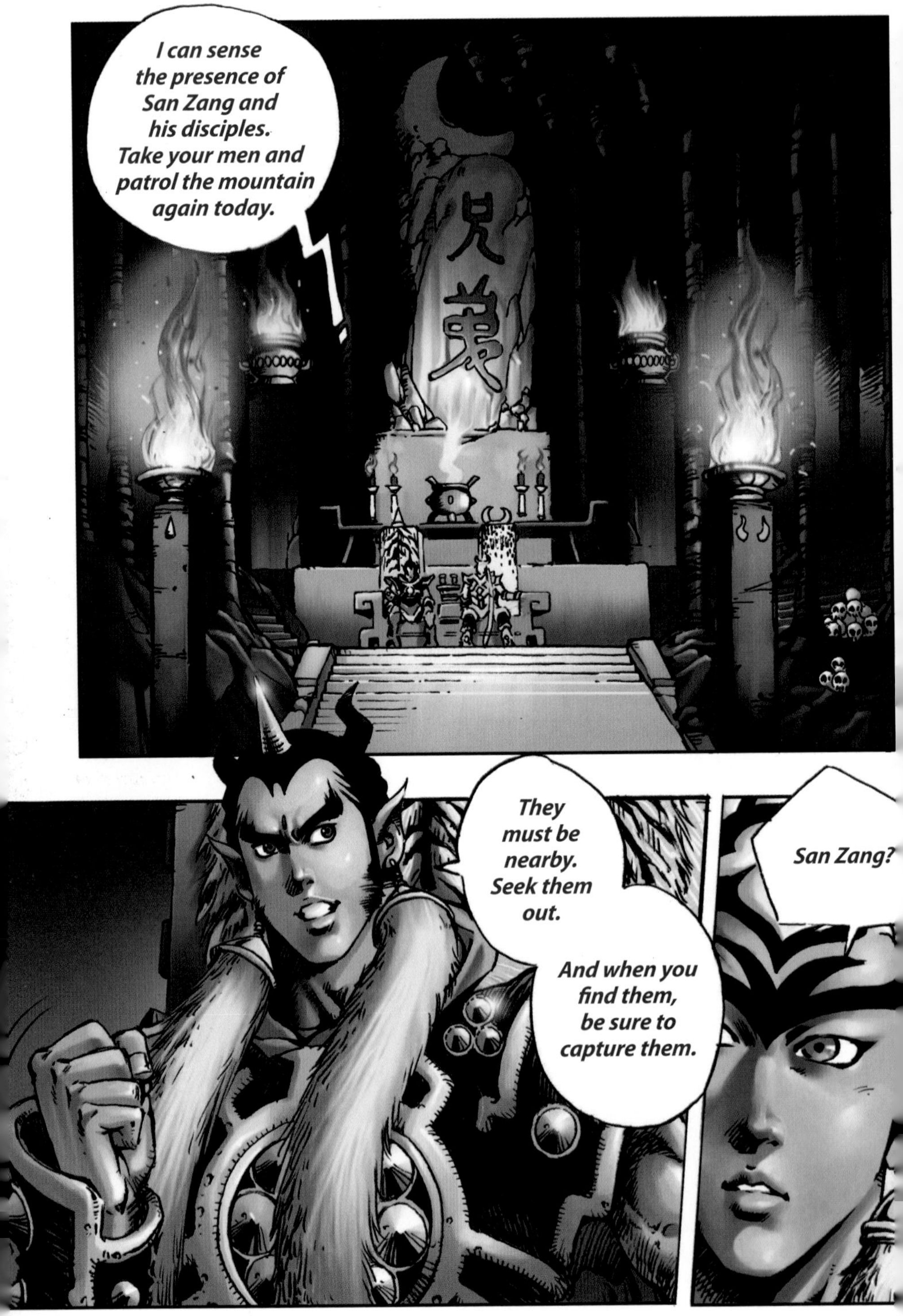
I can sense the presence of San Zang and his disciples. Take your men and patrol the mountain again today.
They must be nearby. Seek them out.
And when you find them, be sure to capture them.
San Zang?

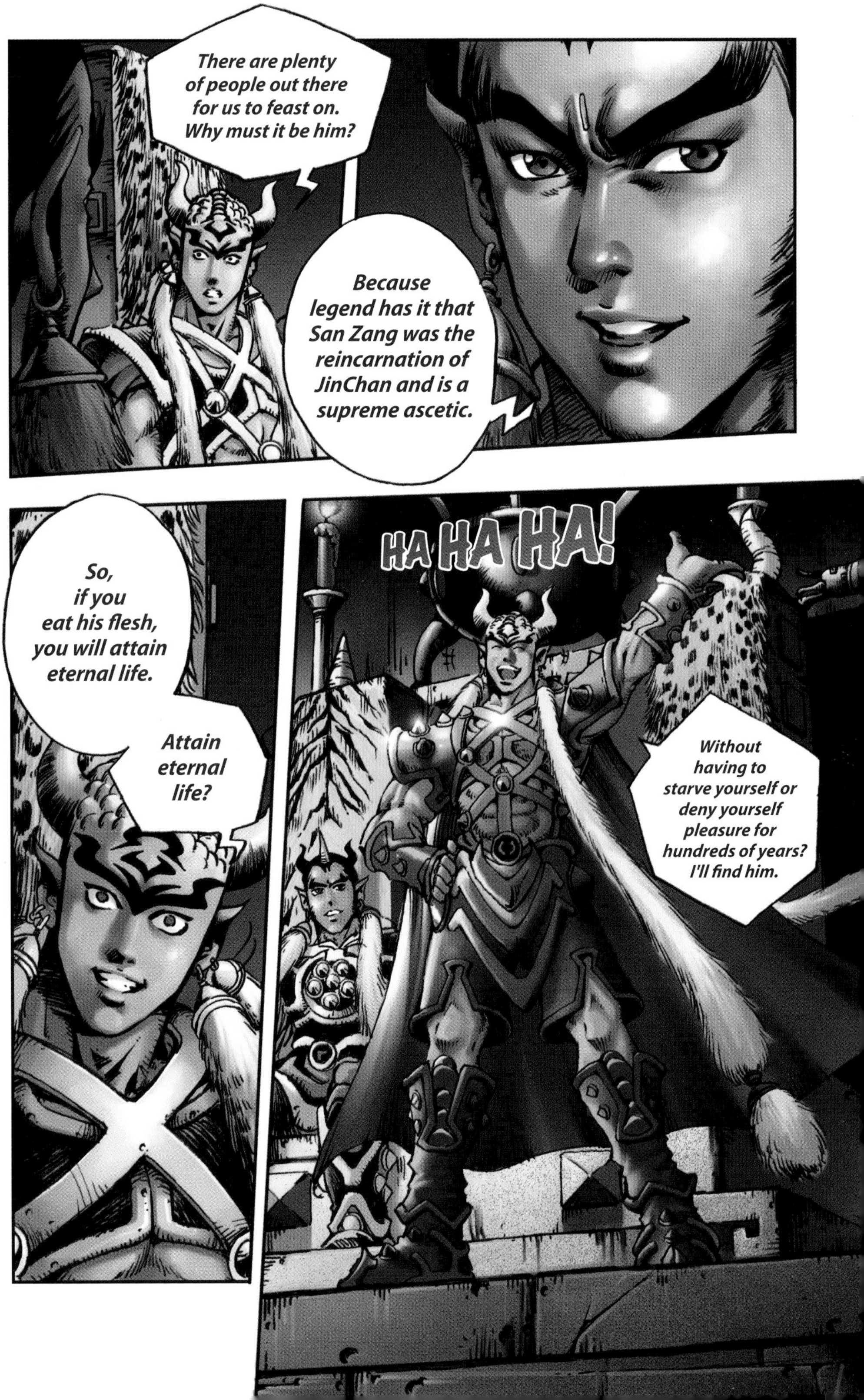
There are plenty of people out there for us to feast on. Why must it be him?
Because legend has it that San Zang was the reincarnation of JinChan and is a supreme ascetic.
So, if you eat his flesh, you will attain eternal life.
Attain eternal life?
HA HA HA!
Without having to starve yourself or deny yourself pleasure for hundreds of years? I'll find him.

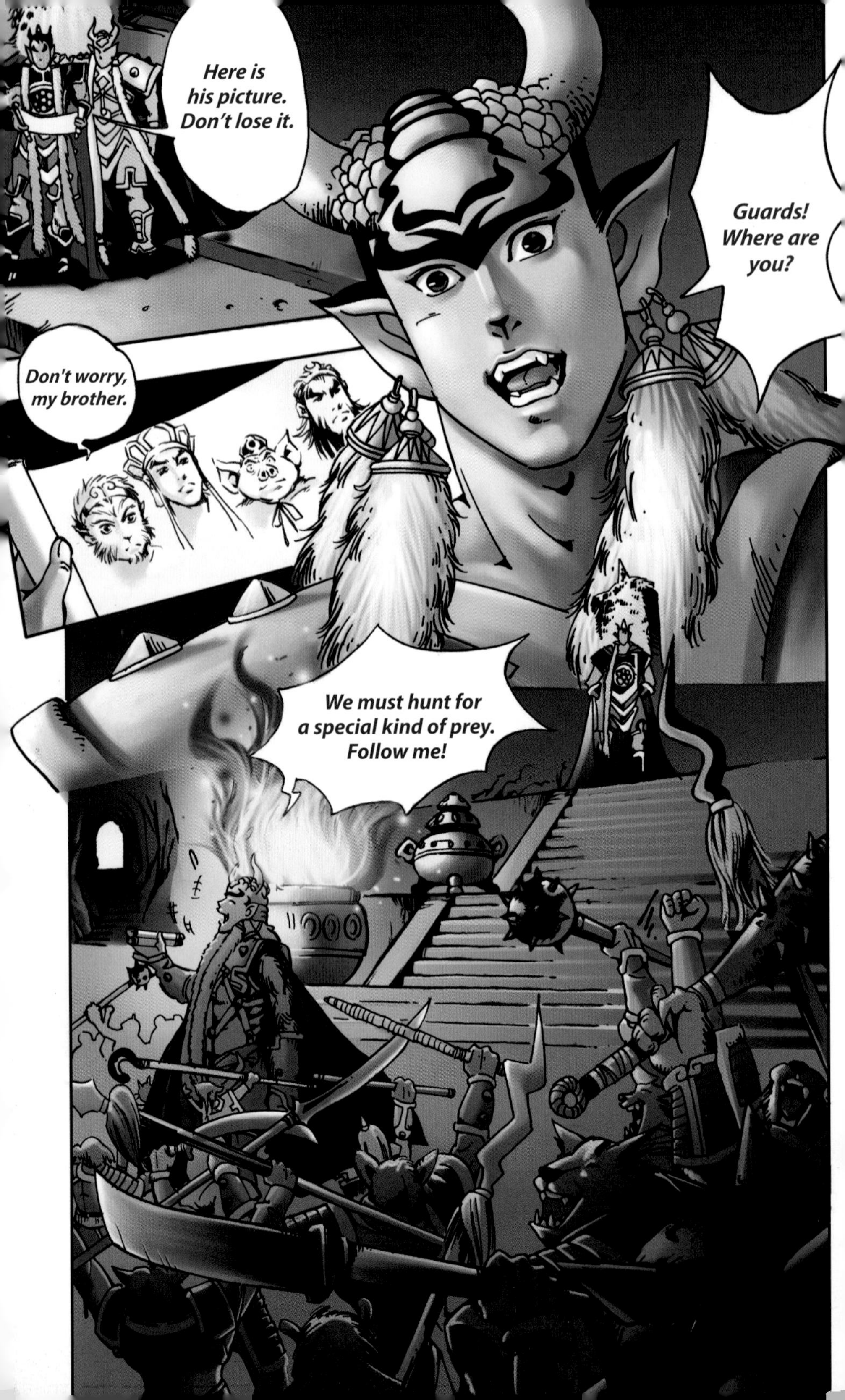
Here is his picture. Don't lose it.
Guards! Where are you?
Don't worry, my brother.
We must hunt for a special kind of prey. Follow me!

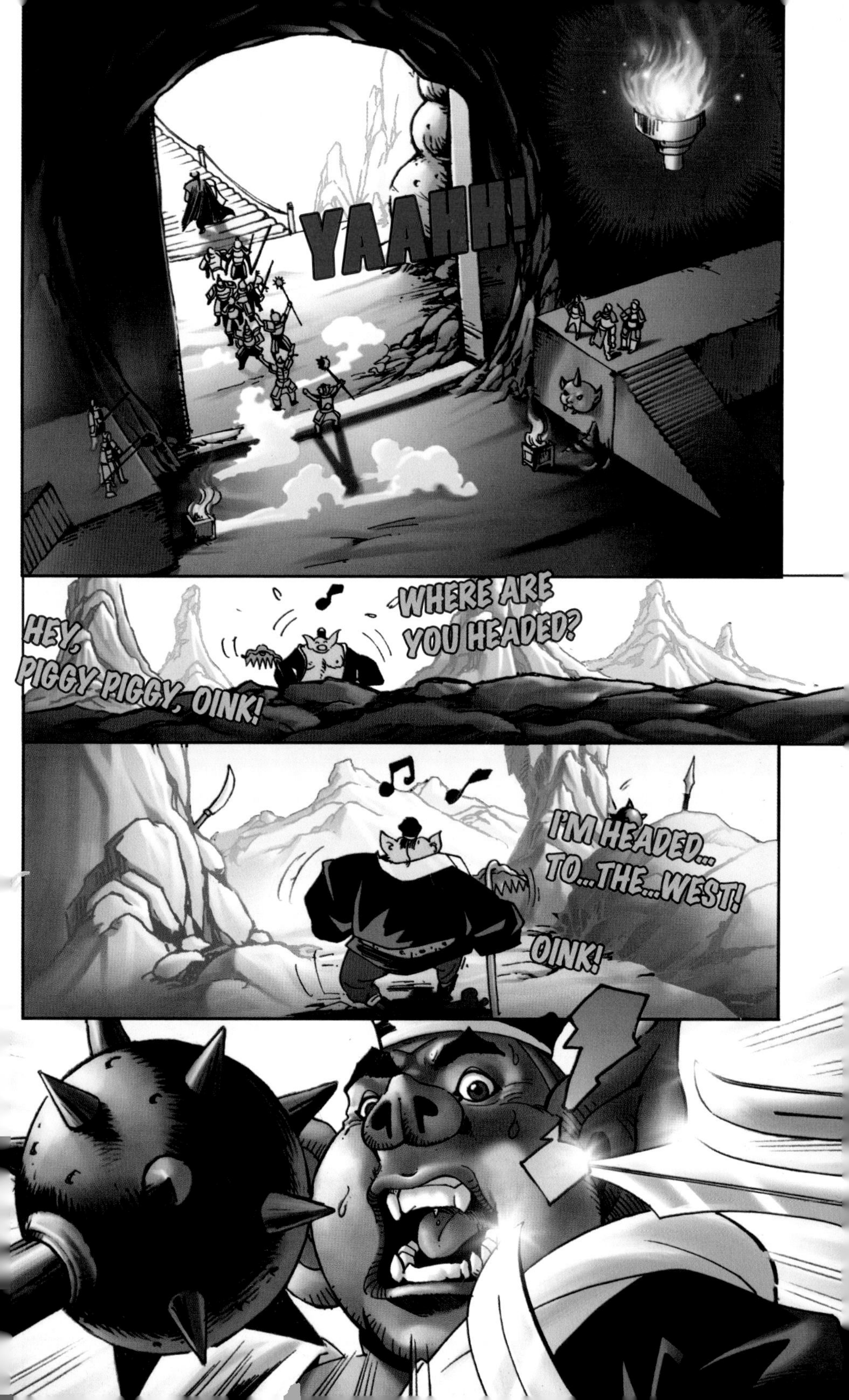
YAAHH!
HEY, PIGGY PIGGY, OINK!
WHERE ARE YOU HEADED?
I'M HEADED... TO...THE...WEST!
OINK!

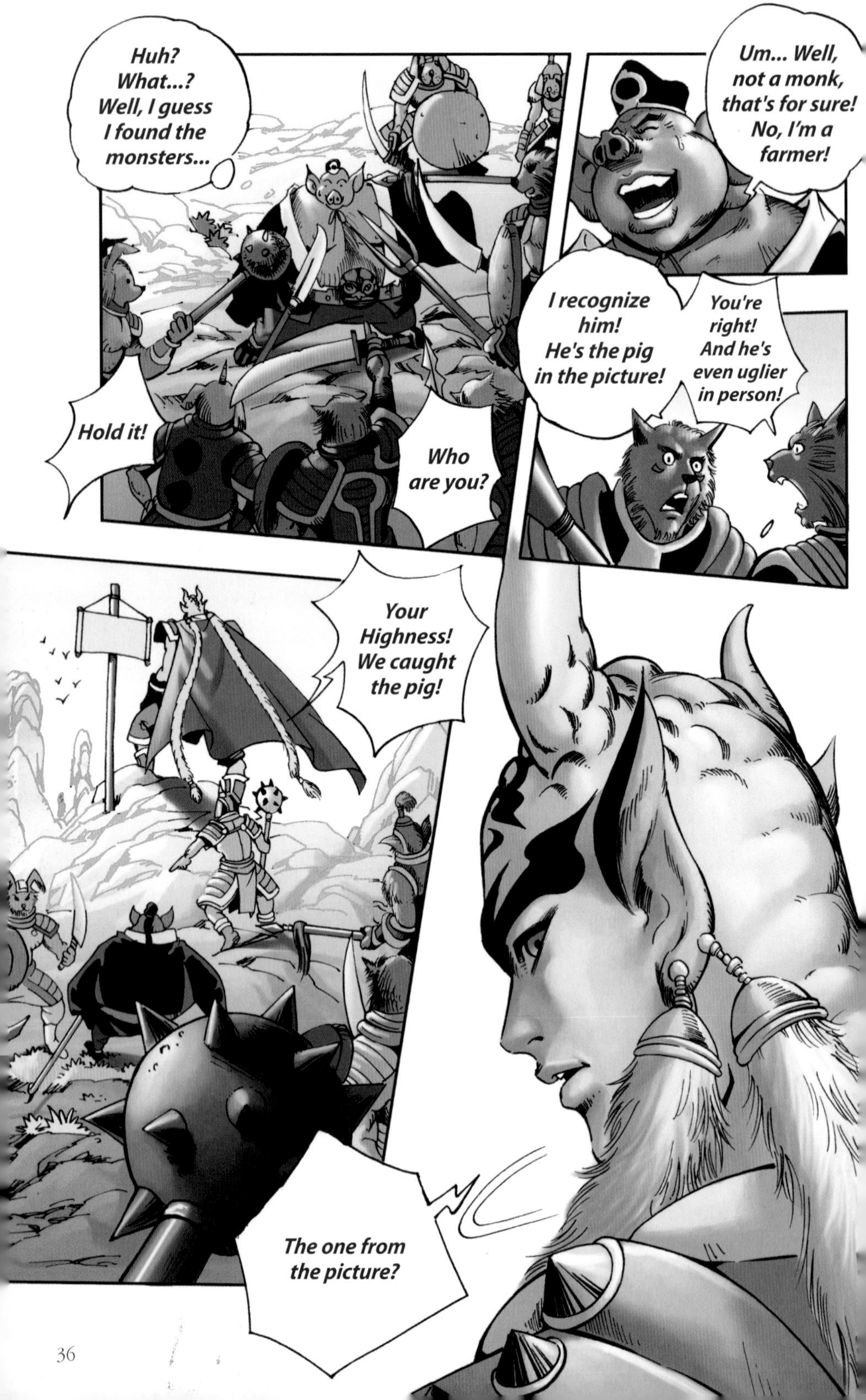
Huh? What...? Well, I guess I found the monsters...
Hold it!
Who are you?
Um... Well, not a monk, that's for sure! No, I'm a farmer!
I recognize him! He's the pig in the picture!
You're right! And he's even uglier in person!
Your Highness! We caught the pig!
The one from the picture?

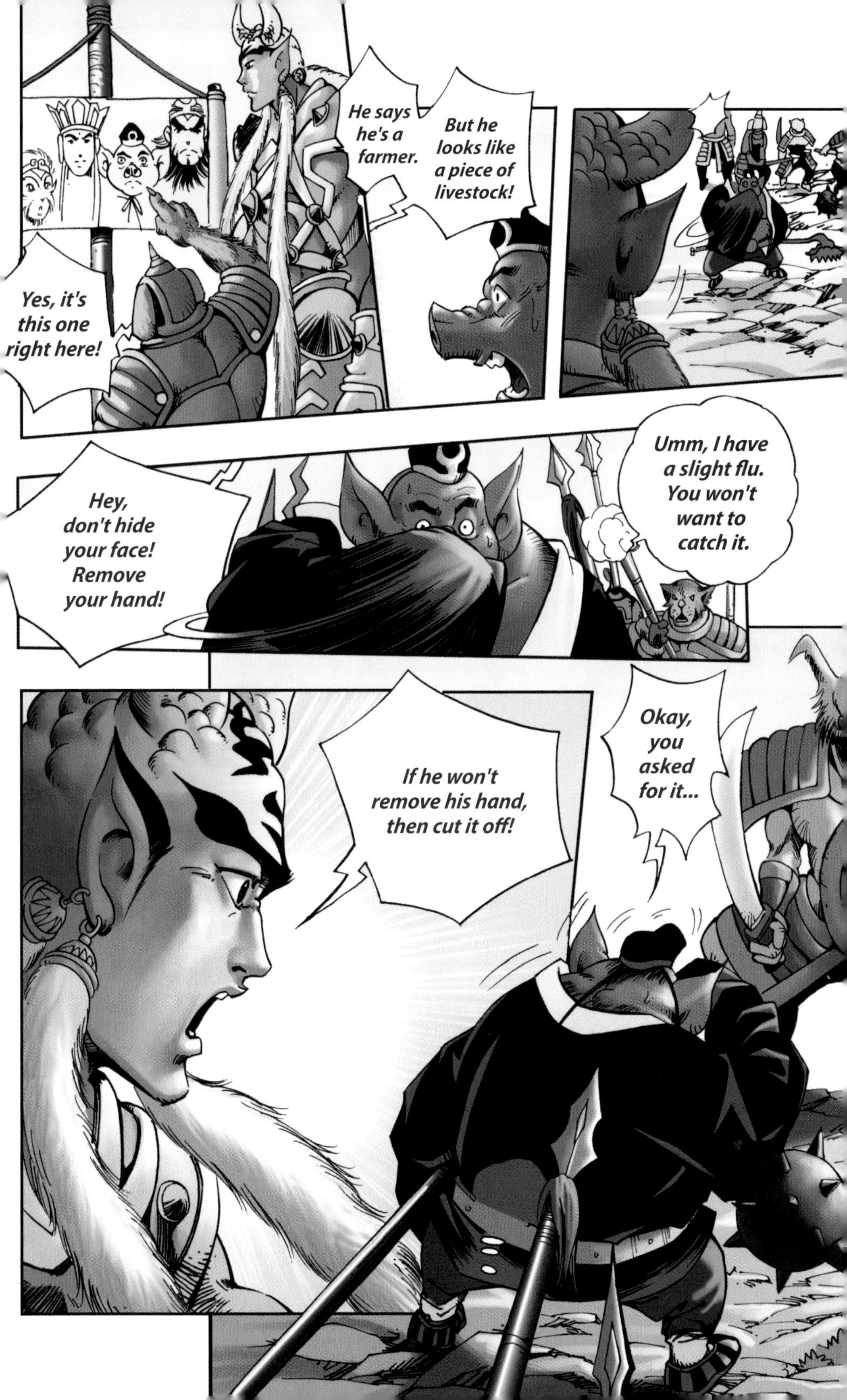
He says he's a farmer.
But he looks like a piece of livestock!
Yes, it's this one right here!
Hey, don't hide your face! Remove your hand!
Umm, I have a slight flu. You won't want to catch it.
If he won't remove his hand, then cut it off!
Okay, you asked for it...

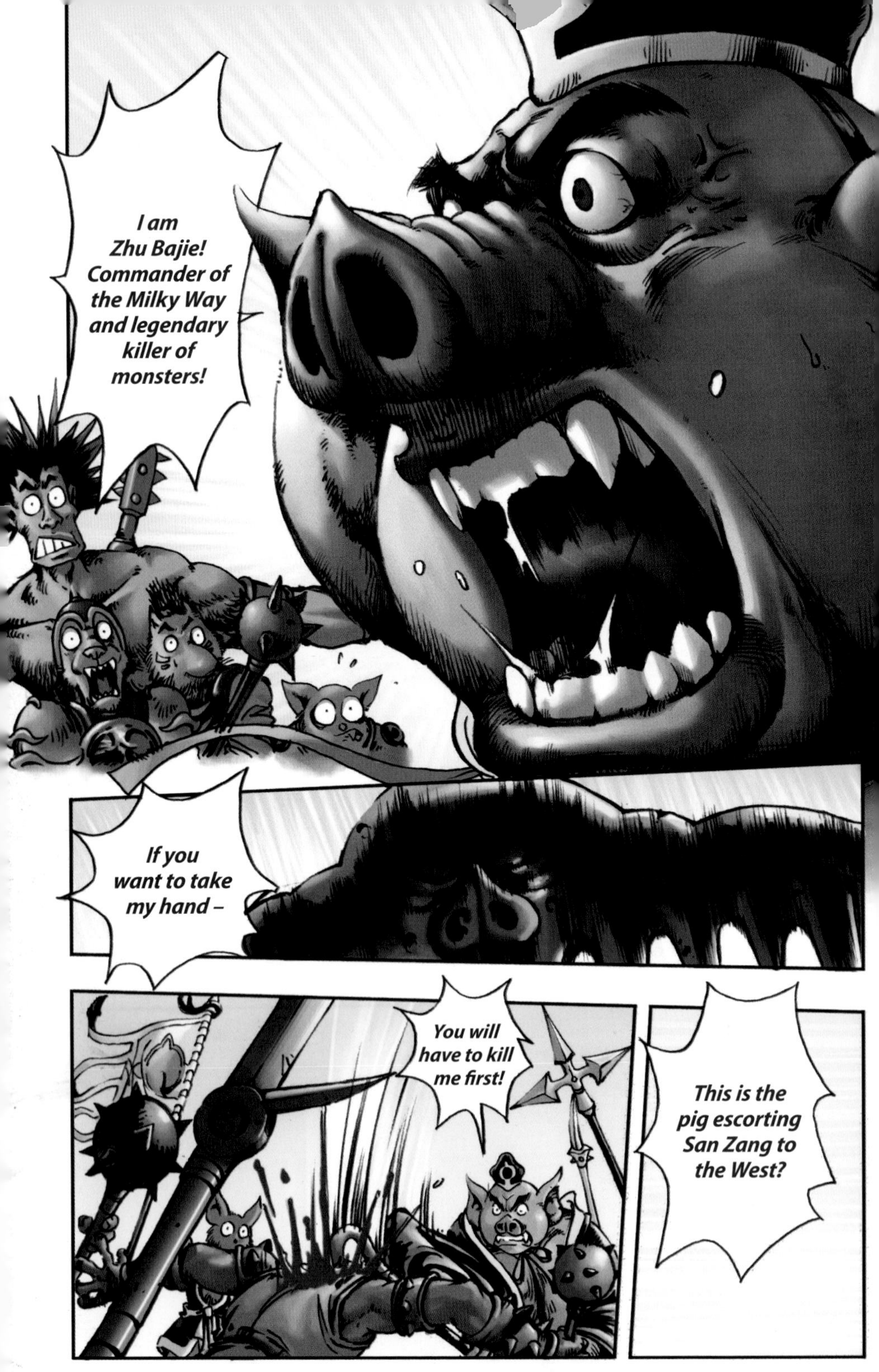
I am Zhu Bajie! Commander of the Milky Way and legendary killer of monsters!
If you want to take my hand –
You will have to kill me first!
This is the pig escorting San Zang to the West?

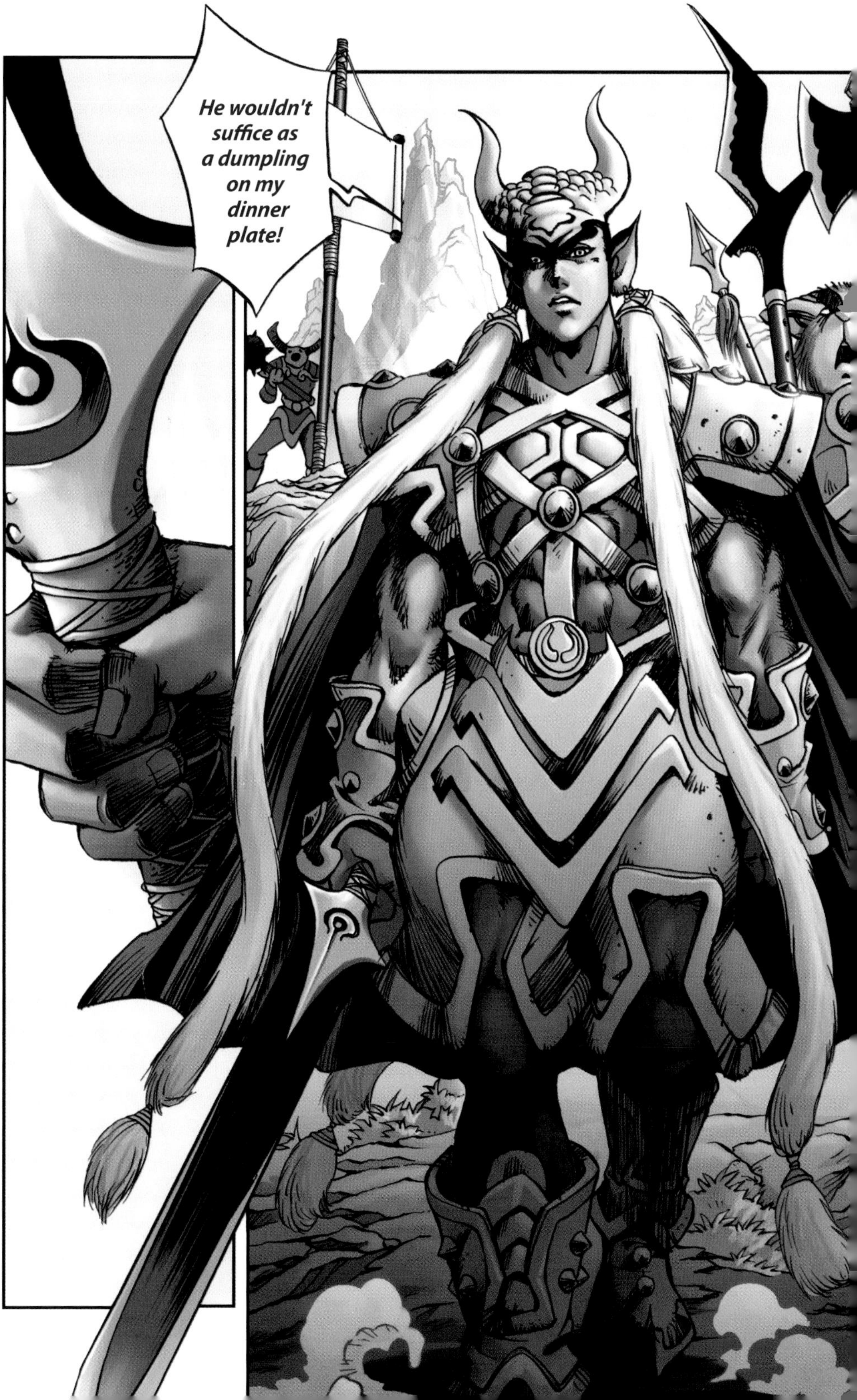
He wouldn't suffice as a dumpling on my dinner plate!

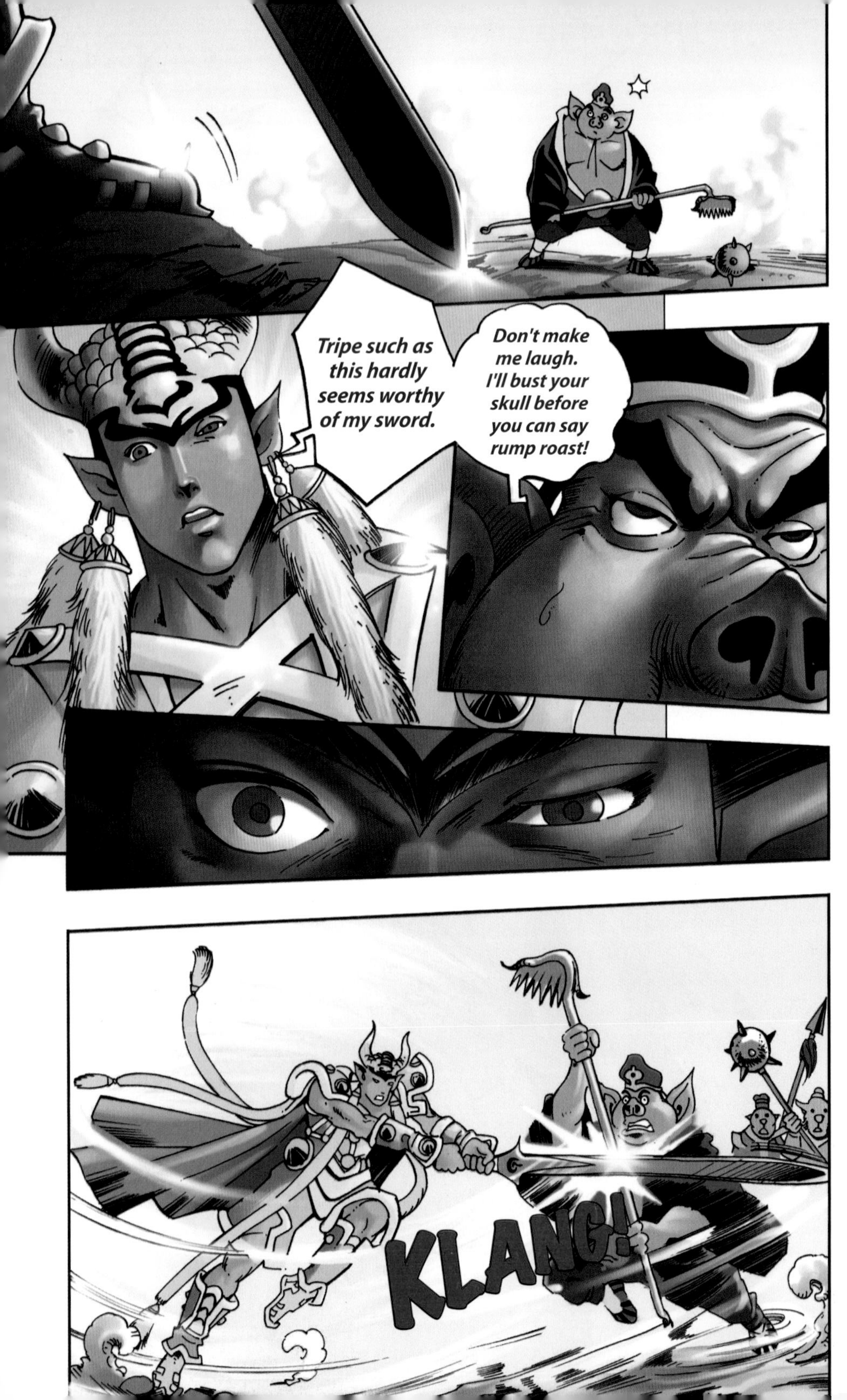
Tripe such as this hardly seems worthy of my sword.
Don't make me laugh. I'll bust your skull before you can say rump roast!
KLANG!

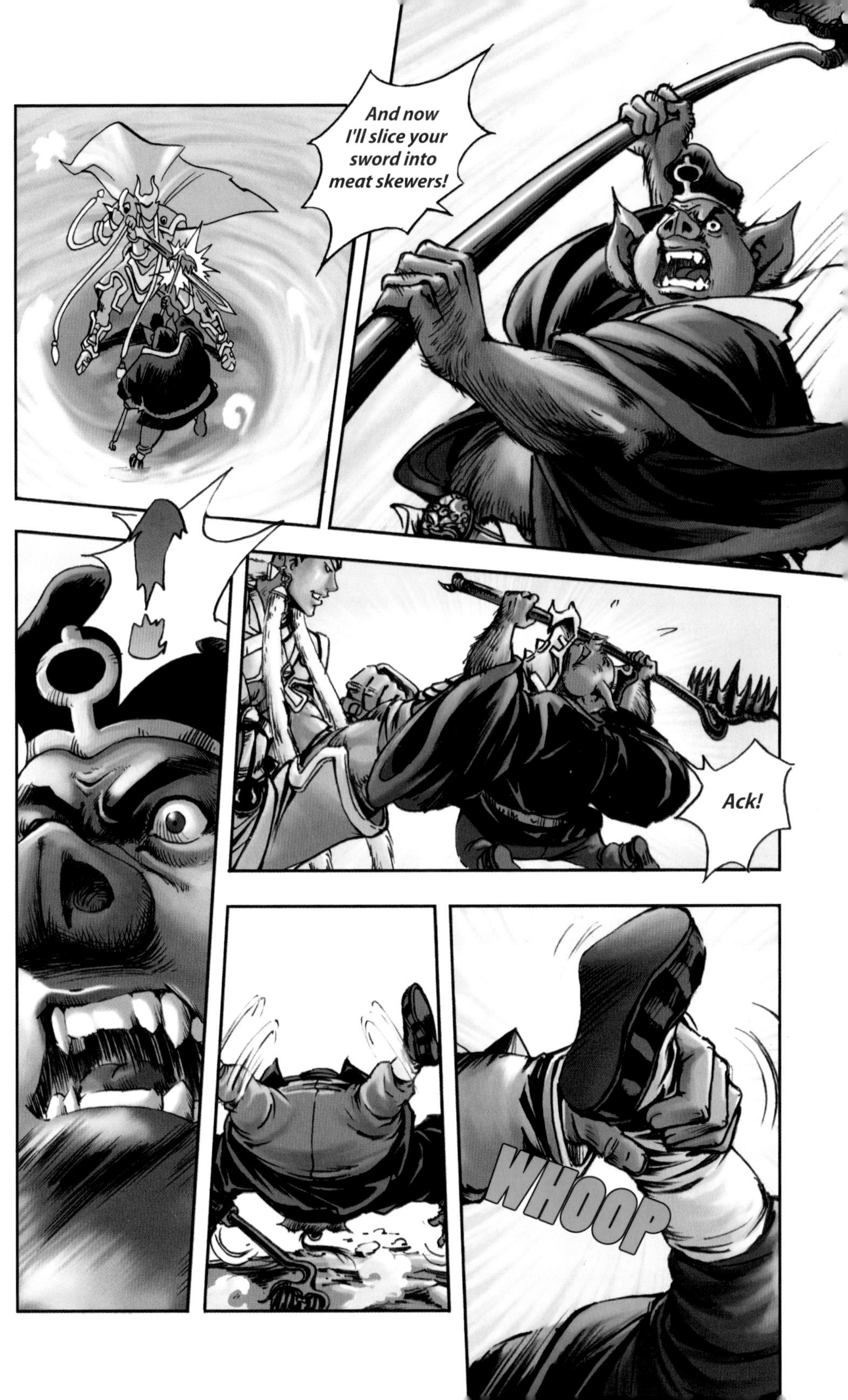
And now I'll slice your sword into meat skewers!
Ack!
WHOOP

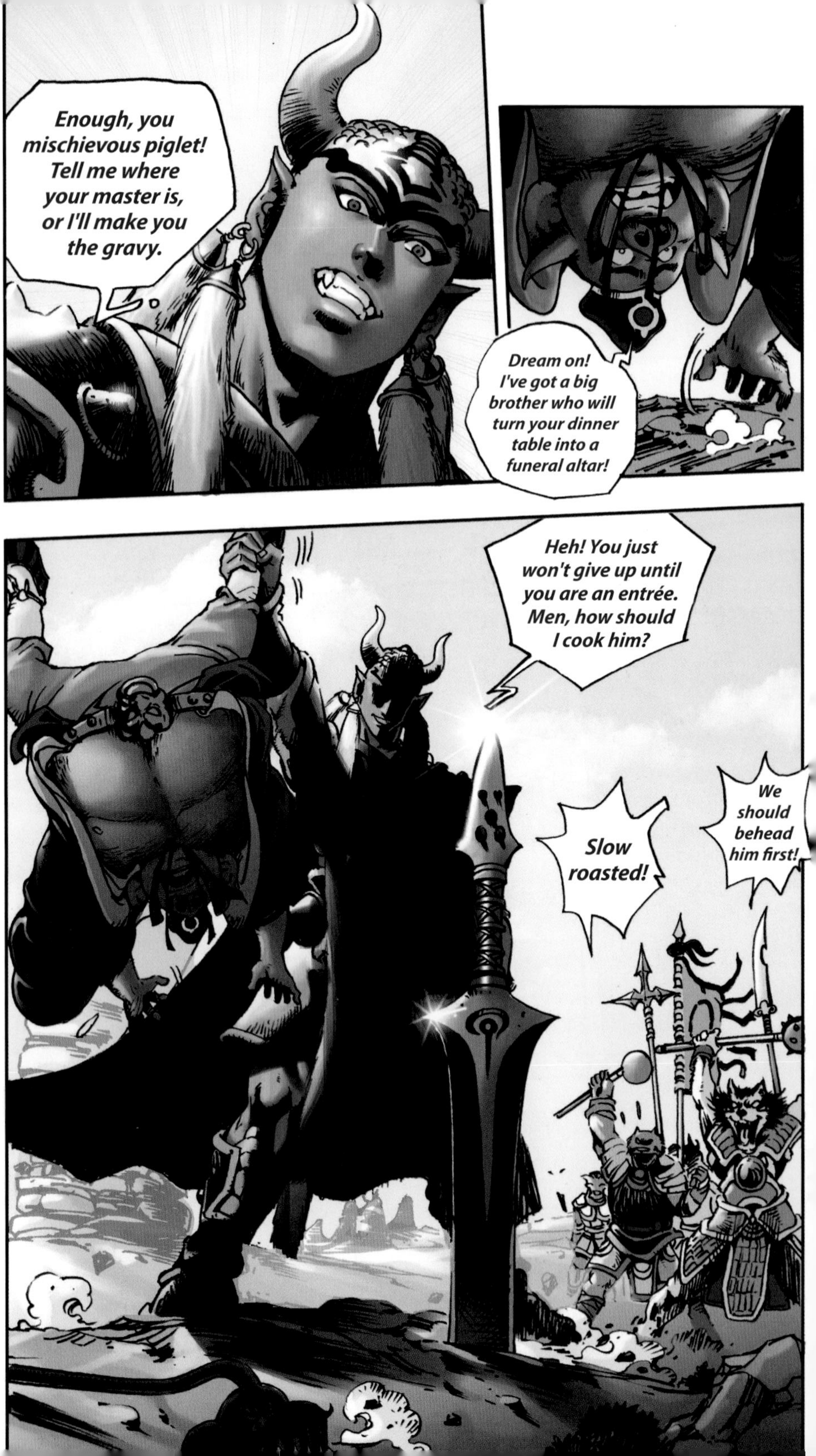
Enough, you mischievous piglet! Tell me where your master is, or I'll make you the gravy.
Dream on! I've got a big brother who will turn your dinner table into a funeral altar!
Heh! You just won't give up until you are an entrée. Men, how should I cook him?
Slow roasted!
We should behead him first!

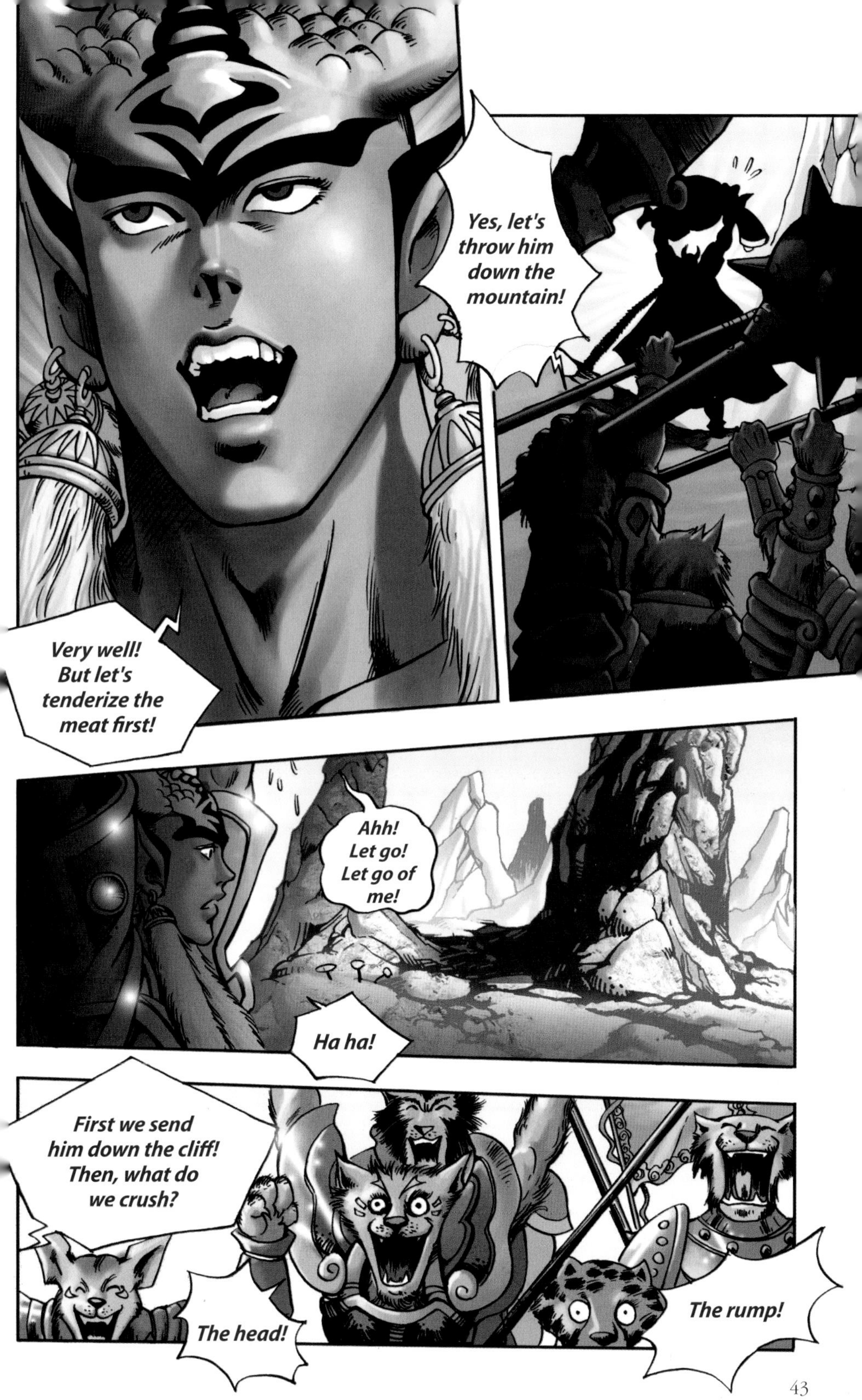
Yes, let's throw him down the mountain!
Very well! But let's tenderize the meat first!
Ahh! Let go! Let go of me!
Ha ha!
First we send him down the cliff! Then, what do we crush?
The head!
The rump!

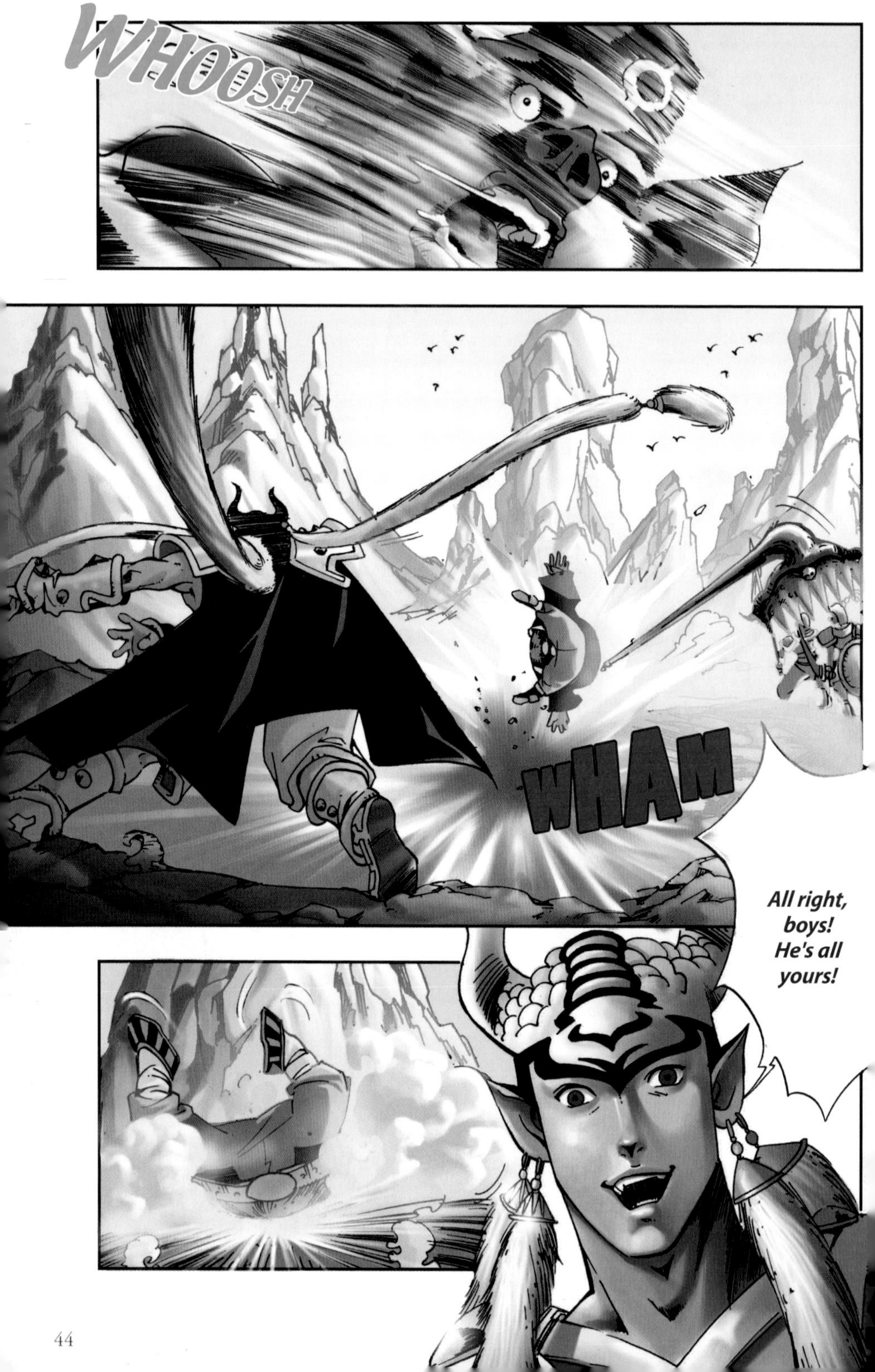
WHOOSH
WHAM
All right, boys! He's all yours!

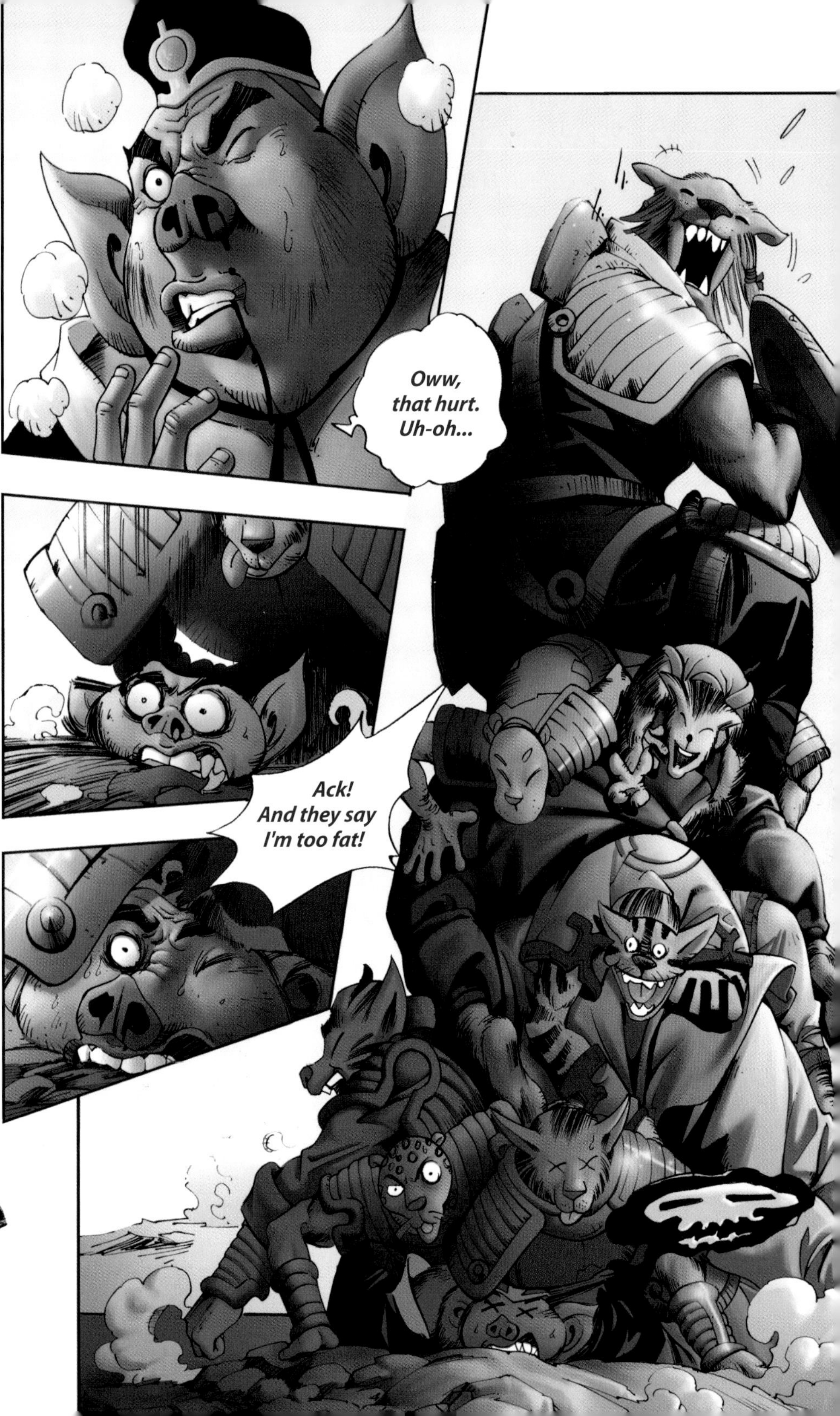
Oww, that hurt. Uh-oh...
Ack! And they say I'm too fat!

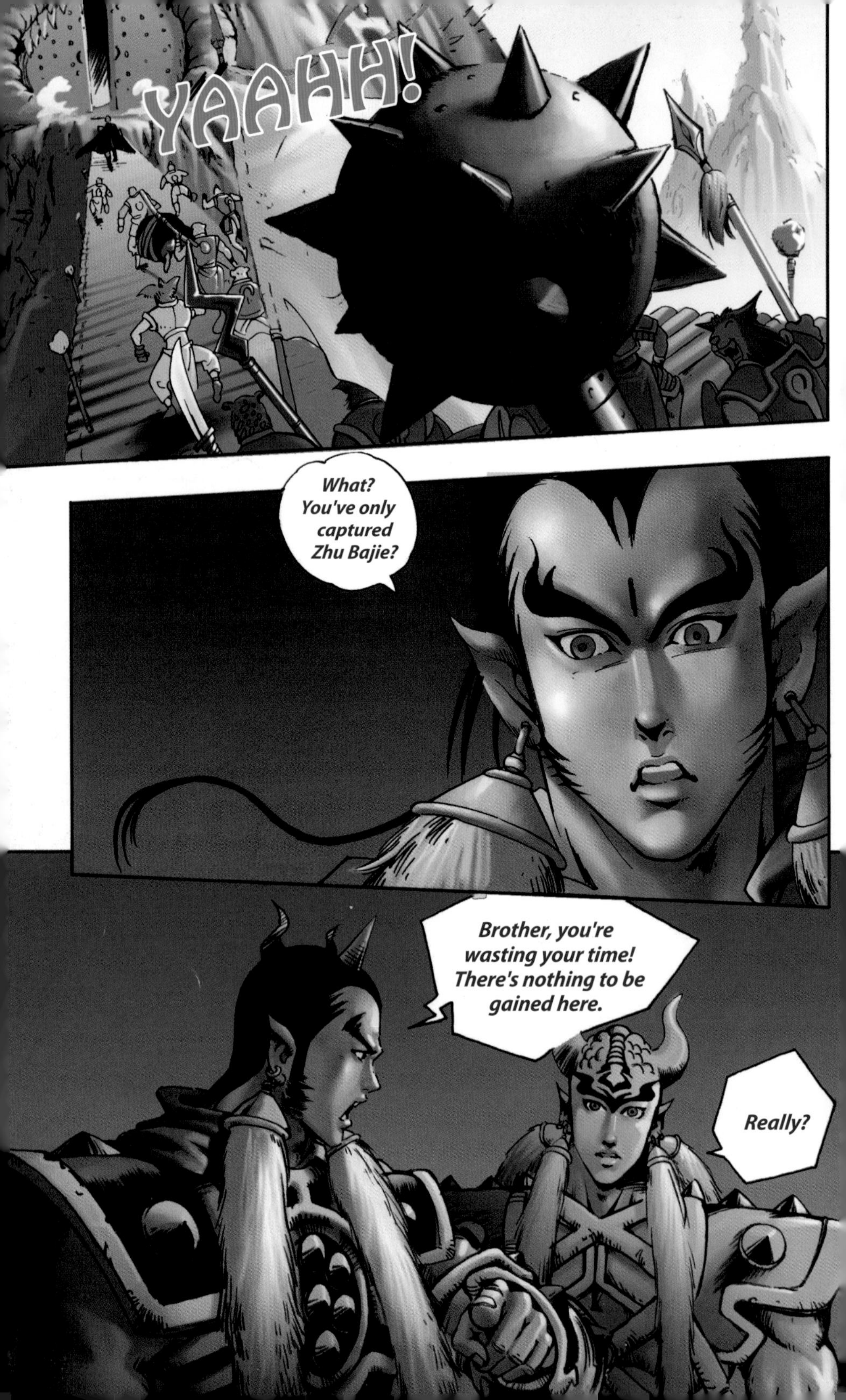
YAAHH!
What? You've only captured Zhu Bajie?
Brother, you're wasting your time! There's nothing to be gained here.
Really?

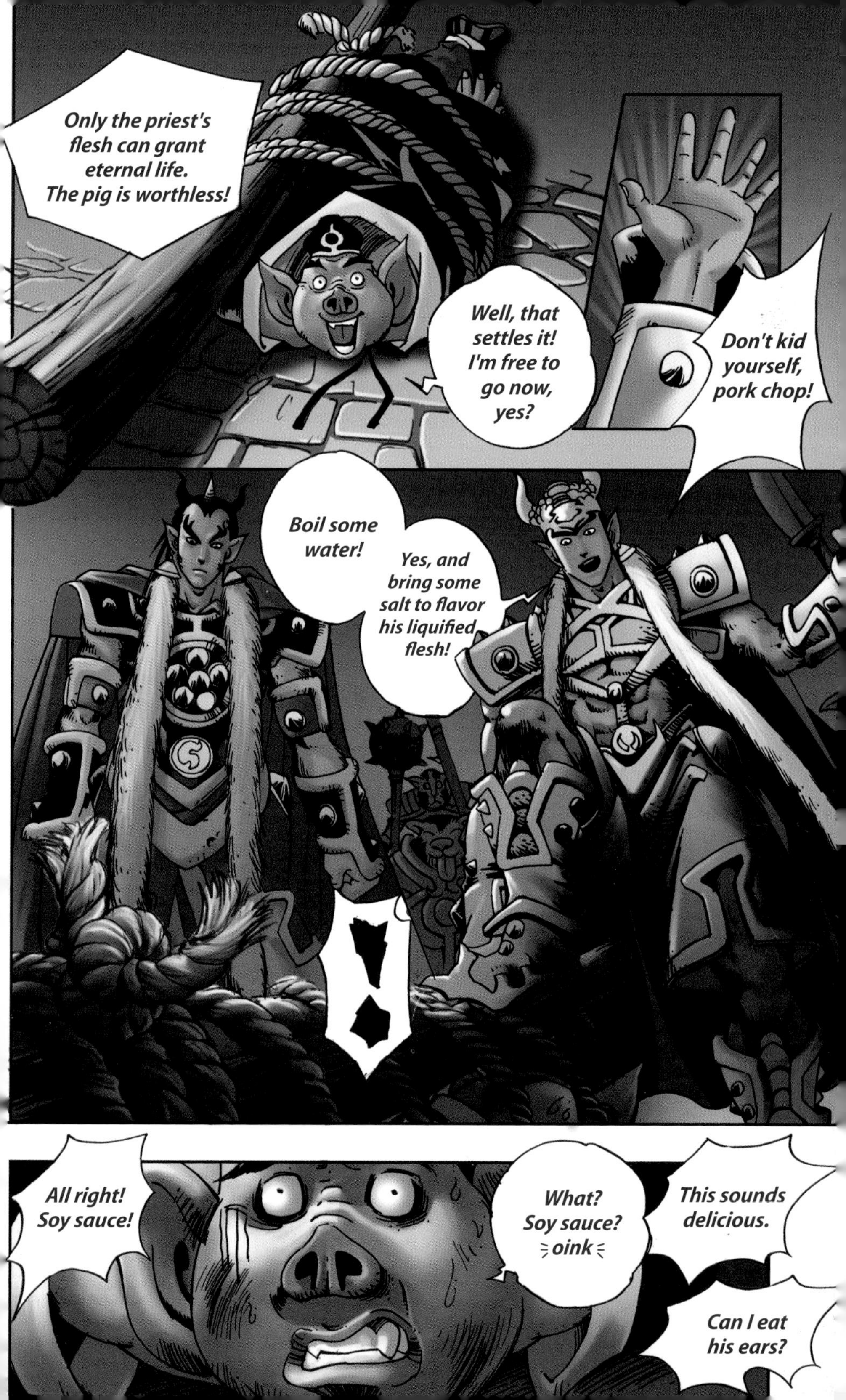
Only the priest's flesh can grant eternal life. The pig is worthless!
Well, that settles it! I'm free to go now, yes?
Don't kid yourself, pork chop!
Boil some water!
Yes, and bring some salt to flavor his liquified flesh!
All right! Soy sauce!
What? Soy sauce? oink
This sounds delicious.
Can I eat his ears?

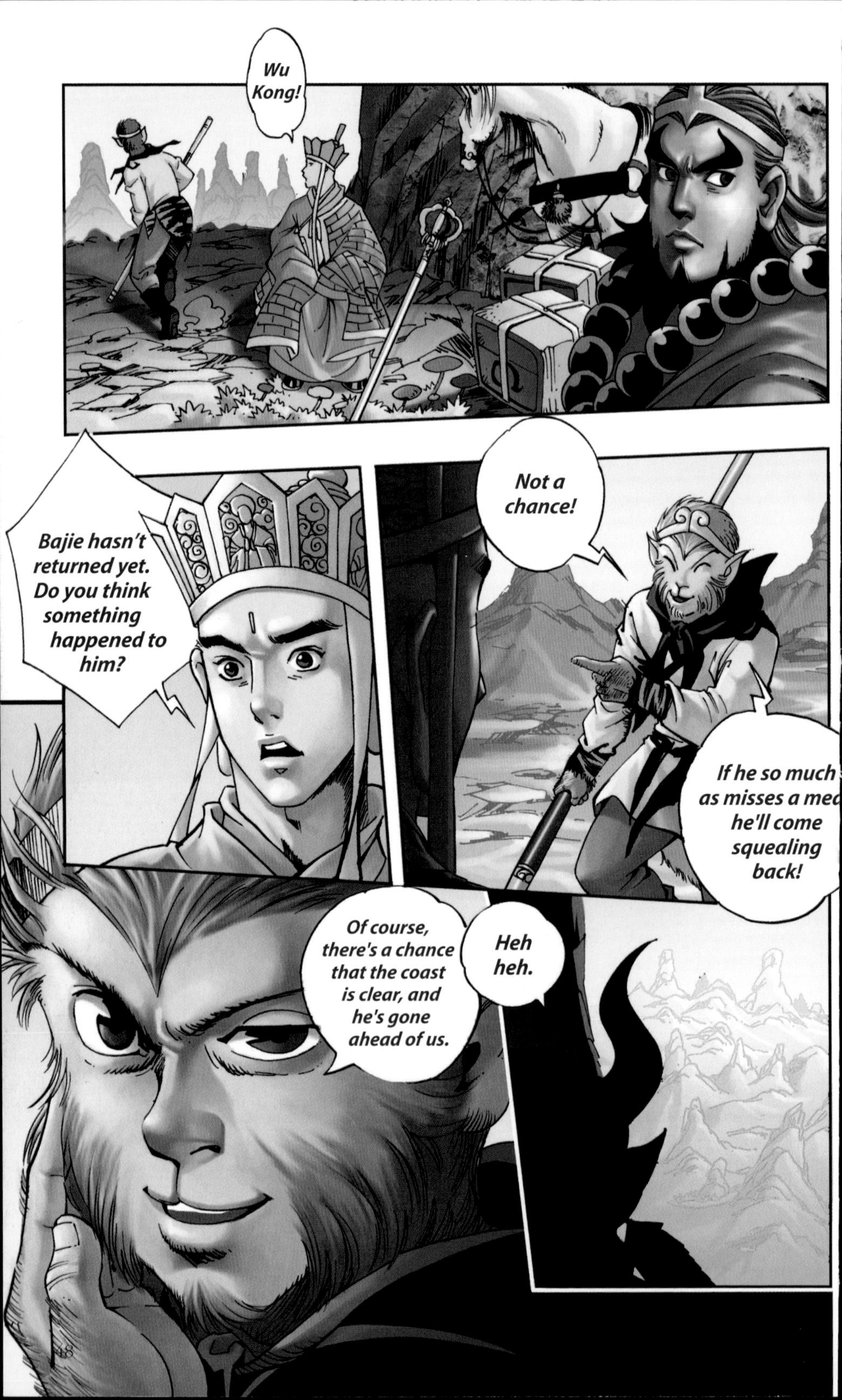
Wu Kong!
Bajie hasn't returned yet. Do you think something happened to him?
Not a chance!
If he so much as misses a mea
he'll come squealing back!
Of course, there's a chance that the coast is clear, and he's gone ahead of us.
Heh heh.

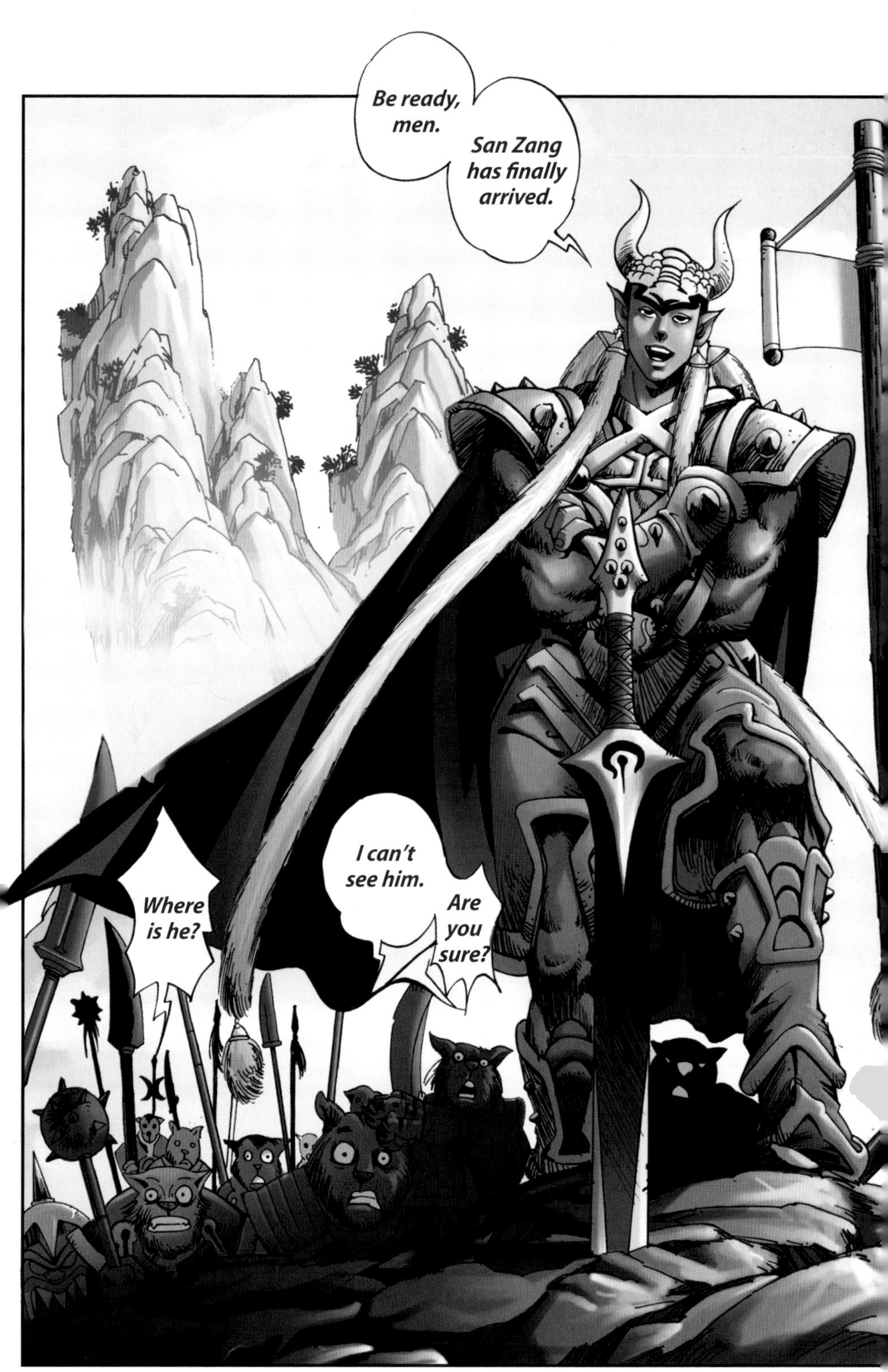
Be ready, men.
San Zang has finally arrived.
Where is he?
I can't see him.
Are you sure?

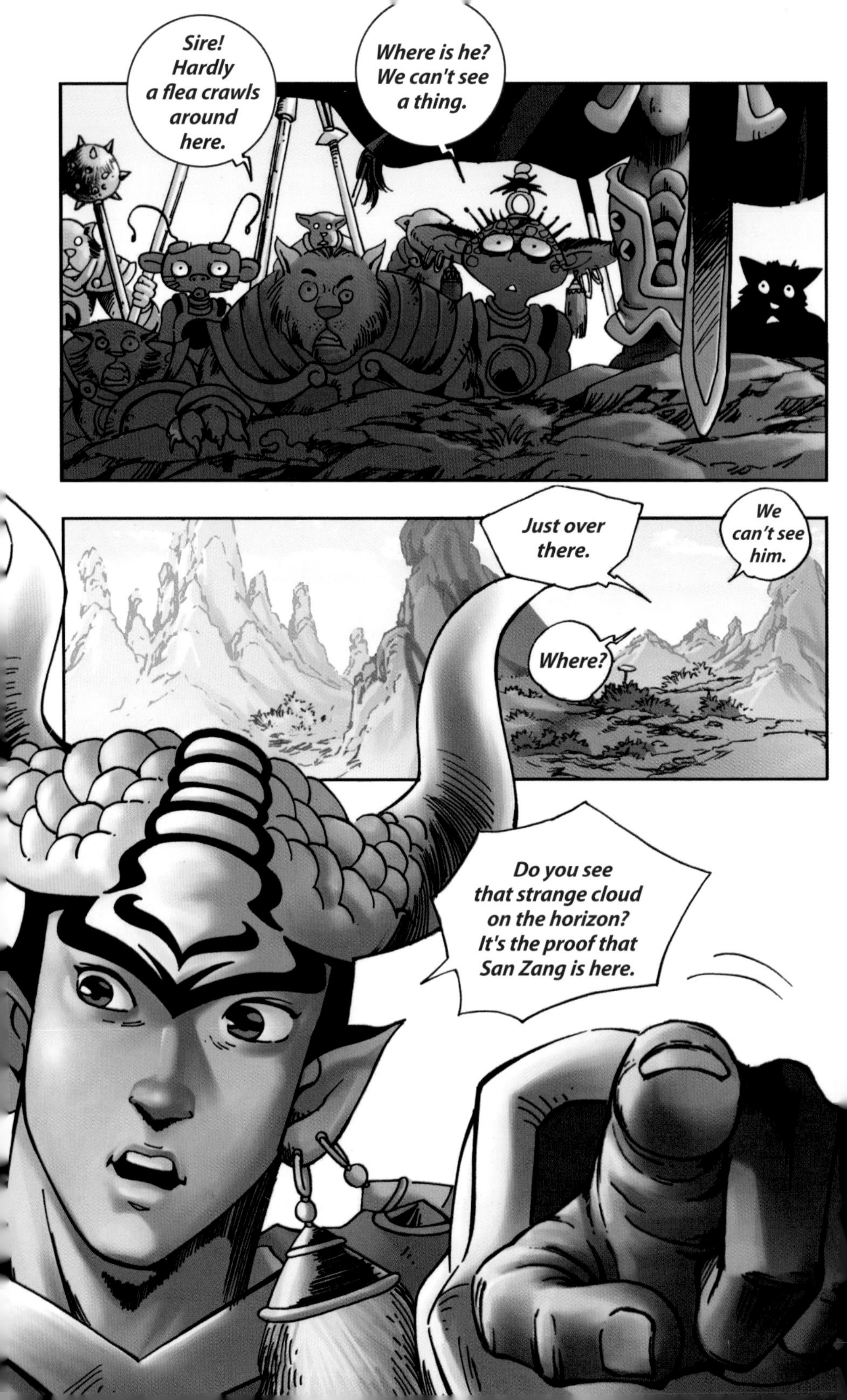
Sire! Hardly a flea crawls around here.
Where is he? We can't see a thing.
Just over there.
We can't see him.
Where?
Do you see that strange cloud on the horizon? It's the proof that San Zang is here.

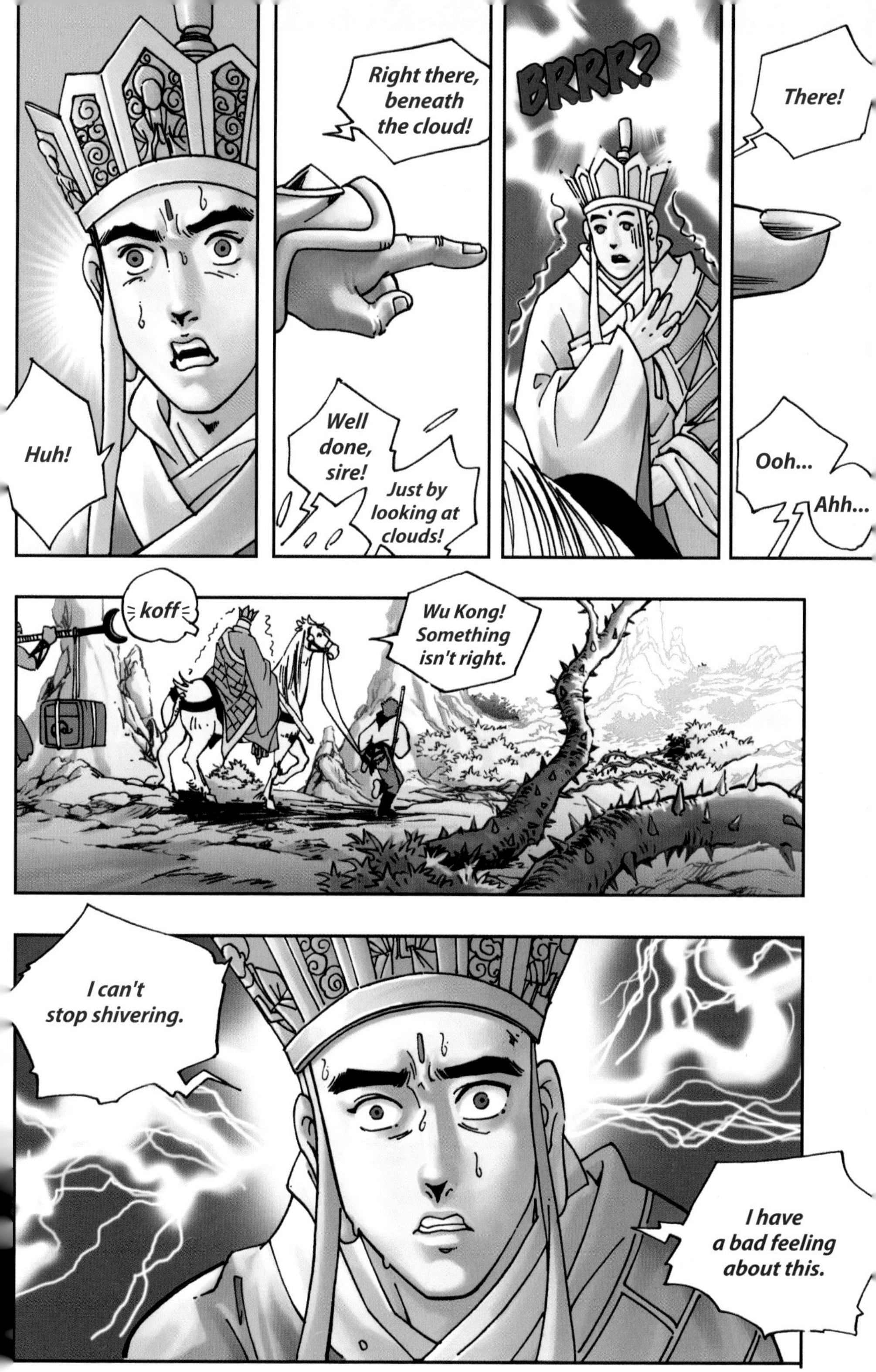
Huh!
Right there, beneath the cloud!
Well done, sire!
Just by looking at clouds!
BRRR?
There!
Ooh...
Ahh...
koff
Wu Kong! Something isn't right.
I can't stop shivering.
I have a bad feeling about this.

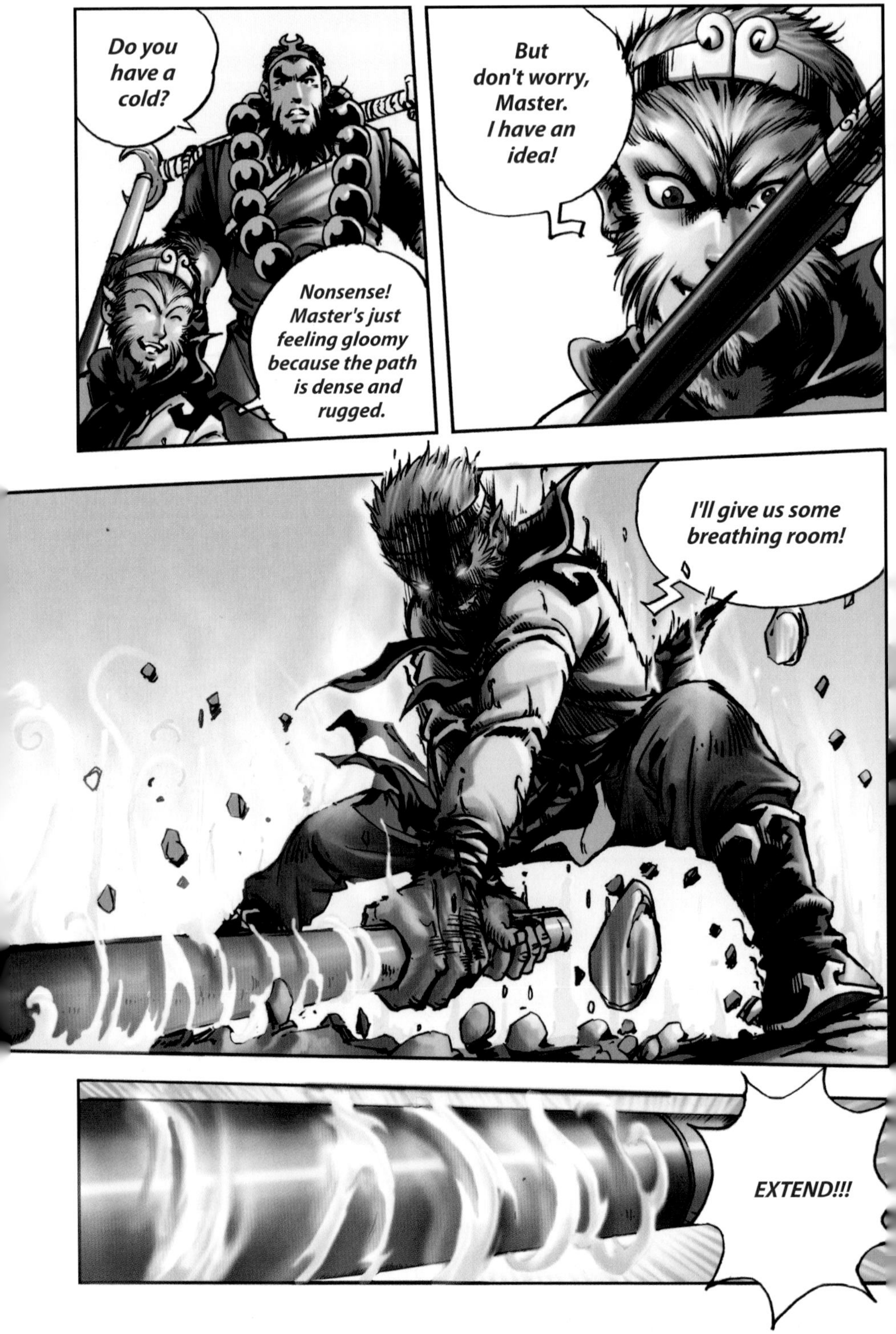
Do you have a cold?
Nonsense! Master's just feeling gloomy because the path is dense and rugged.
But don't worry, Master. I have an idea!
I'll give us some breathing room!
EXTEND!!!

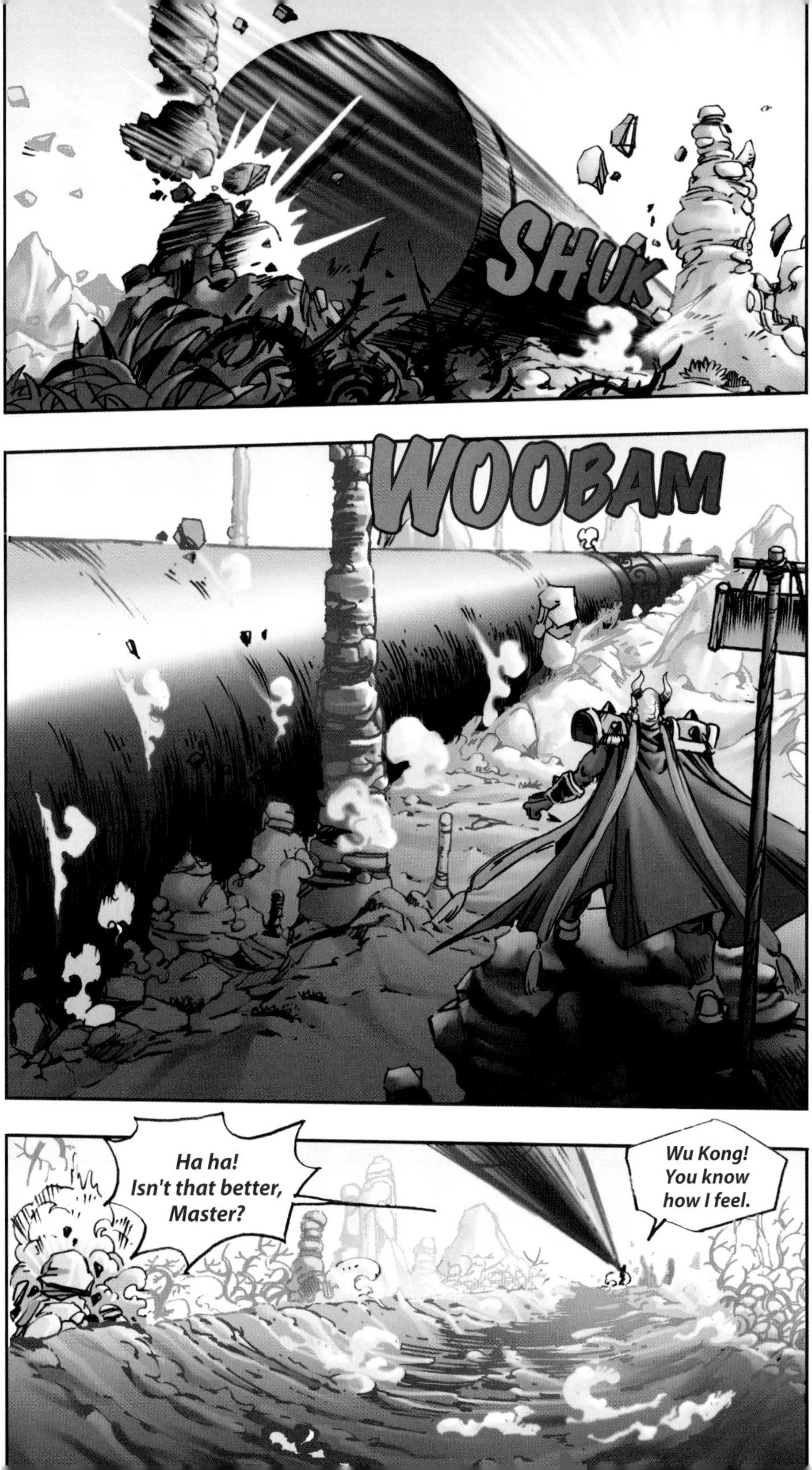
SHUK
WOOBAM
Ha ha! Isn't that better, Master?
Wu Kong! You know how I feel.

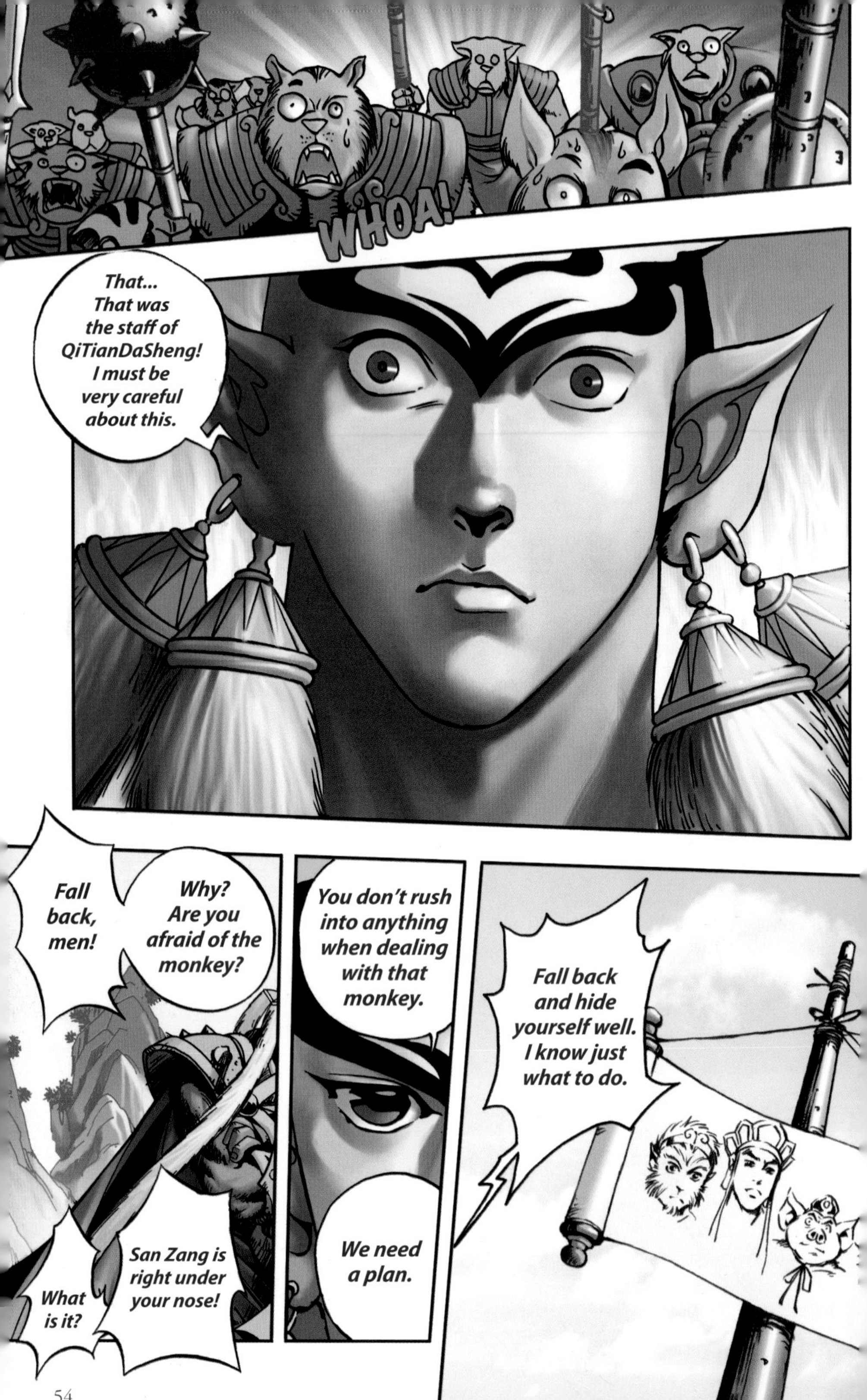
WHOA!
That... That was the staff of QiTianDaSheng! I must be very careful about this.
Fall back, men!
Why? Are you afraid of the monkey?
What is it?
San Zang is right under your nose!
You don't rush into anything when dealing with that monkey.
We need a plan.
Fall back and hide yourself well. I know just what to do.

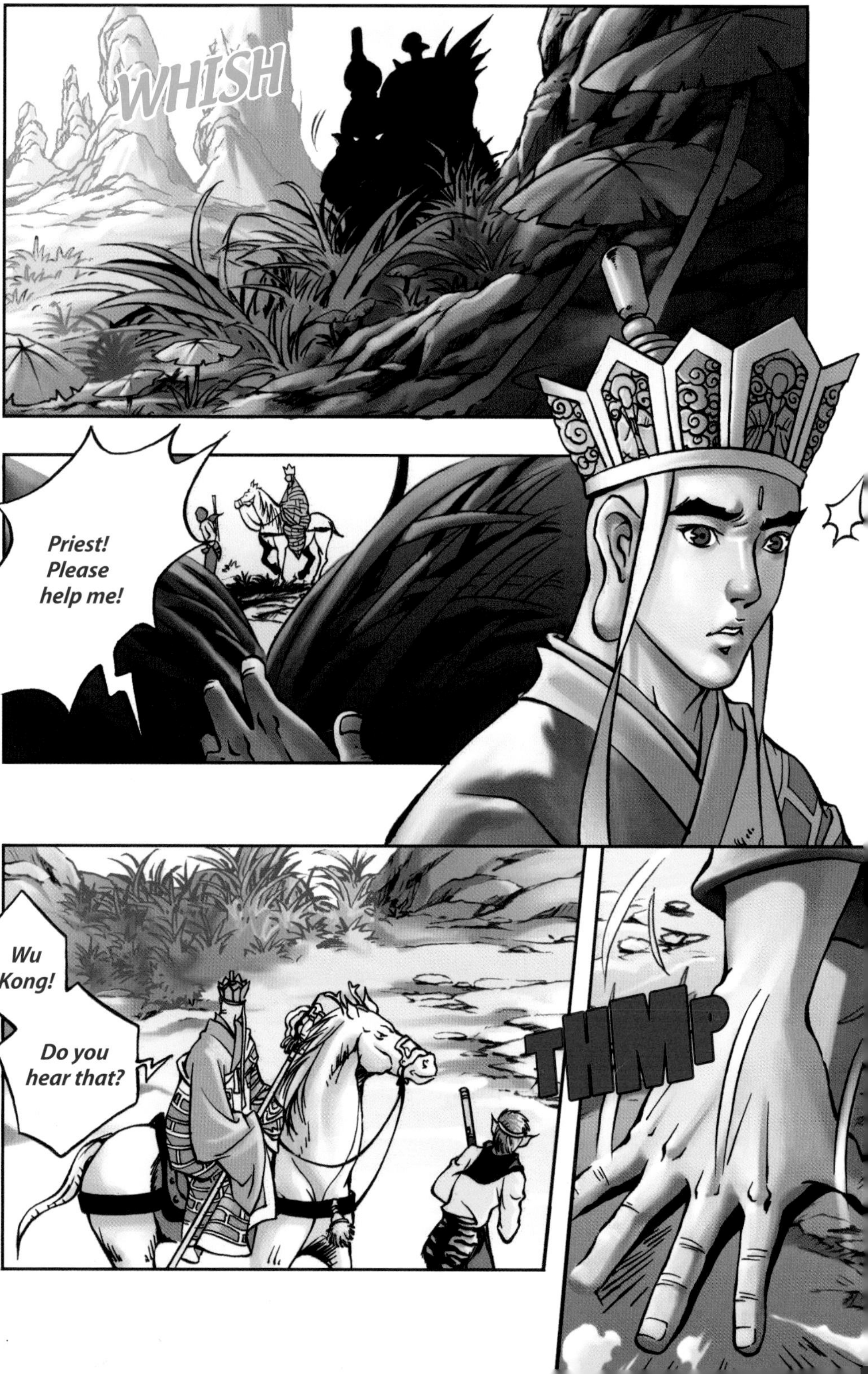
WHISH
Priest! Please help me!
Wu Kong!
Do you hear that?
THMP

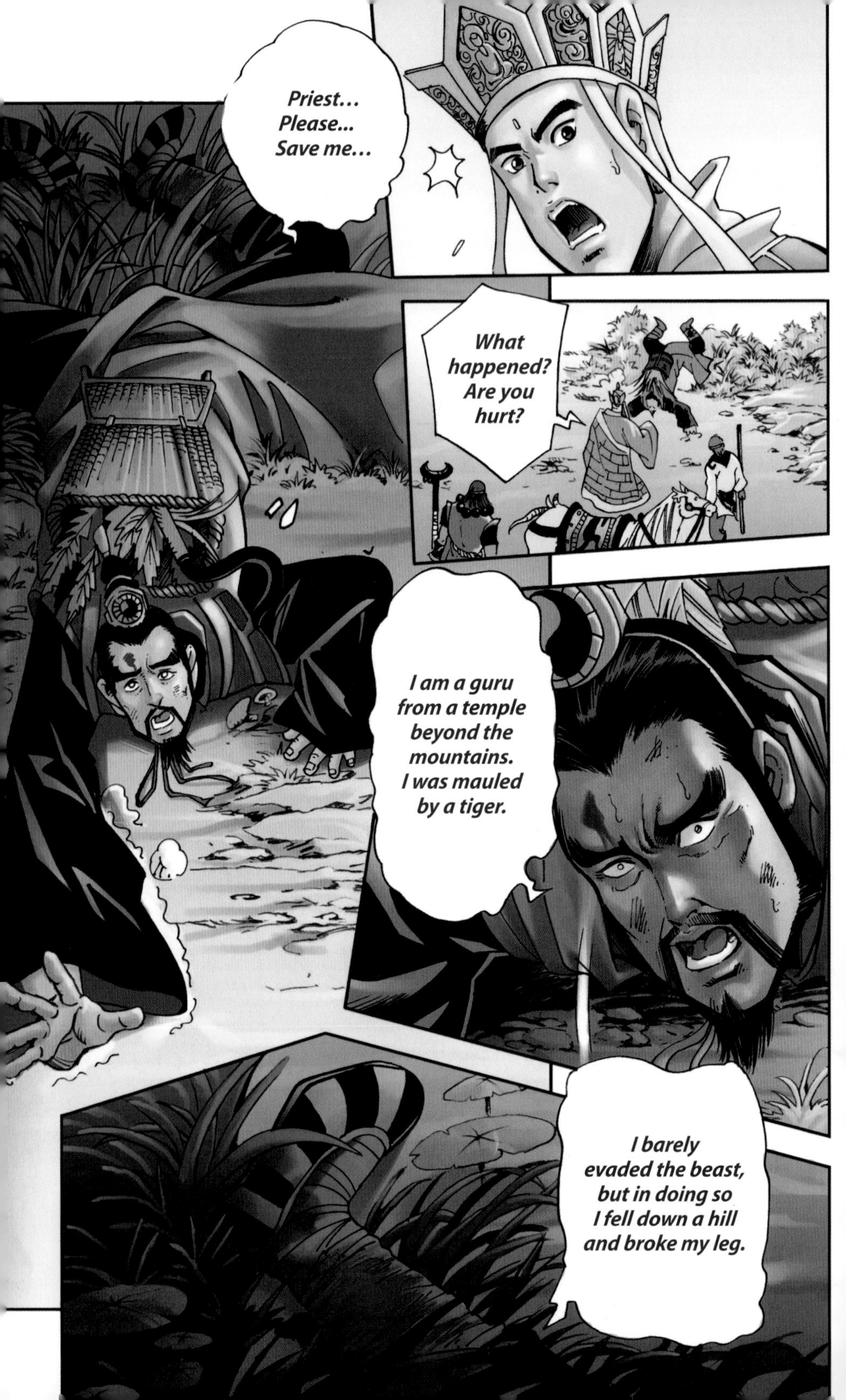
Priest… Please… Save me…
What happened? Are you hurt?
I am a guru from a temple beyond the mountains. I was mauled by a tiger.
I barely evaded the beast, but in doing so I fell down a hill and broke my leg.

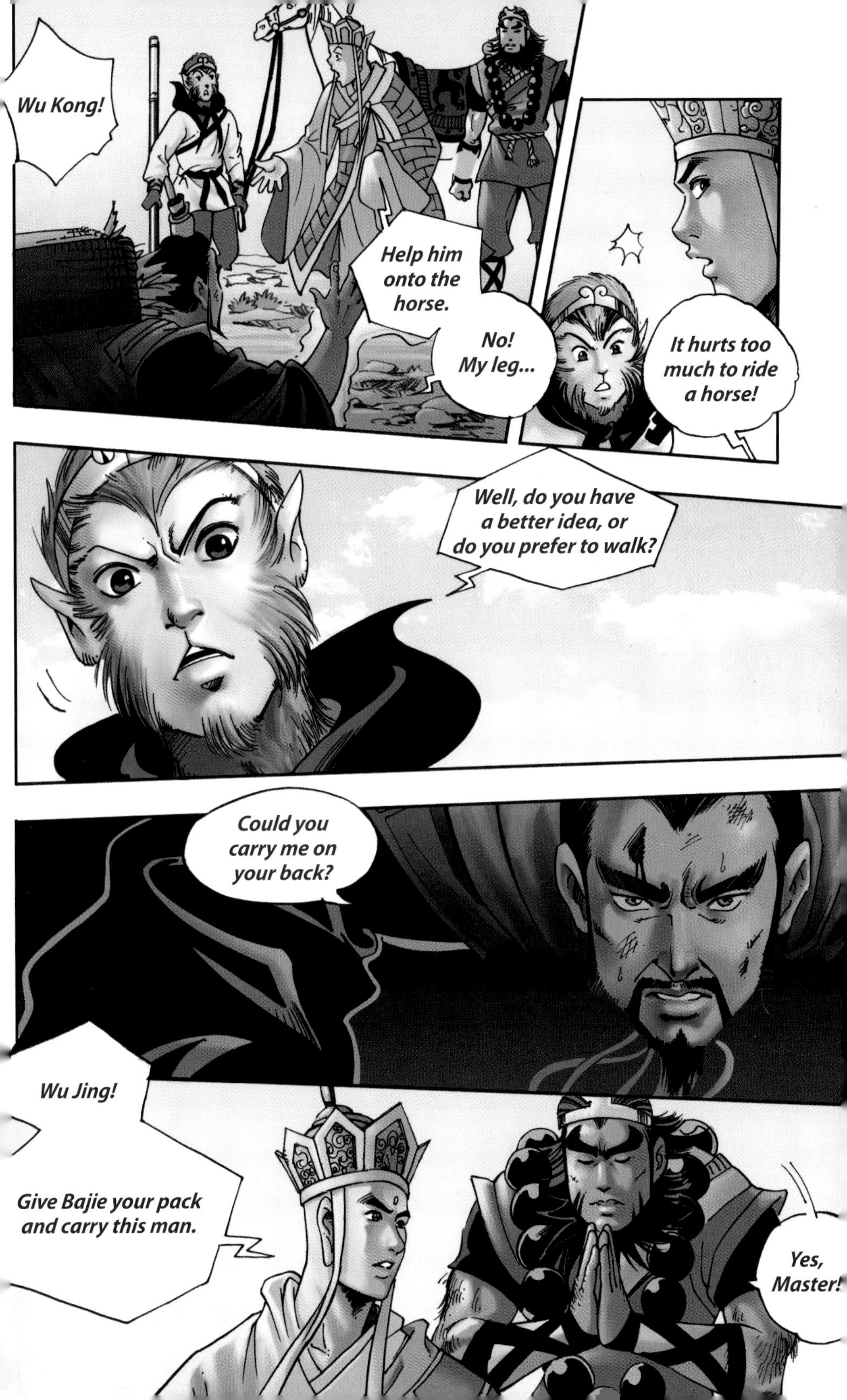
Wu Kong!
Help him onto the horse.
No! My leg...
It hurts too much to ride a horse!
Well, do you have a better idea, or do you prefer to walk?
Could you carry me on your back?
Wu Jing!
Give Bajie your pack and carry this man.
Yes, Master!

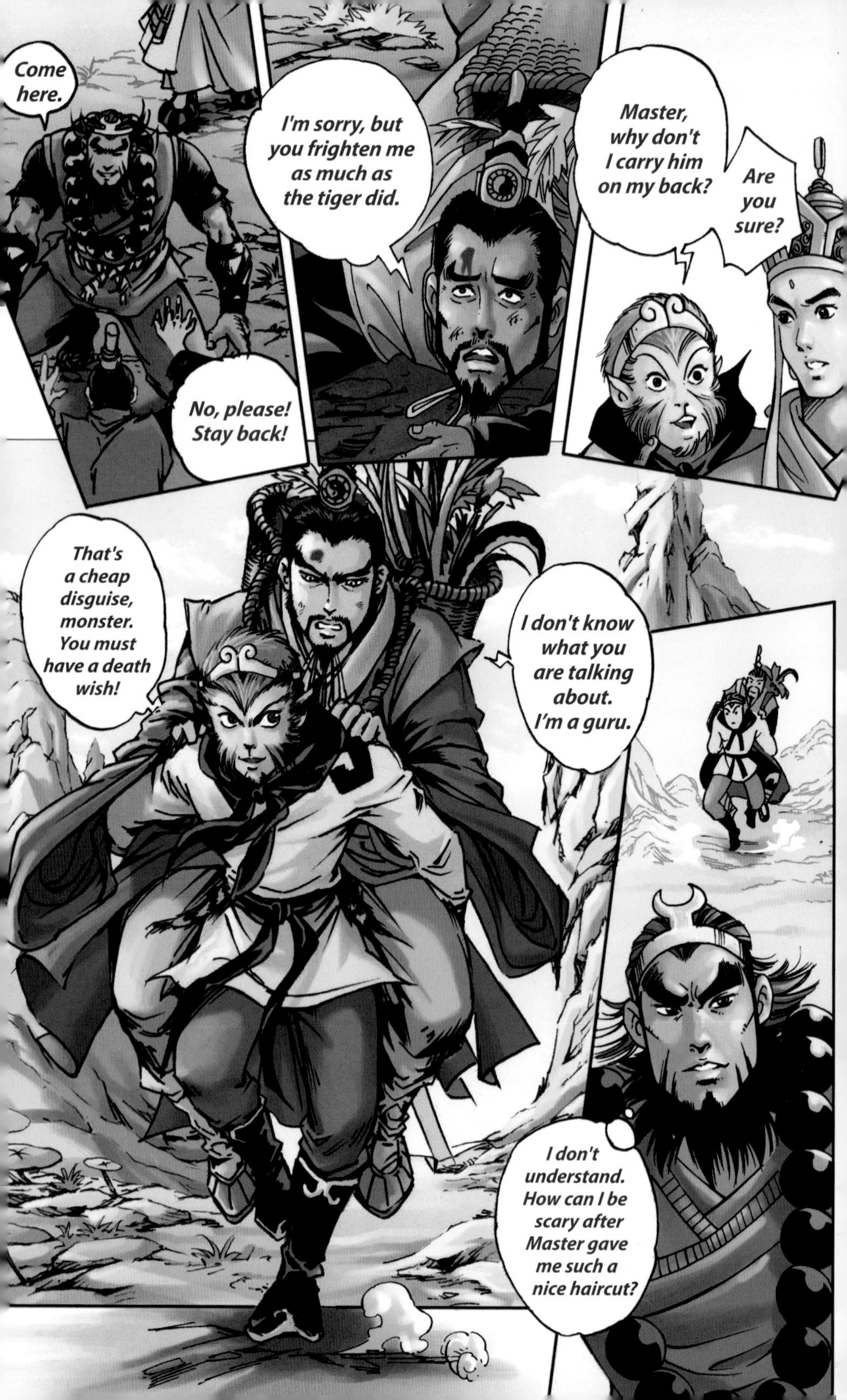
Come here.
No, please! Stay back!
I'm sorry, but you frighten me as much as the tiger did.
Master, why don't I carry him on my back?
Are you sure?
That's a cheap disguise, monster. You must have a death wish!
I don't know what you are talking about. I'm a guru.
I don't understand. How can I be scary after Master gave me such a nice haircut?

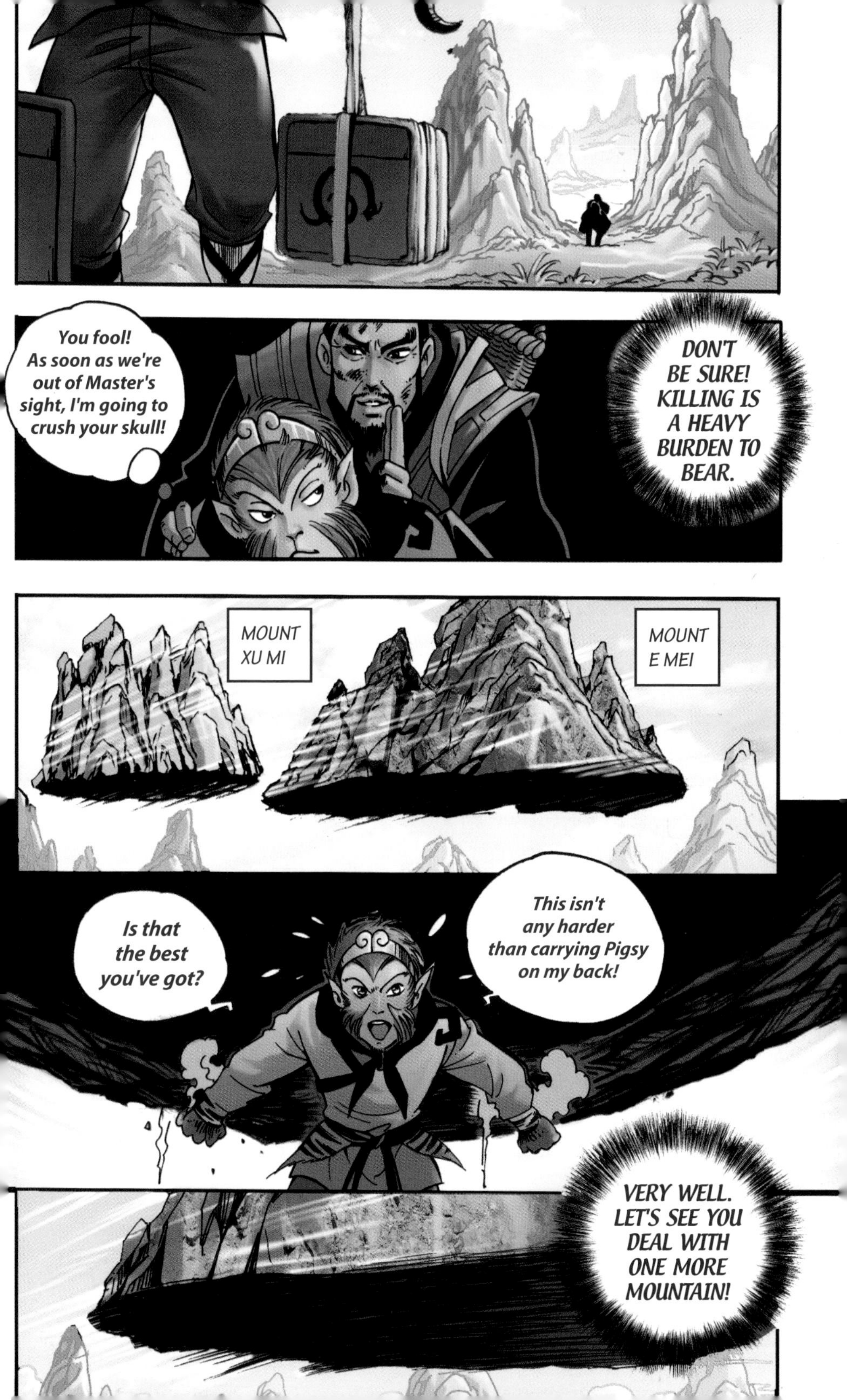
You fool!
As soon as we're out of Master's sight, I'm going to crush your skull!
DON'T BE SURE! KILLING IS A HEAVY BURDEN TO BEAR.
MOUNT XU MI
MOUNT E MEI
Is that the best you've got?
This isn't any harder than carrying Pigsy on my back!
VERY WELL. LET'S SEE YOU DEAL WITH ONE MORE MOUNTAIN!

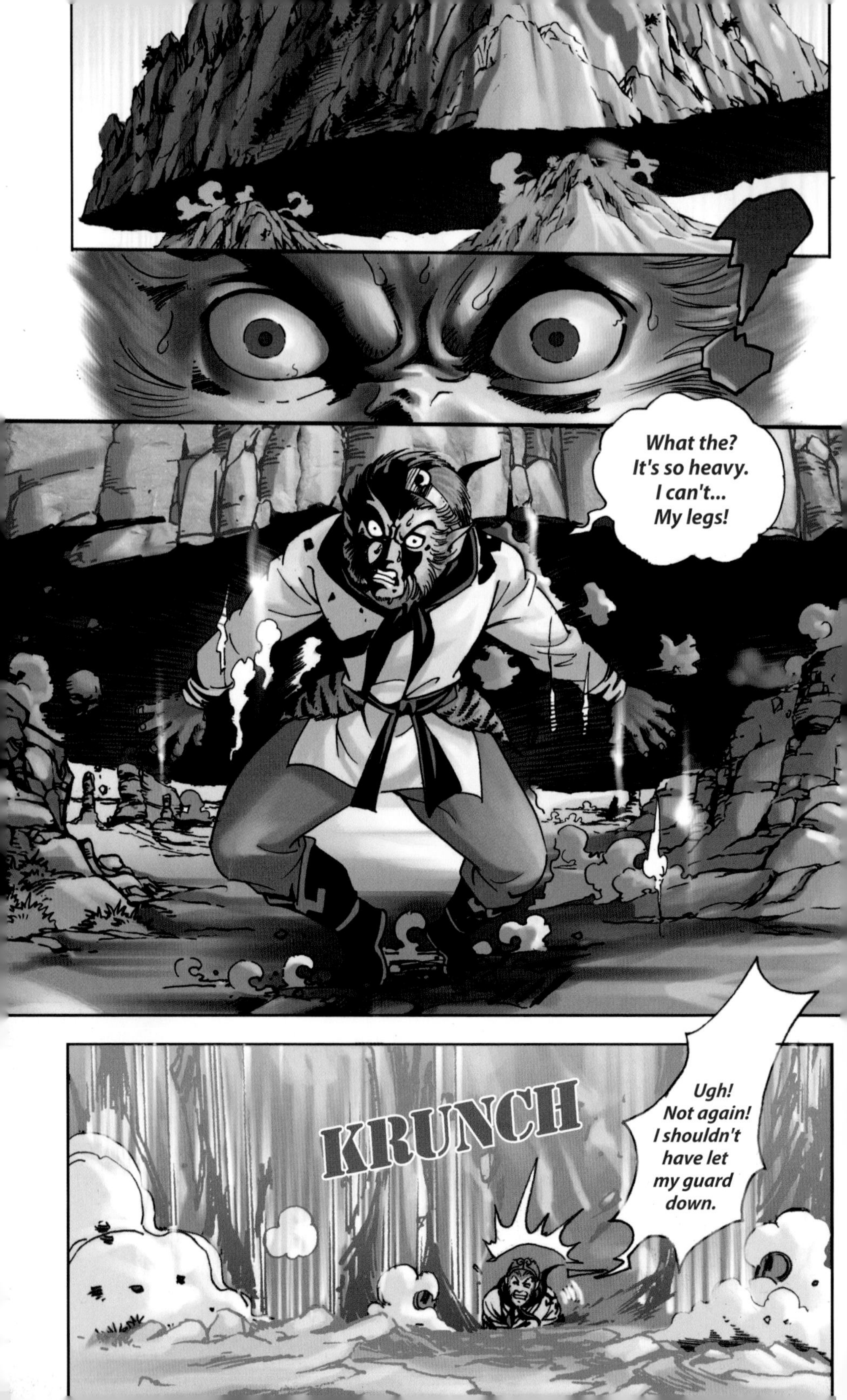
What the? It's so heavy. I can't... My legs!
KRUNCH
Ugh! Not again! I shouldn't have let my guard down.

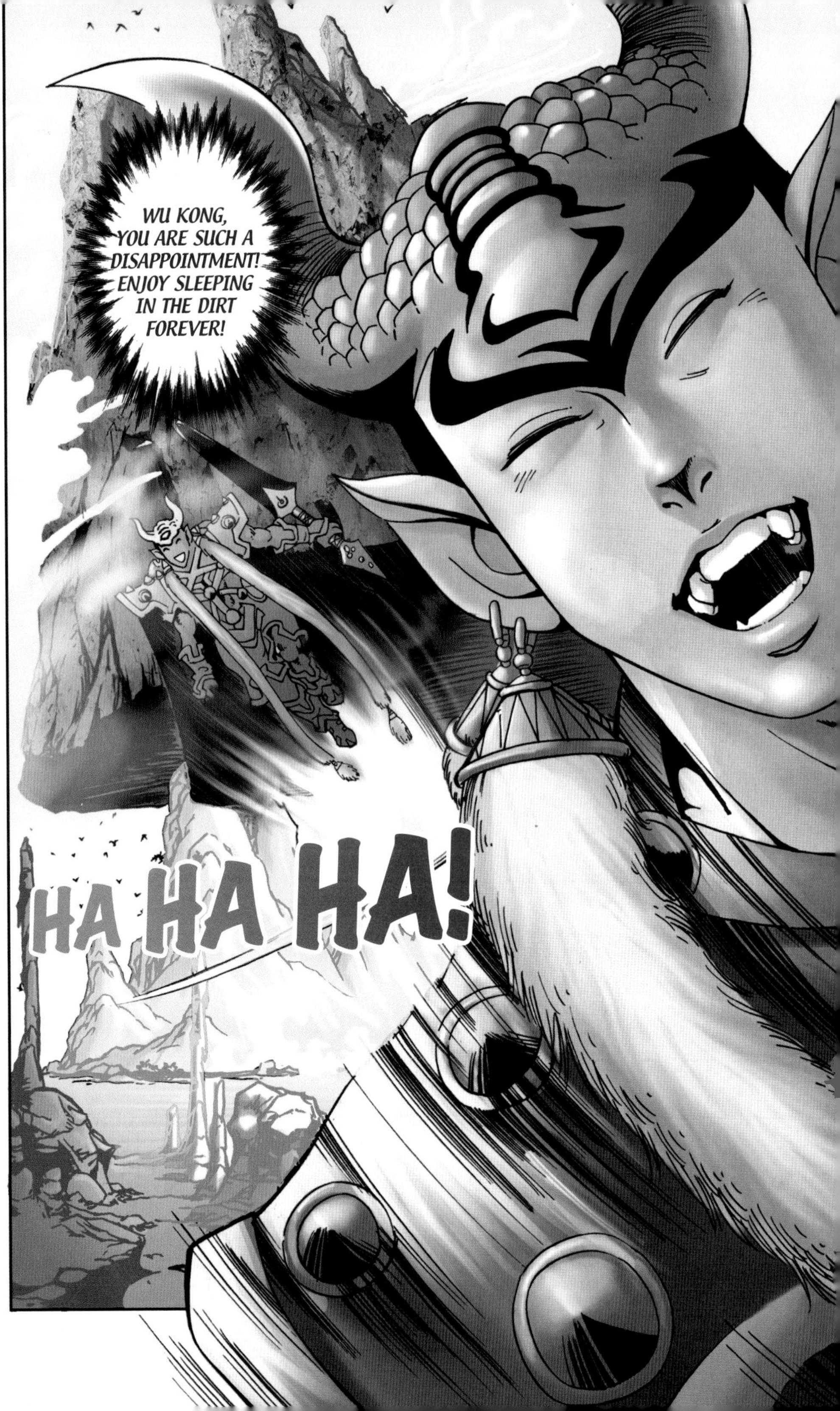
WU KONG, YOU ARE SUCH A DISAPPOINTMENT! ENJOY SLEEPING IN THE DIRT FOREVER!
HA HA HA!

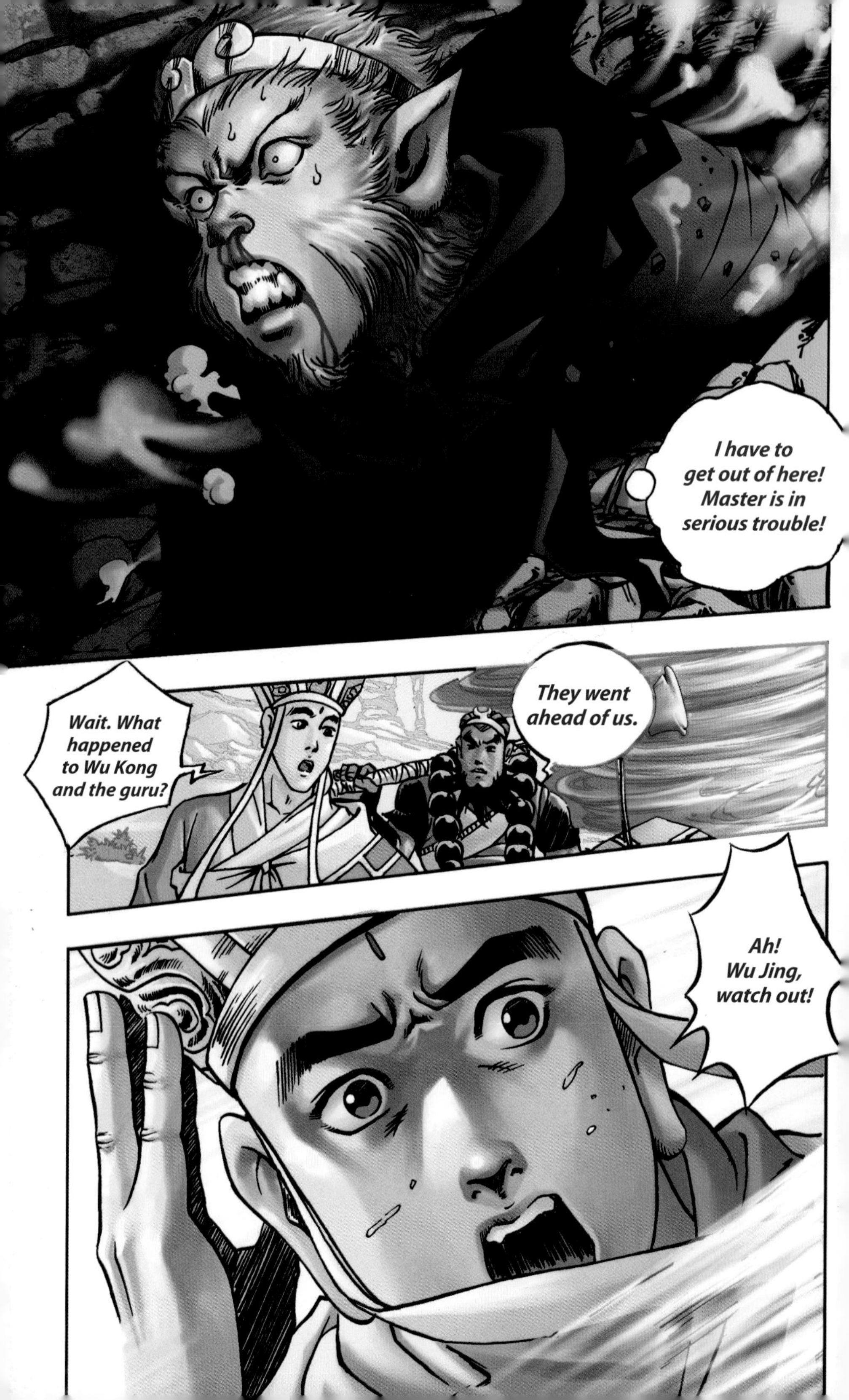
I have to get out of here! Master is in serious trouble!
Wait. What happened to Wu Kong and the guru?
They went ahead of us.
Ah! Wu Jing, watch out!

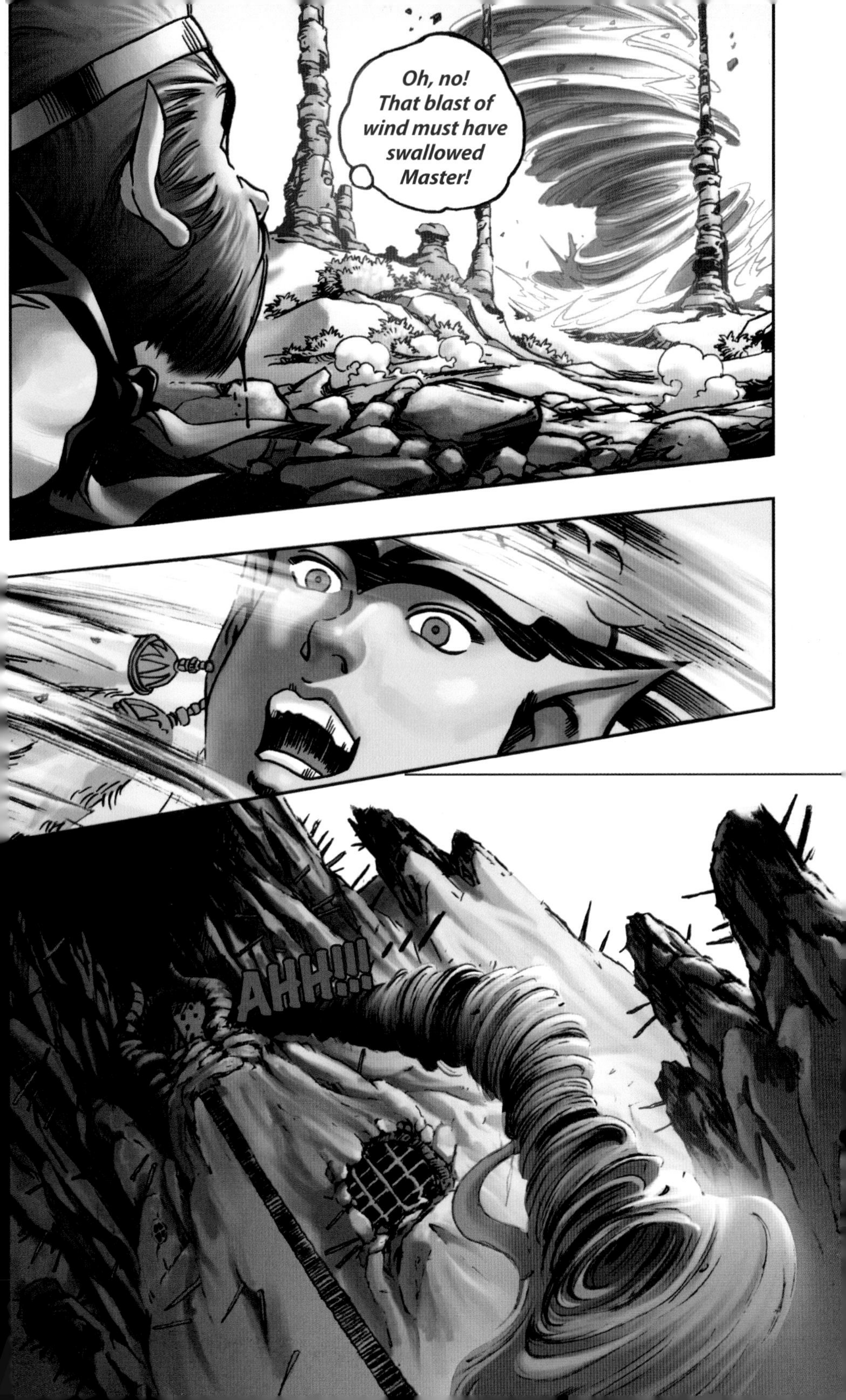
Oh, no! That blast of wind must have swallowed Master!
AHH!!!

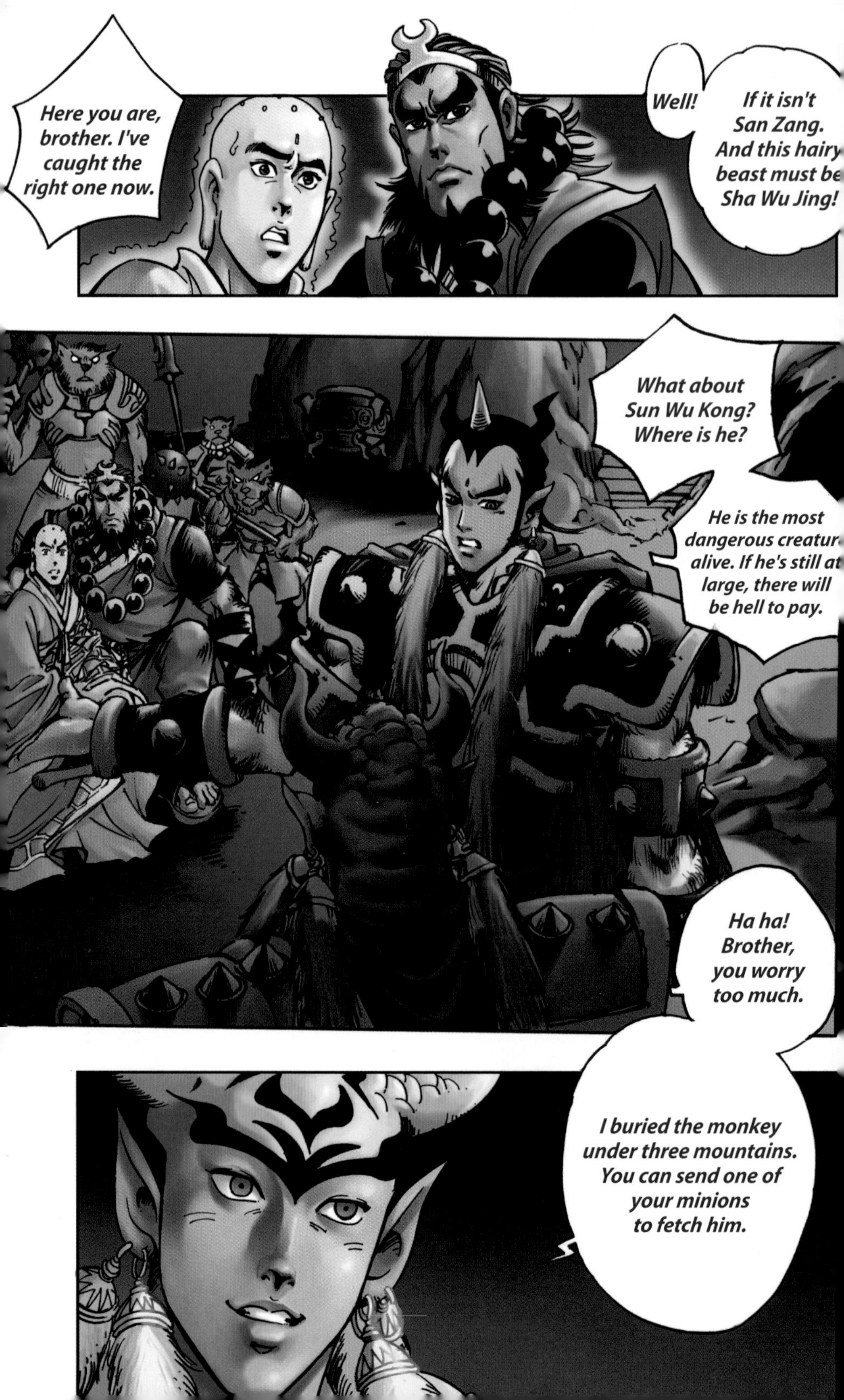
Here you are, brother. I've caught the right one now.
Well!
If it isn't San Zang. And this hairy beast must be Sha Wu Jing!
What about Sun Wu Kong? Where is he?
He is the most dangerous creature alive. If he's still at large, there will be hell to pay.
Ha ha! Brother, you worry too much.
I buried the monkey under three mountains. You can send one of your minions to fetch him.

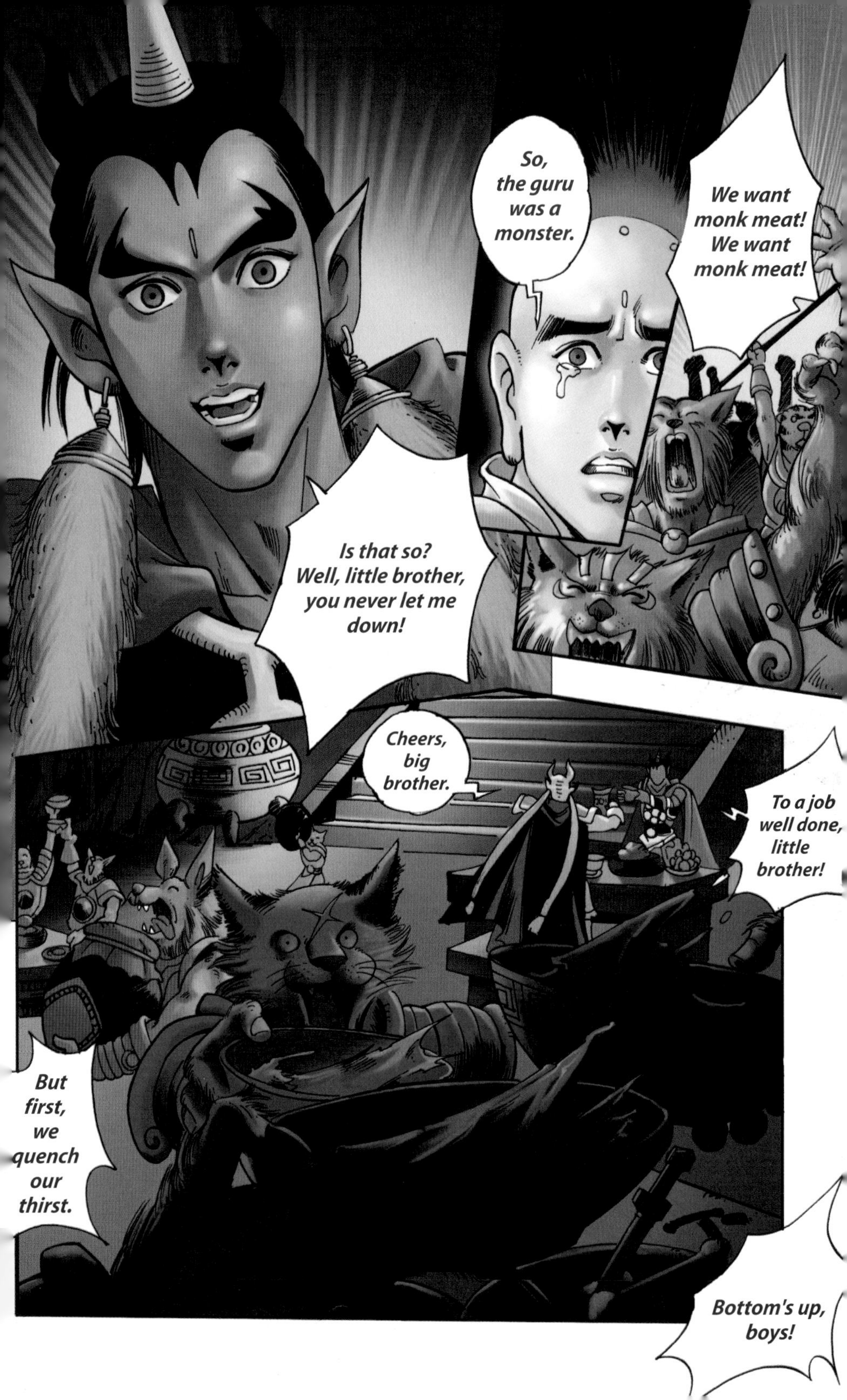
So, the guru was a monster.
We want monk meat! We want monk meat!
Is that so? Well, little brother, you never let me down!
Cheers, big brother.
To a job well done, little brother!
But first, we quench our thirst.
Bottom's up, boys!

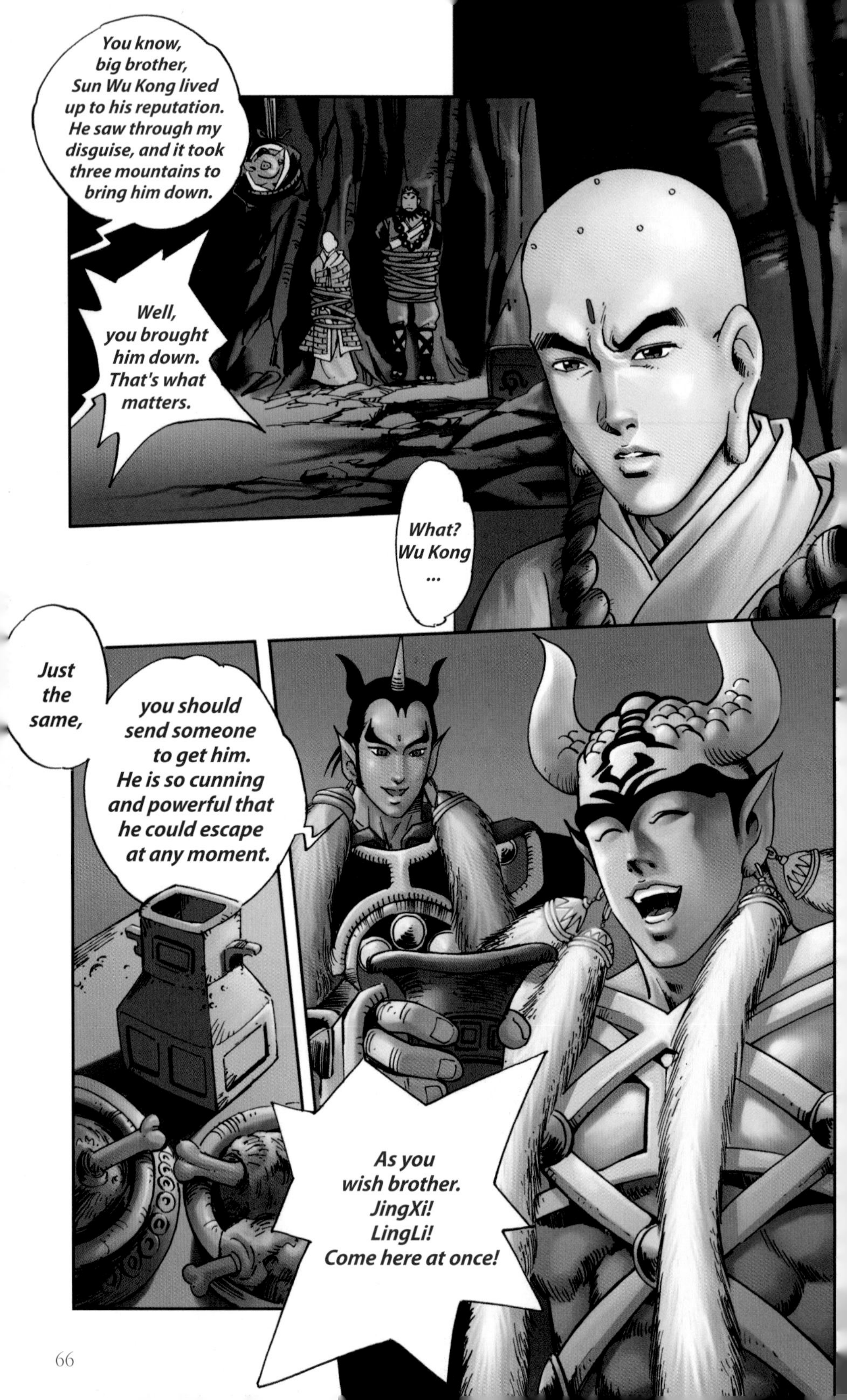
You know, big brother, Sun Wu Kong lived up to his reputation. He saw through my disguise, and it took three mountains to bring him down.
Well, you brought him down. That's what matters.
What? Wu Kong ...
Just the same,
you should send someone to get him. He is so cunning and powerful that he could escape at any moment.
As you wish brother. JingXi! LingLi! Come here at once!

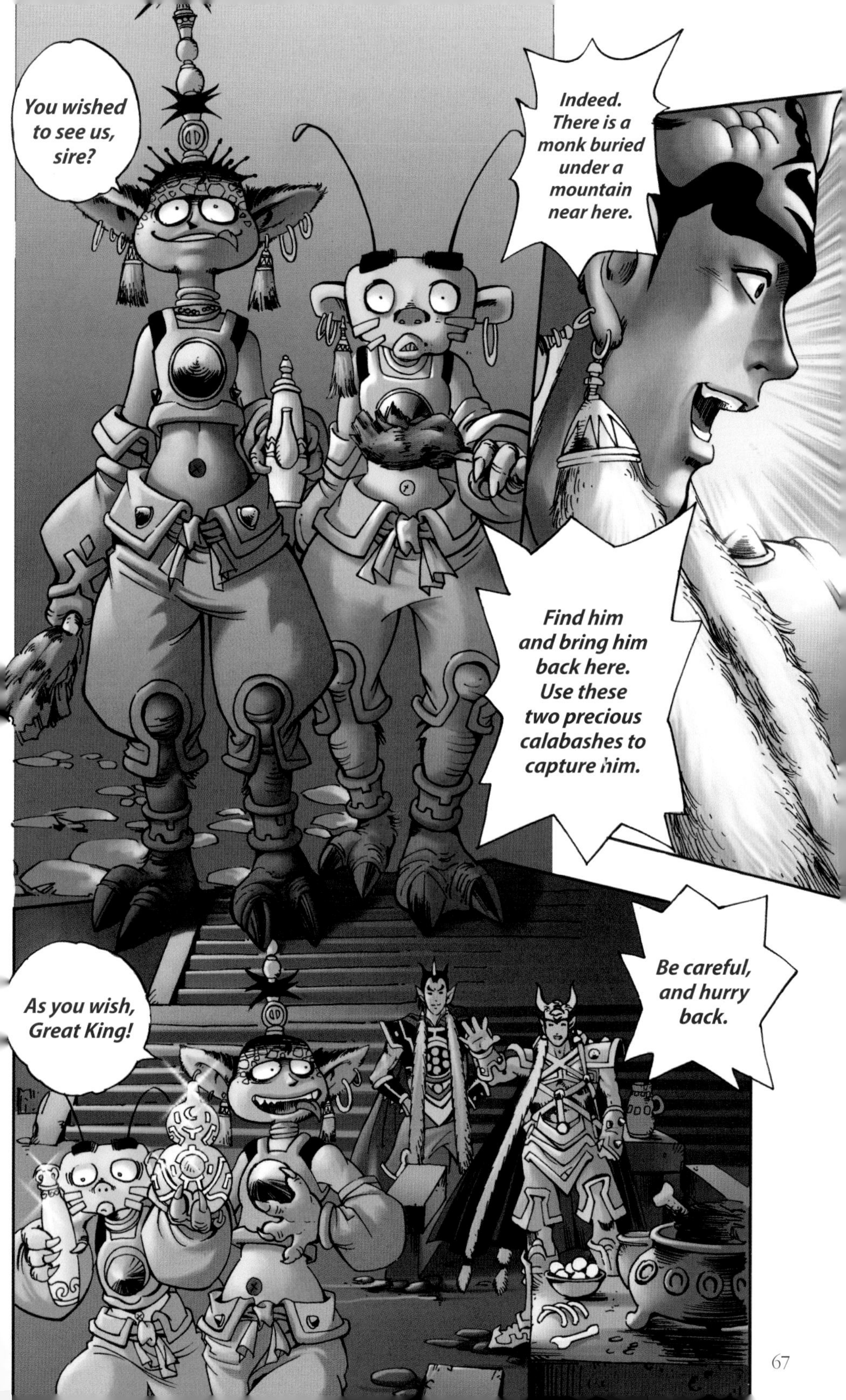
You wished to see us, sire?
Indeed. There is a monk buried under a mountain near here.
Find him and bring him back here. Use these two precious calabashes to capture him.
As you wish, Great King!
Be careful, and hurry back.

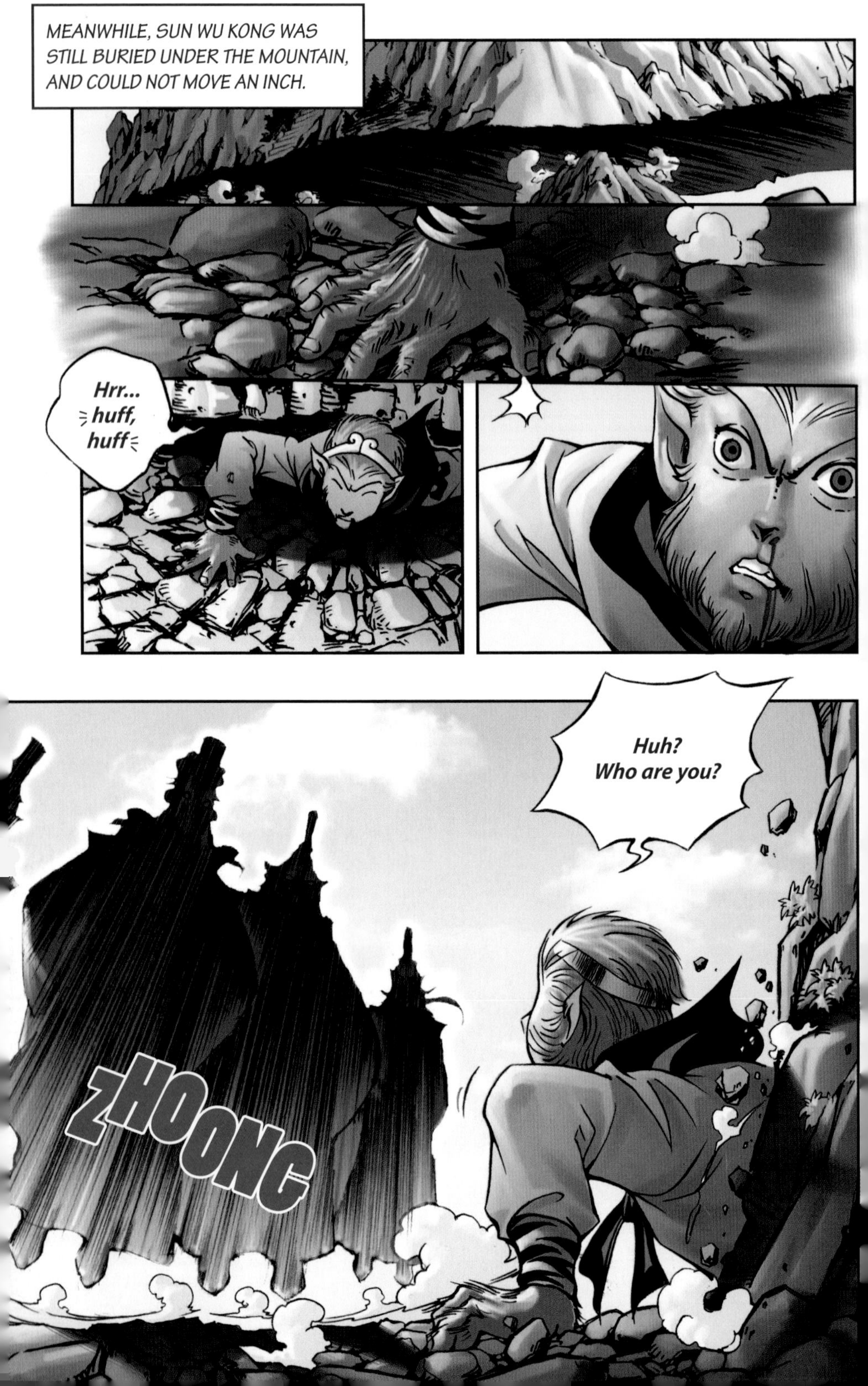
MEANWHILE, SUN WU KONG WAS STILL BURIED UNDER THE MOUNTAIN, AND COULD NOT MOVE AN INCH.
Hrr... huff, huff
Huh? Who are you?
ZHOONG

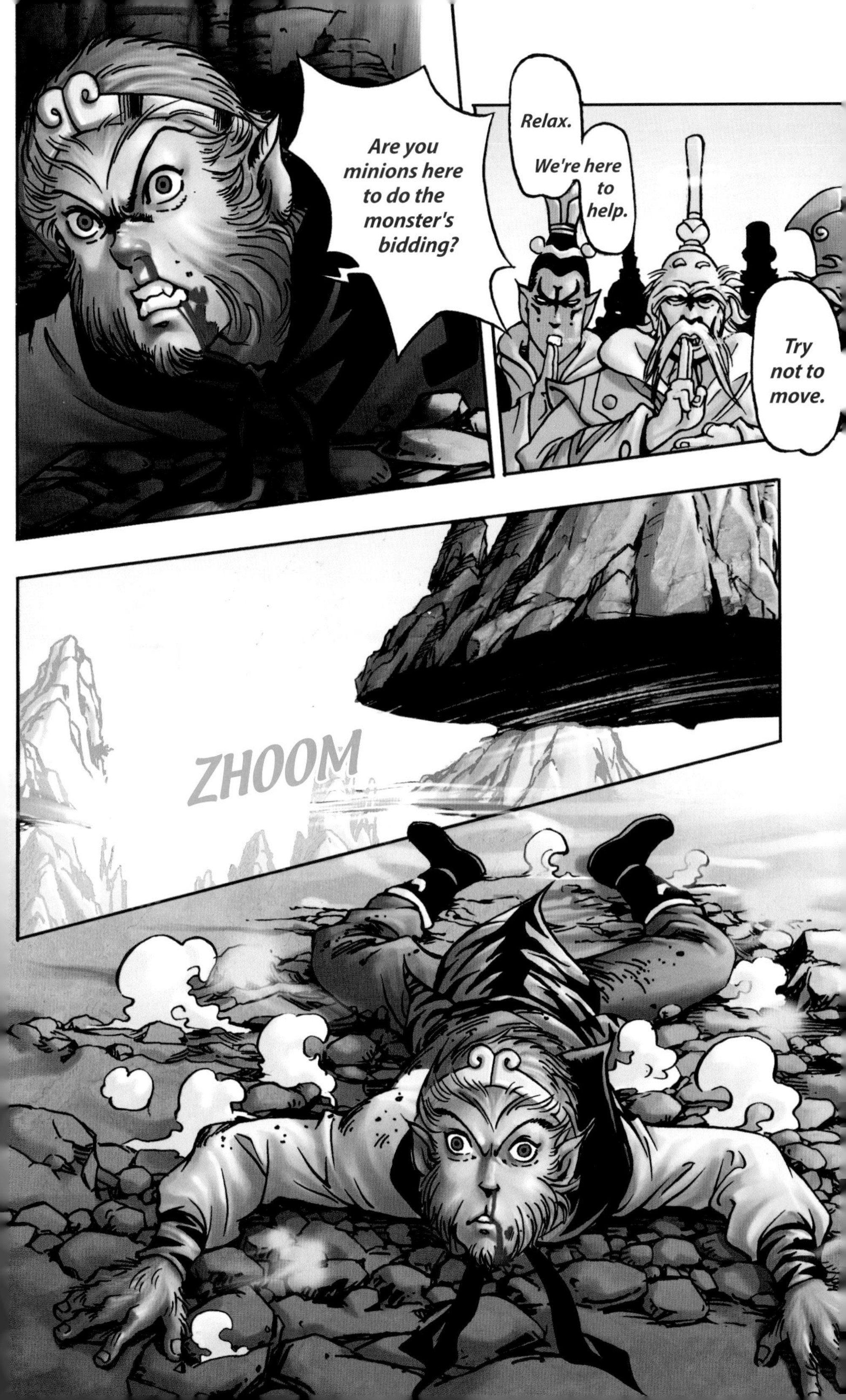
Are you minions here to do the monster's bidding?
Relax.
We're here to help.
Try not to move.
ZHOOM

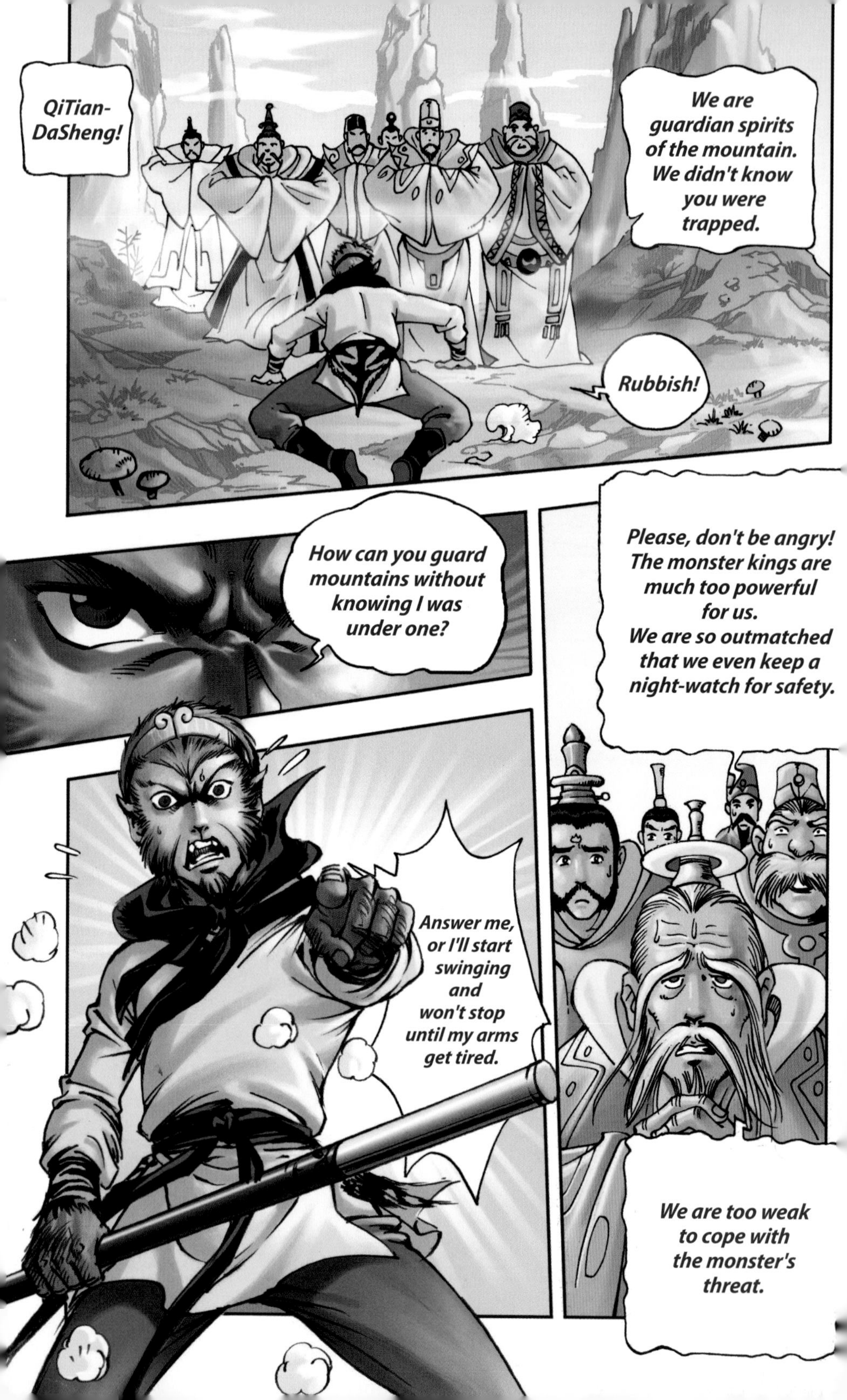

QiTian-DaSheng!
We are guardian spirits of the mountain. We didn't know you were trapped.
Rubbish!
How can you guard mountains without knowing I was under one?
Please, don't be angry! The monster kings are much too powerful for us. We are so outmatched that we even keep a night-watch for safety.
Answer me, or I'll start swinging and won't stop until my arms get tired.
We are too weak to cope with the monster's threat.

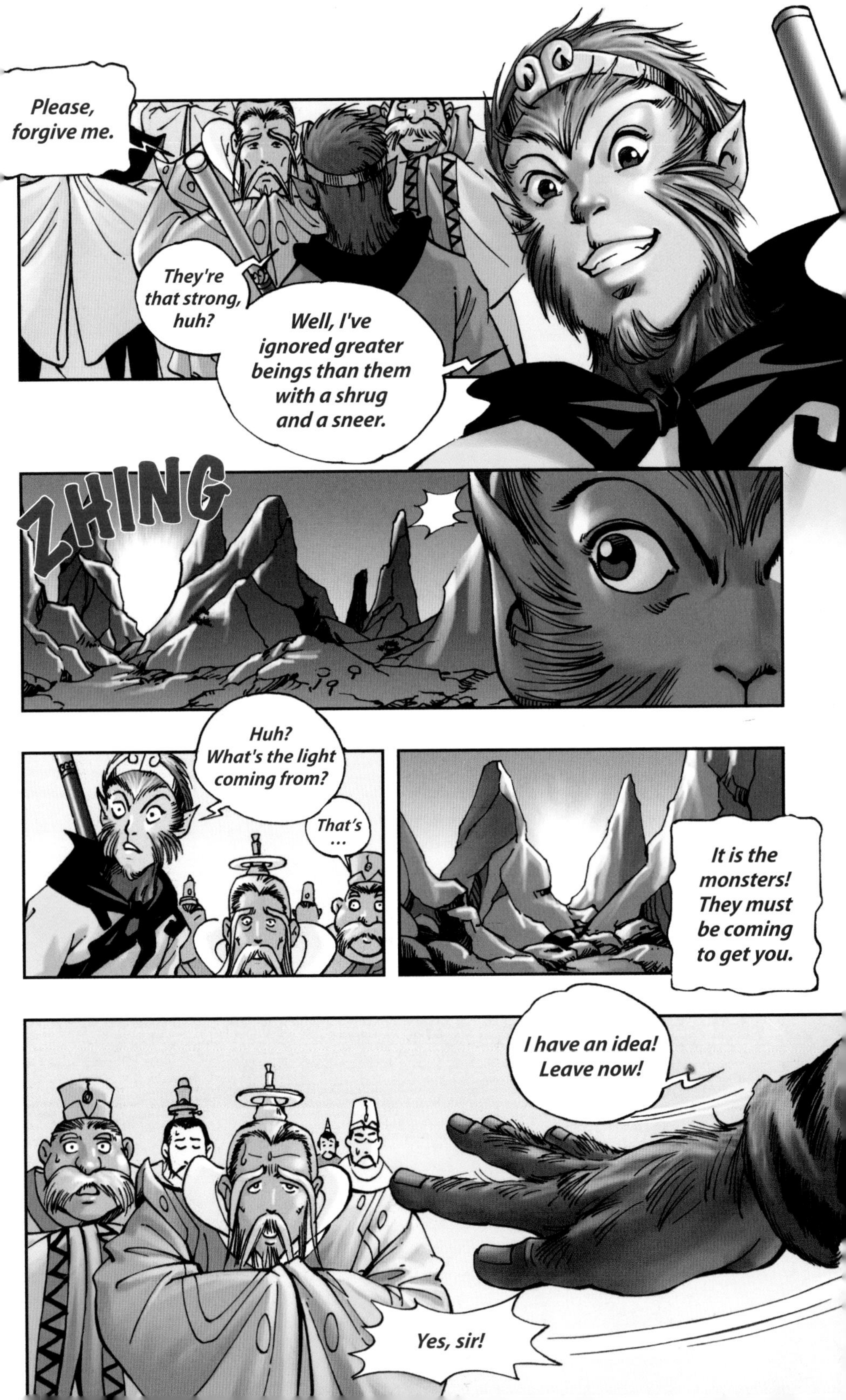
Please, forgive me.
They're that strong, huh?
Well, I've ignored greater beings than them with a shrug and a sneer.
ZHING
Huh? What's the light coming from?
That's ...
It is the monsters! They must be coming to get you.
I have an idea! Leave now!
Yes, sir!

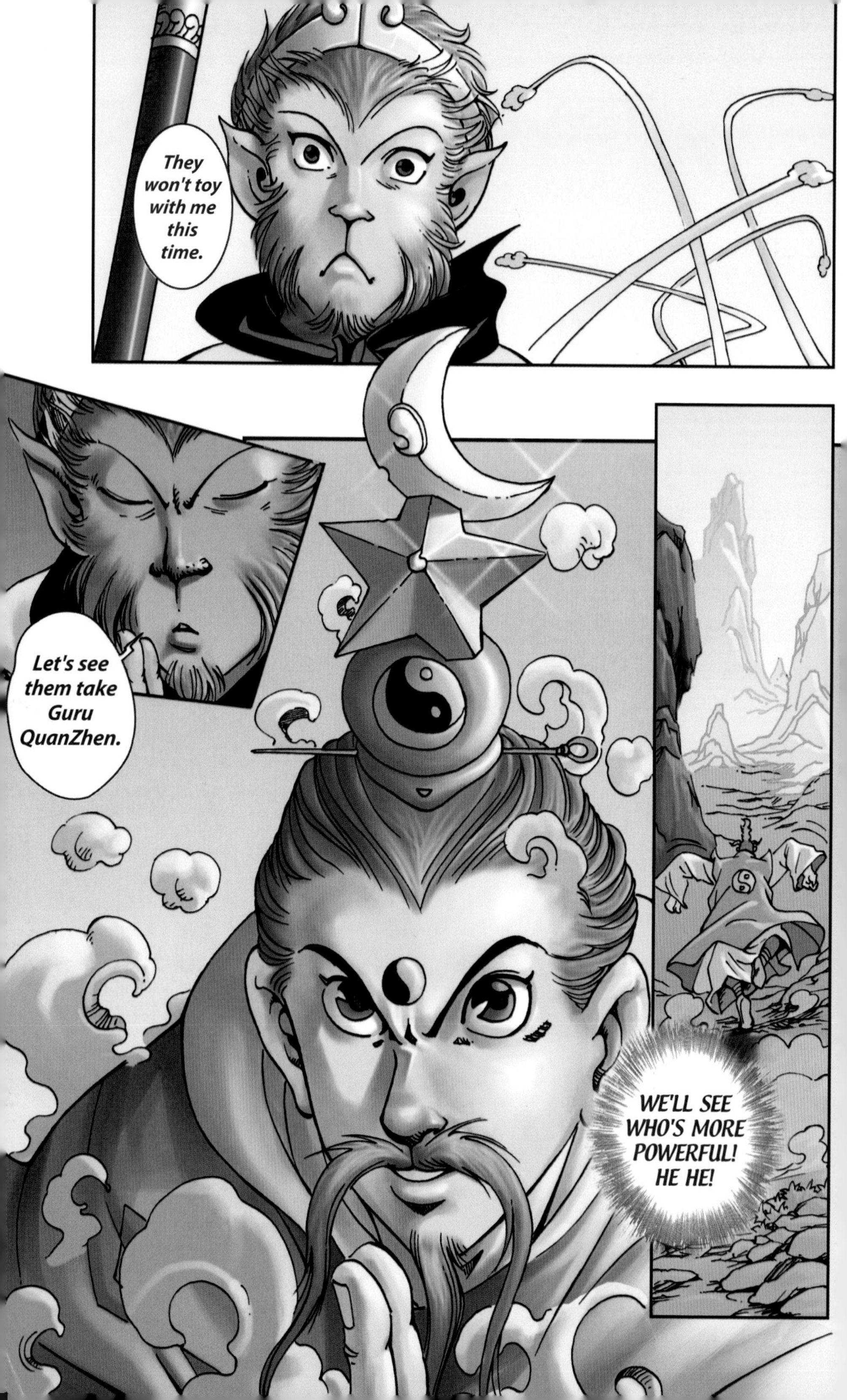

They won't toy with me this time.
Let's see them take Guru QuanZhen.
WE'LL SEE WHO'S MORE POWERFUL! HE HE!

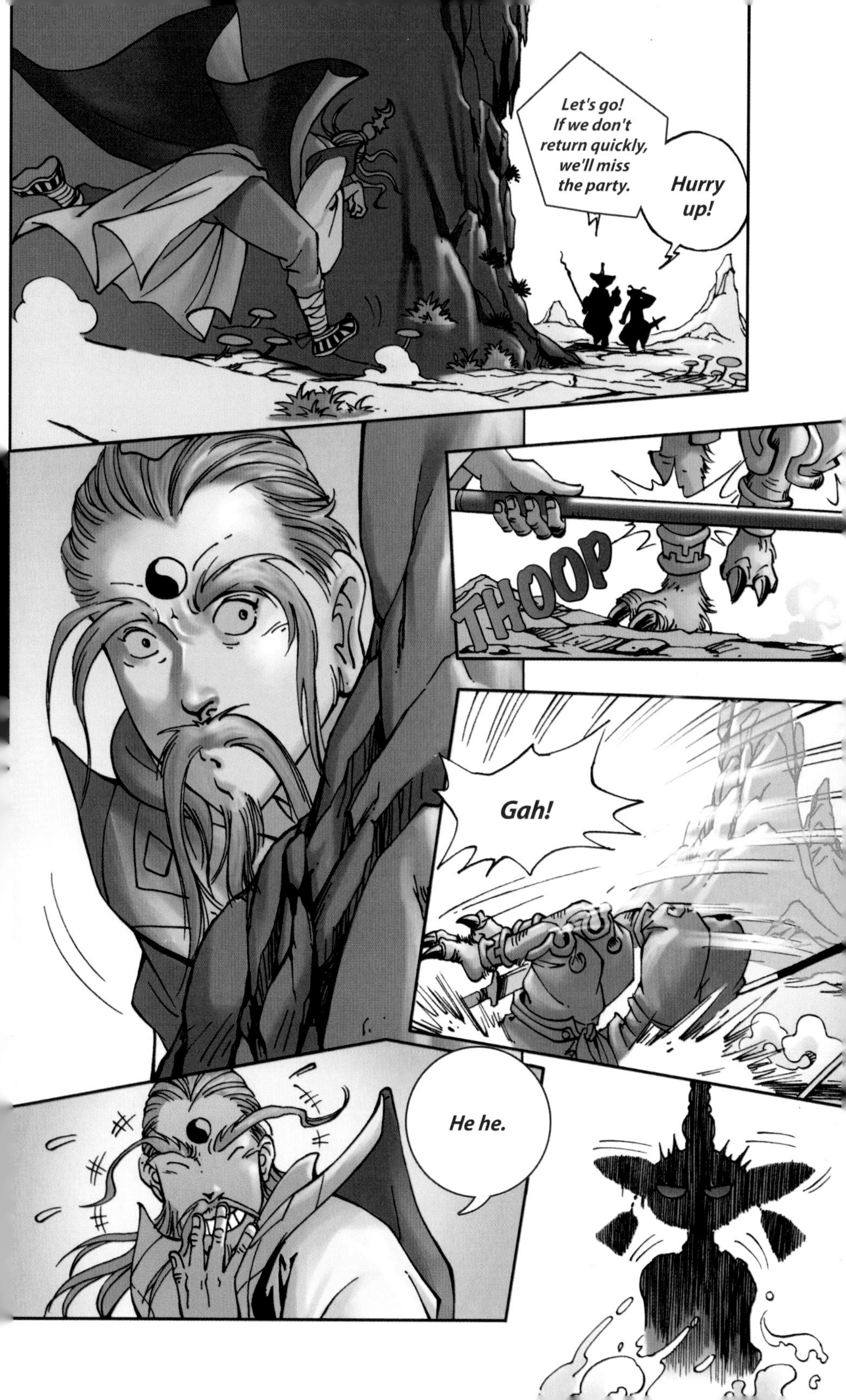
Let's go! If we don't return quickly, we'll miss the party.
Hurry up!
THOOP
Gah!
He he.

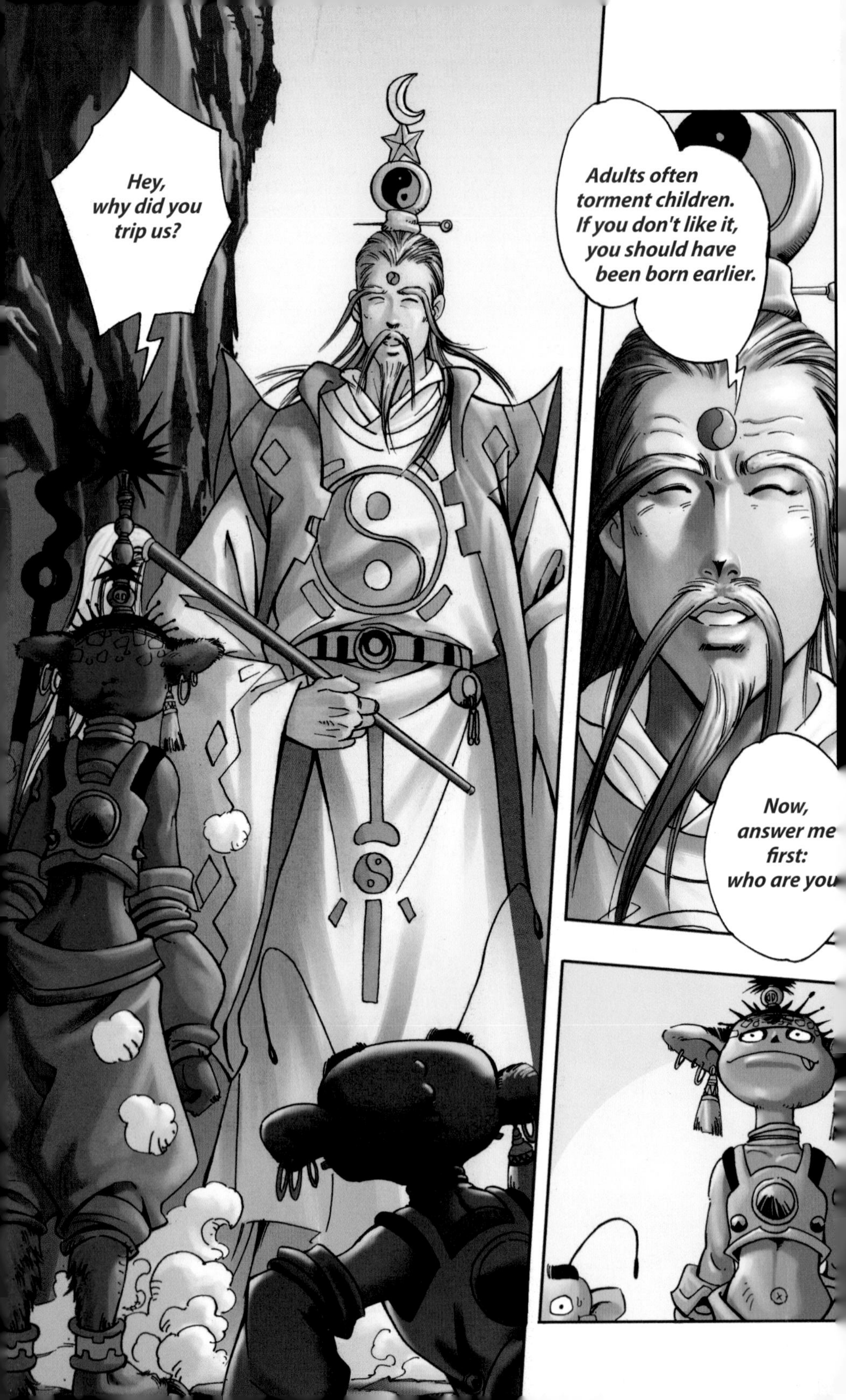
Hey, why did you trip us?
Adults often torment children. If you don't like it, you should have been born earlier.
Now, answer me first: who are you

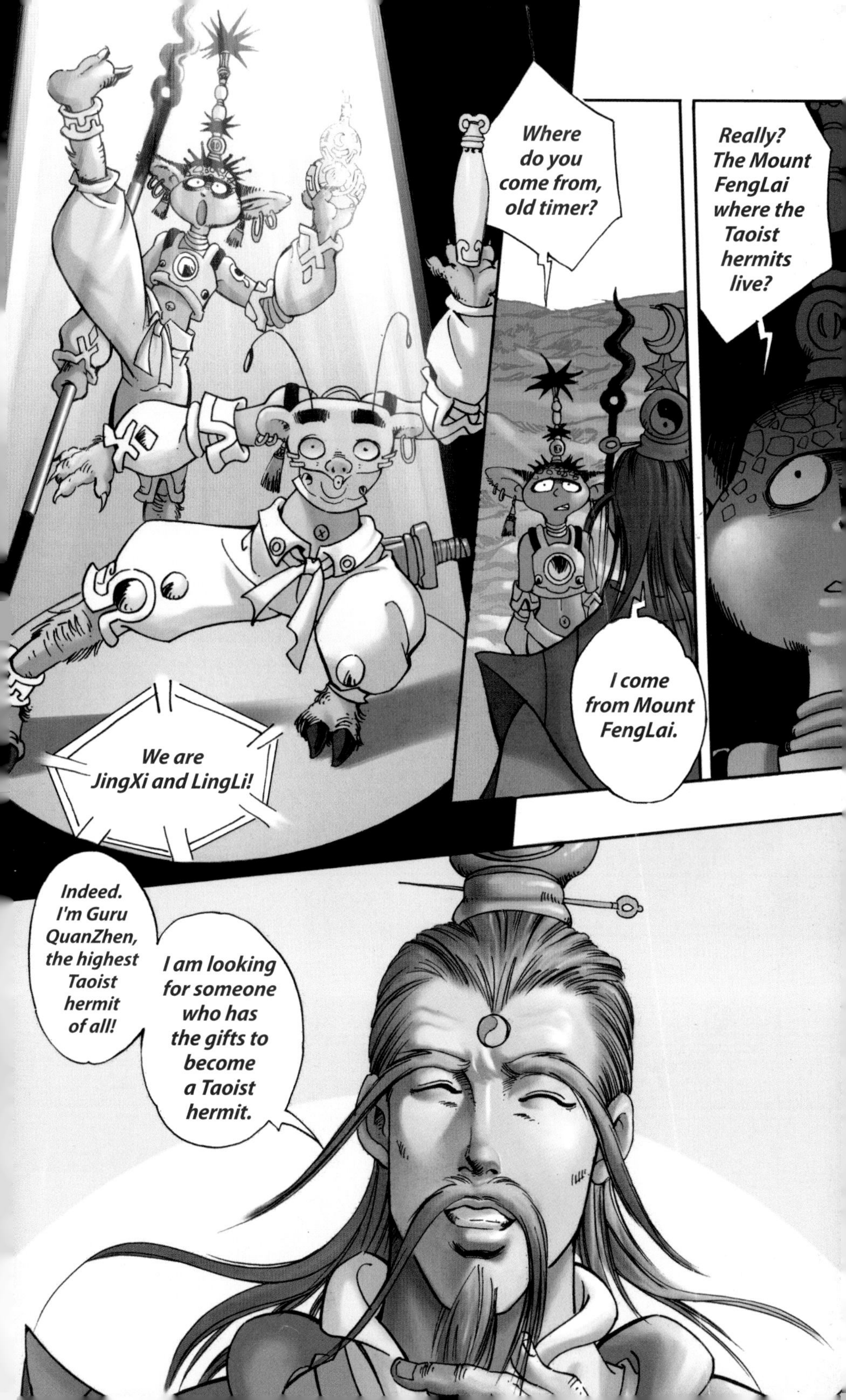
We are JingXi and LingLi!
Where do you come from, old timer?
I come from Mount FengLai.
Really? The Mount FengLai where the Taoist hermits live?
Indeed. I'm Guru QuanZhen, the highest Taoist hermit of all!
I am looking for someone who has the gifts to become a Taoist hermit.

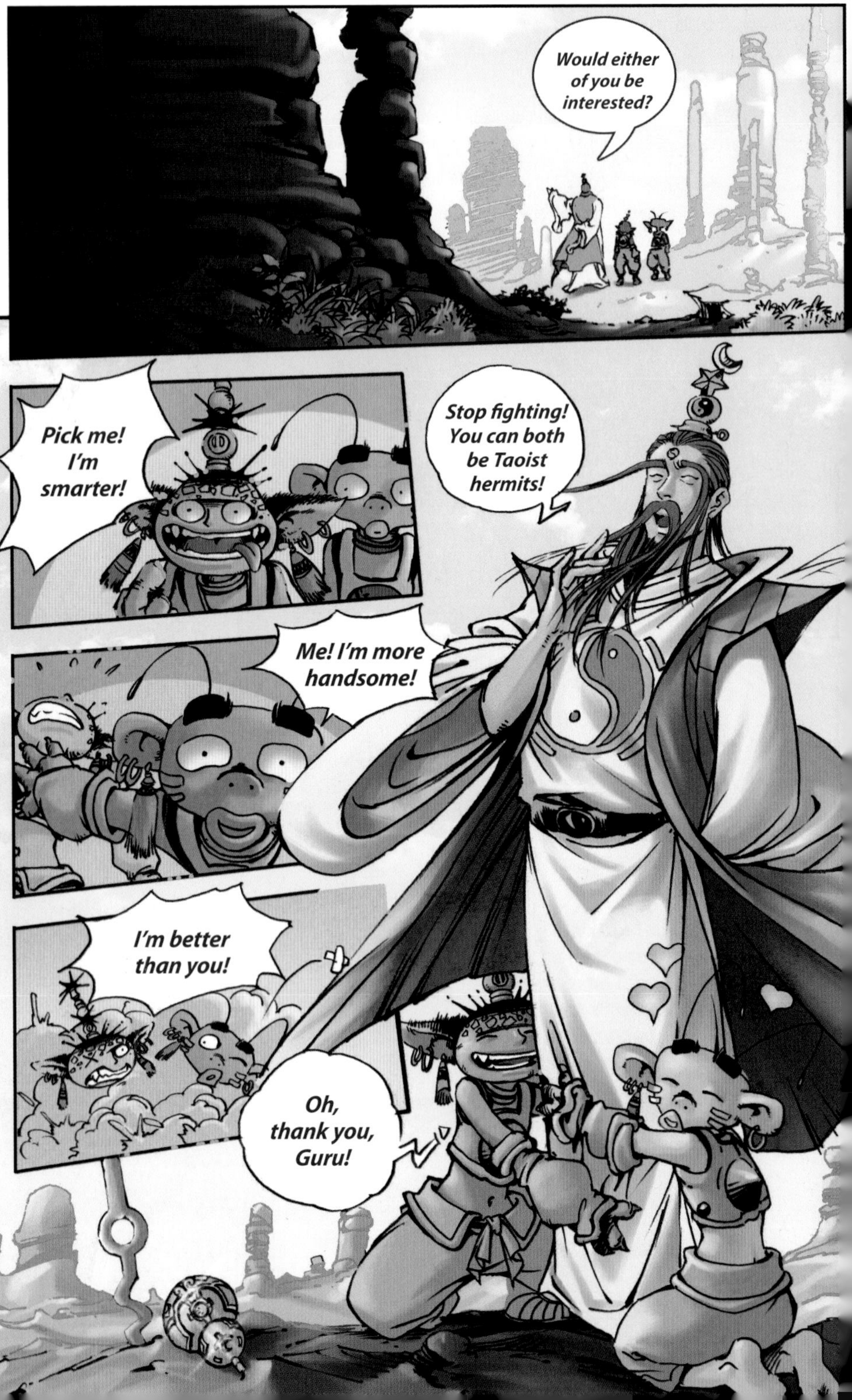
Would either of you be interested?
Pick me! I'm smarter!
Stop fighting! You can both be Taoist hermits!
Me! I'm more handsome!
I'm better than you!
Oh, thank you, Guru!

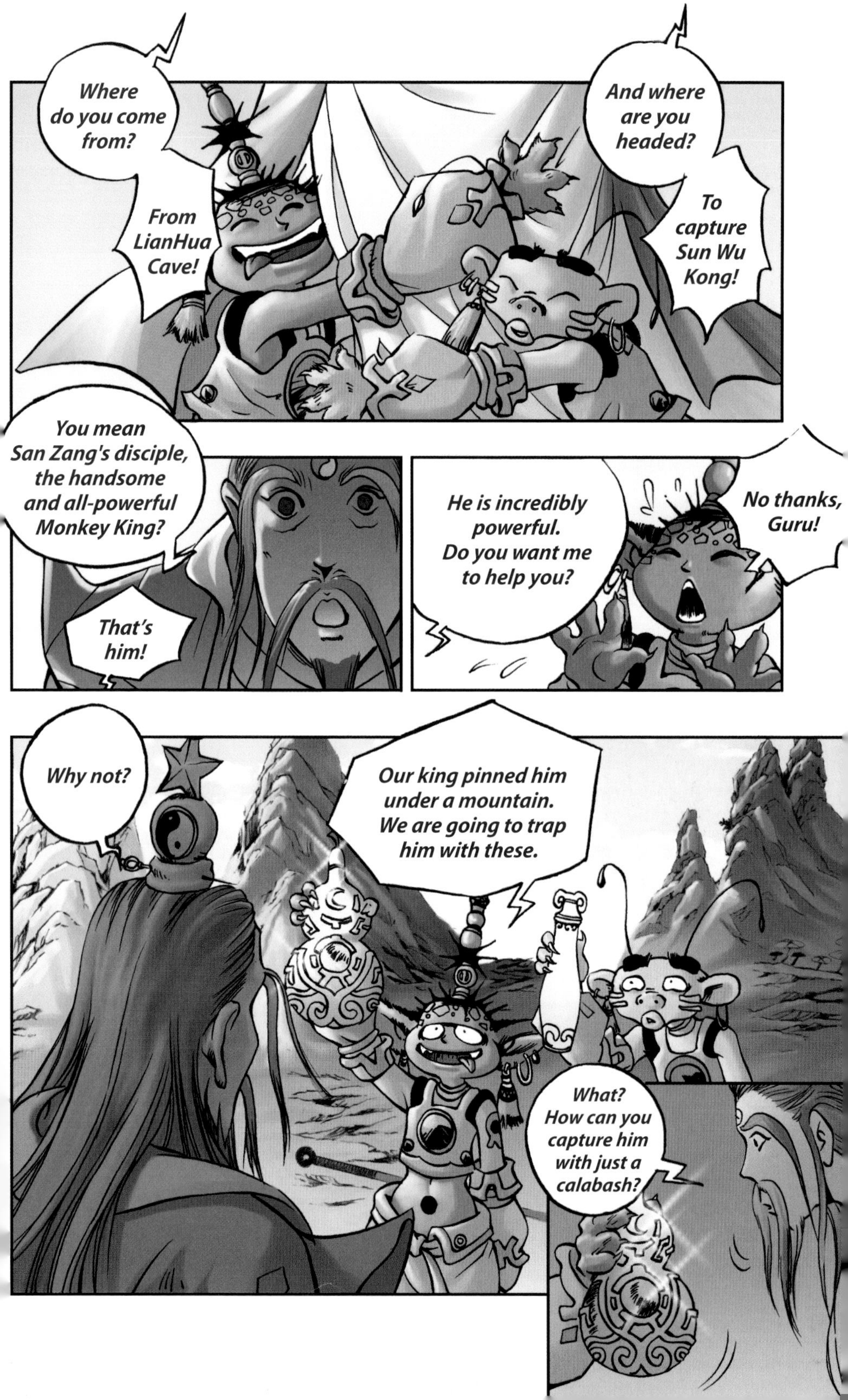
Where do you come from?
From LianHua Cave!
And where are you headed?
To capture Sun Wu Kong!
You mean San Zang's disciple, the handsome and all-powerful Monkey King?
That's him!
He is incredibly powerful. Do you want me to help you?
No thanks, Guru!
Why not?
Our king pinned him under a mountain. We are going to trap him with these.
What? How can you capture him with just a calabash?

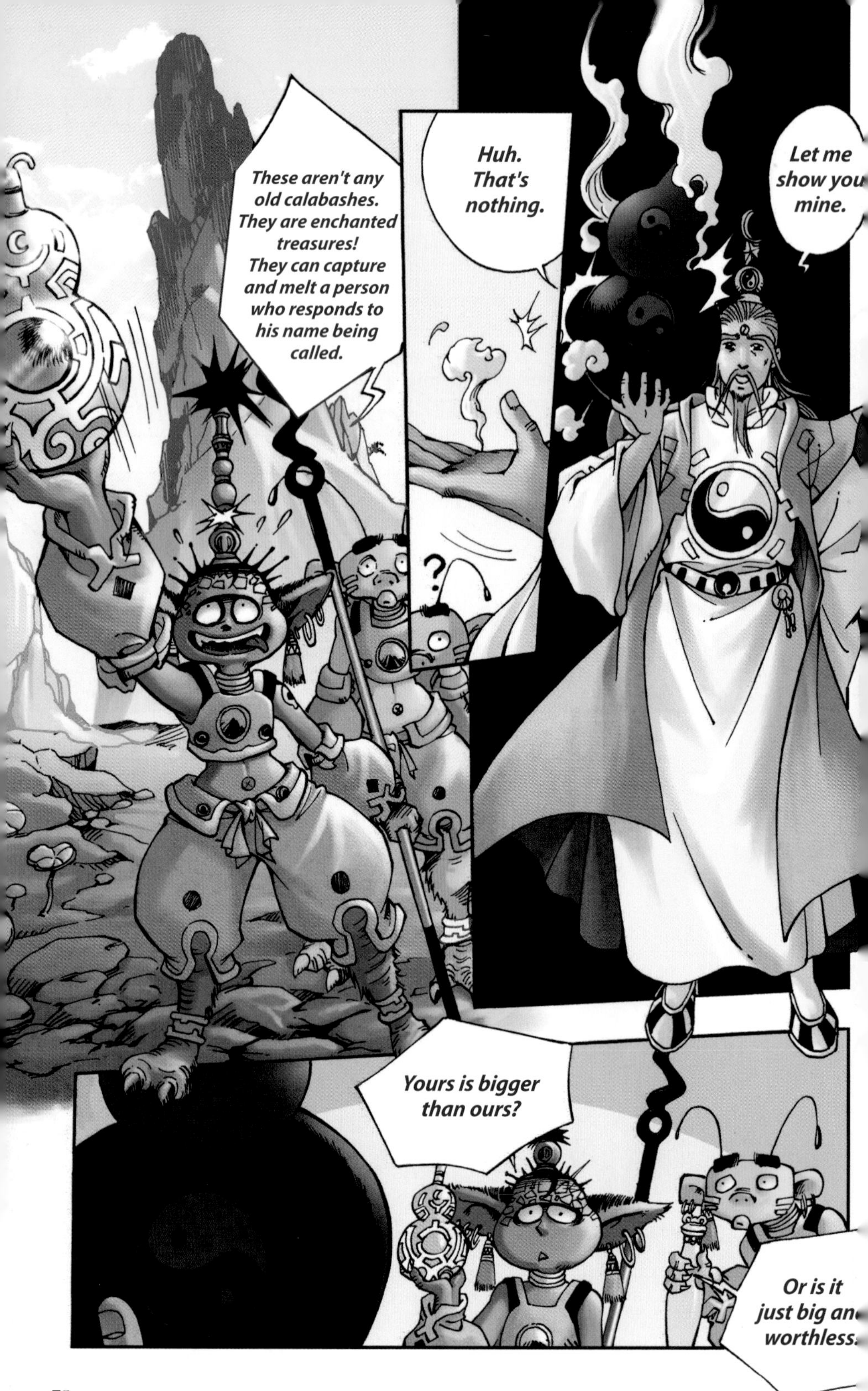
These aren't any old calabashes. They are enchanted treasures! They can capture and melt a person who responds to his name being called.
Huh. That's nothing.
Let me show you mine.
Yours is bigger than ours?
Or is it just big an worthless.

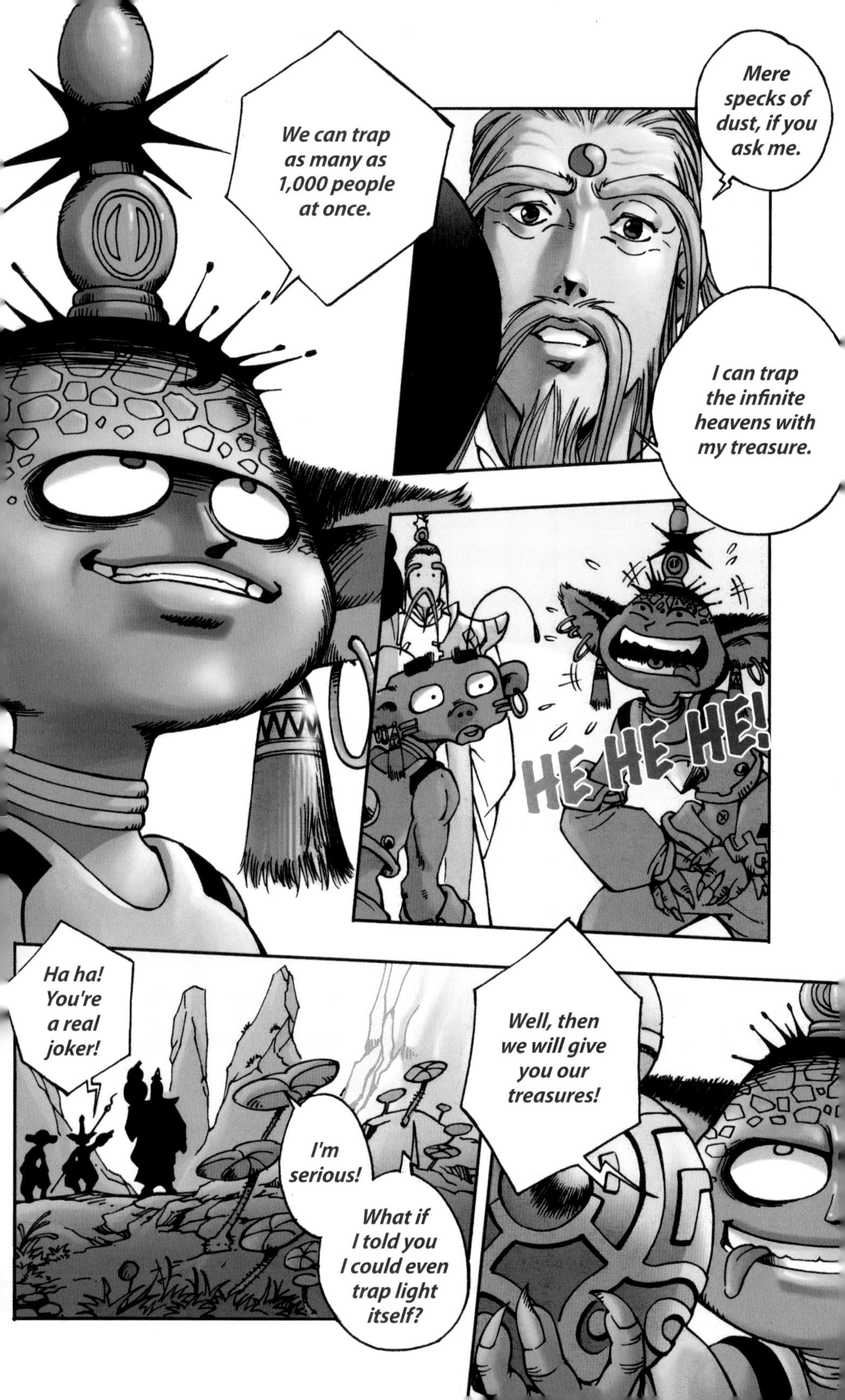
We can trap as many as 1,000 people at once.
Mere specks of dust, if you ask me.
I can trap the infinite heavens with my treasure.
HE HE HE!
Ha ha! You're a real joker!
I'm serious!
What if I told you I could even trap light itself?
Well, then we will give you our treasures!

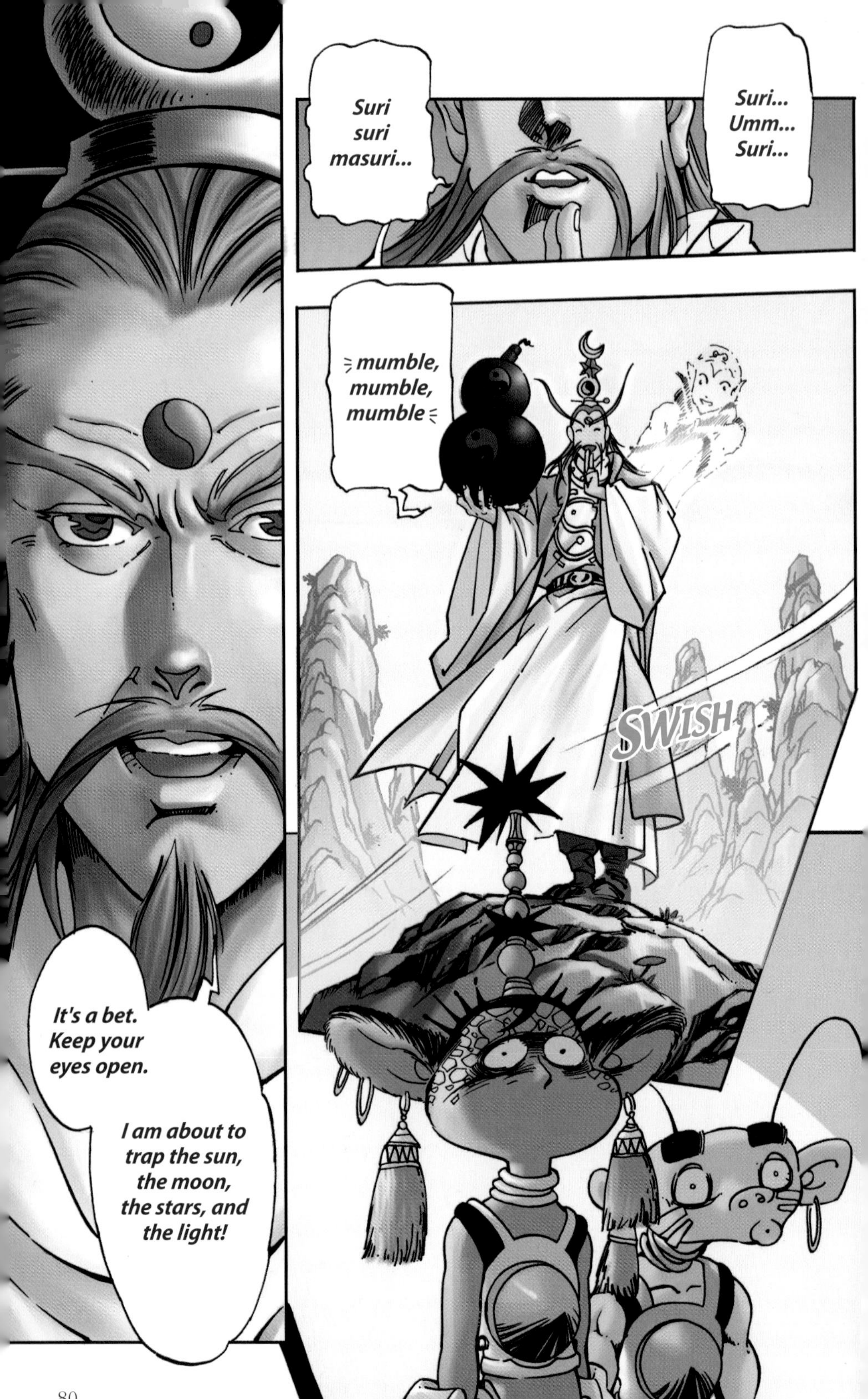
Suri suri masuri...
Suri... Umm... Suri...
mumble, mumble, mumble
SWISH
It's a bet. Keep your eyes open.
I am about to trap the sun, the moon, the stars, and the light!

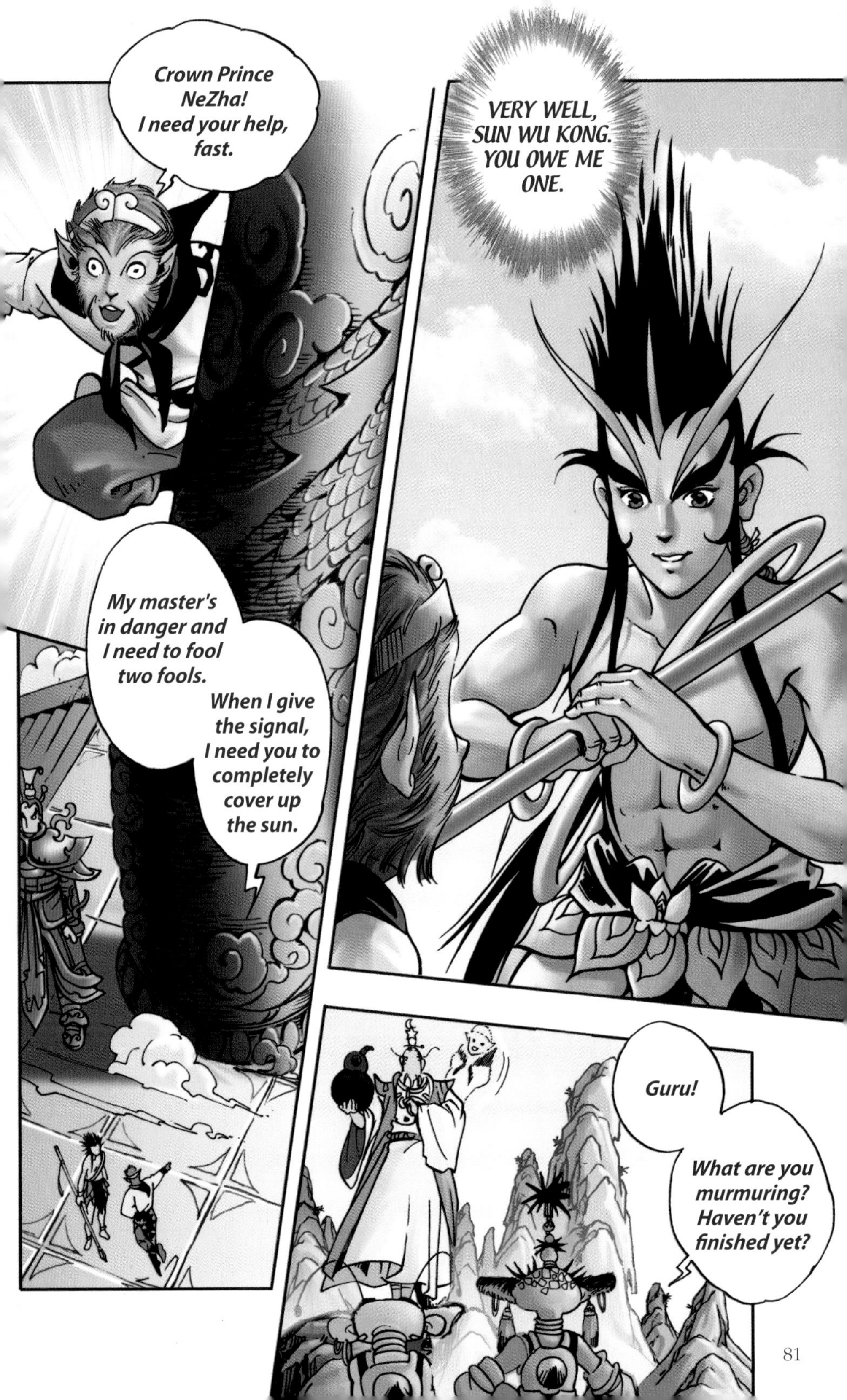
Crown Prince NeZha! I need your help, fast.
VERY WELL, SUN WU KONG. YOU OWE ME ONE.
My master's in danger and I need to fool two fools.
When I give the signal, I need you to completely cover up the sun.
Guru!
What are you murmuring? Haven't you finished yet?

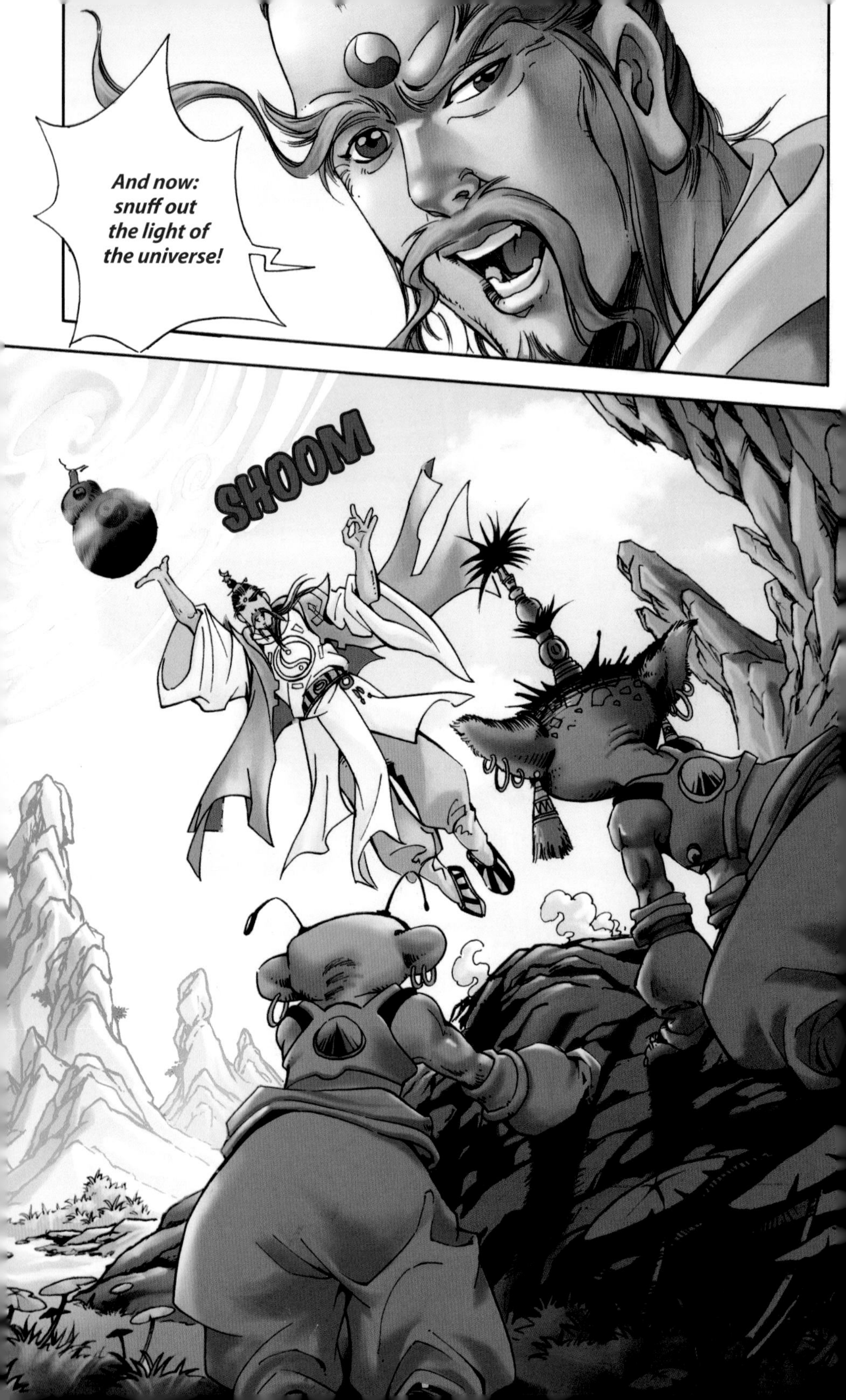
And now: snuff out the light of the universe!
SHOOM

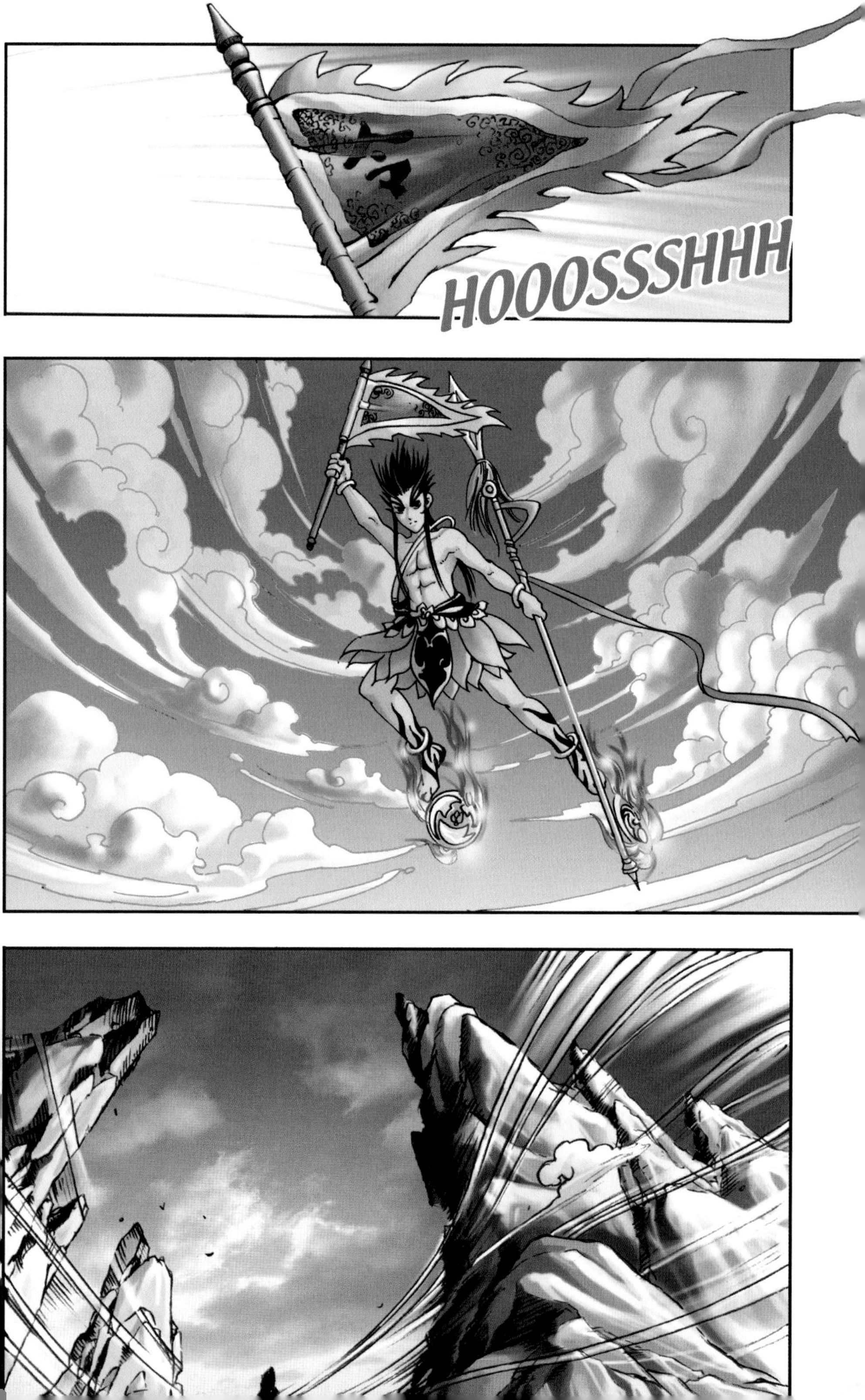
HOOOSSSHHH

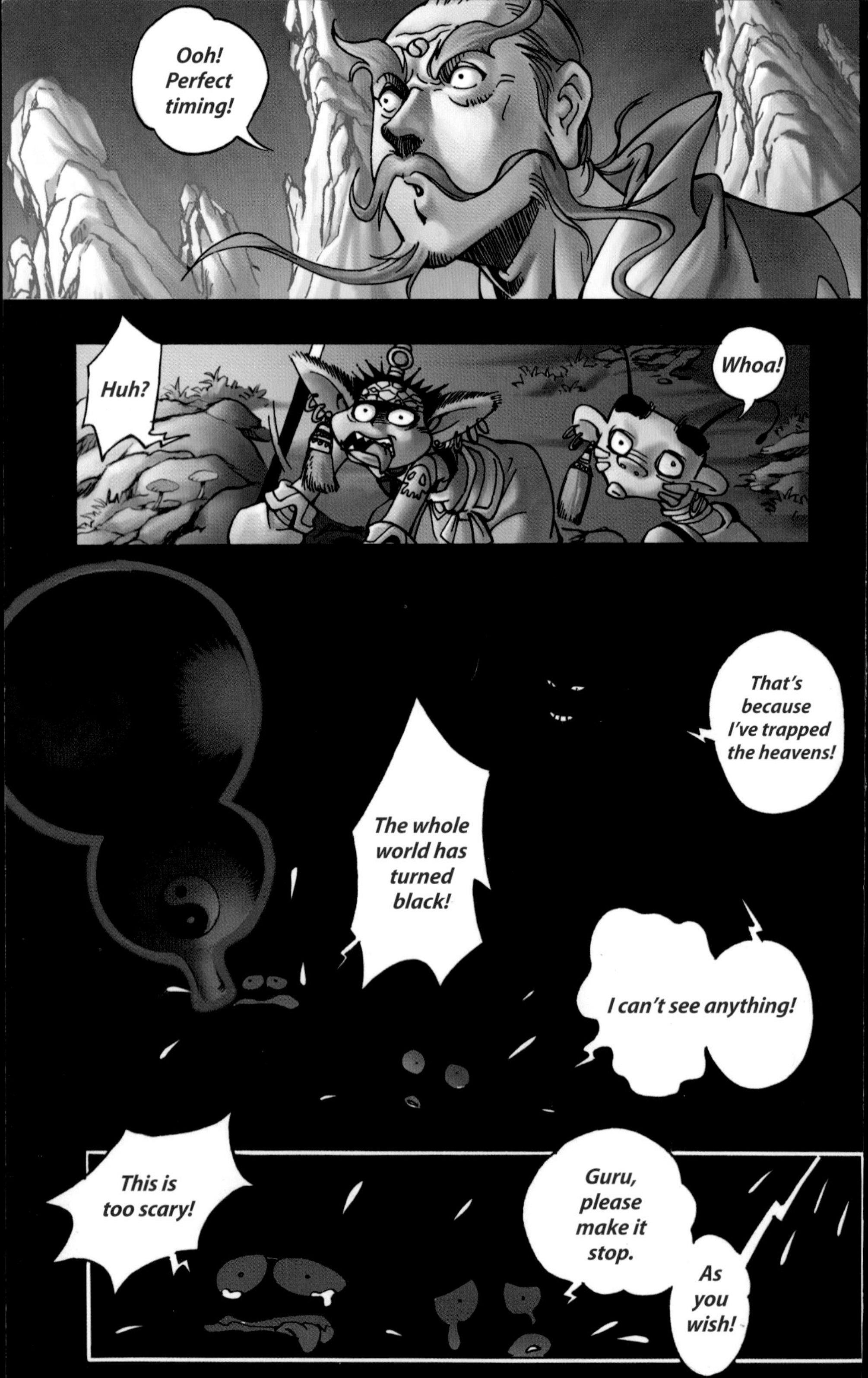
Ooh! Perfect timing!
Huh?
Whoa!
That's because I've trapped the heavens!
The whole world has turned black!
I can't see anything!
This is too scary!
Guru, please make it stop.
As you wish!

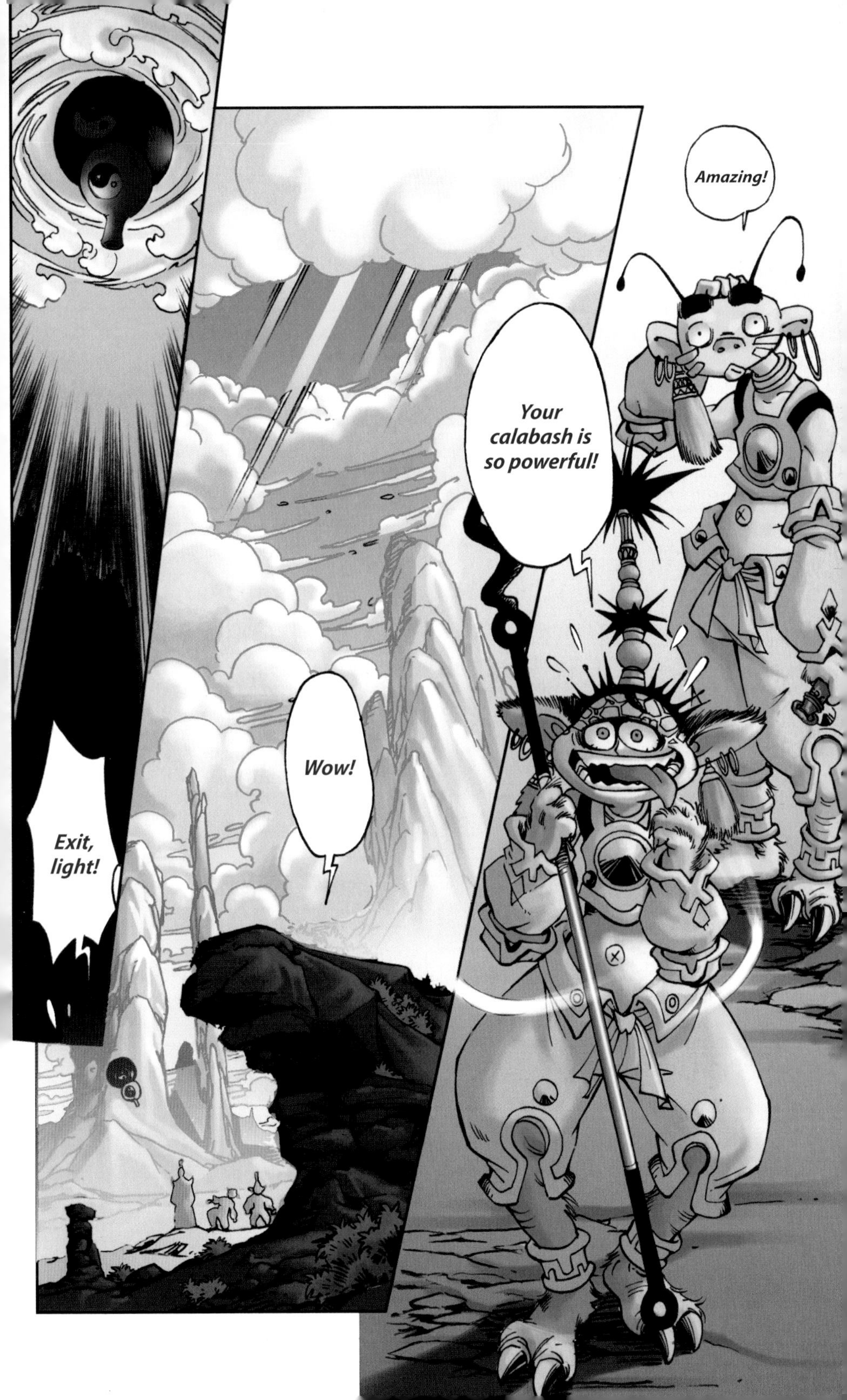
Exit, light!
Wow!
Your calabash is so powerful!
Amazing!

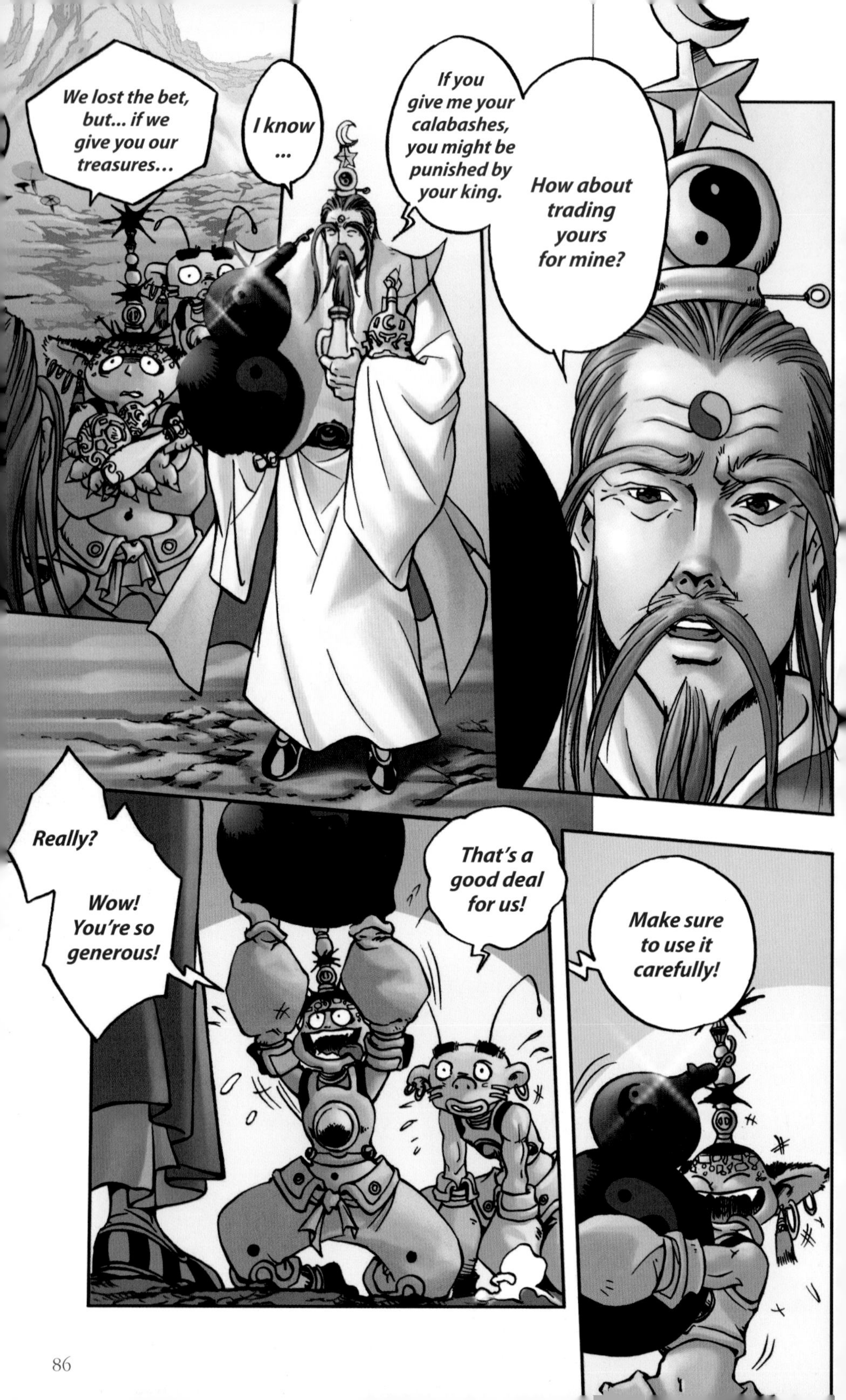
We lost the bet, but... if we give you our treasures...
I know ...
If you give me your calabashes, you might be punished by your king.
How about trading yours for mine?
Really?
Wow! You're so generous!
That's a good deal for us!
Make sure to use it carefully!

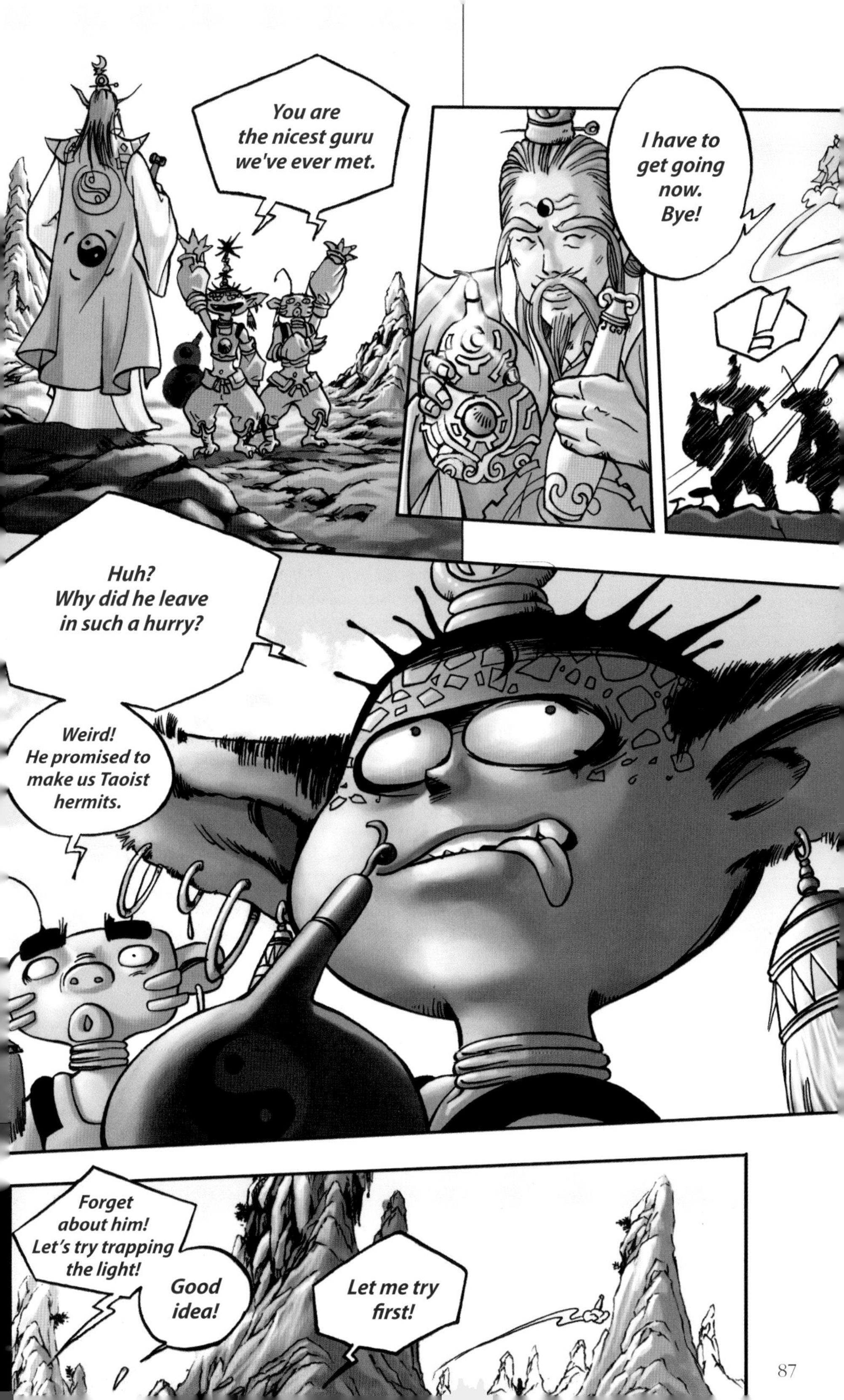
You are the nicest guru we've ever met.
I have to get going now. Bye!
!
Huh? Why did he leave in such a hurry?
Weird! He promised to make us Taoist hermits.
Forget about him! Let's try trapping the light!
Good idea!
Let me try first!

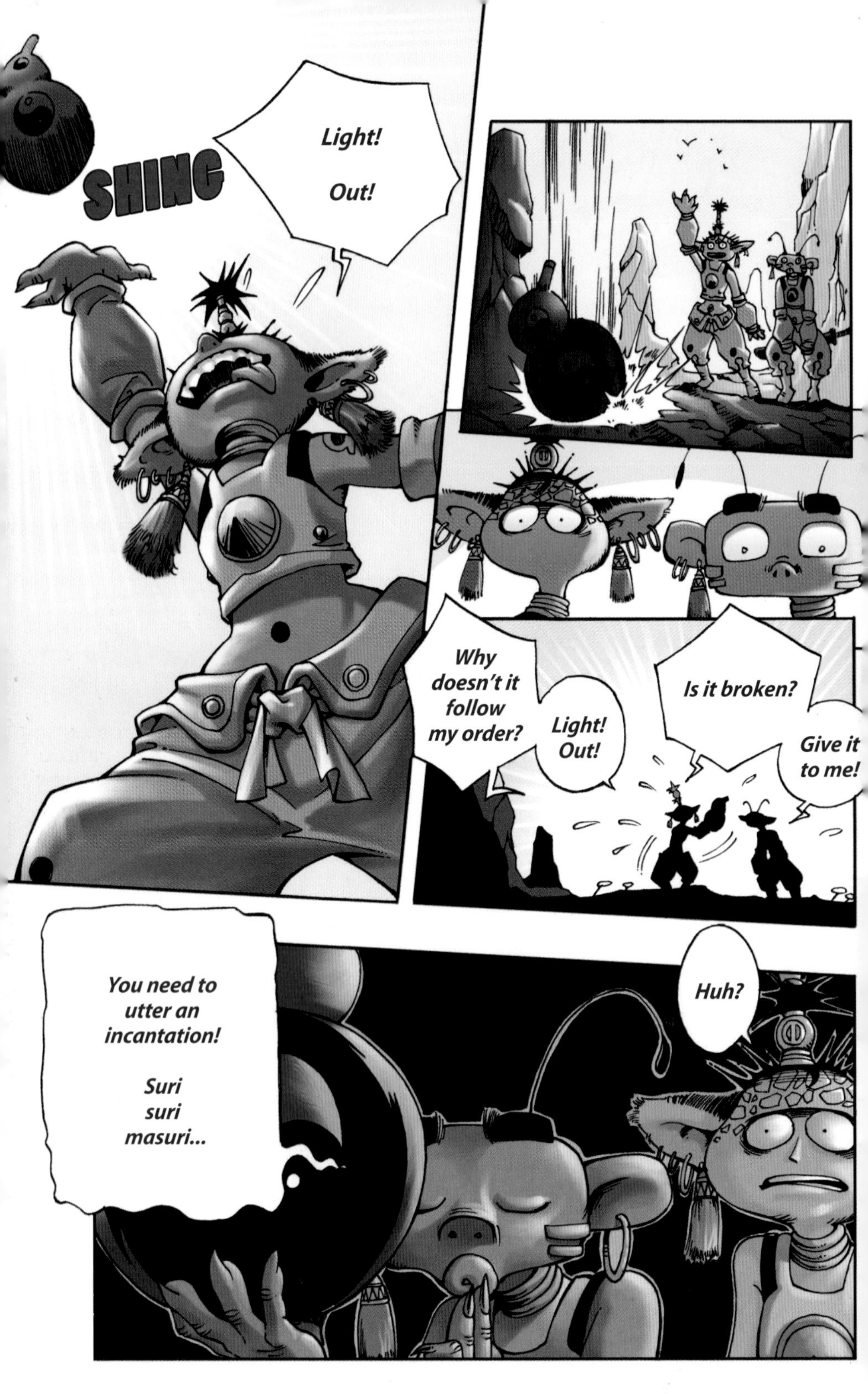
SHING
Light! Out!
Why doesn't it follow my order?
Light! Out!
Is it broken?
Give it to me!
You need to utter an incantation! Suri suri masuri...
Huh?

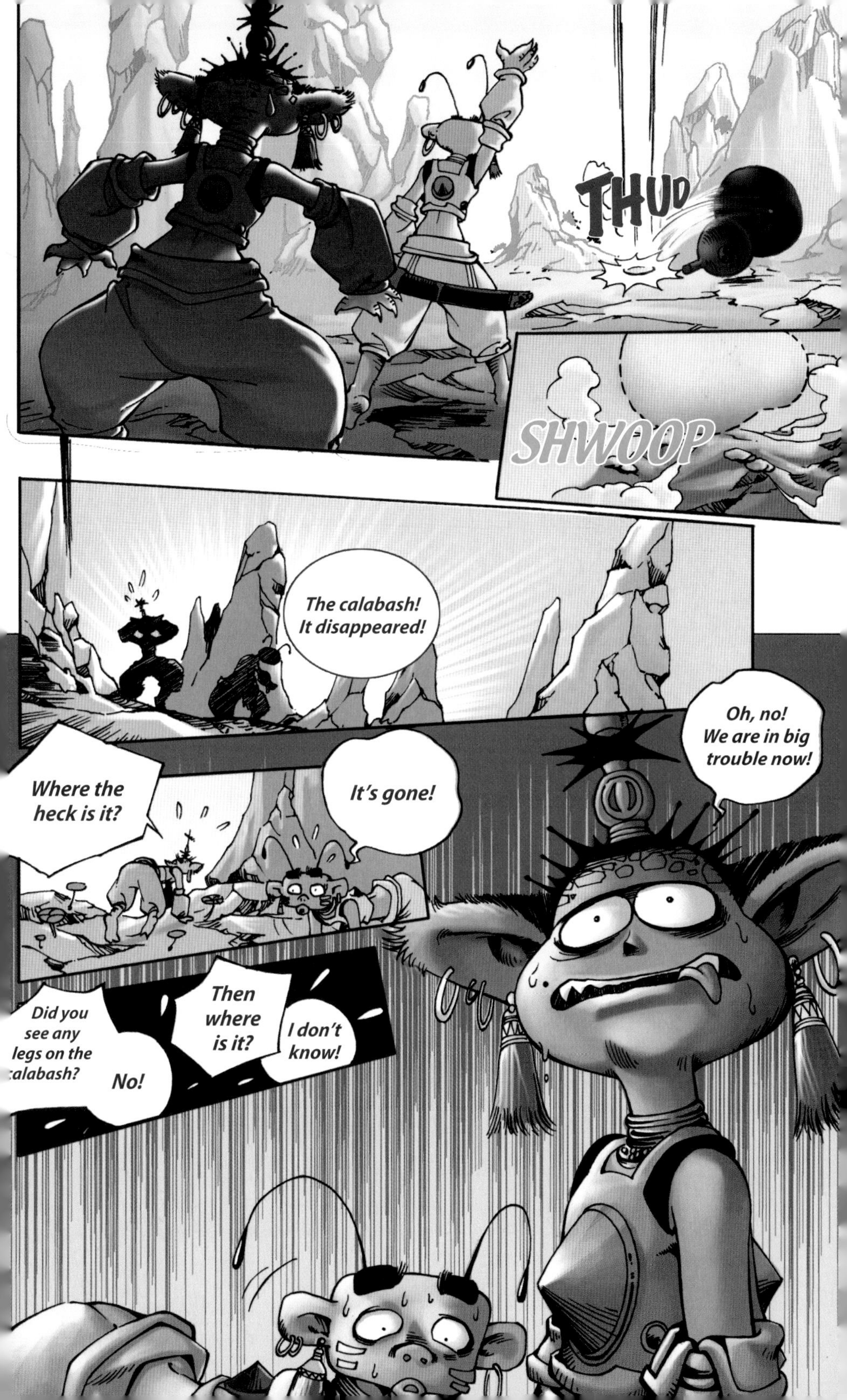
THUD
SHWOOP
The calabash! It disappeared!
Oh, no! We are in big trouble now!
Where the heck is it?
It's gone!
Did you see any legs on the calabash?
No!
Then where is it?
I don't know!

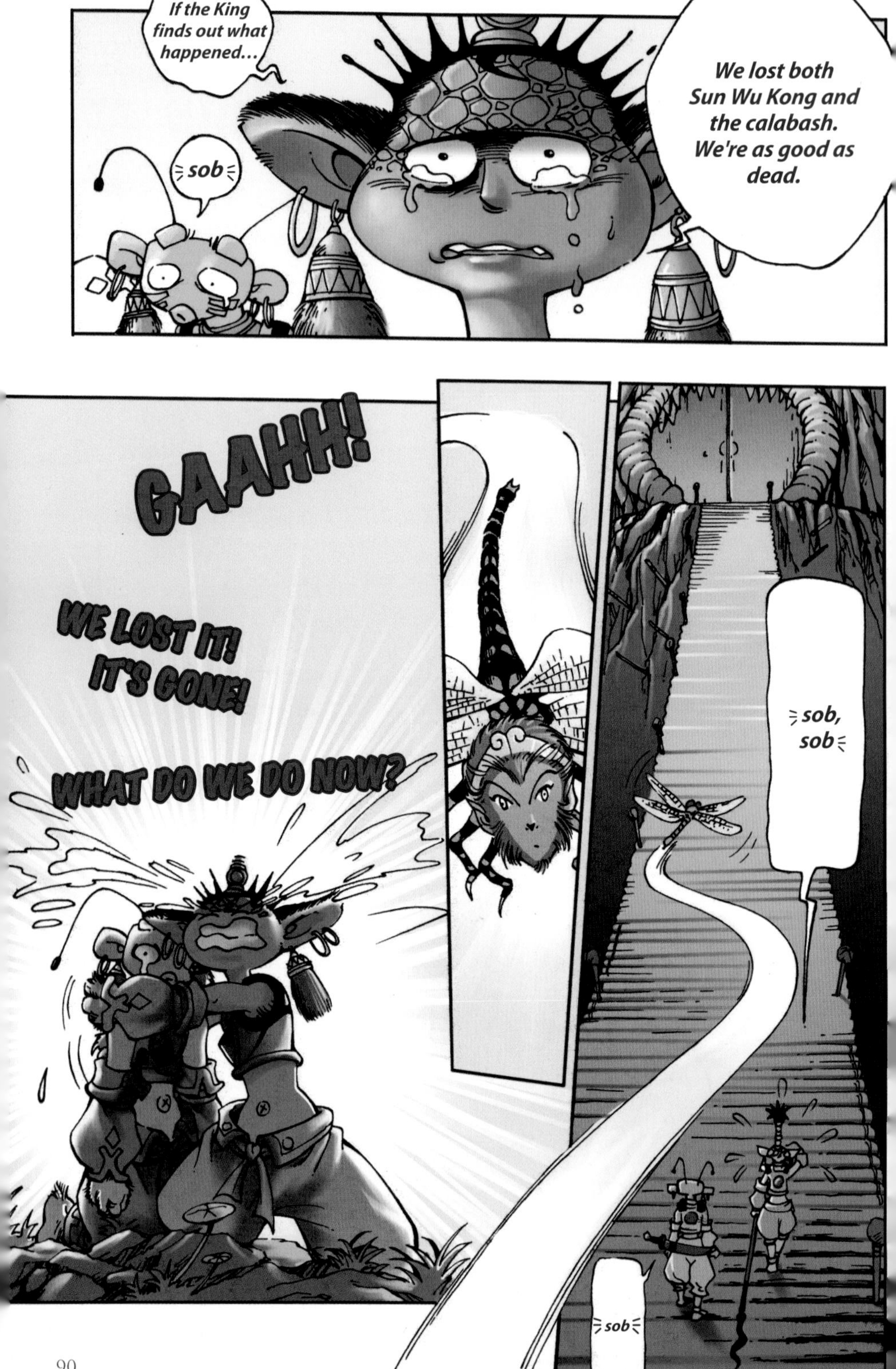
If the King finds out what happened...
sob
We lost both Sun Wu Kong and the calabash. We're as good as dead.
GAAHH!
WE LOST IT! IT'S GONE!
WHAT DO WE DO NOW?
sob, sob
sob

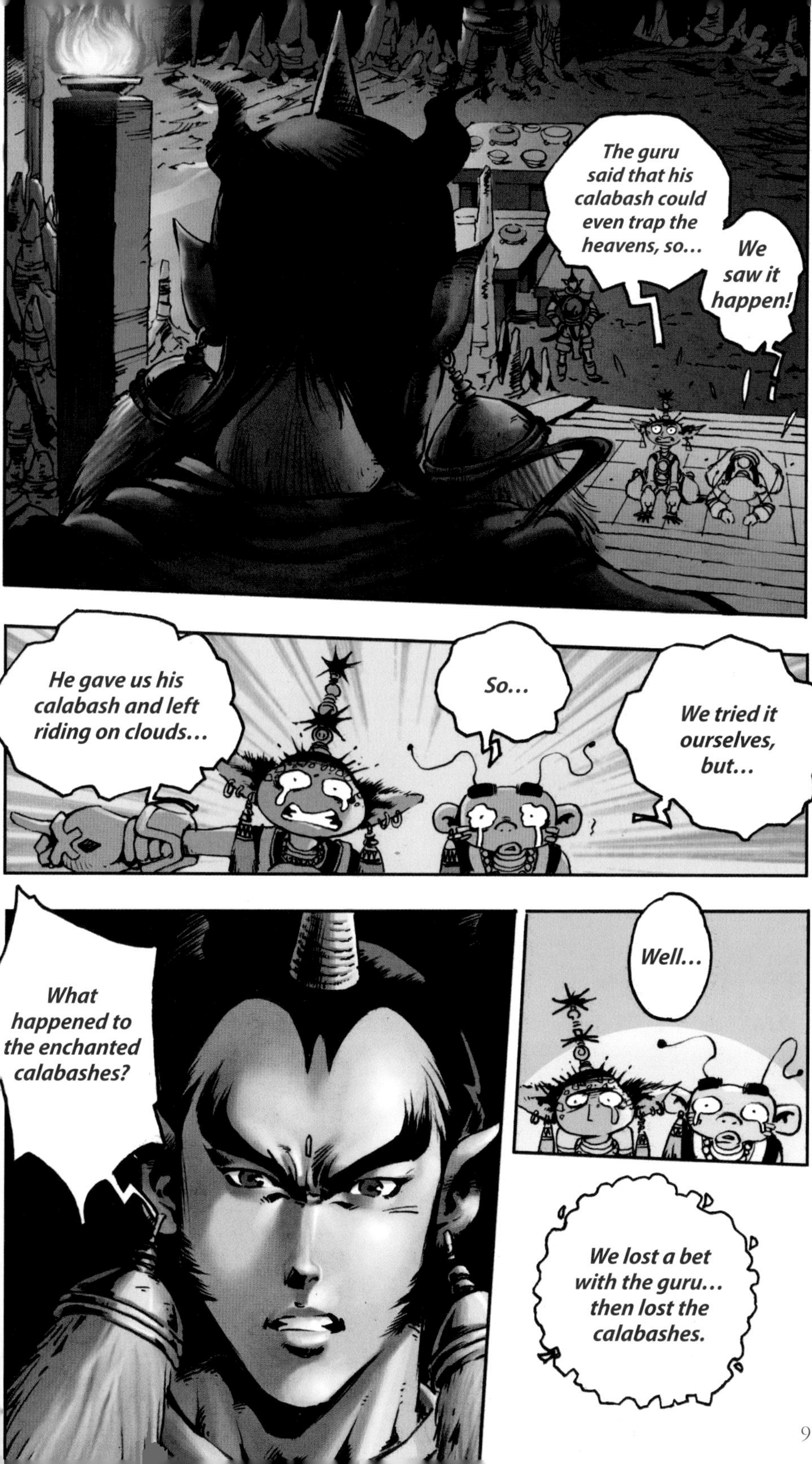
The guru said that his calabash could even trap the heavens, so...
We saw it happen!
He gave us his calabash and left riding on clouds...
So...
We tried it ourselves, but...
What happened to the enchanted calabashes?
Well...
We lost a bet with the guru... then lost the calabashes.

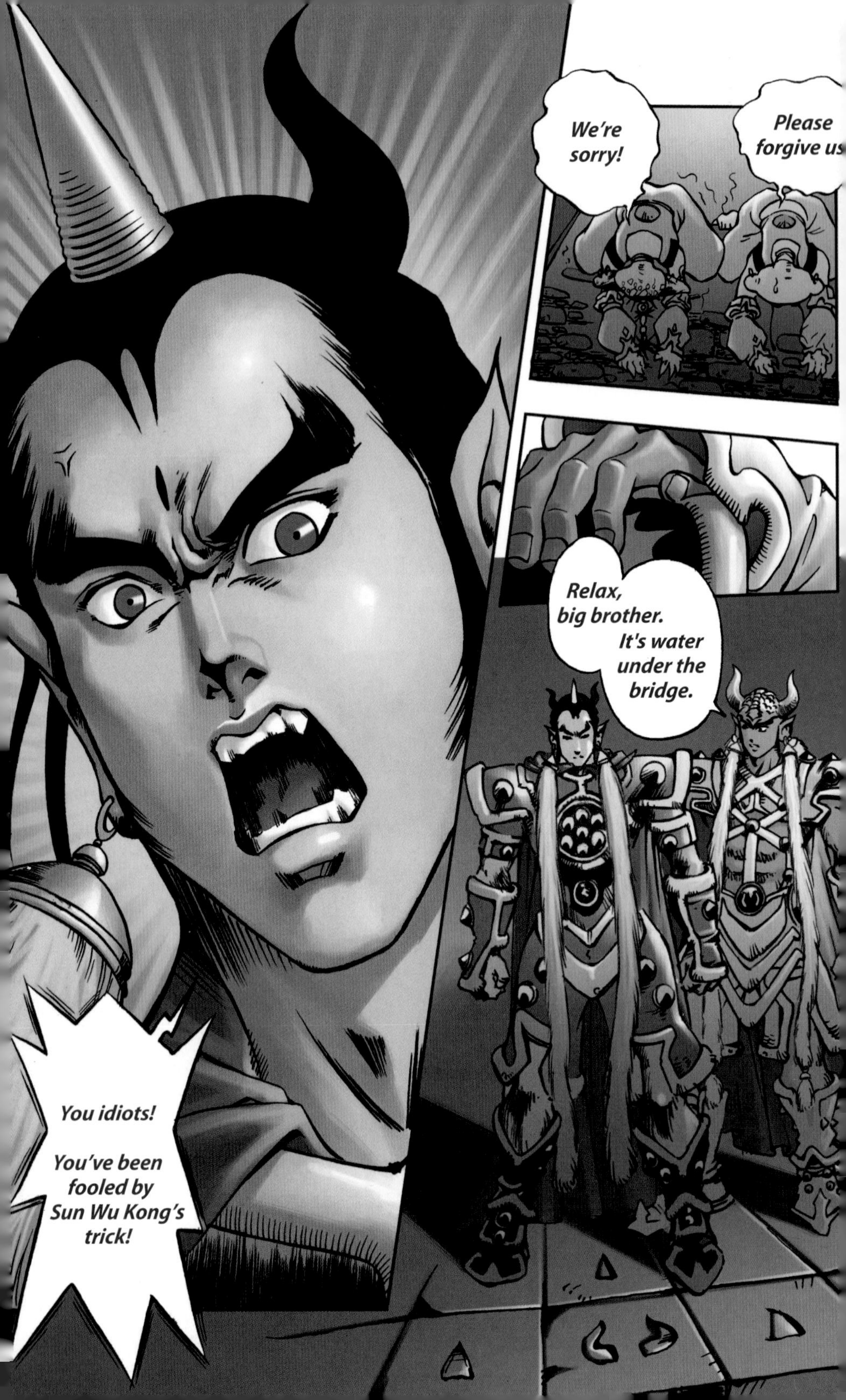

You idiots!
You've been fooled by Sun Wu Kong's trick!
We're sorry!
Please forgive us
Relax, big brother.
It's water under the bridge.

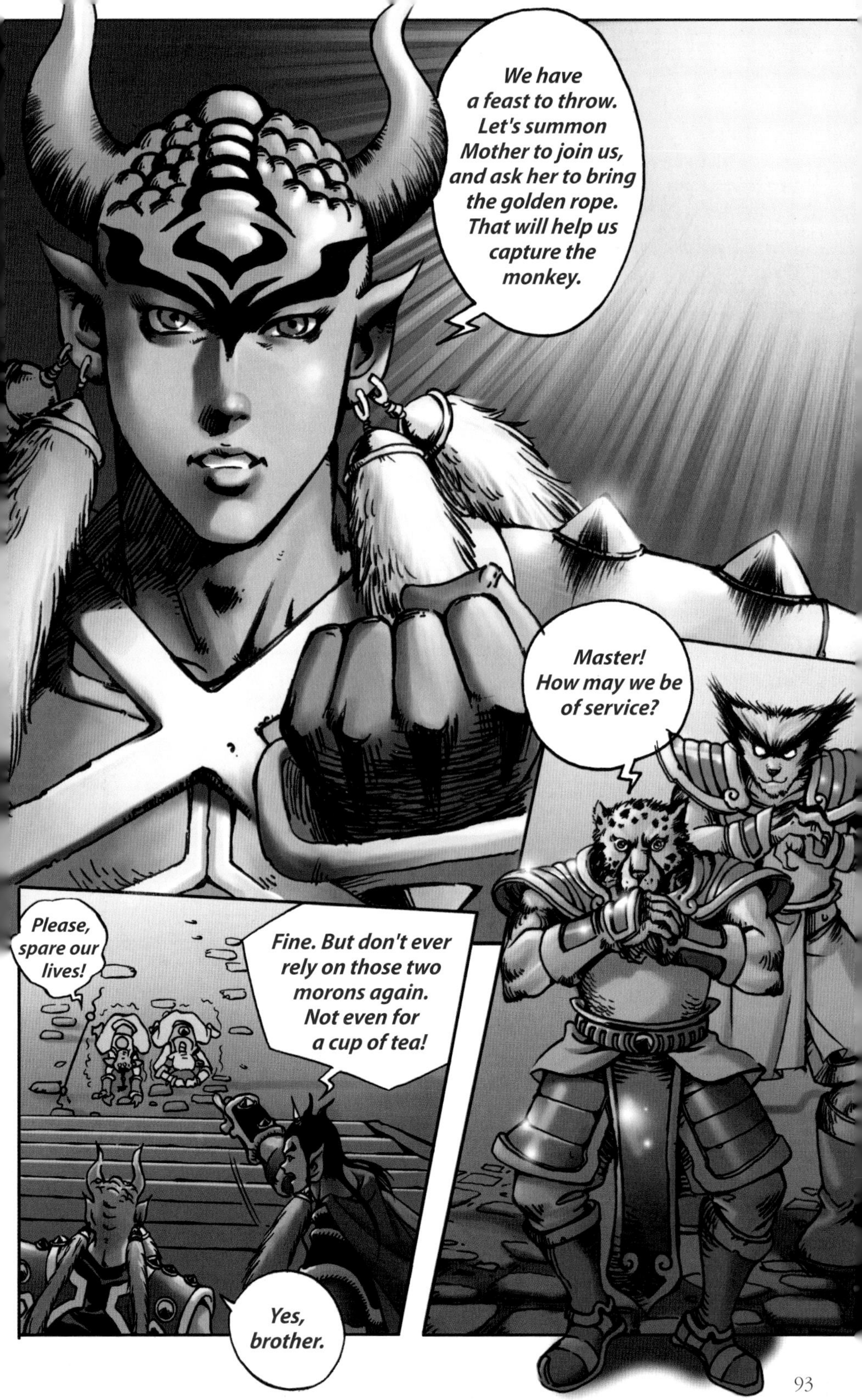

We have a feast to throw. Let's summon Mother to join us, and ask her to bring the golden rope. That will help us capture the monkey.
Master! How may we be of service?
Please, spare our lives!
Fine. But don't ever rely on those two morons again. Not even for a cup of tea!
Yes, brother.

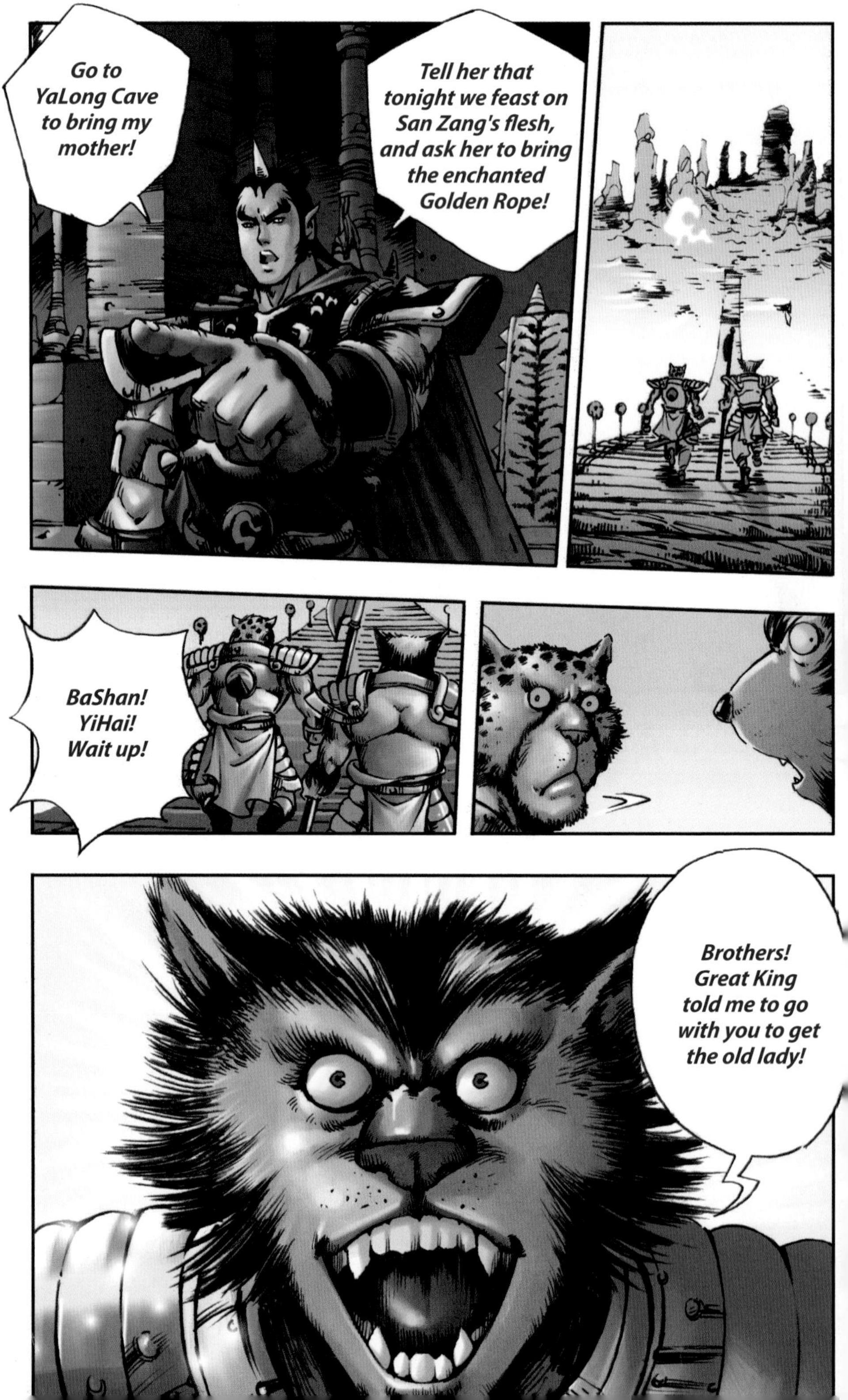
Go to YaLong Cave to bring my mother!
Tell her that tonight we feast on San Zang's flesh, and ask her to bring the enchanted Golden Rope!
BaShan! YiHai! Wait up!
Brothers! Great King told me to go with you to get the old lady!

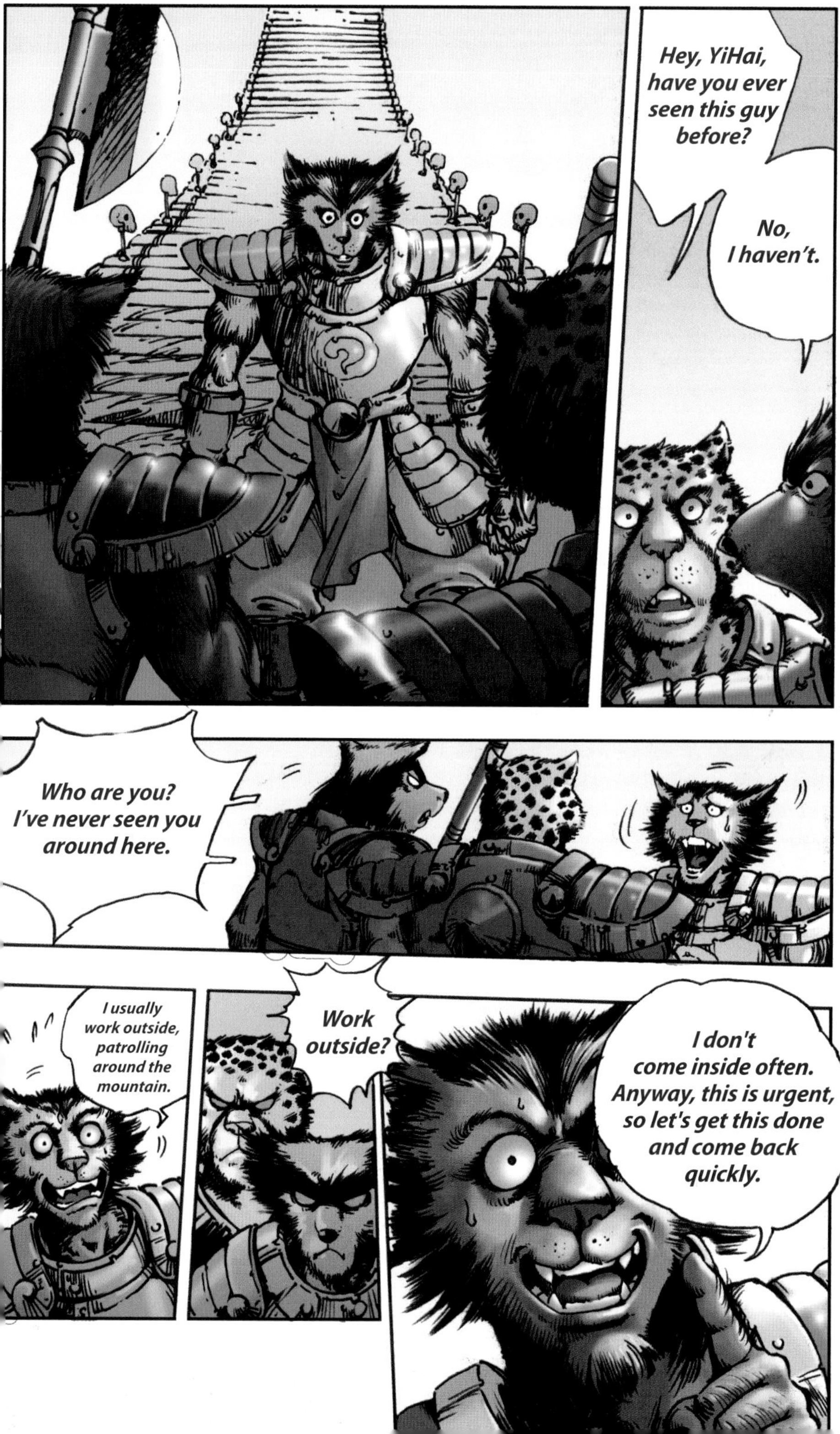
Hey, YiHai, have you ever seen this guy before?
No, I haven't.
Who are you? I've never seen you around here.
I usually work outside, patrolling around the mountain.
Work outside?
I don't come inside often. Anyway, this is urgent, so let's get this done and come back quickly.

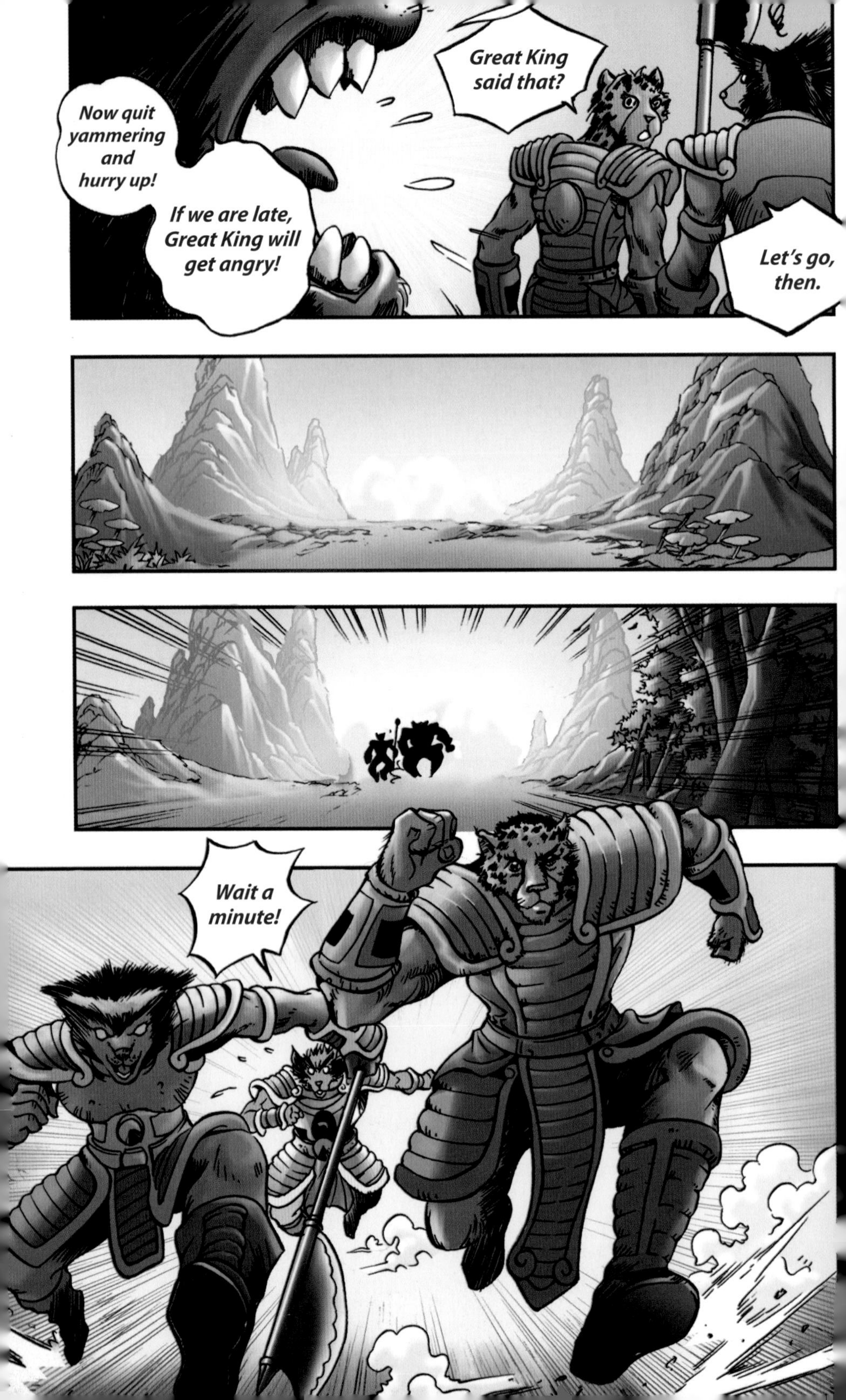
Great King said that?
Now quit yammering and hurry up!
If we are late, Great King will get angry!
Let's go, then.
Wait a minute!

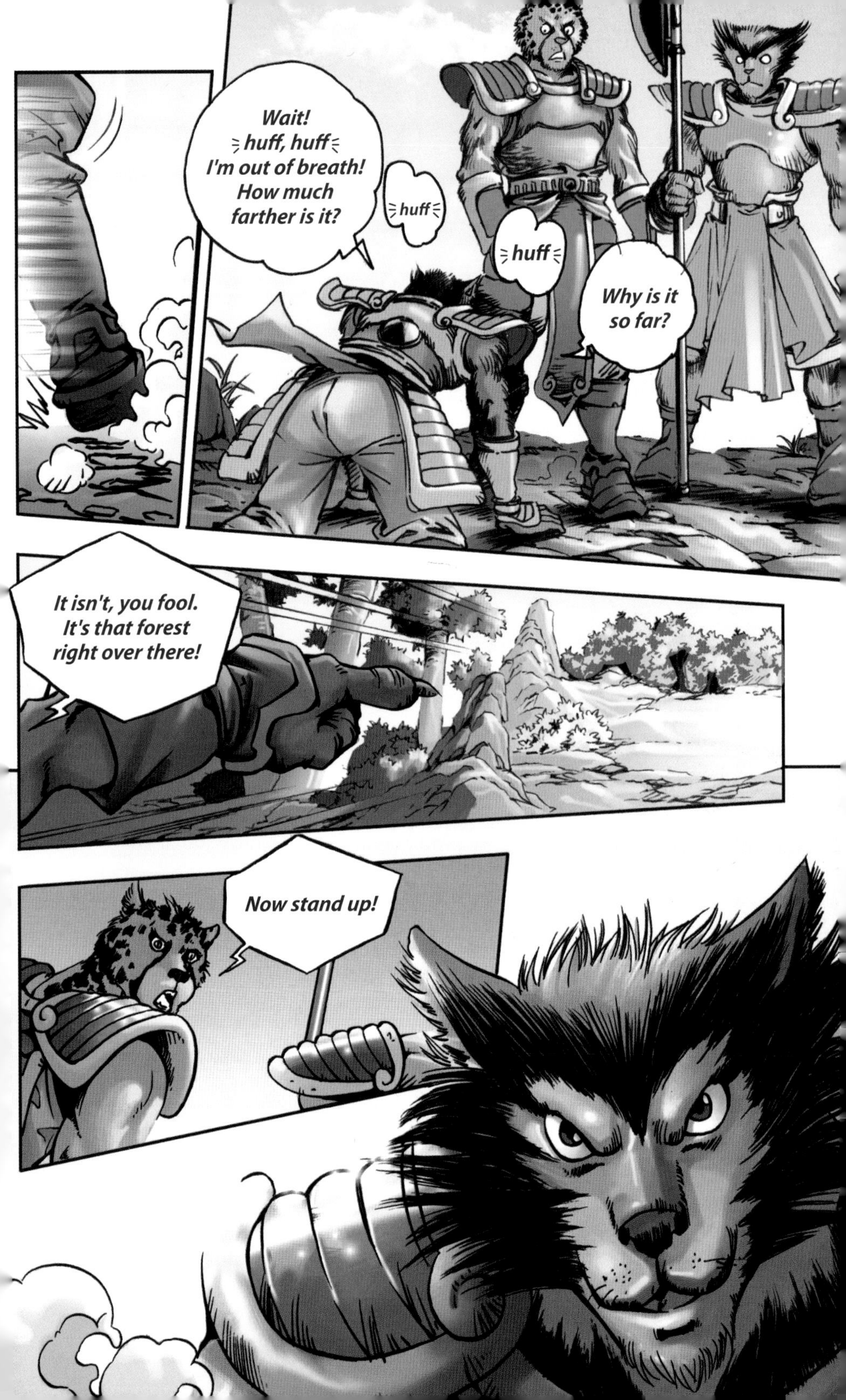
Wait!
huff, huff
I'm out of breath!
How much farther is it?
huff
huff
Why is it so far?
It isn't, you fool.
It's that forest right over there!
Now stand up!

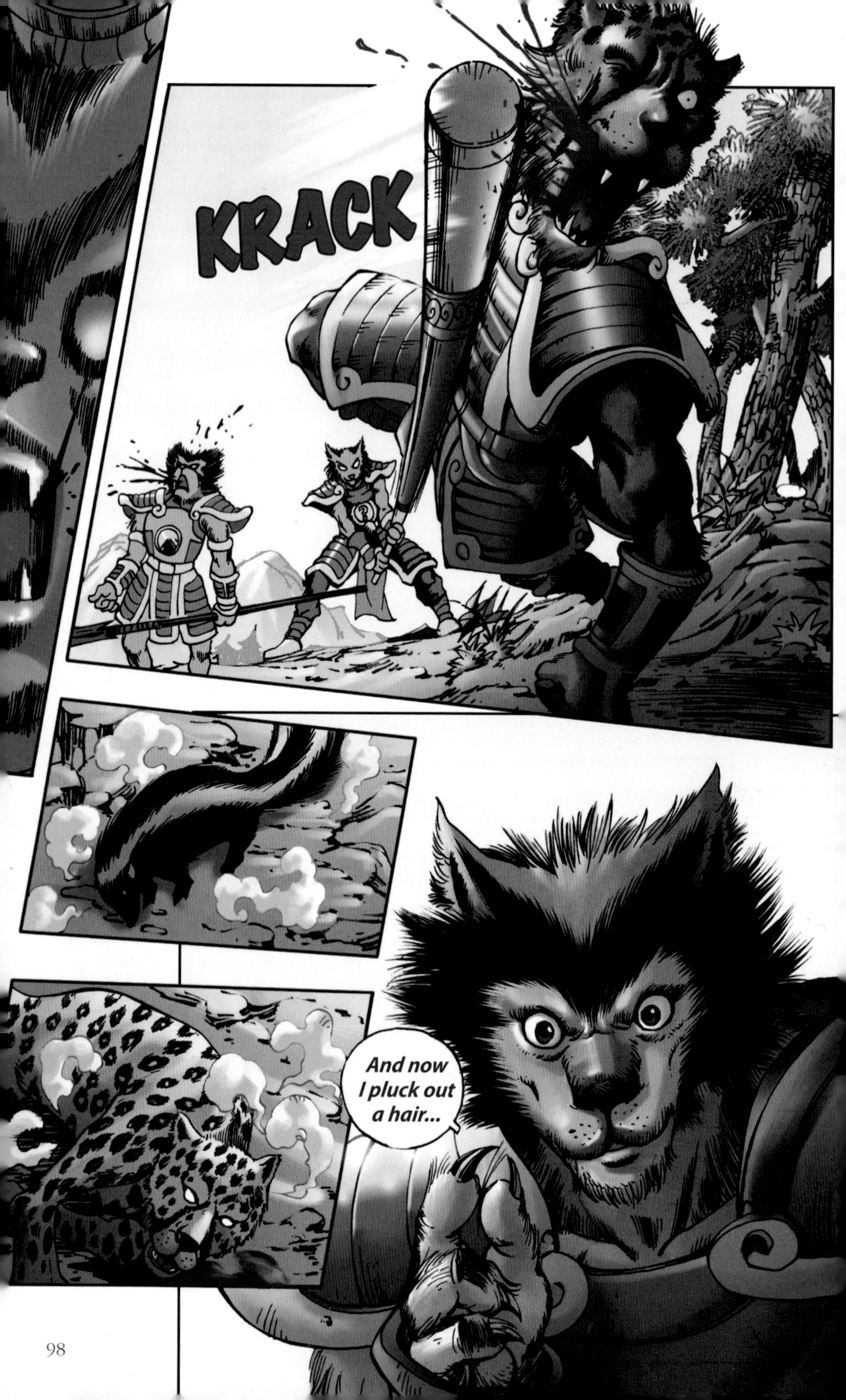
KRACK
And now I pluck out a hair...

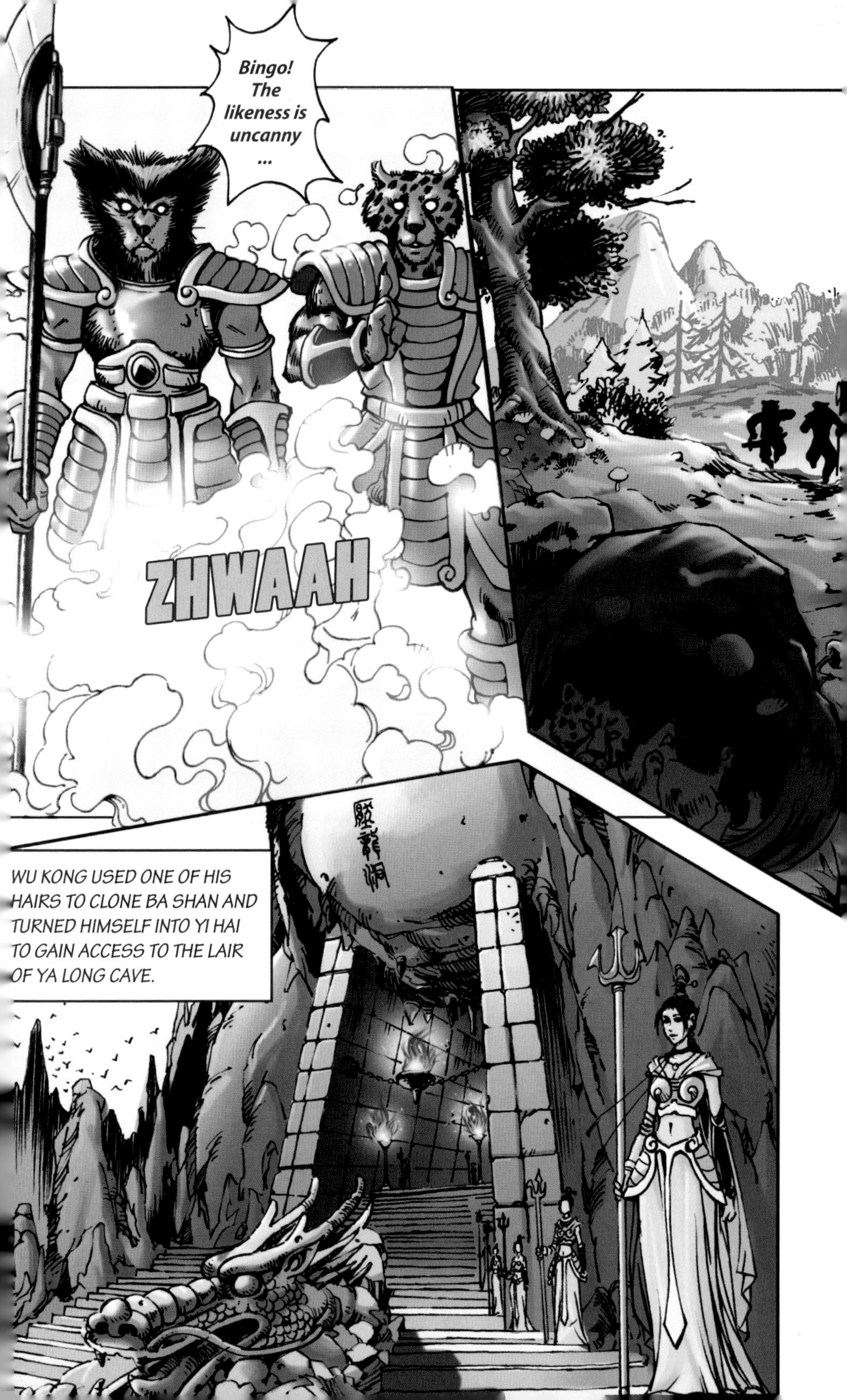
Bingo! The likeness is uncanny ...
ZHWAAH
WU KONG USED ONE OF HIS HAIRS TO CLONE BA SHAN AND TURNED HIMSELF INTO YI HAI TO GAIN ACCESS TO THE LAIR OF YA LONG CAVE.
壓龍洞

Your Highness!
We come on behalf of
your two sons to deliver
an urgent message!

Stand up!

Why are you in such a hurry?

The Great Kings
have captured San Zang
and ask you to join them
for a feast.

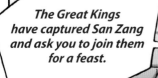

They also
seek to capture
Sun Wu Kong, an
ask you to bring
the golden rope.

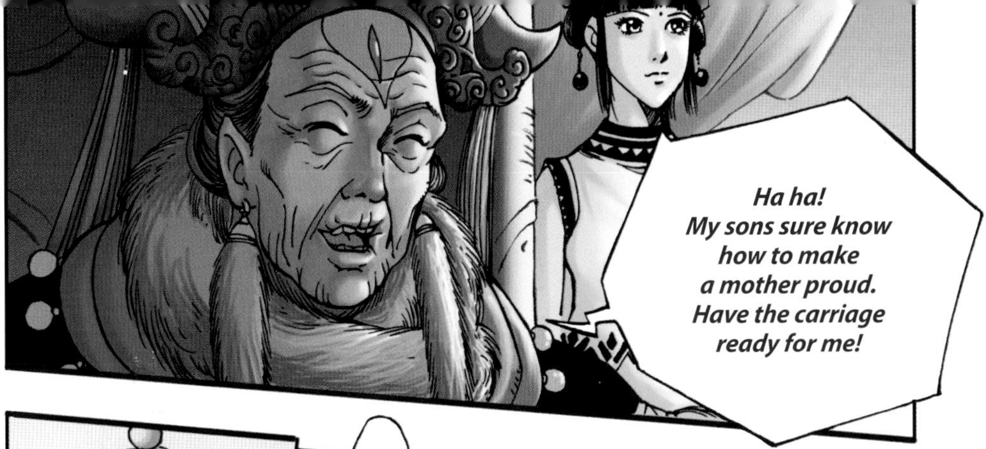
Ha ha!
My sons sure know how to make a mother proud. Have the carriage ready for me!

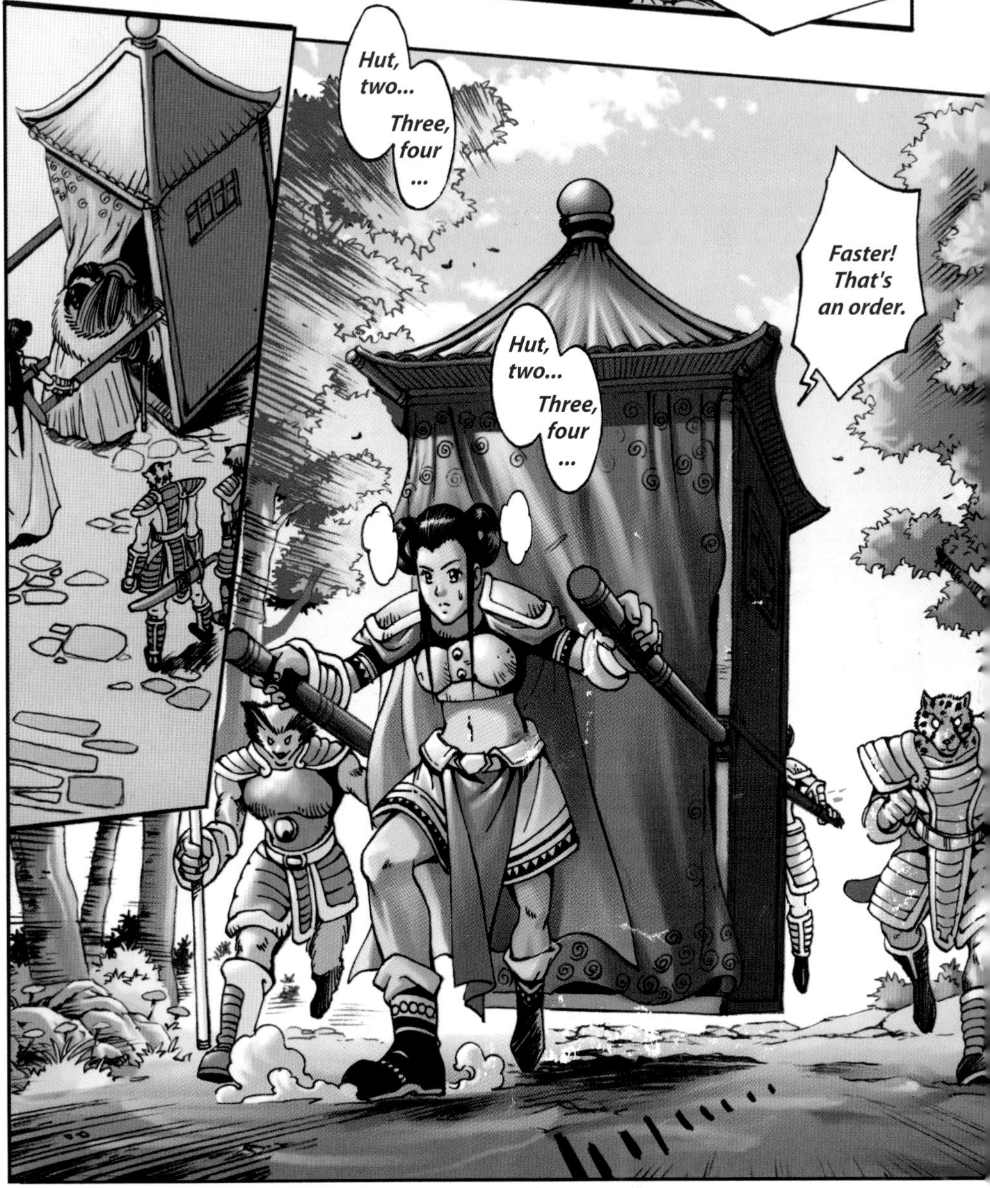
Hut, two... Three, four ...
Faster! That's an order.
Hut, two... Three, four ...

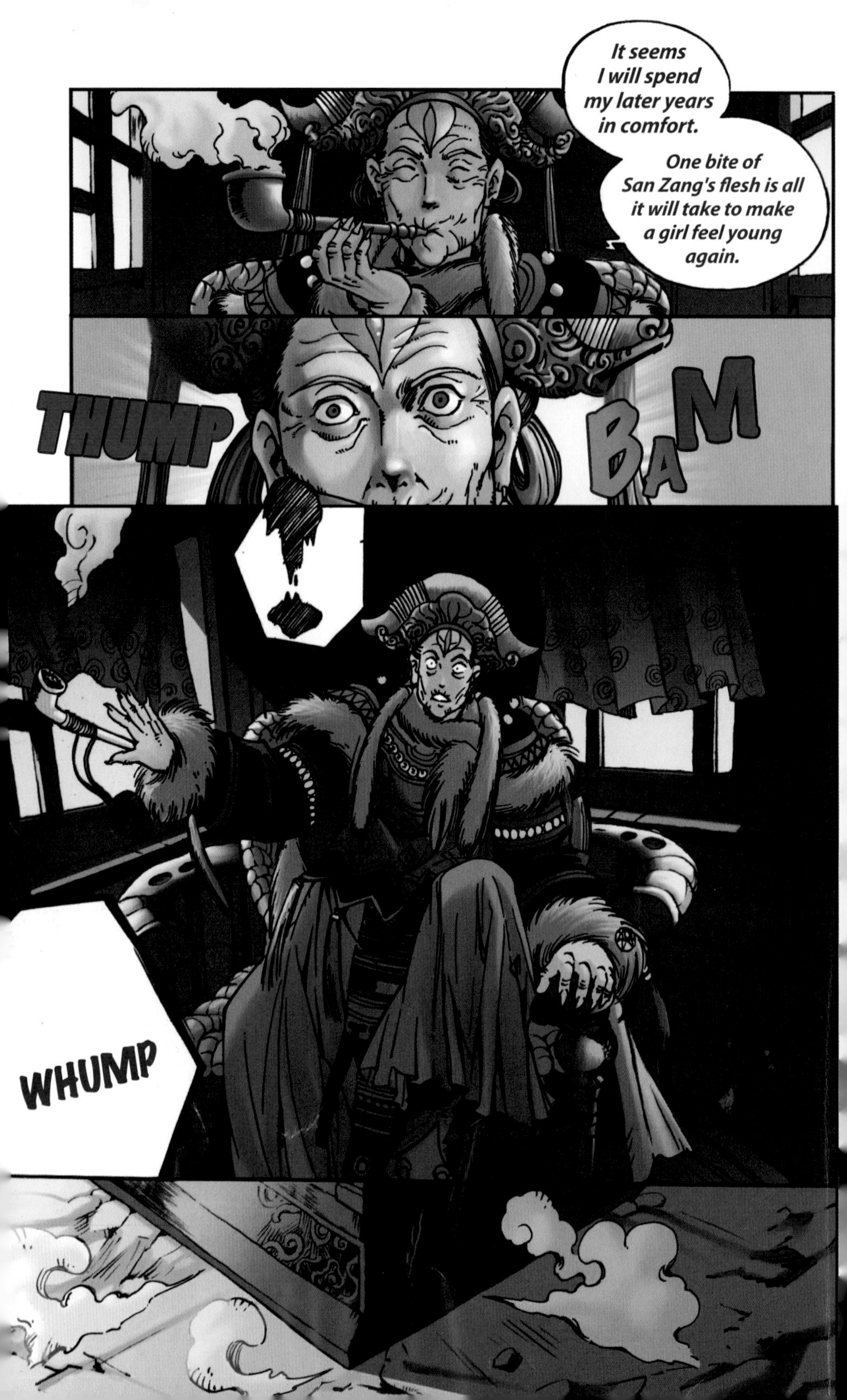
It seems I will spend my later years in comfort.
One bite of San Zang's flesh is all it will take to make a girl feel young again.
THUMP
BAM
!
WHUMP

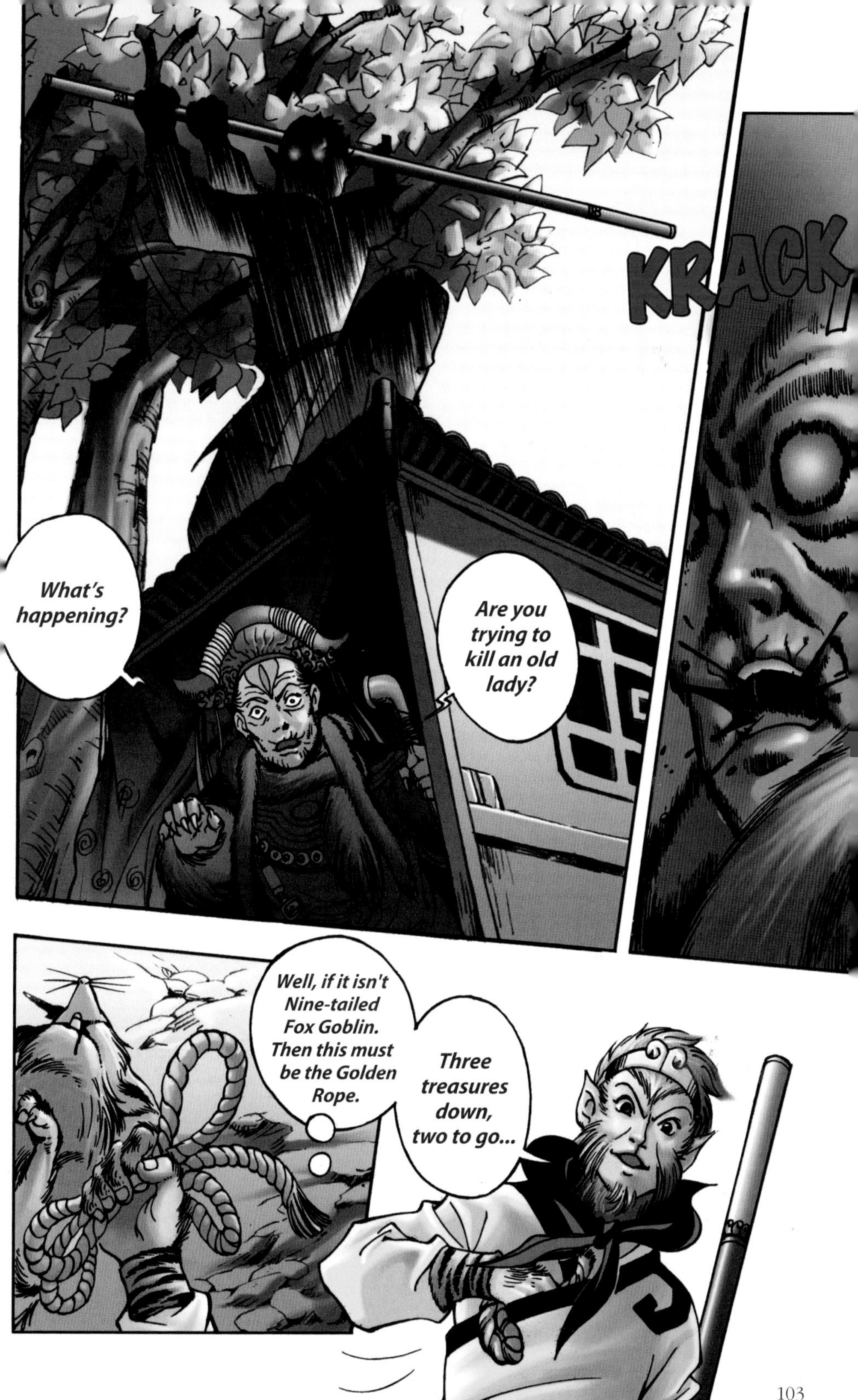
KRACK
What's happening?
Are you trying to kill an old lady?
Well, if it isn't Nine-tailed Fox Goblin. Then this must be the Golden Rope.
Three treasures down, two to go...

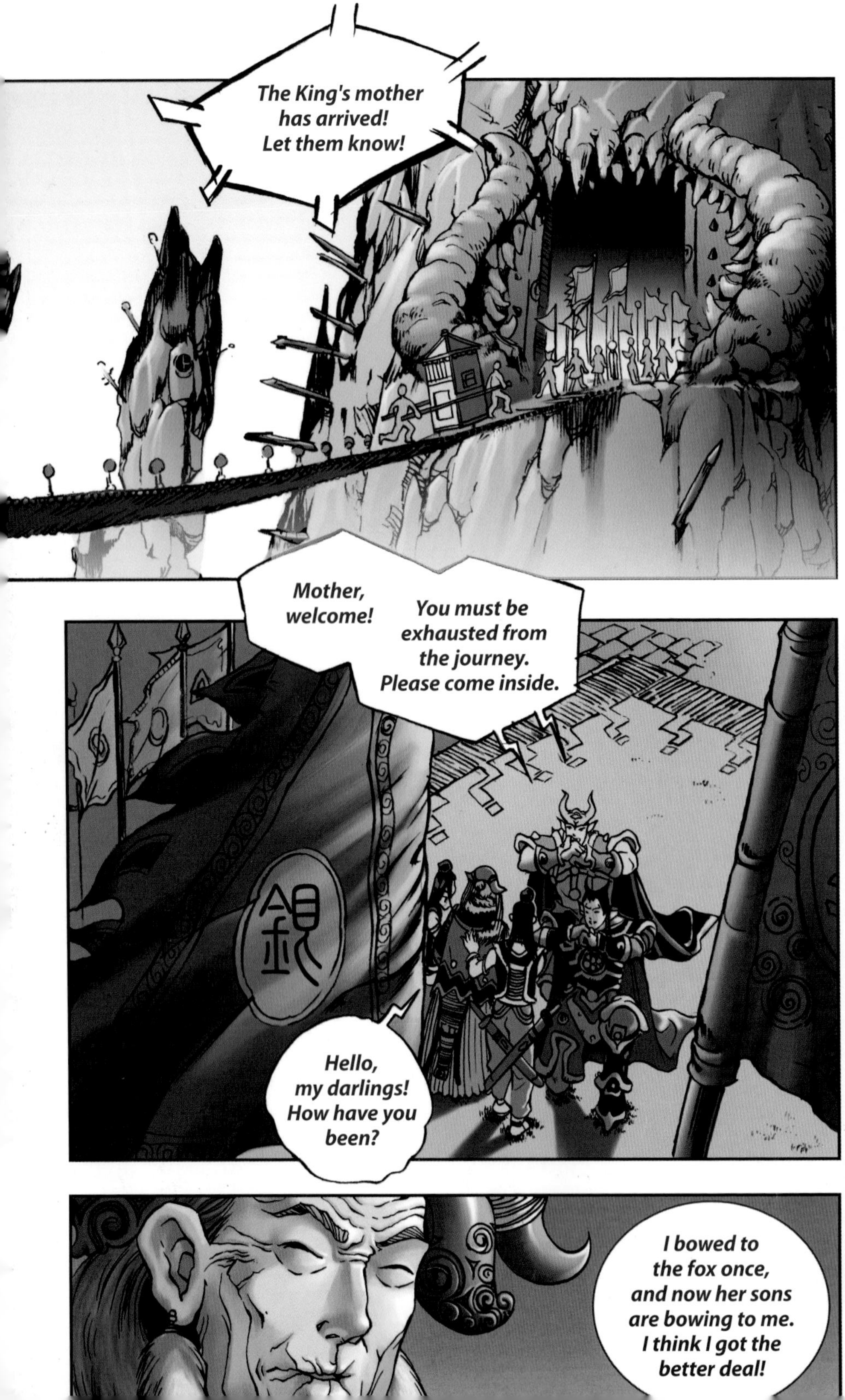
The King's mother has arrived! Let them know!
Mother, welcome!
You must be exhausted from the journey. Please come inside.
Hello, my darlings! How have you been?
I bowed to the fox once, and now her sons are bowing to me. I think I got the better deal!

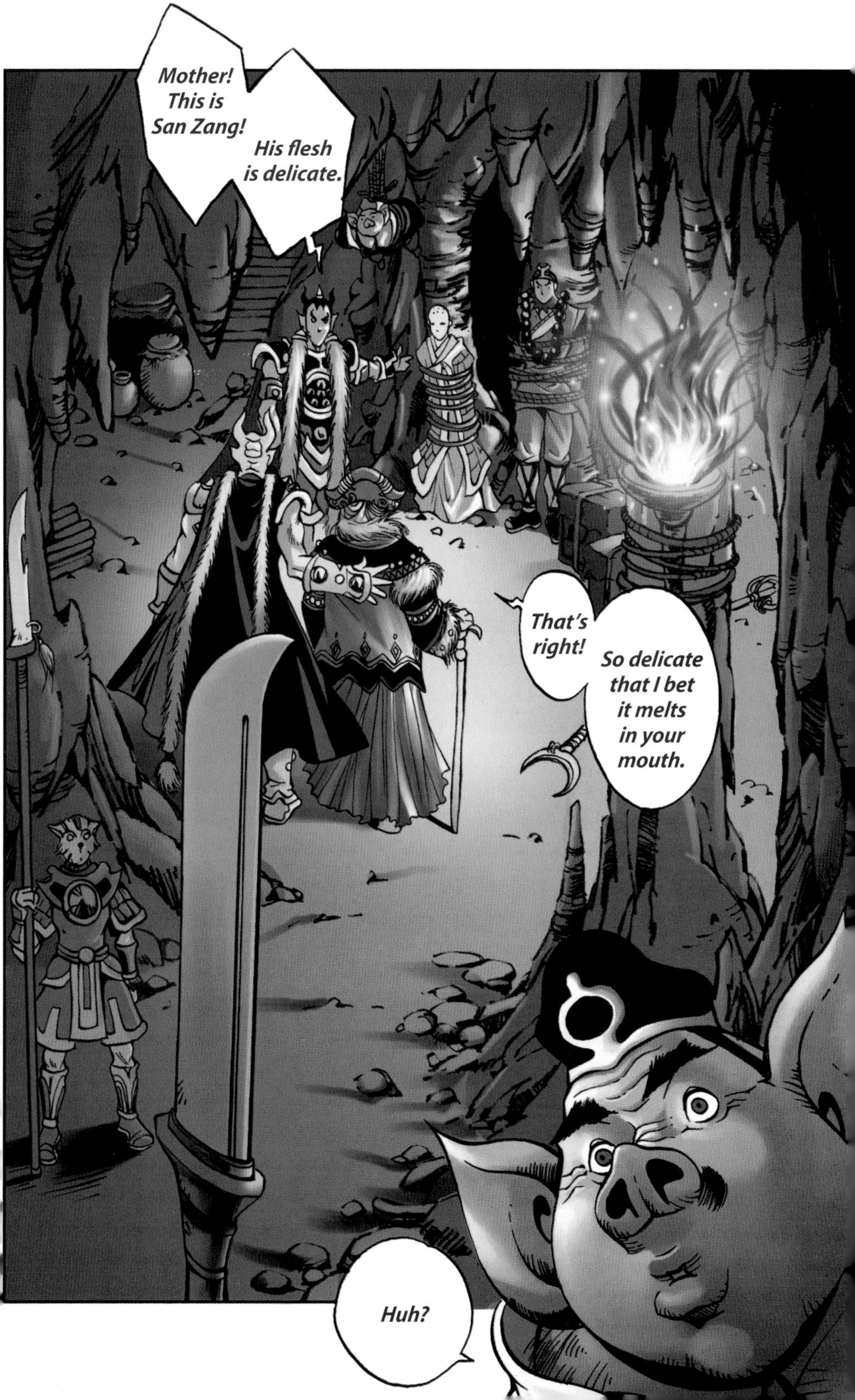
Mother! This is San Zang!
His flesh is delicate.
That's right!
So delicate that I bet it melts in your mouth.
Huh?

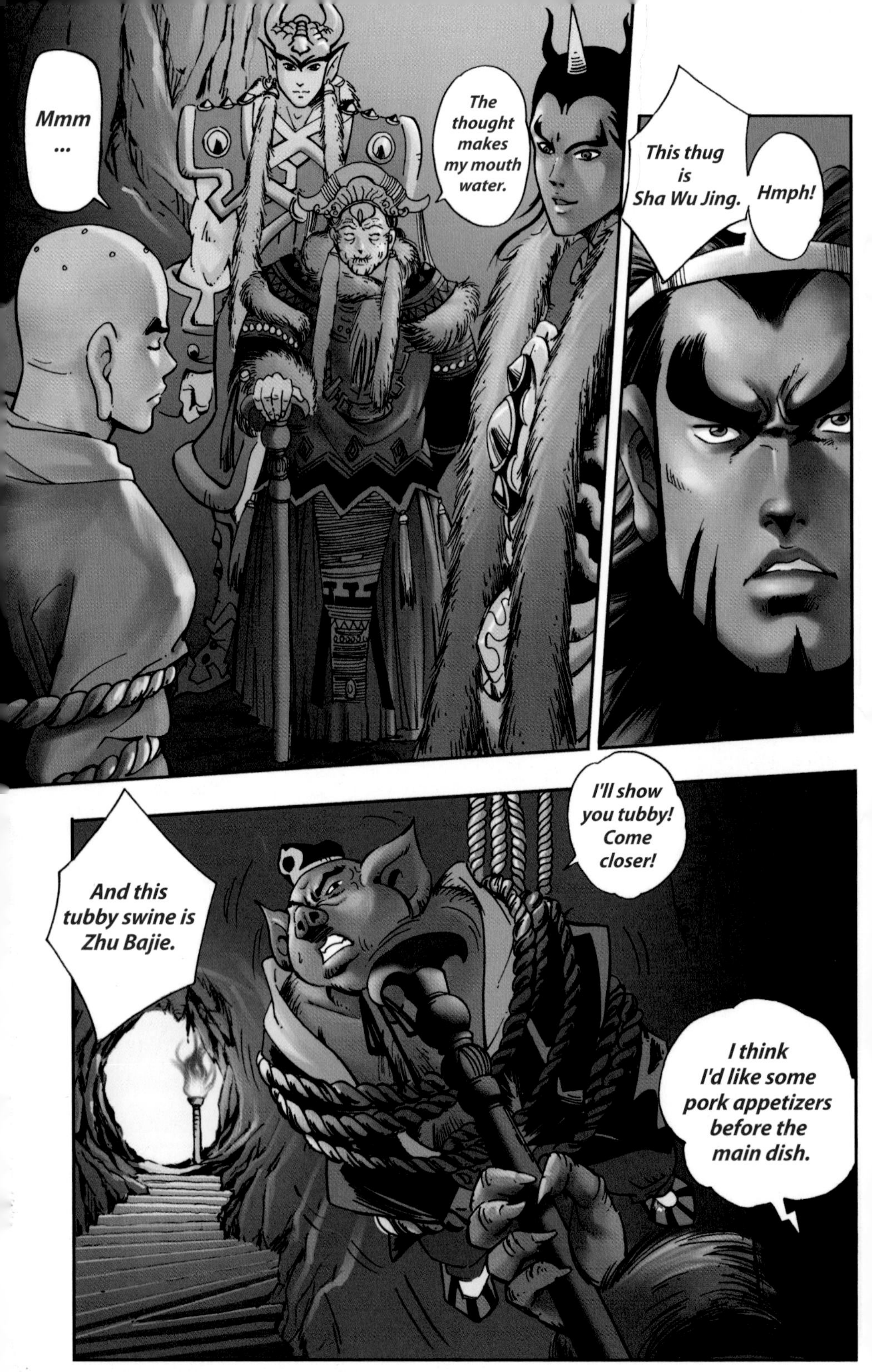
Mmm
...
The thought makes my mouth water.
This thug is Sha Wu Jing.
Hmph!
And this tubby swine is Zhu Bajie.
I'll show you tubby! Come closer!
I think I'd like some pork appetizers before the main dish.

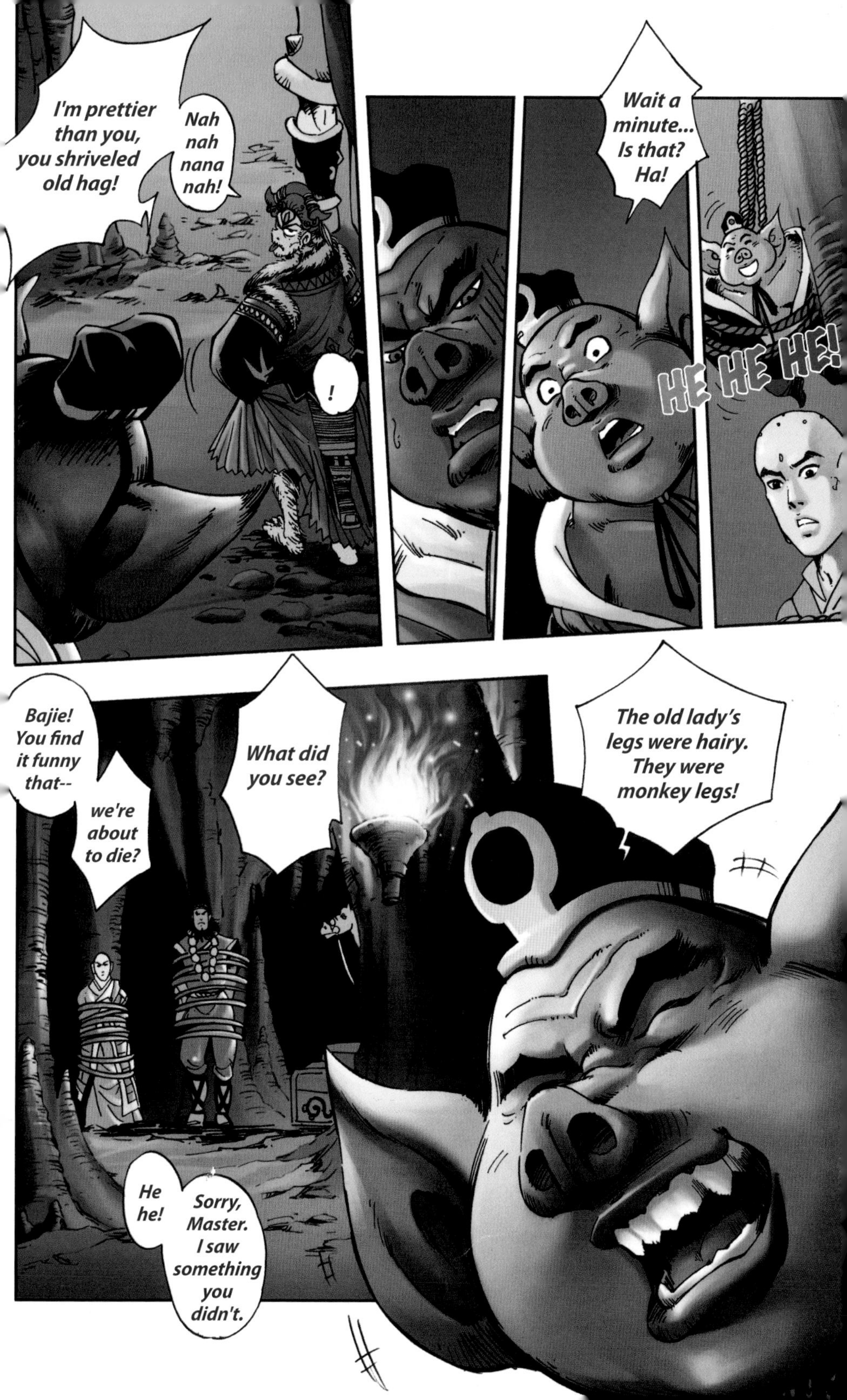
I'm prettier than you, you shriveled old hag!
Nah nah nana nah!
!
Wait a minute... Is that? Ha!
HE HE HE!
Bajie! You find it funny that--
we're about to die?
What did you see?
He he!
Sorry, Master. I saw something you didn't.
The old lady's legs were hairy. They were monkey legs!

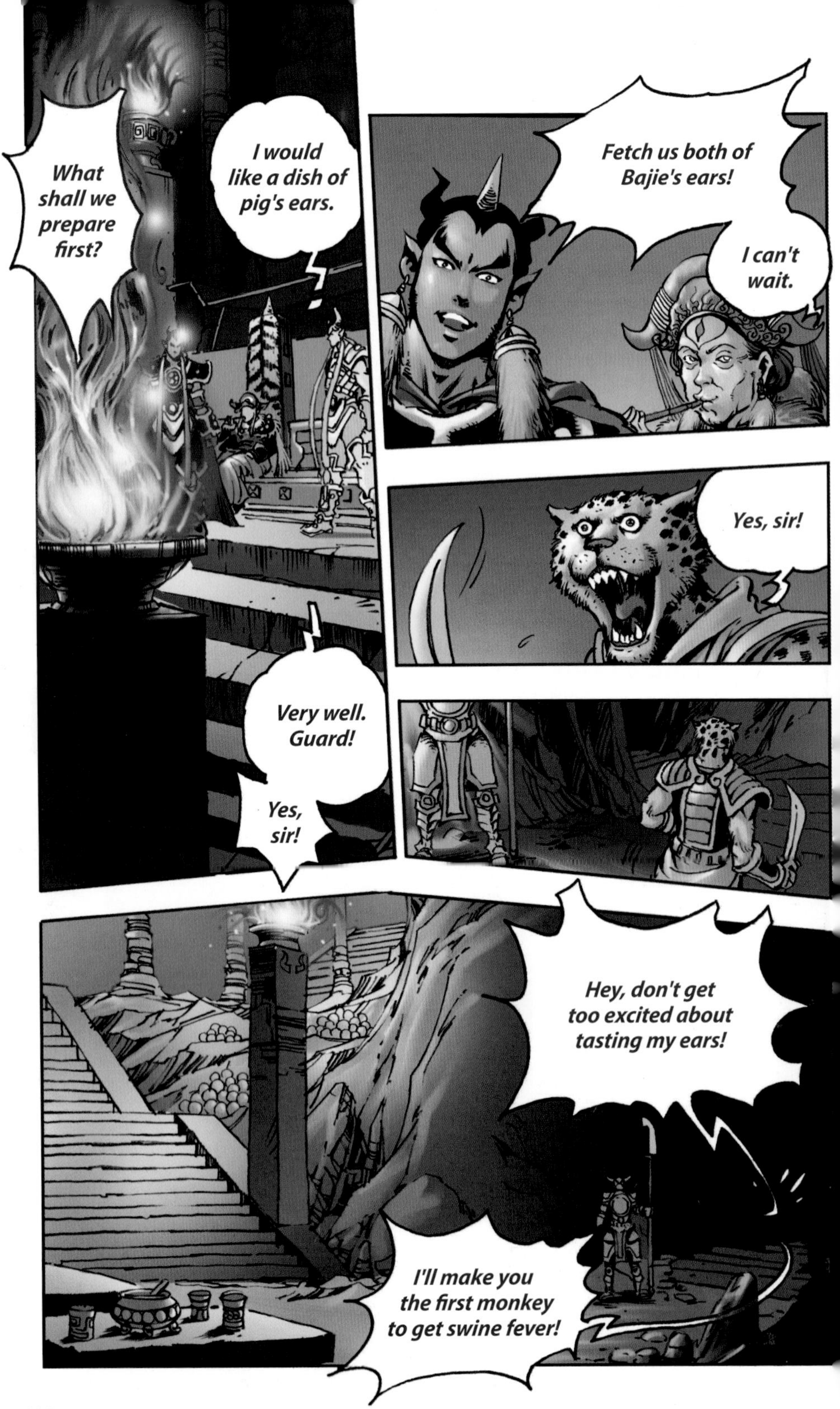
What shall we prepare first?
I would like a dish of pig's ears.
Fetch us both of Bajie's ears!
I can't wait.
Yes, sir!
Very well. Guard!
Yes, sir!
Hey, don't get too excited about tasting my ears!
I'll make you the first monkey to get swine fever!

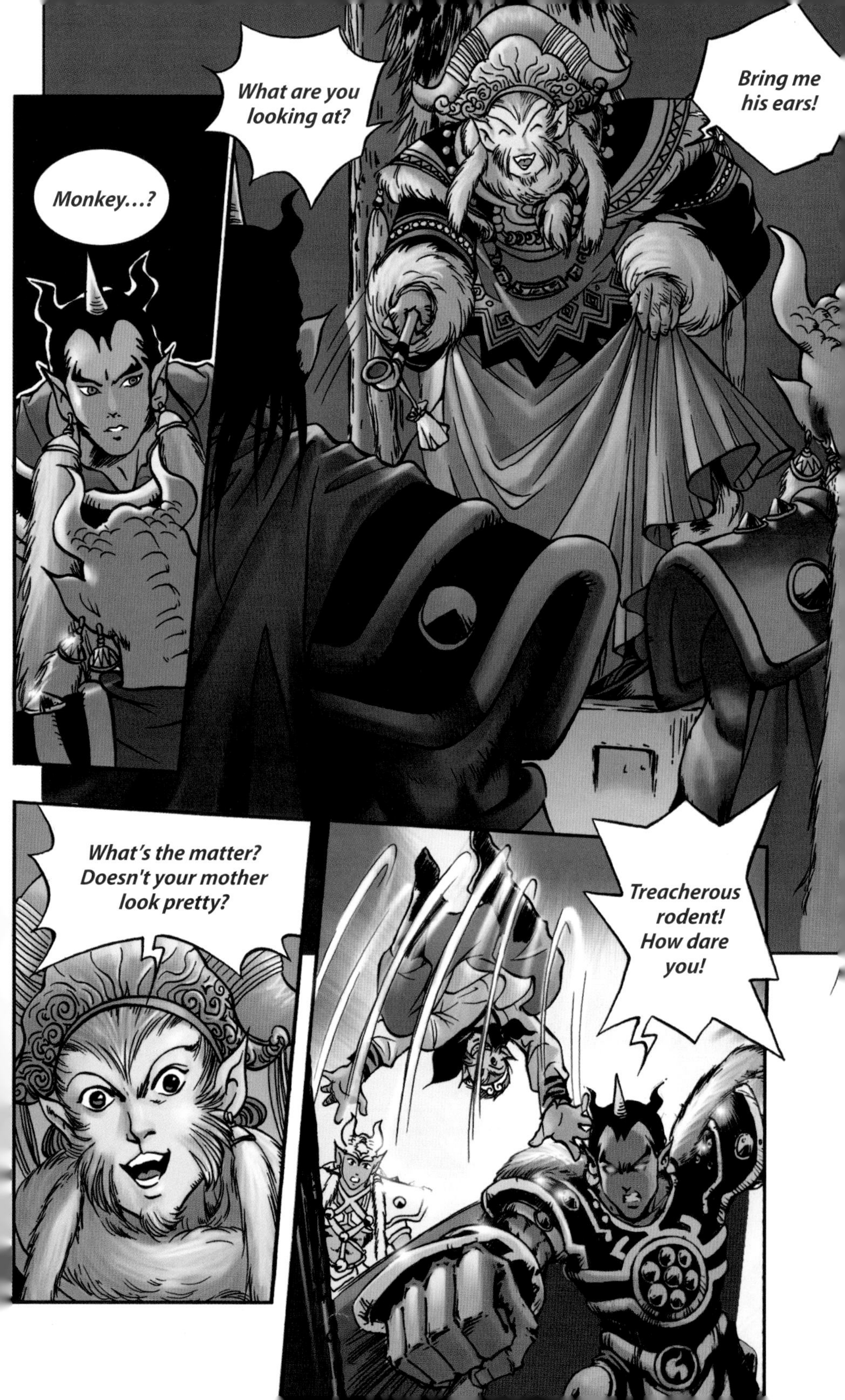
What are you looking at?
Bring me his ears!
Monkey...?
What's the matter? Doesn't your mother look pretty?
Treacherous rodent! How dare you!

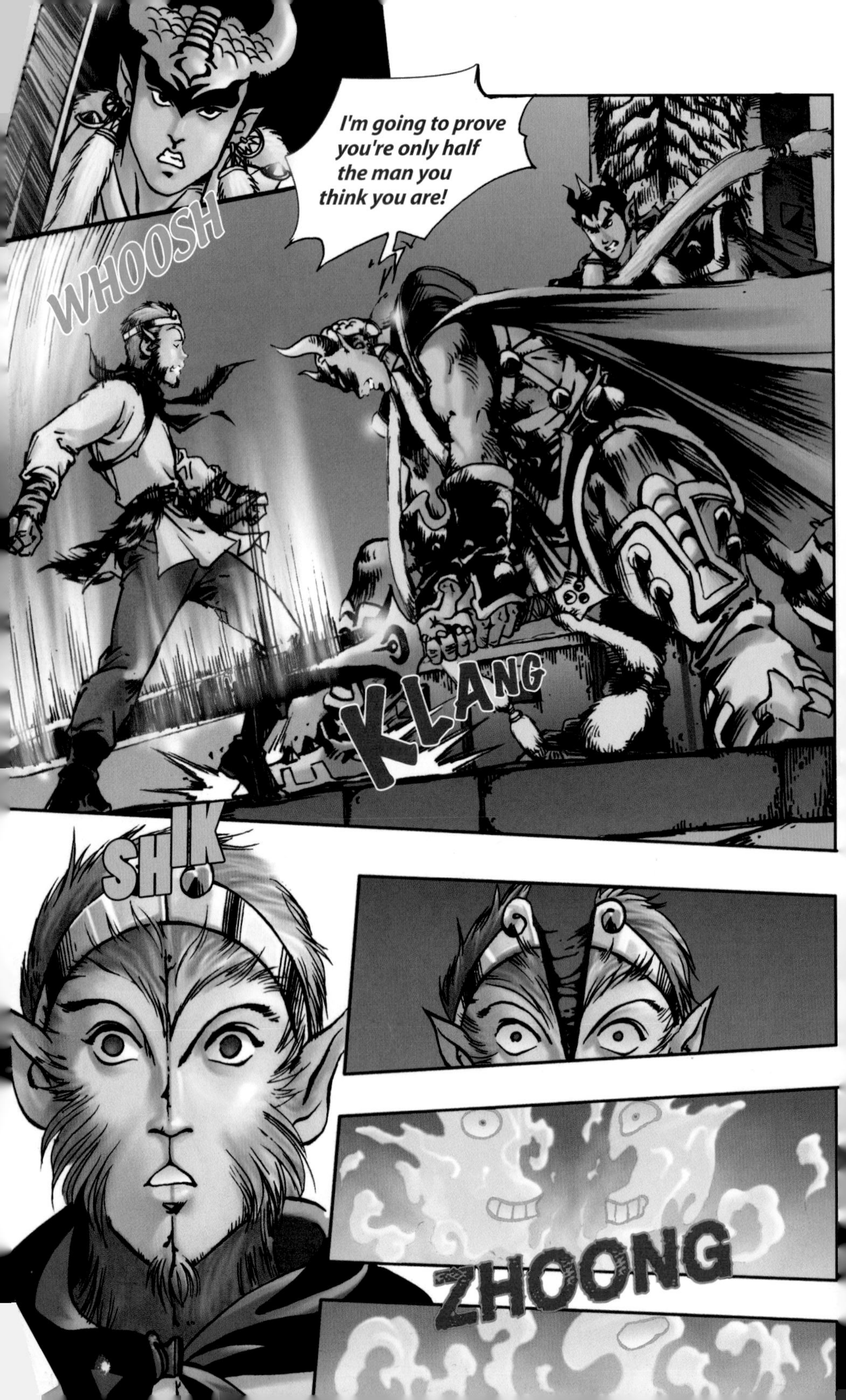
I'm going to prove you're only half the man you think you are!
WHOOSH
KLANG
SHIK
ZHOONG

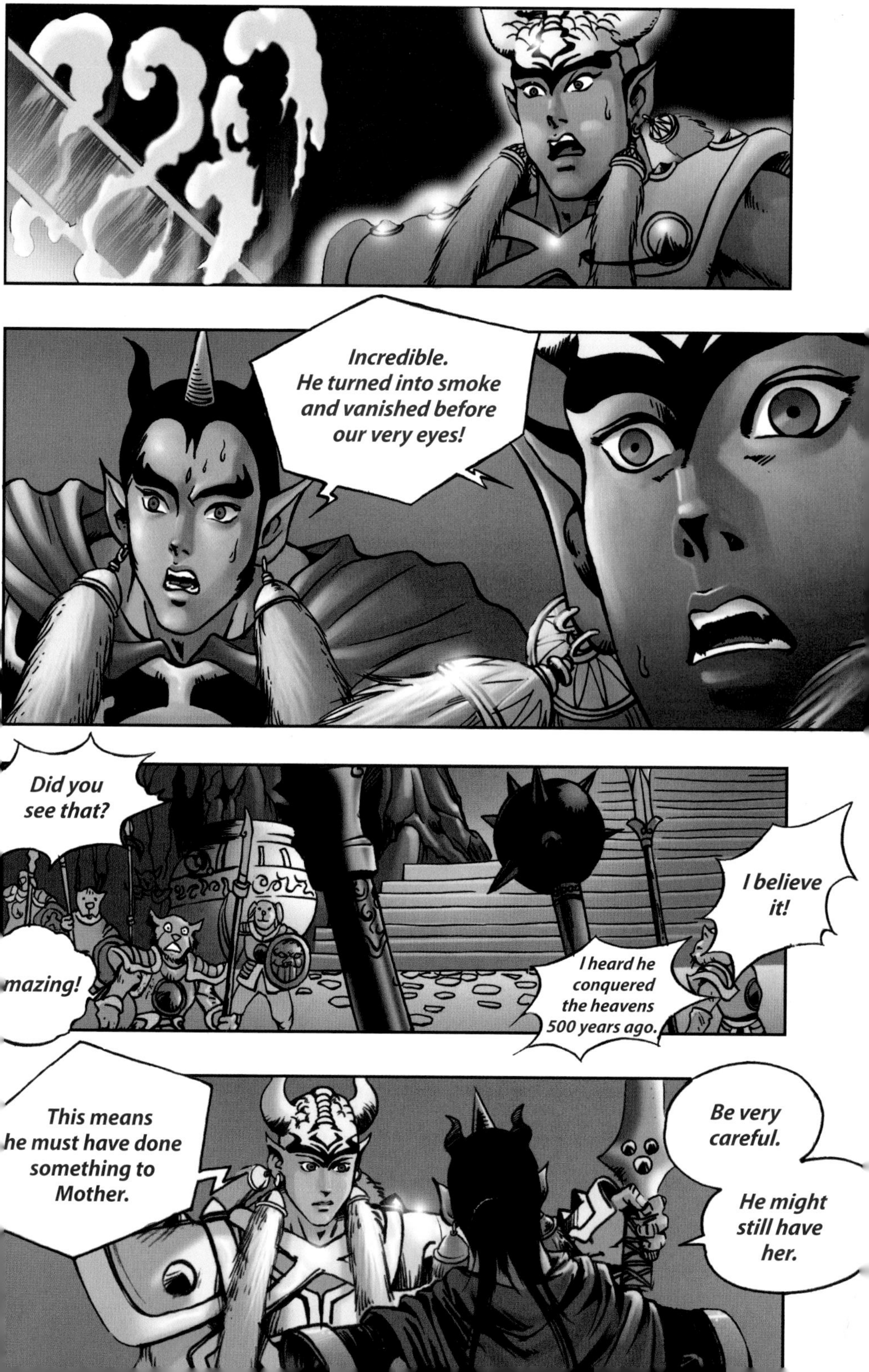
Incredible. He turned into smoke and vanished before our very eyes!
Did you see that?
I believe it!
mazing!
I heard he conquered the heavens 500 years ago.
This means he must have done something to Mother.
Be very careful.
He might still have her.

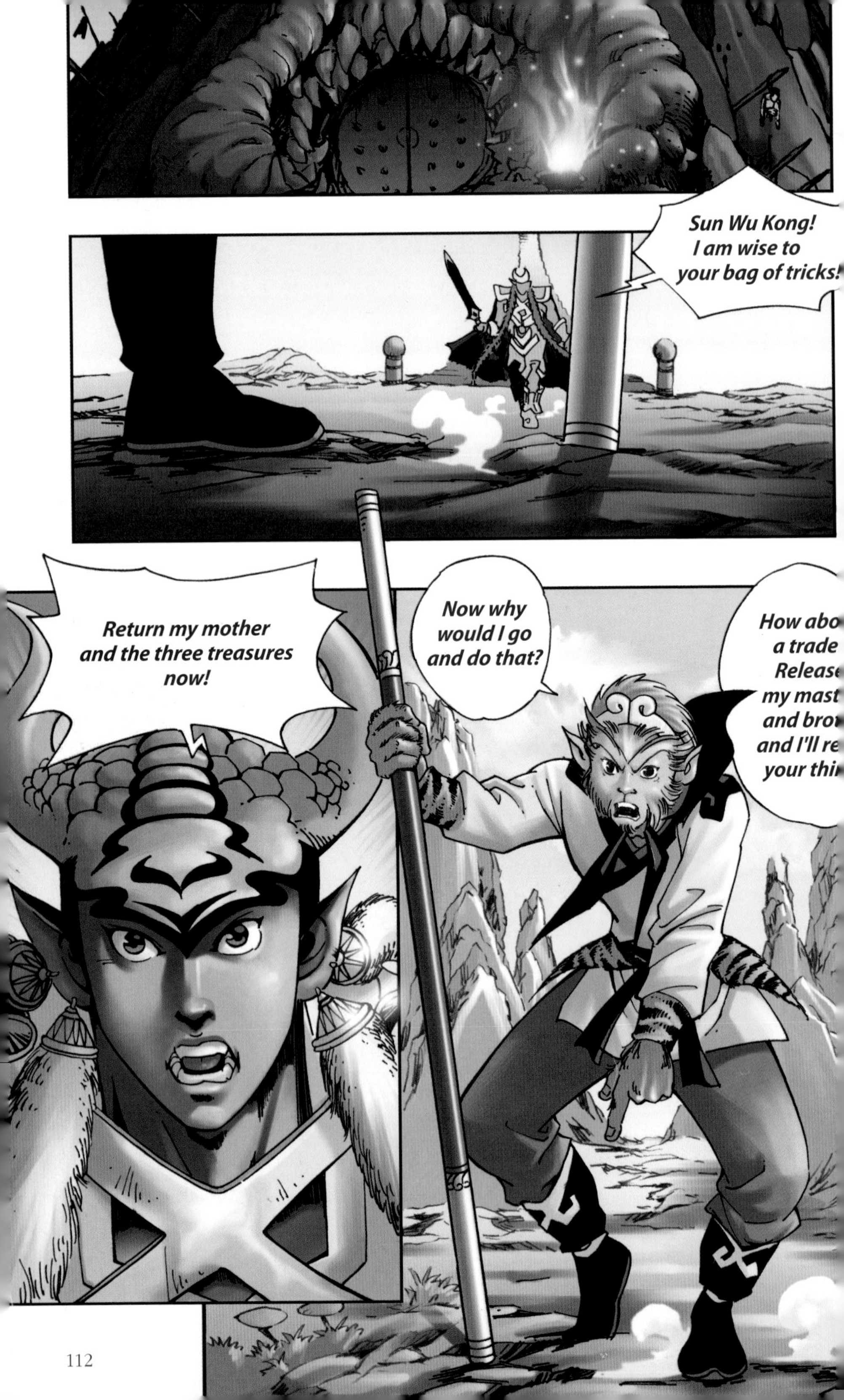
Sun Wu Kong! I am wise to your bag of tricks!
Return my mother and the three treasures now!
Now why would I go and do that?
How abo a trade Releas my mast and bro and I'll re your thi

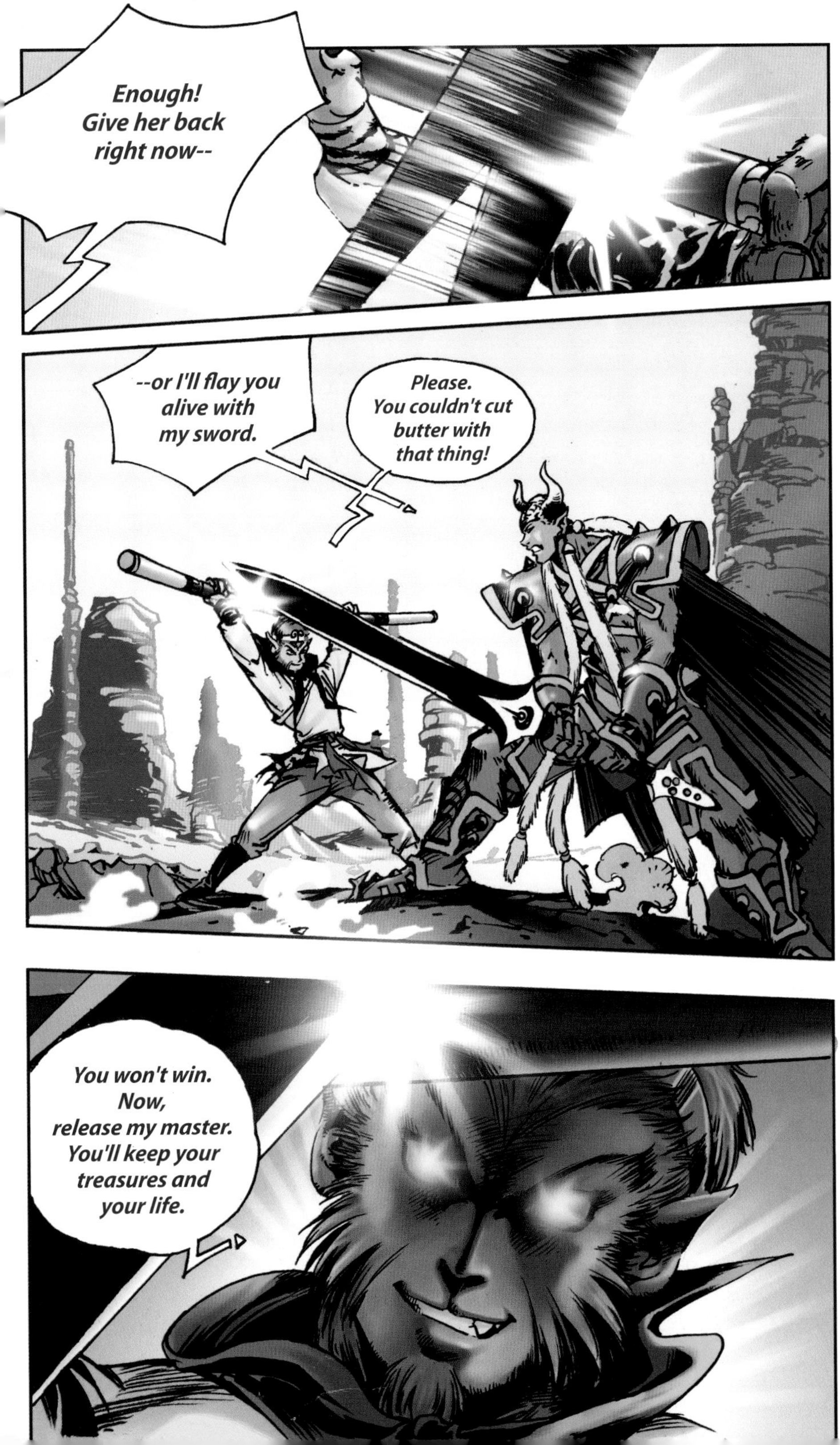
Enough! Give her back right now--
--or I'll flay you alive with my sword.
Please. You couldn't cut butter with that thing!
You won't win. Now, release my master. You'll keep your treasures and your life.

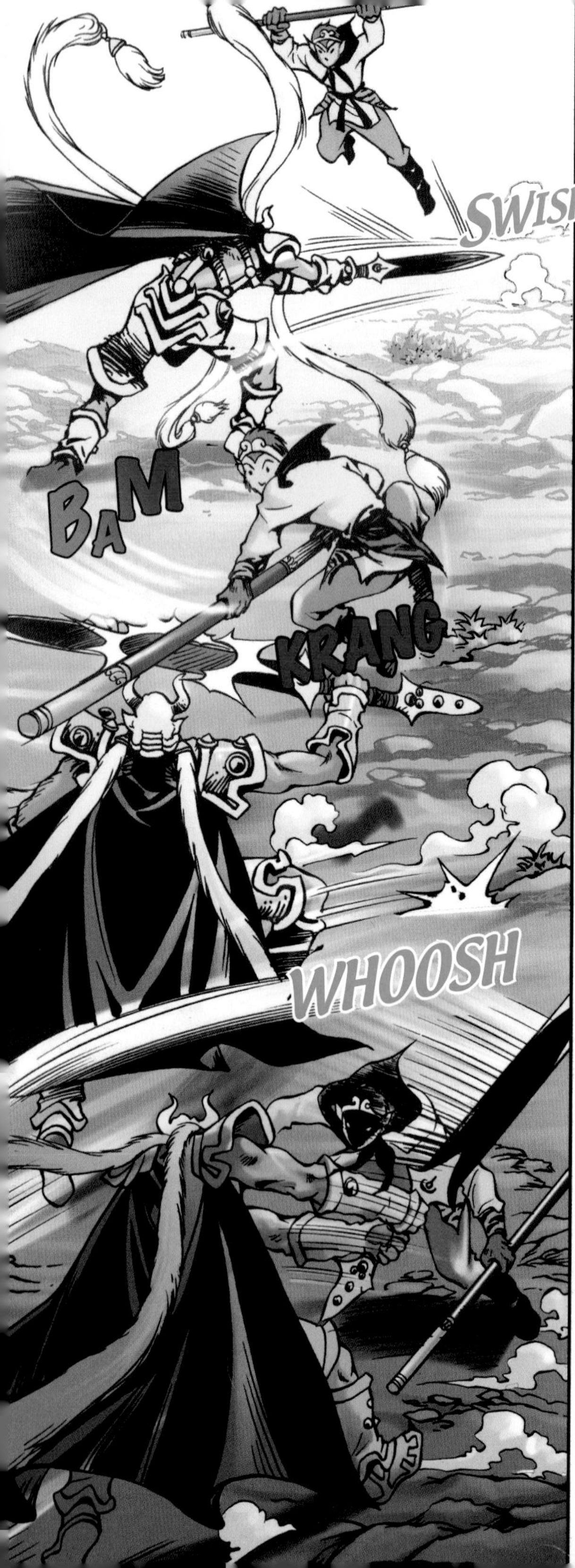
SWISH
BAM
KRANG
WHOOSH

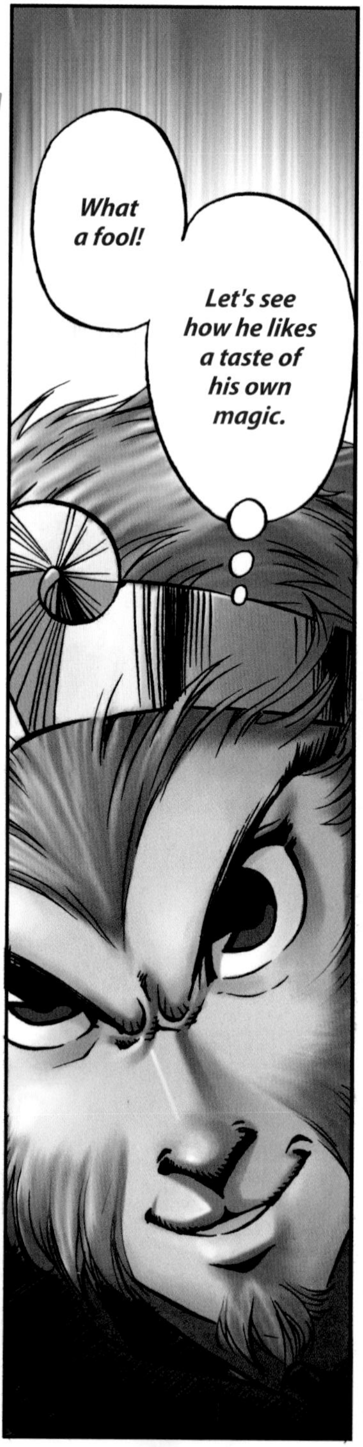
What a fool!
Let's see how he likes a taste of his own magic.

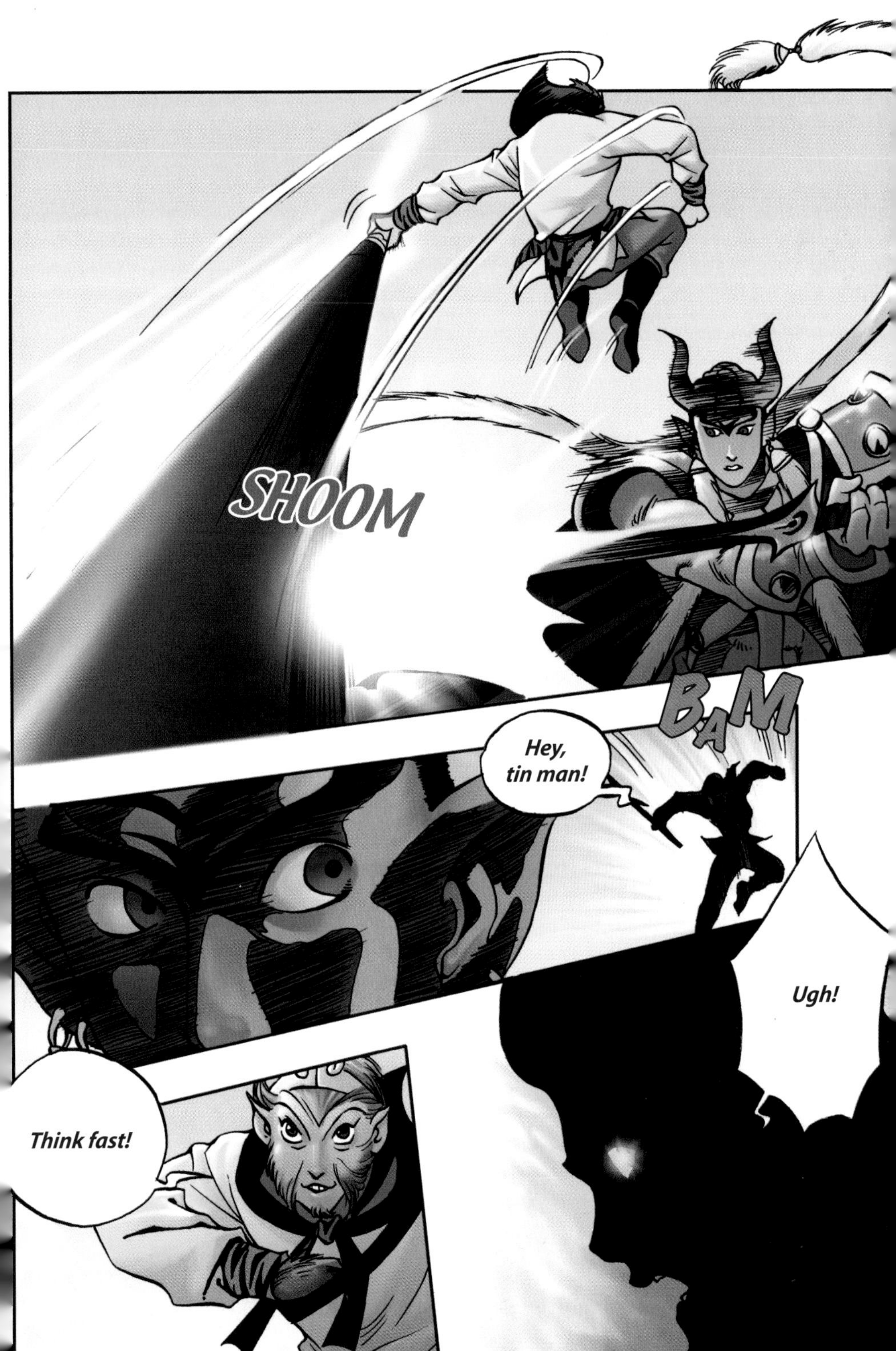
SHOOM
BAM
Hey, tin man!
Ugh!
Think fast!

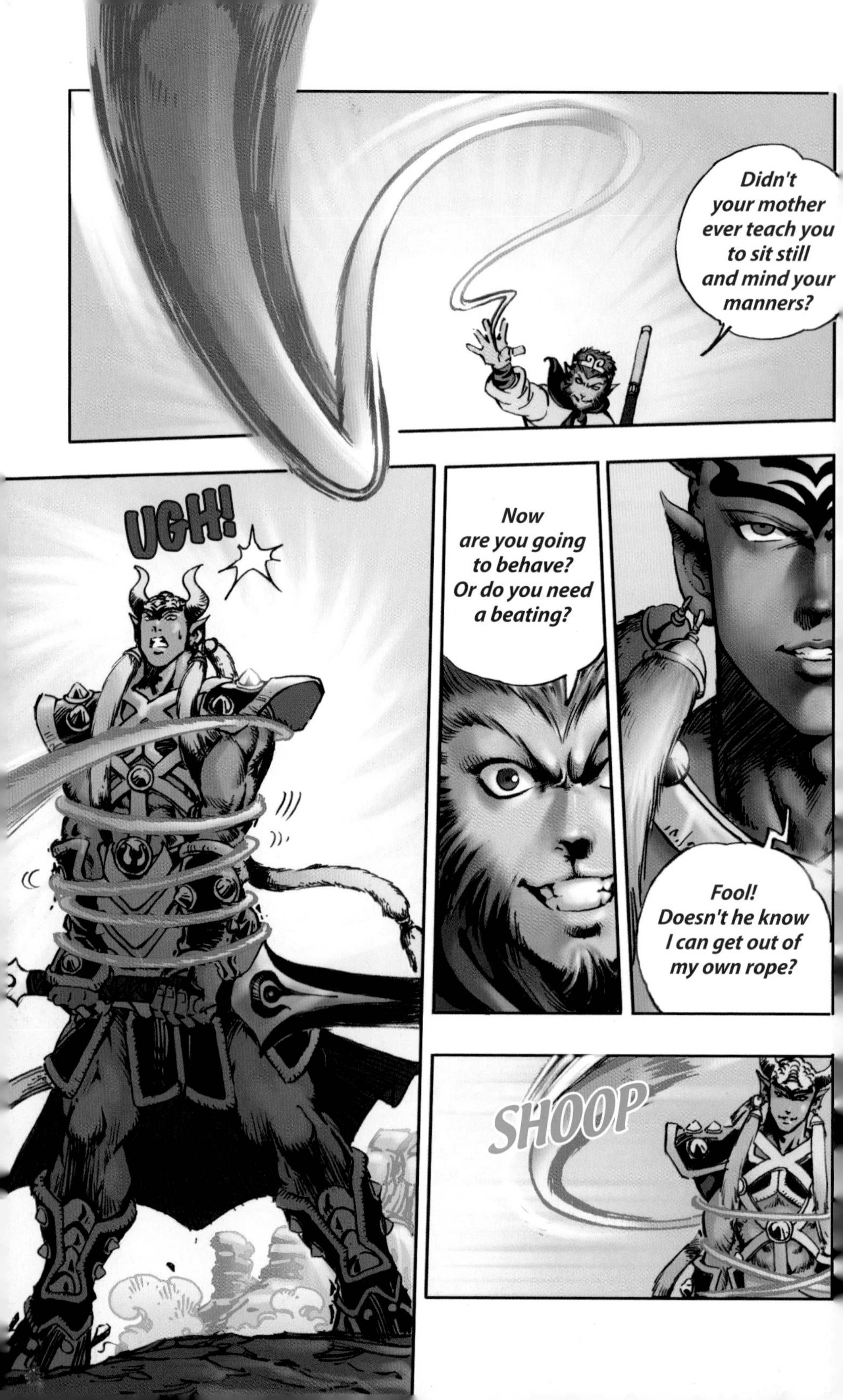
Didn't your mother ever teach you to sit still and mind your manners?
UGH!
Now are you going to behave? Or do you need a beating?
Fool! Doesn't he know I can get out of my own rope?
SHOOP

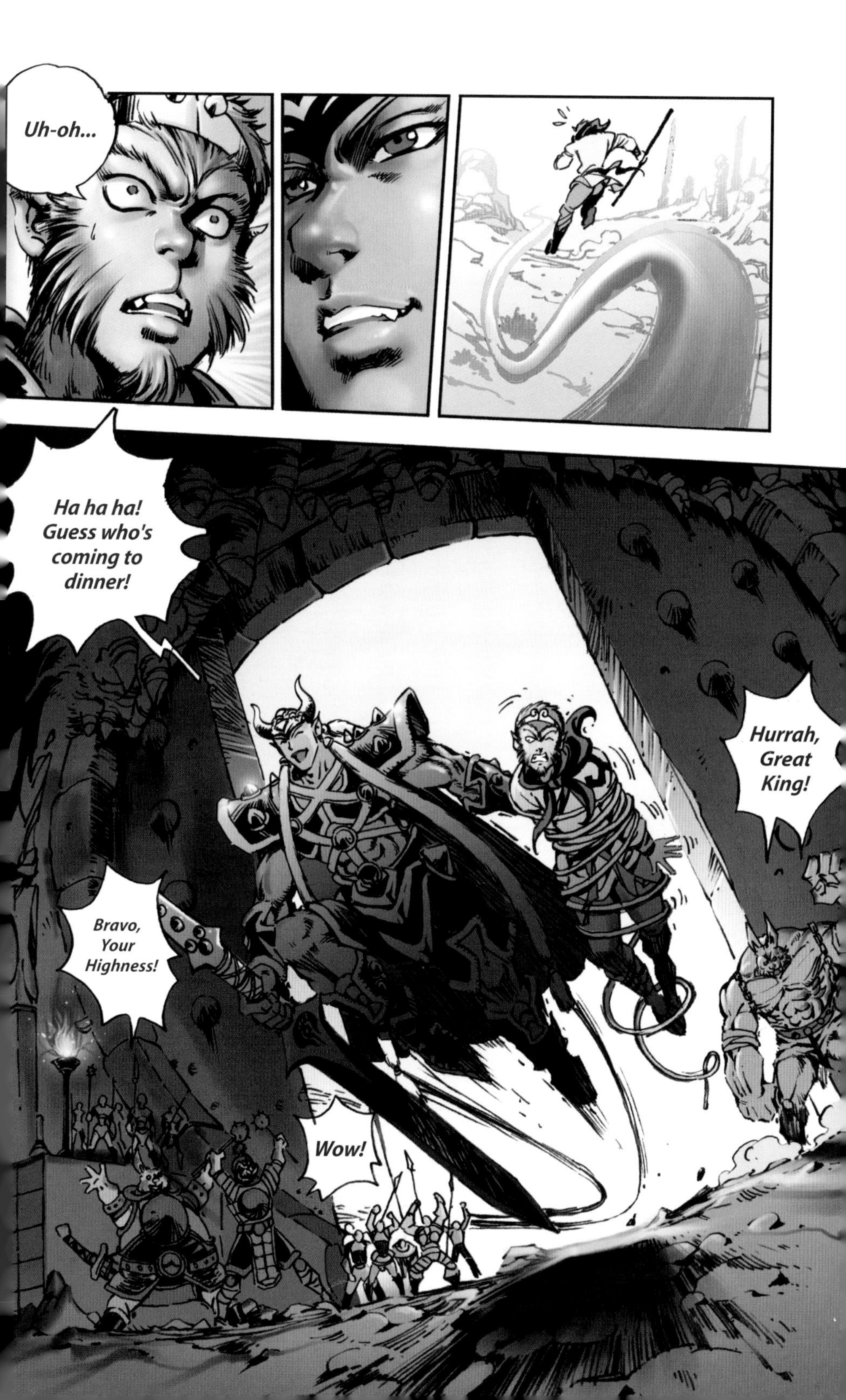
Uh-oh...
Ha ha ha! Guess who's coming to dinner!
Hurrah, Great King!
Bravo, Your Highness!
Wow!

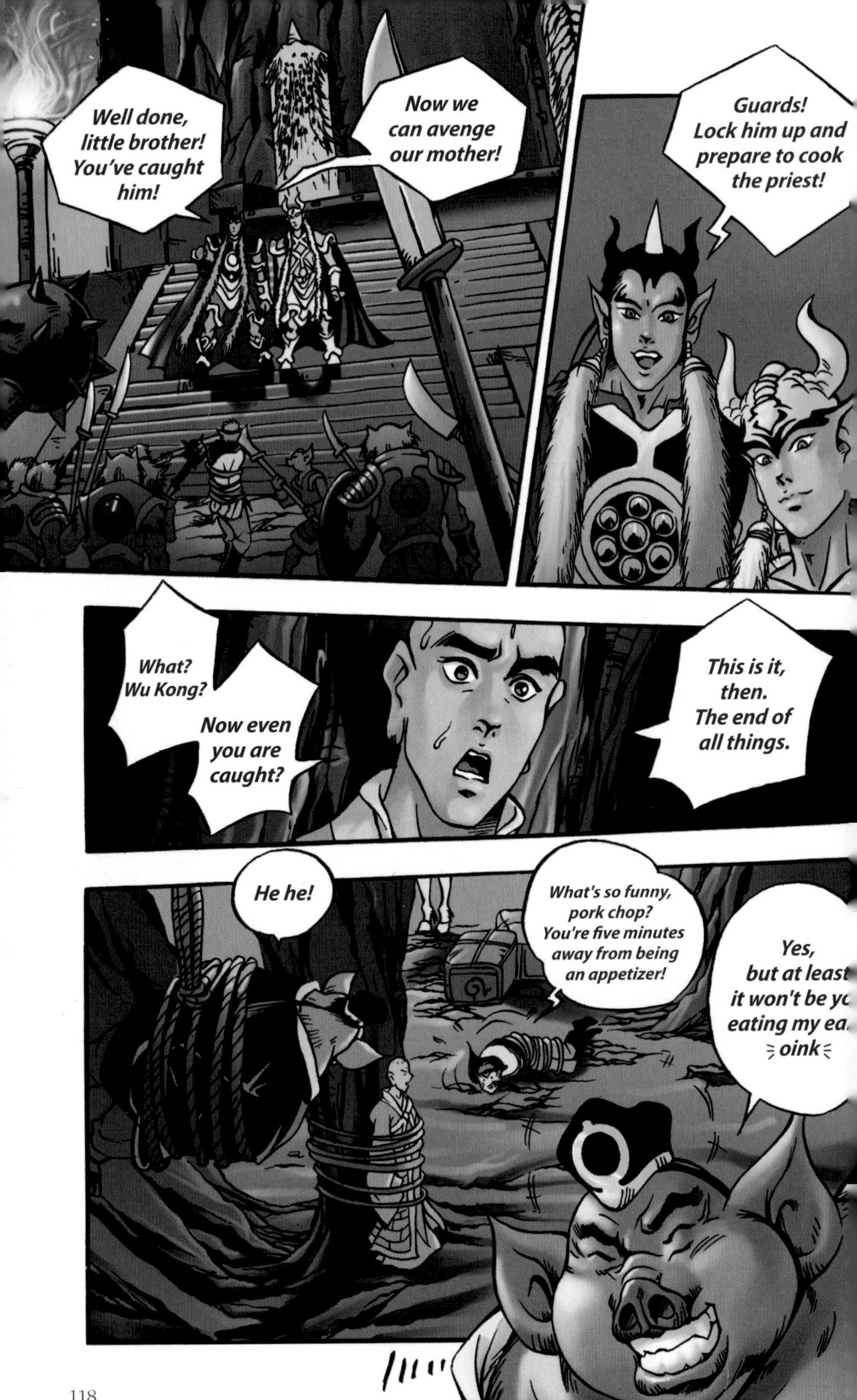
Well done, little brother! You've caught him!
Now we can avenge our mother!
Guards! Lock him up and prepare to cook the priest!
What? Wu Kong?
Now even you are caught?
This is it, then. The end of all things.
He he!
What's so funny, pork chop? You're five minutes away from being an appetizer!
Yes, but at least it won't be yo eating my ea
oink

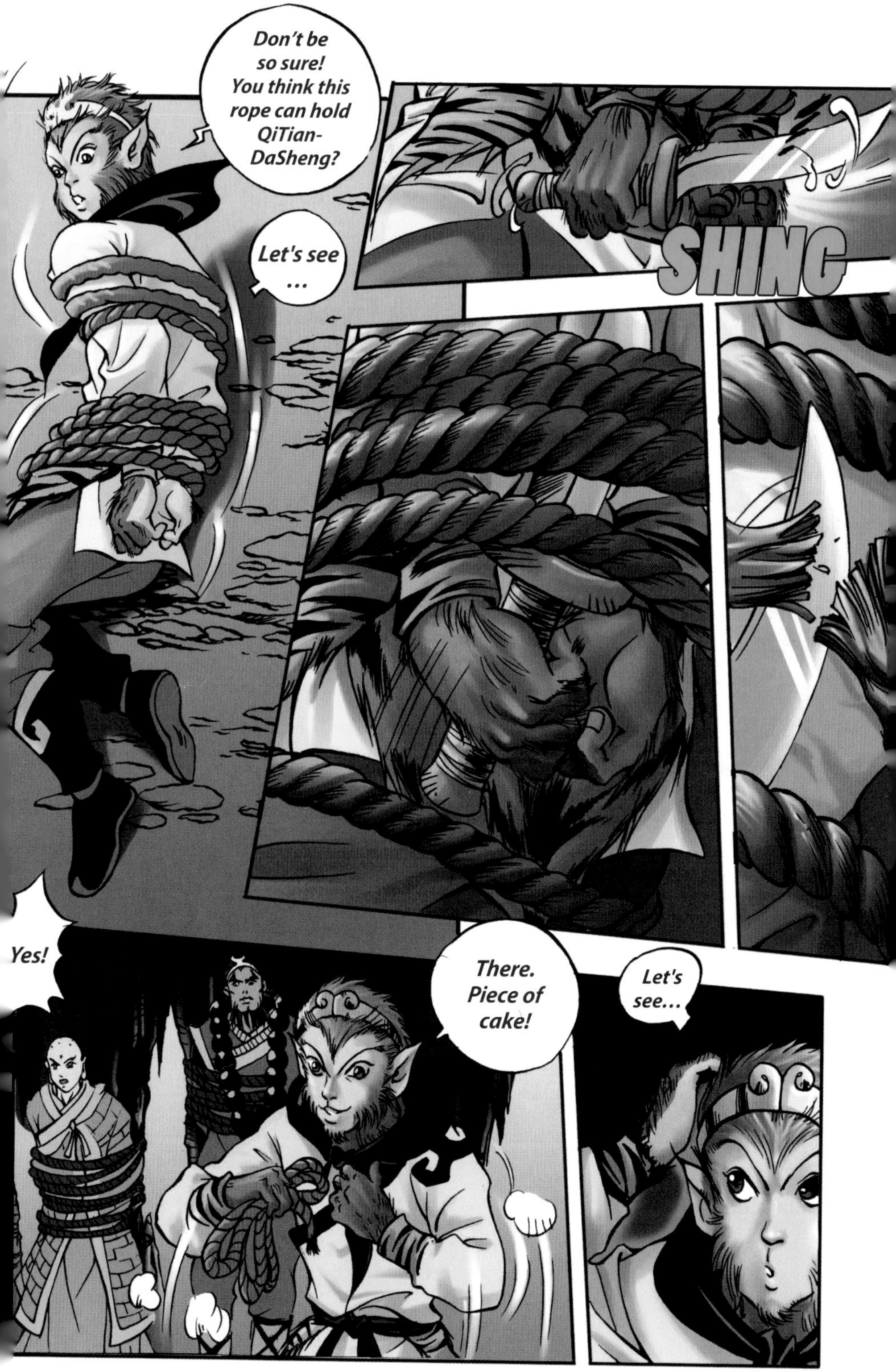
Don't be so sure! You think this rope can hold QiTian-DaSheng?
Let's see …
SHING
Yes!
There. Piece of cake!
Let's see…

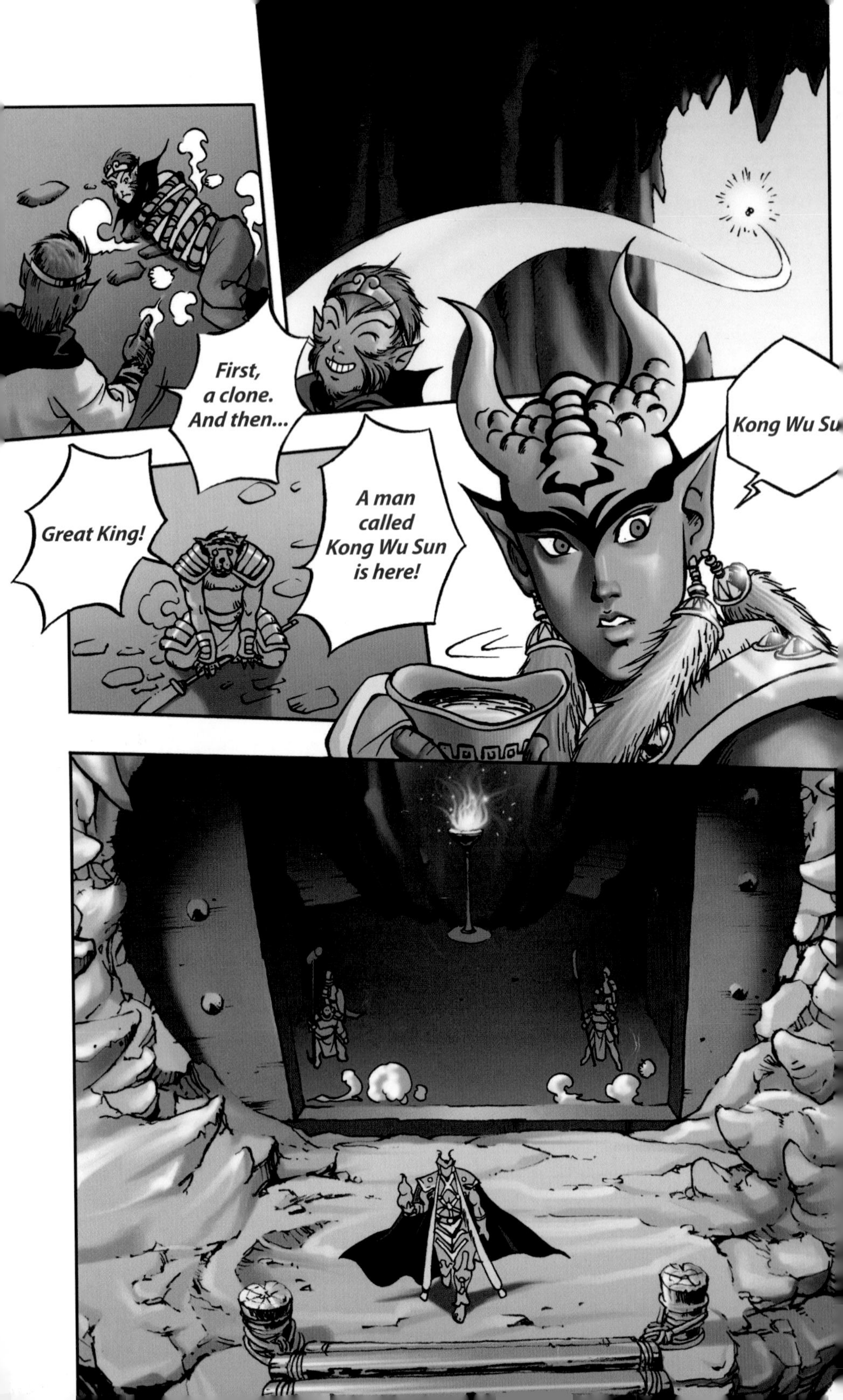
First, a clone. And then...
Kong Wu Su
Great King!
A man called Kong Wu Sun is here!

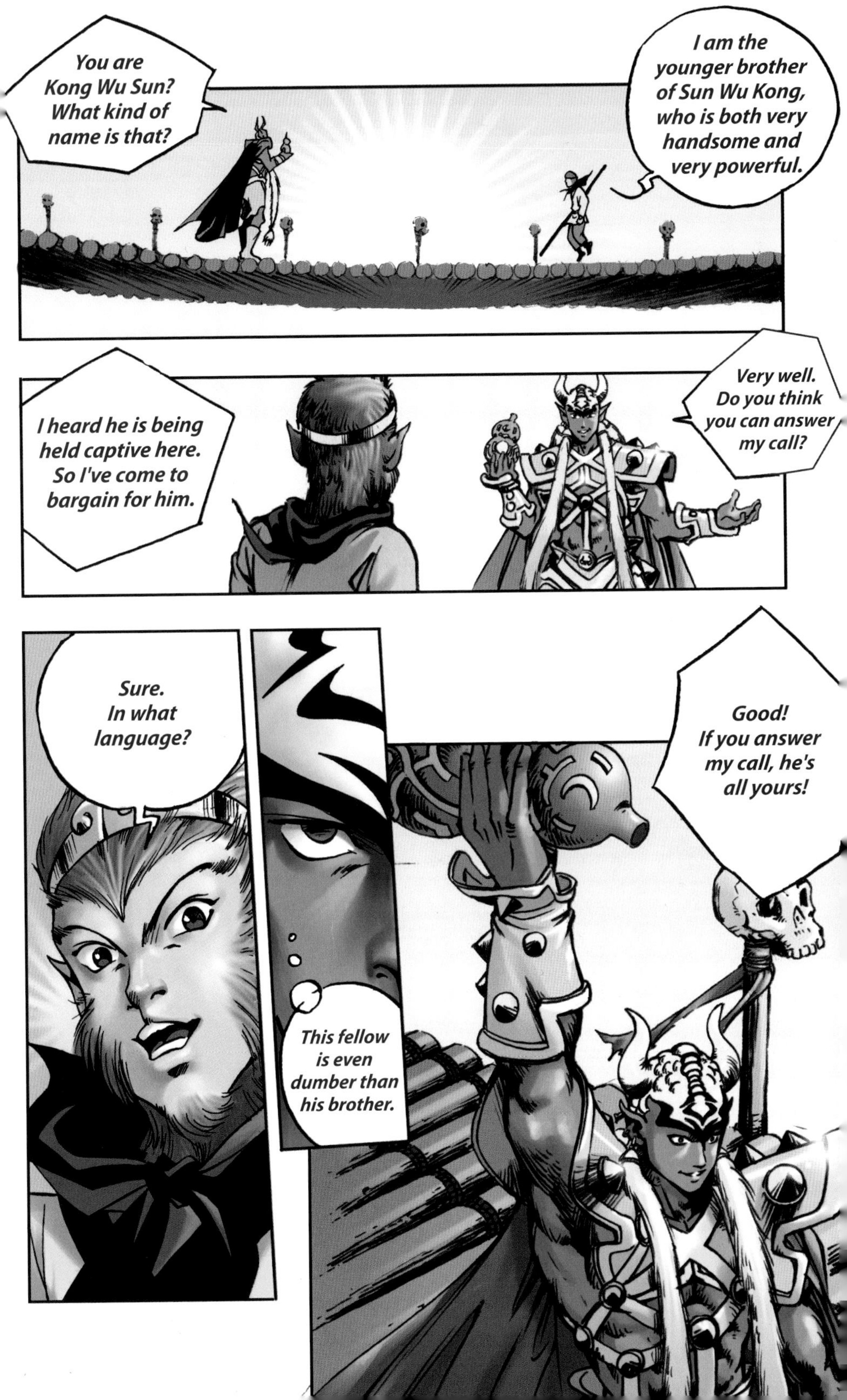
You are Kong Wu Sun? What kind of name is that?
I am the younger brother of Sun Wu Kong, who is both very handsome and very powerful.
I heard he is being held captive here. So I've come to bargain for him.
Very well. Do you think you can answer my call?
Sure. In what language?
This fellow is even dumber than his brother.
Good! If you answer my call, he's all yours!

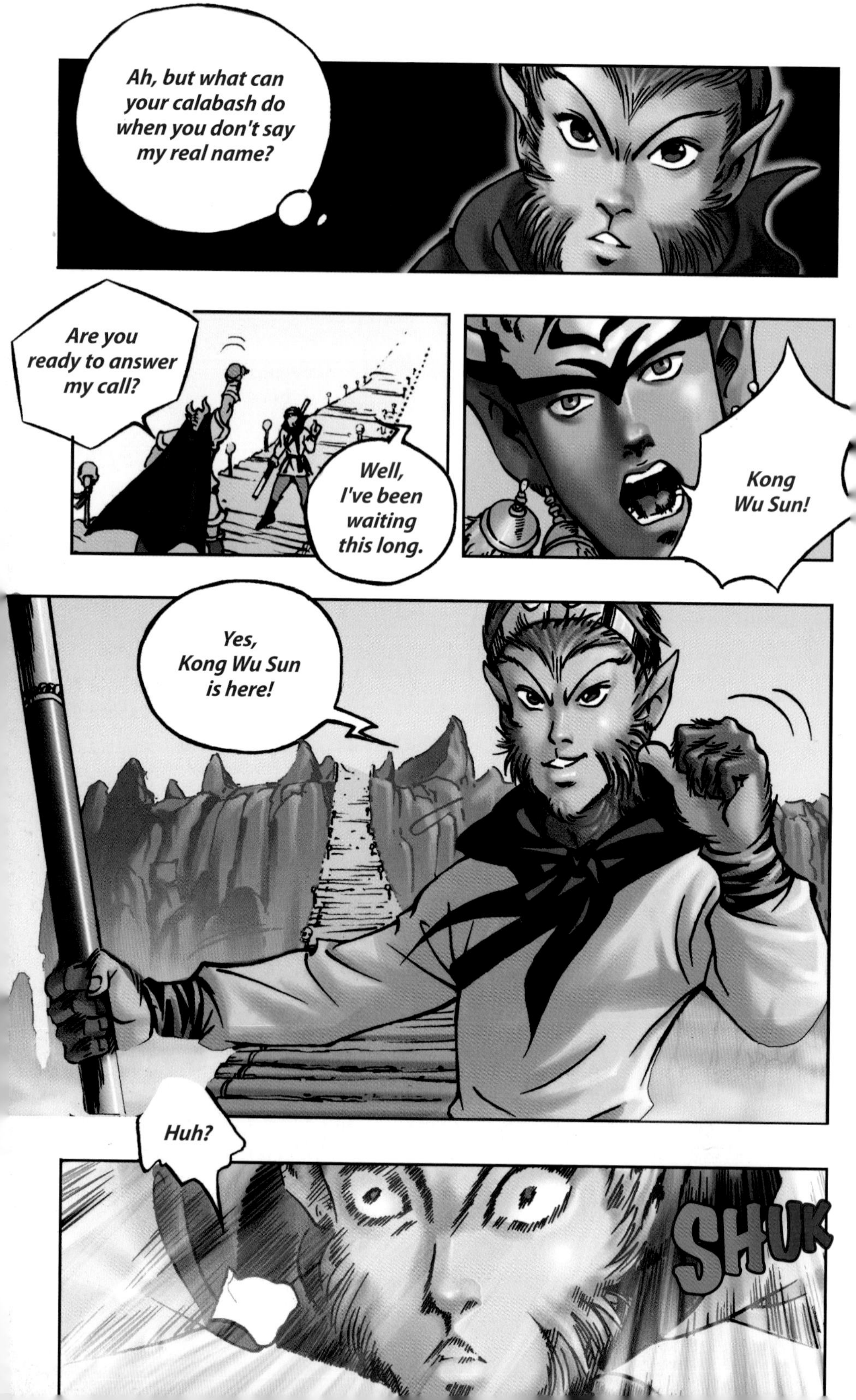
Ah, but what can your calabash do when you don't say my real name?
Are you ready to answer my call?
Well, I've been waiting this long.
Kong Wu Sun!
Yes, Kong Wu Sun is here!
Huh?
SHUK

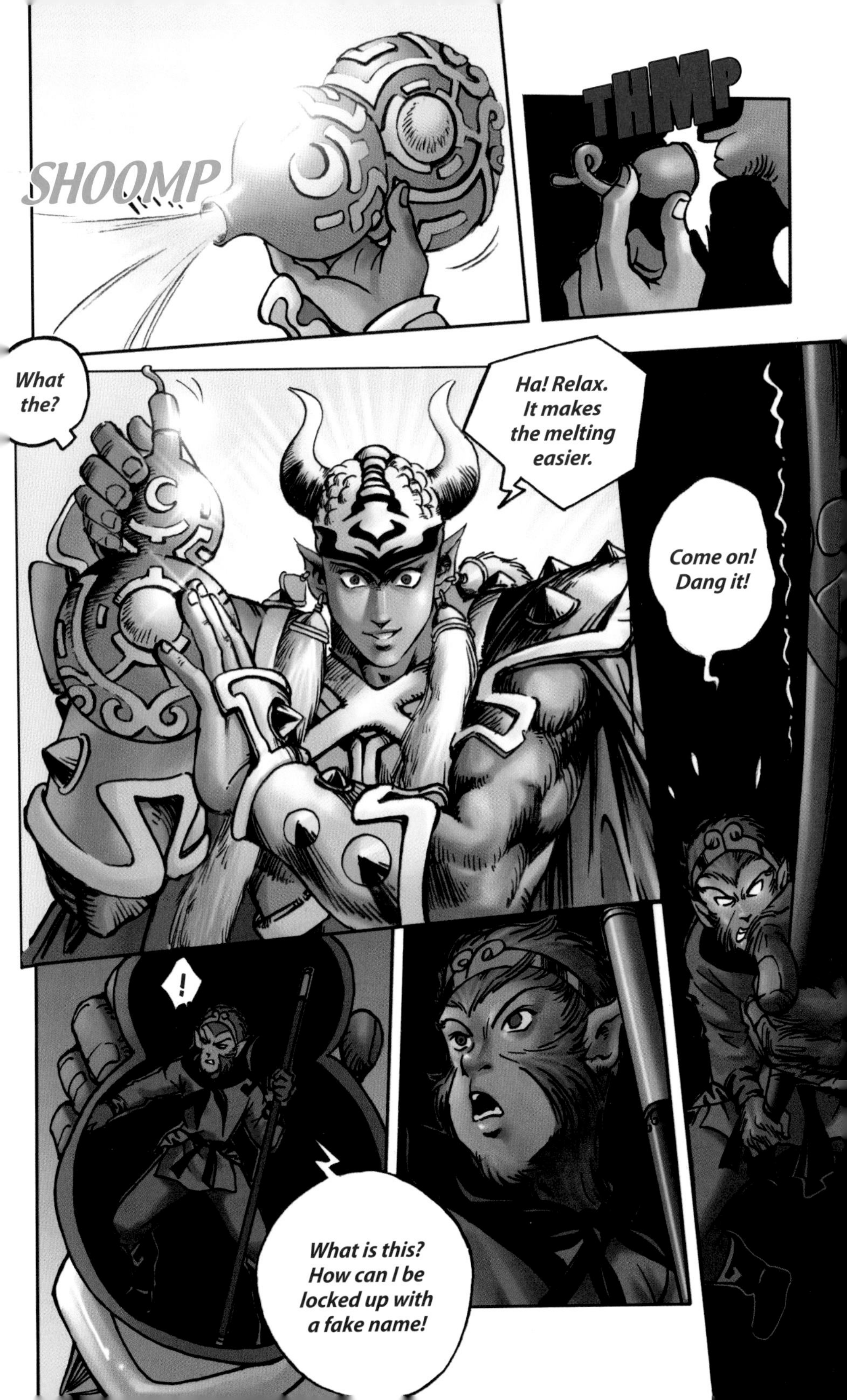
SHOOMP
THMP
What the?
Ha! Relax. It makes the melting easier.
Come on! Dang it!
!
What is this? How can I be locked up with a fake name!

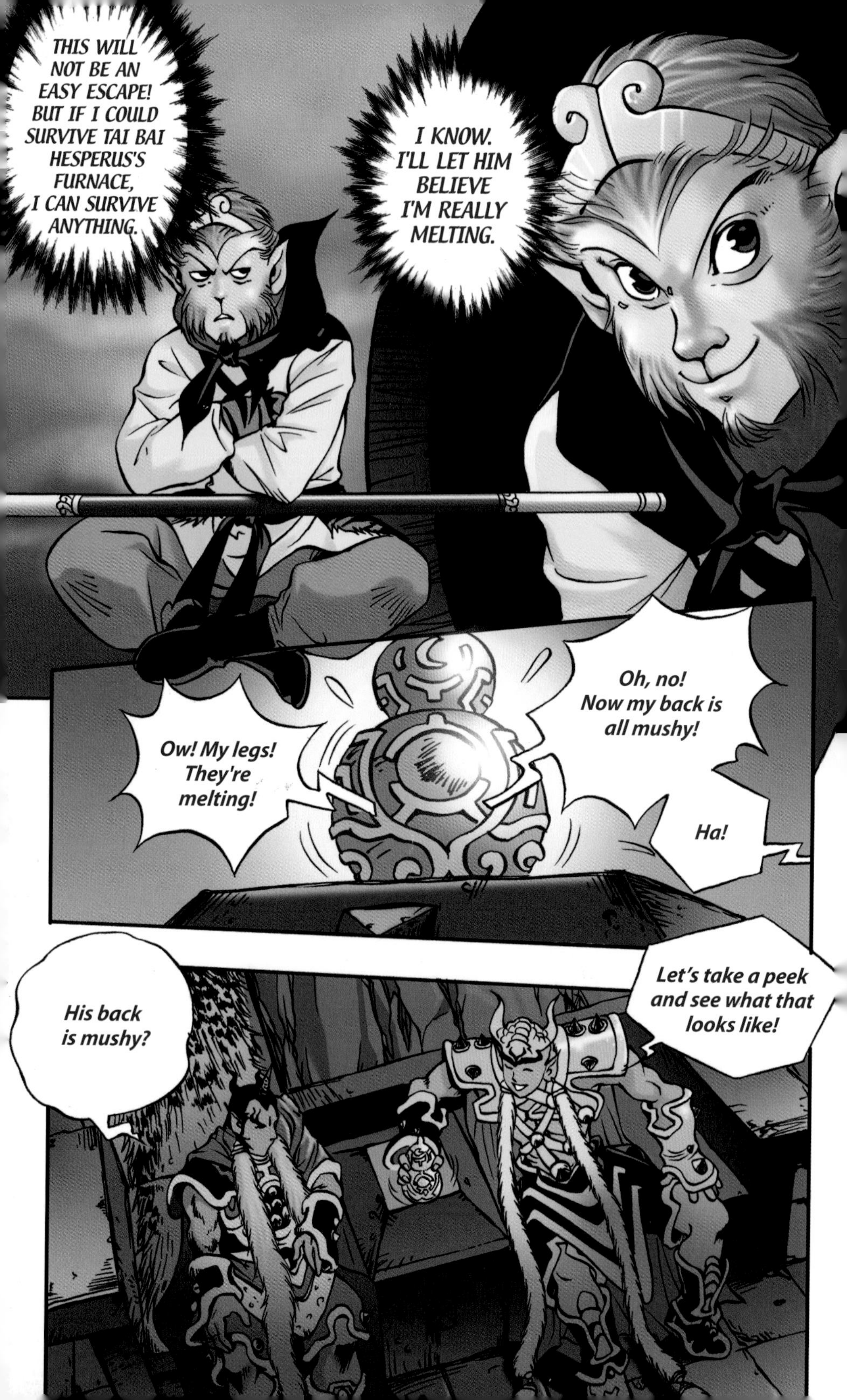
THIS WILL NOT BE AN EASY ESCAPE! BUT IF I COULD SURVIVE TAI BAI HESPERUS'S FURNACE, I CAN SURVIVE ANYTHING.
I KNOW. I'LL LET HIM BELIEVE I'M REALLY MELTING.
Ow! My legs! They're melting!
Oh, no! Now my back is all mushy!
Ha!
His back is mushy?
Let's take a peek and see what that looks like!

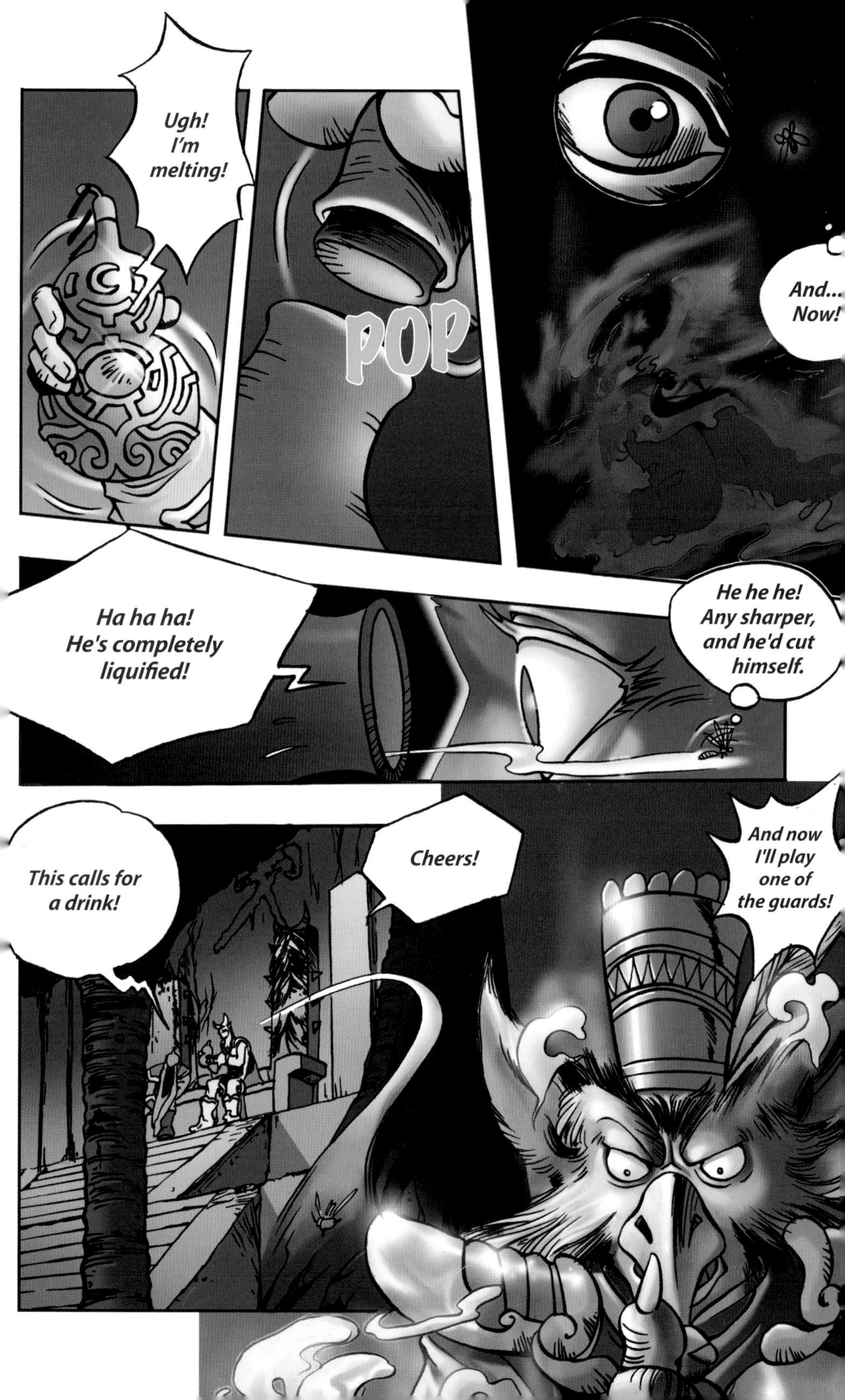
Ugh! I'm melting!
POP
And... Now!
Ha ha ha! He's completely liquified!
He he he! Any sharper, and he'd cut himself.
This calls for a drink!
Cheers!
And now I'll play one of the guards!

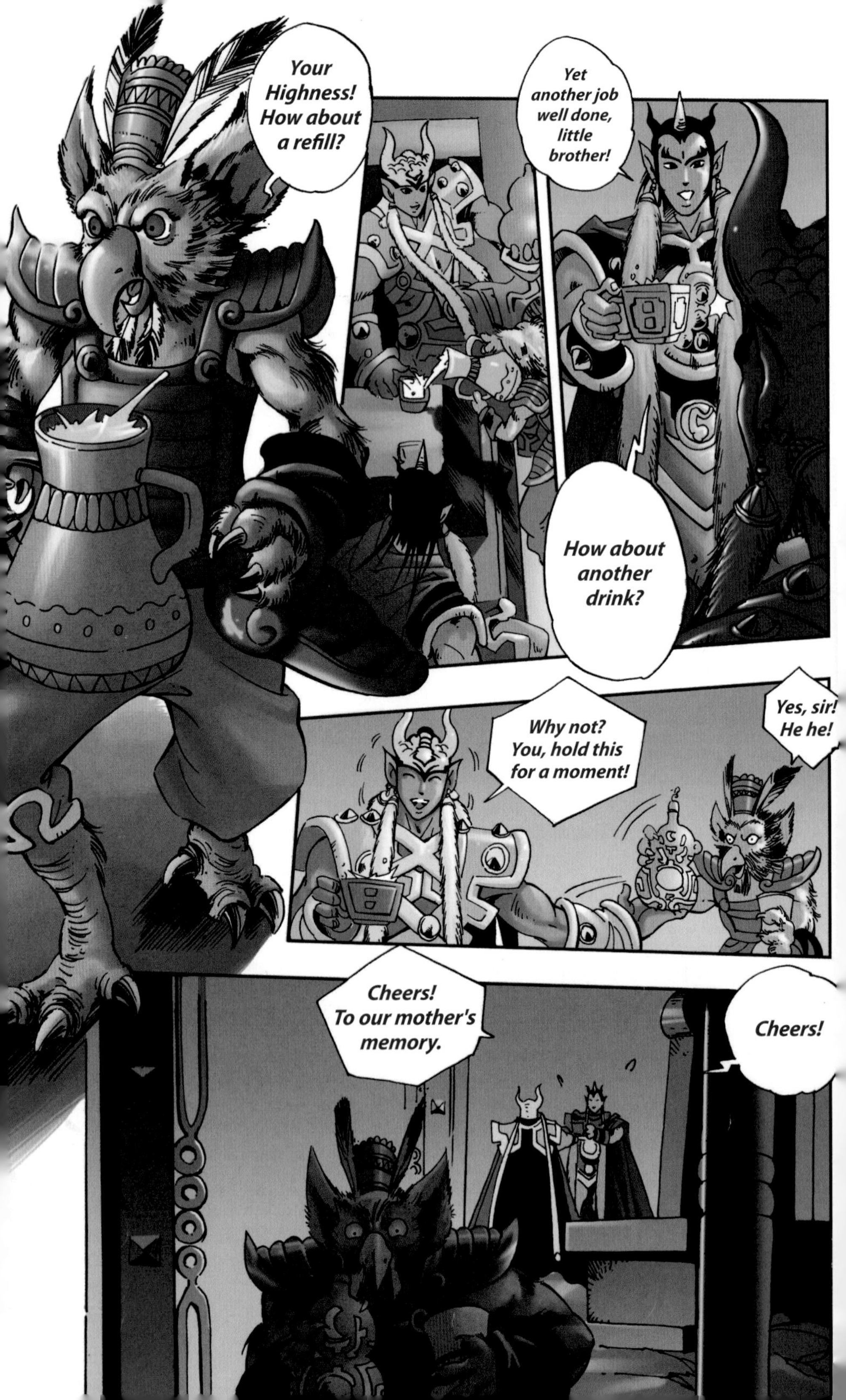
Your Highness! How about a refill?
Yet another job well done, little brother!
How about another drink?
Why not? You, hold this for a moment!
Yes, sir! He he!
Cheers! To our mother's memory.
Cheers!

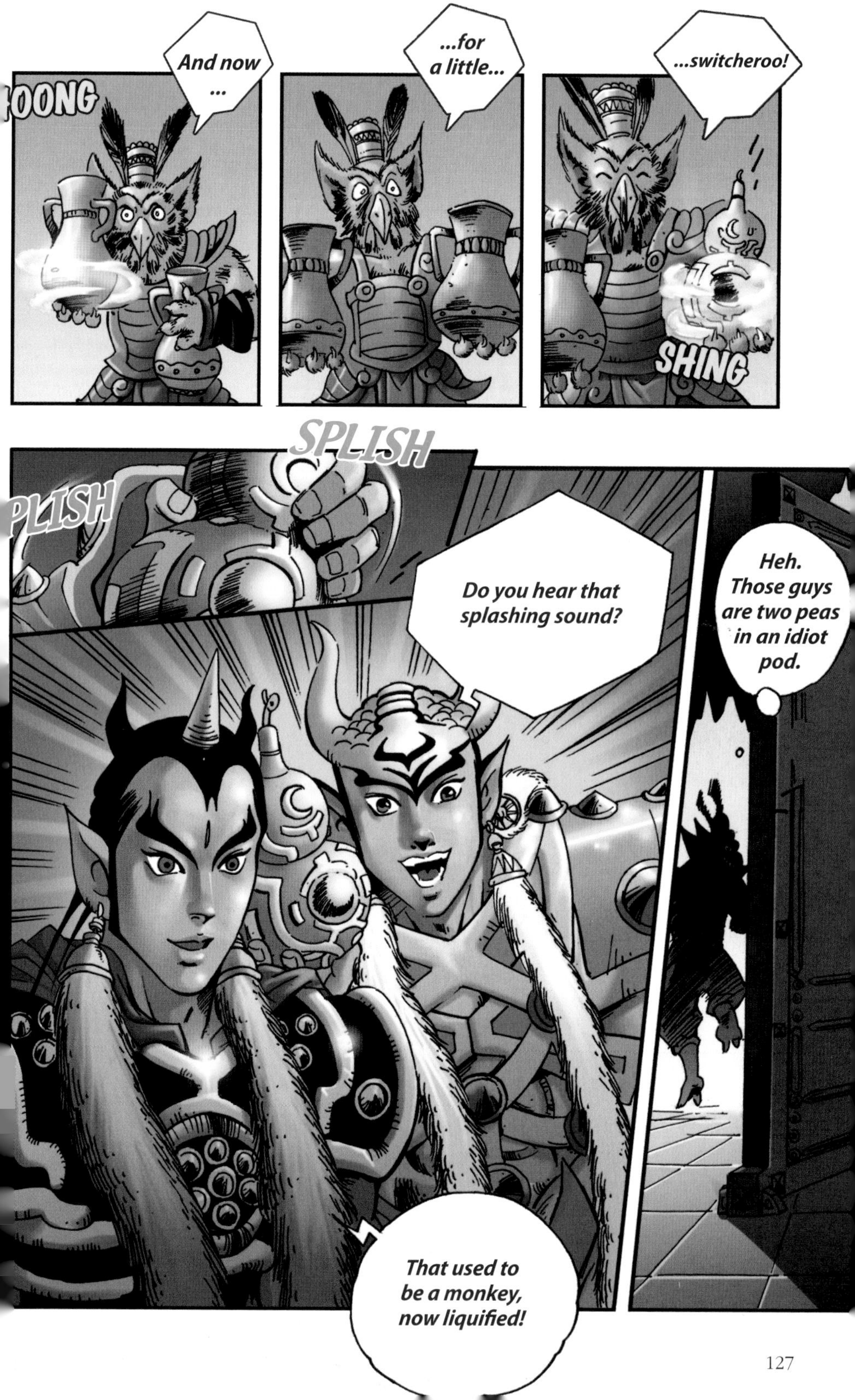
OONG
And now ...
...for a little...
...switcheroo!
SHING
SPLISH
SPLISH
Do you hear that splashing sound?
Heh. Those guys are two peas in an idiot pod.
That used to be a monkey, now liquified!

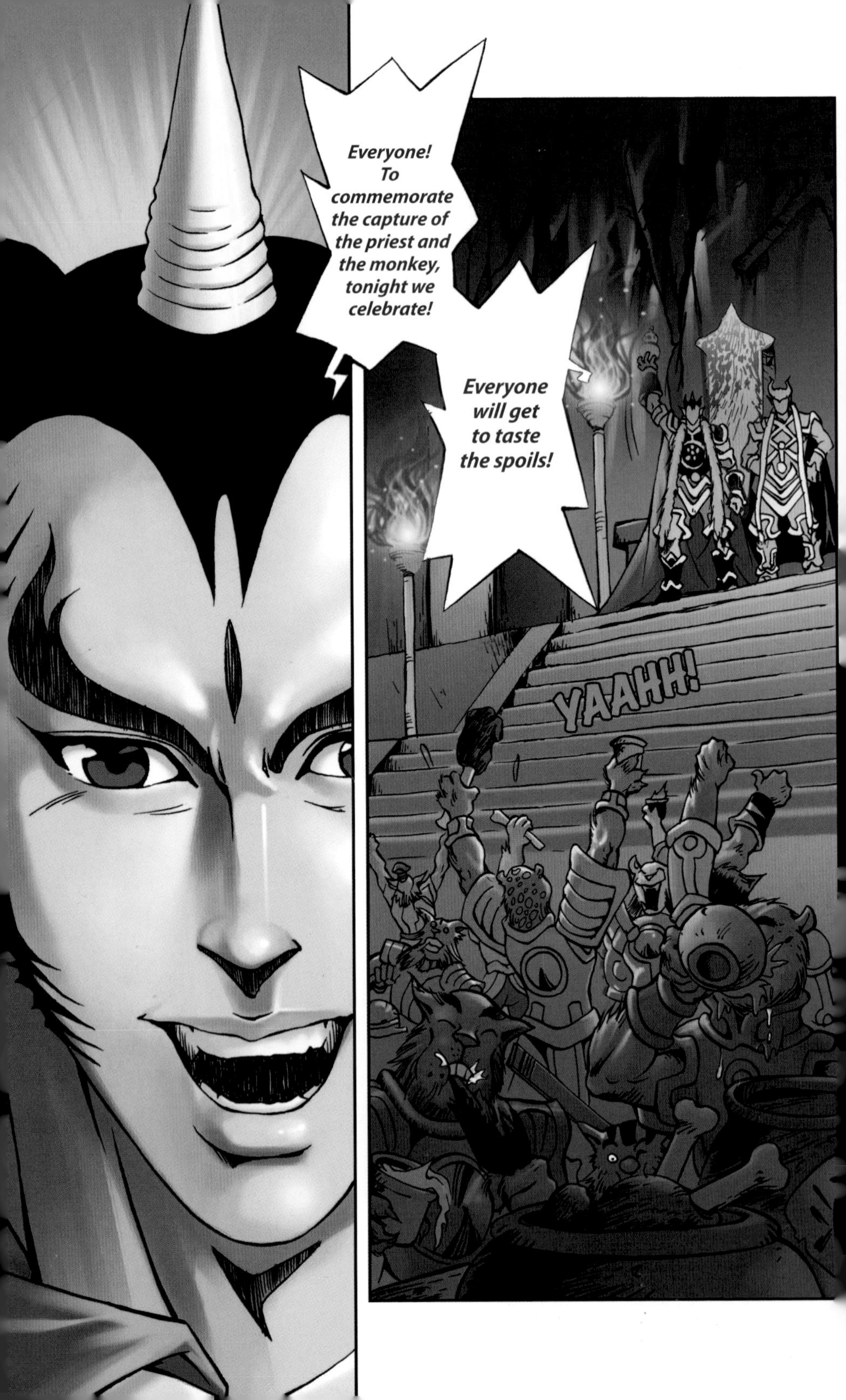
Everyone! To commemorate the capture of the priest and the monkey, tonight we celebrate!
Everyone will get to taste the spoils!
YAAHH!

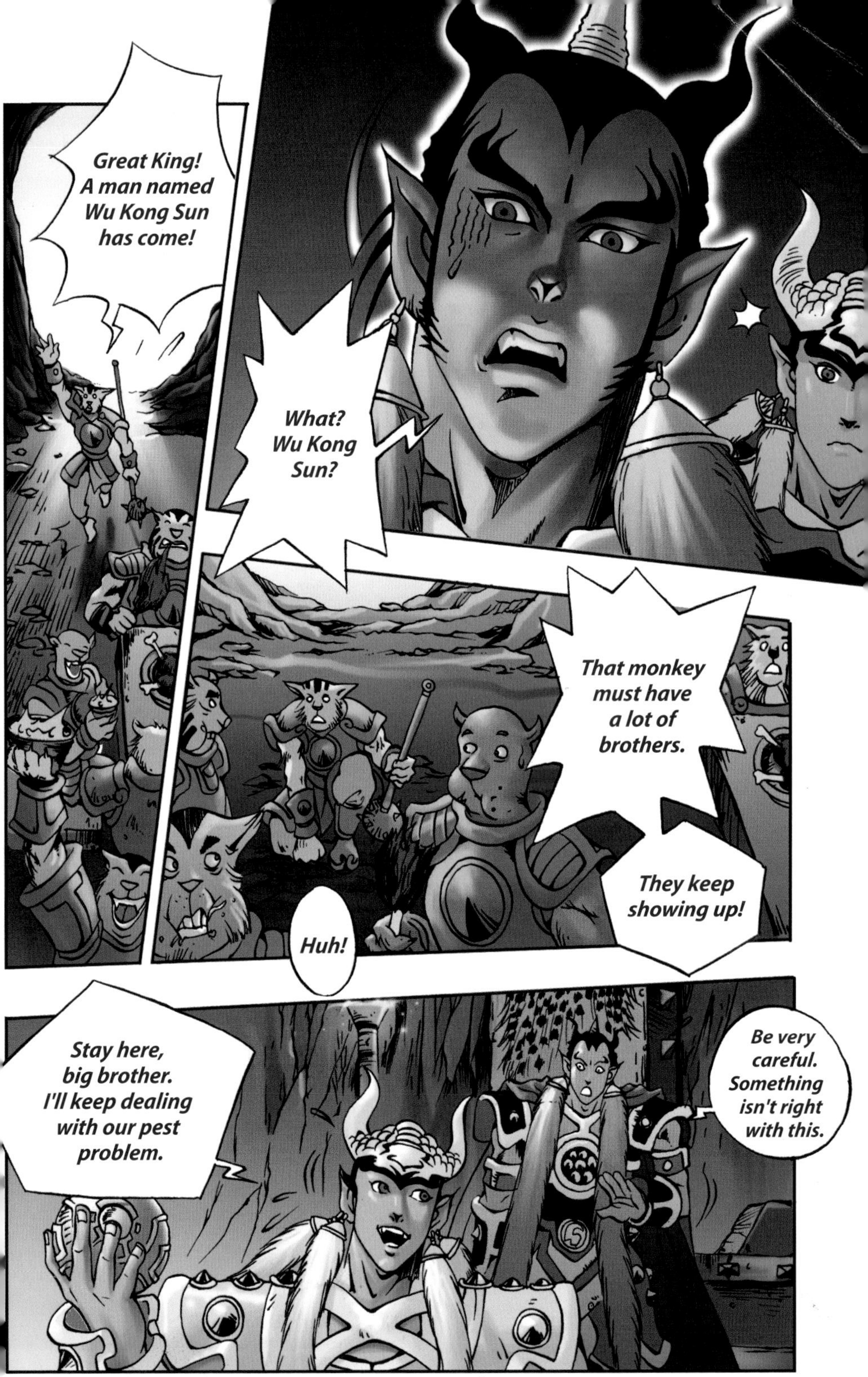

Great King! A man named Wu Kong Sun has come!
What? Wu Kong Sun?
That monkey must have a lot of brothers.
They keep showing up!
Huh!
Stay here, big brother. I'll keep dealing with our pest problem.
Be very careful. Something isn't right with this.

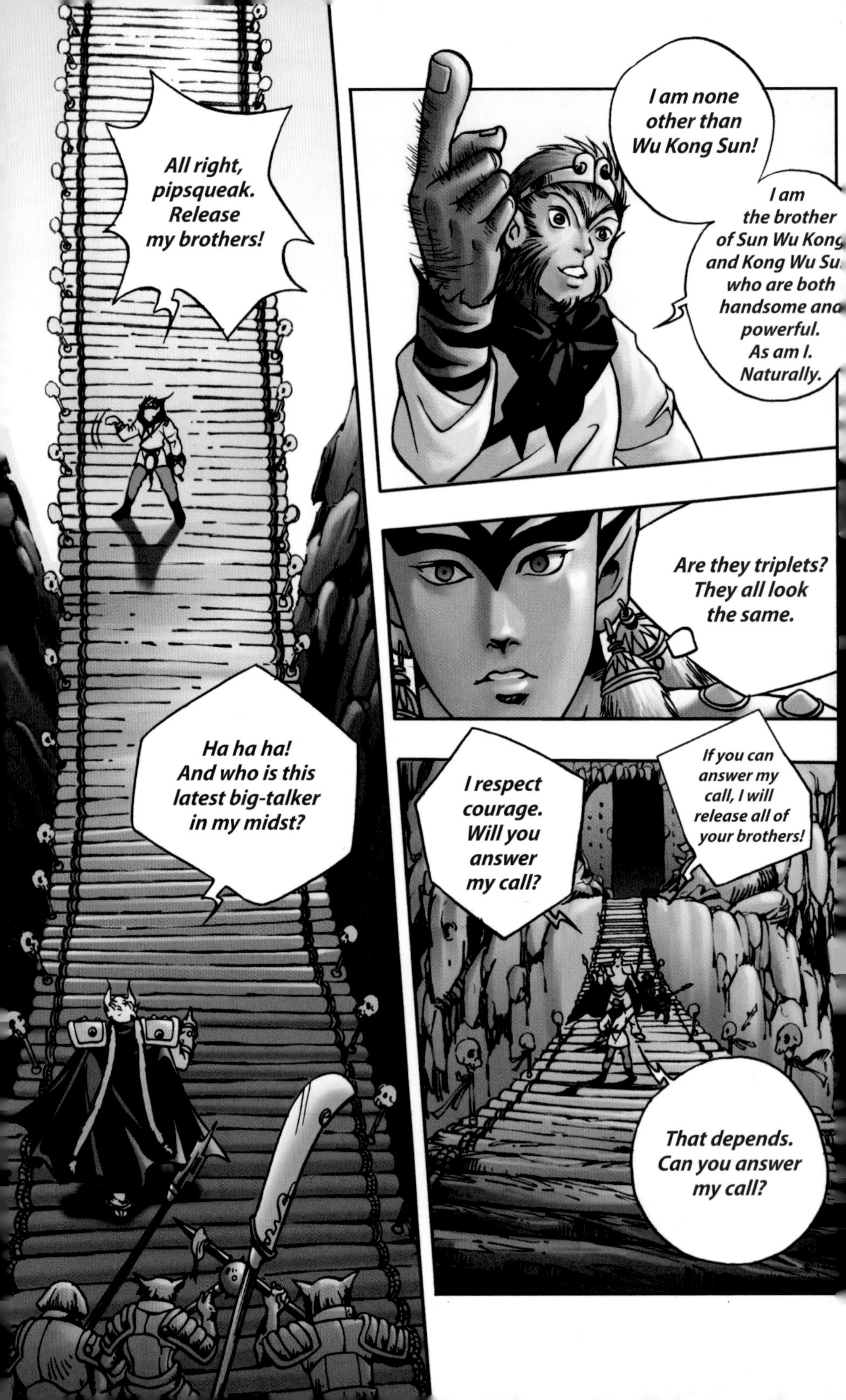
All right, pipsqueak. Release my brothers!
Ha ha ha! And who is this latest big-talker in my midst?
I am none other than Wu Kong Sun!
I am the brother of Sun Wu Kong and Kong Wu Su who are both handsome and powerful. As am I. Naturally.
Are they triplets? They all look the same.
I respect courage. Will you answer my call?
If you can answer my call, I will release all of your brothers!
That depends. Can you answer my call?

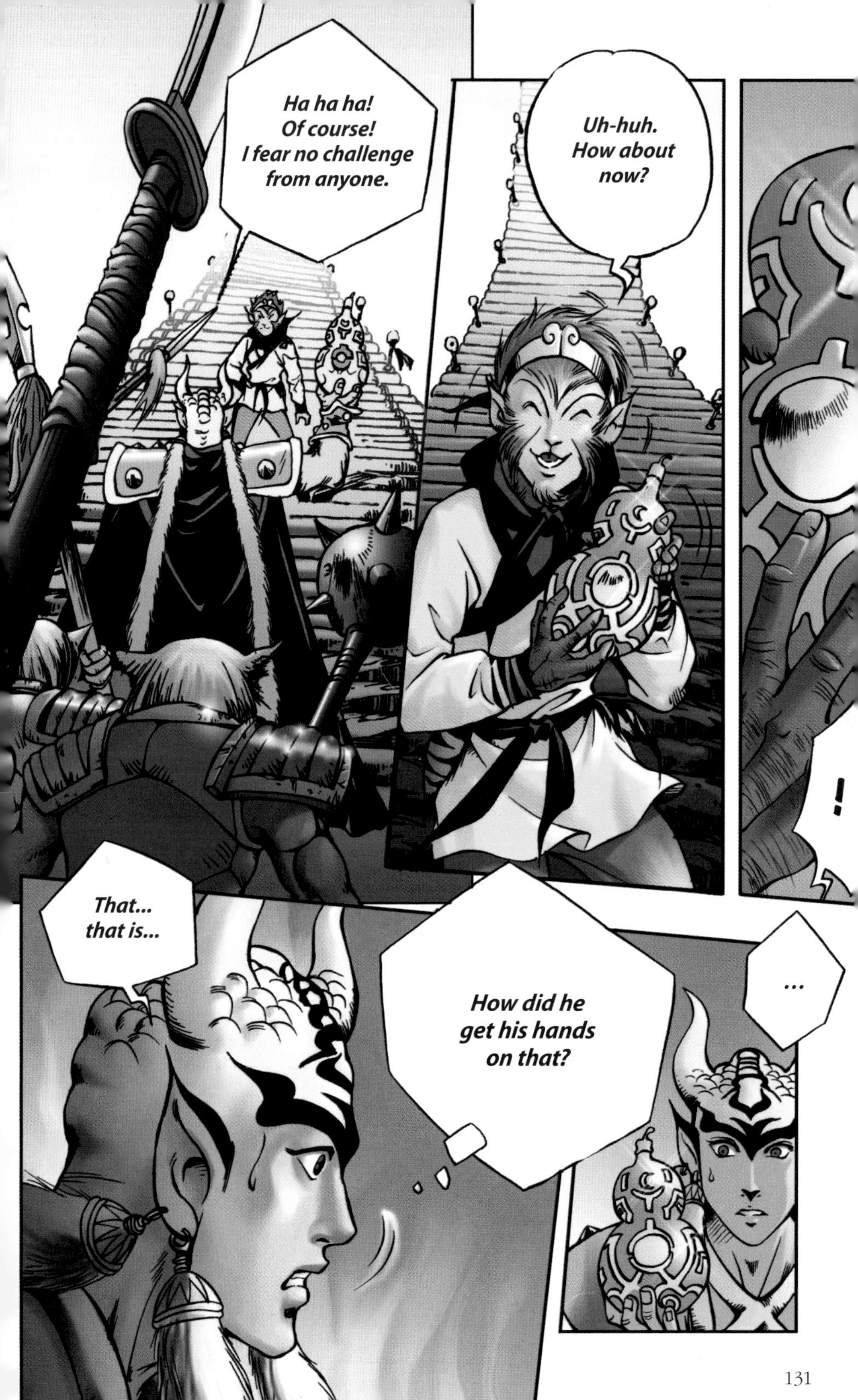
Ha ha ha!
Of course!
I fear no challenge
from anyone.
Uh-huh.
How about
now?
!
That...
that is...
How did he
get his hands
on that?
...

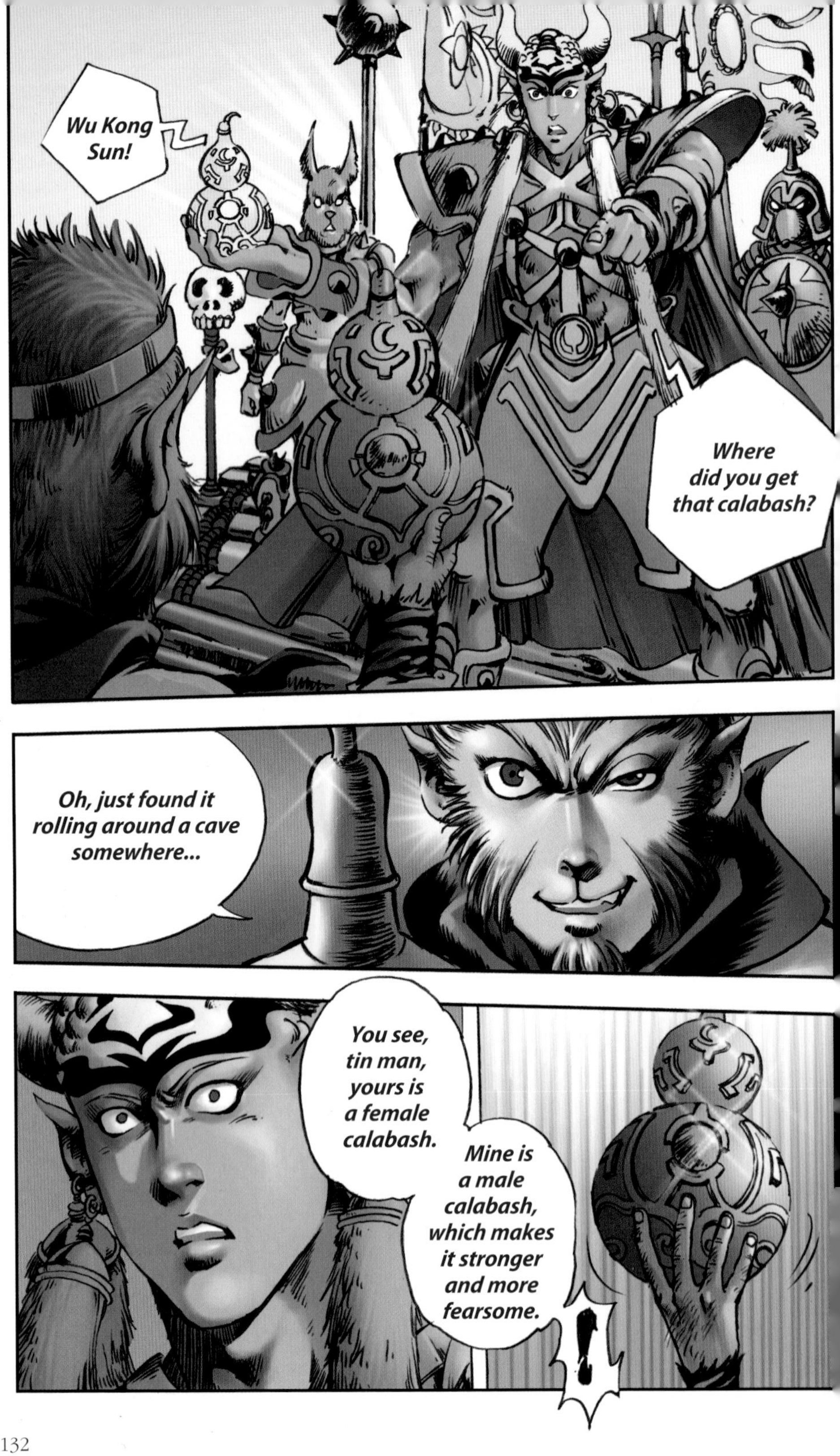

Wu Kong Sun!
Where did you get that calabash?
Oh, just found it rolling around a cave somewhere...
You see, tin man, yours is a female calabash.
Mine is a male calabash, which makes it stronger and more fearsome.
!

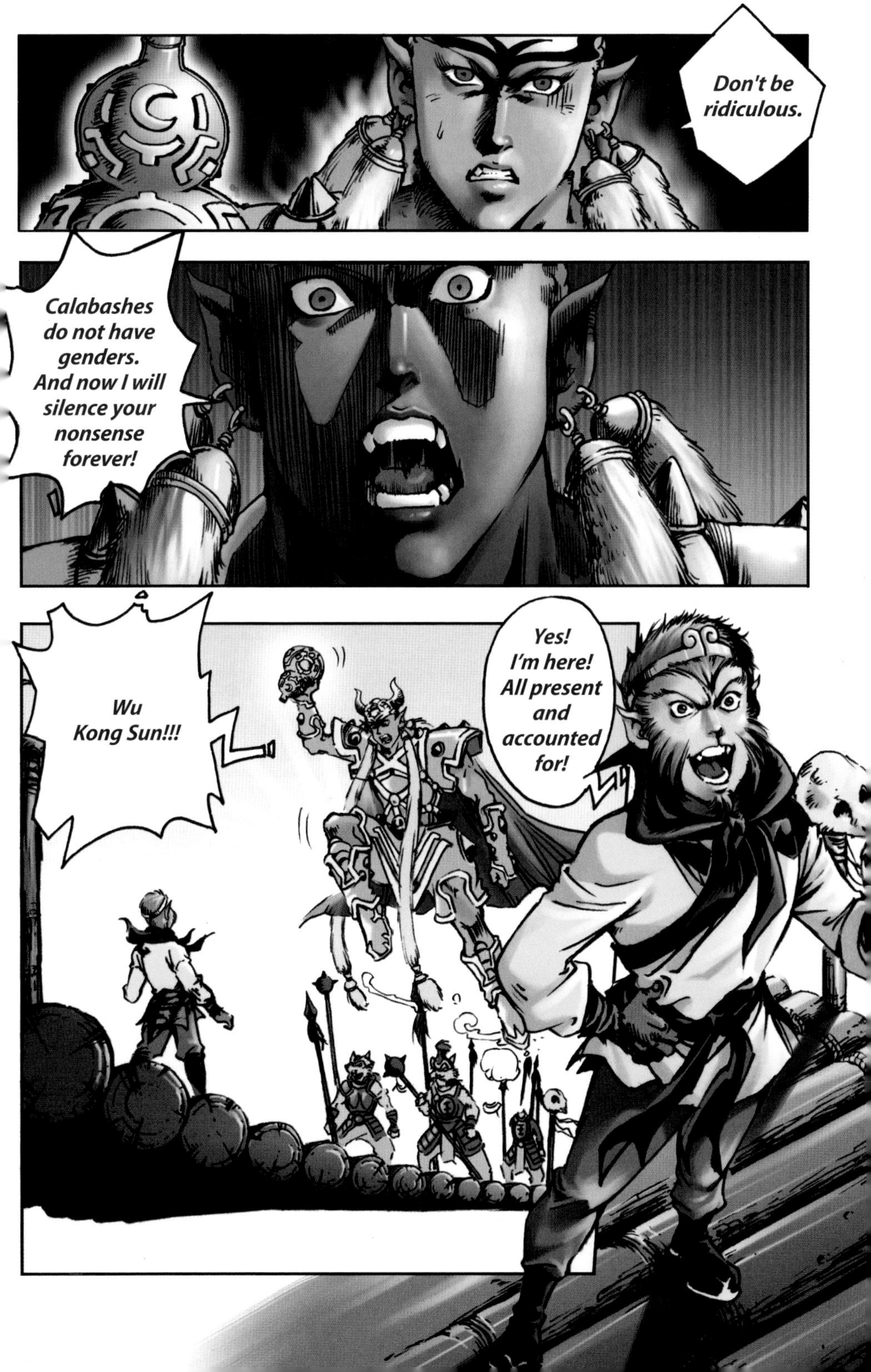
Don't be ridiculous.
Calabashes do not have genders. And now I will silence your nonsense forever!
Wu Kong Sun!!!
Yes! I'm here! All present and accounted for!

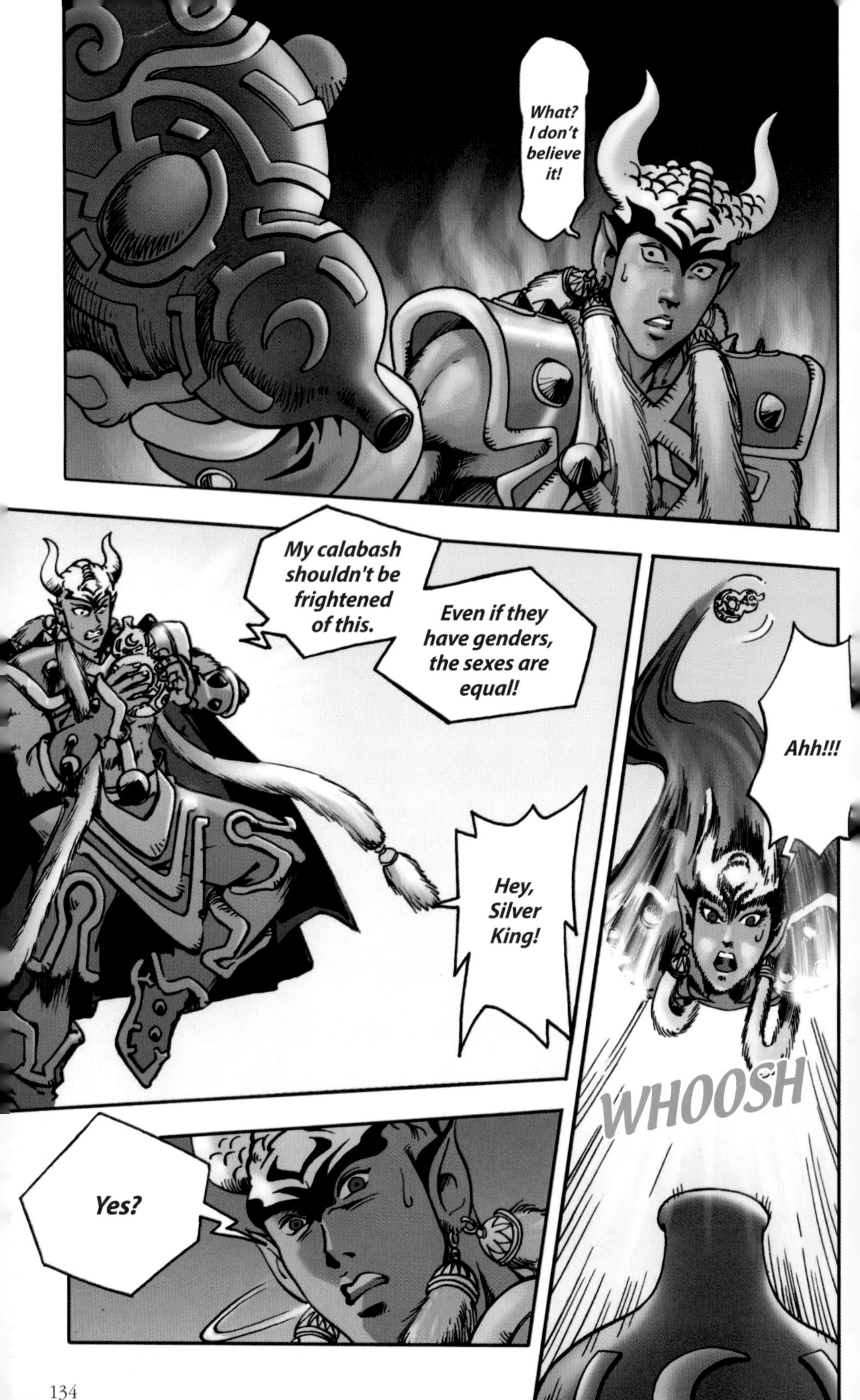
What? I don't believe it!
My calabash shouldn't be frightened of this.
Even if they have genders, the sexes are equal!
Hey, Silver King!
Yes?
Ahh!!!
WHOOSH

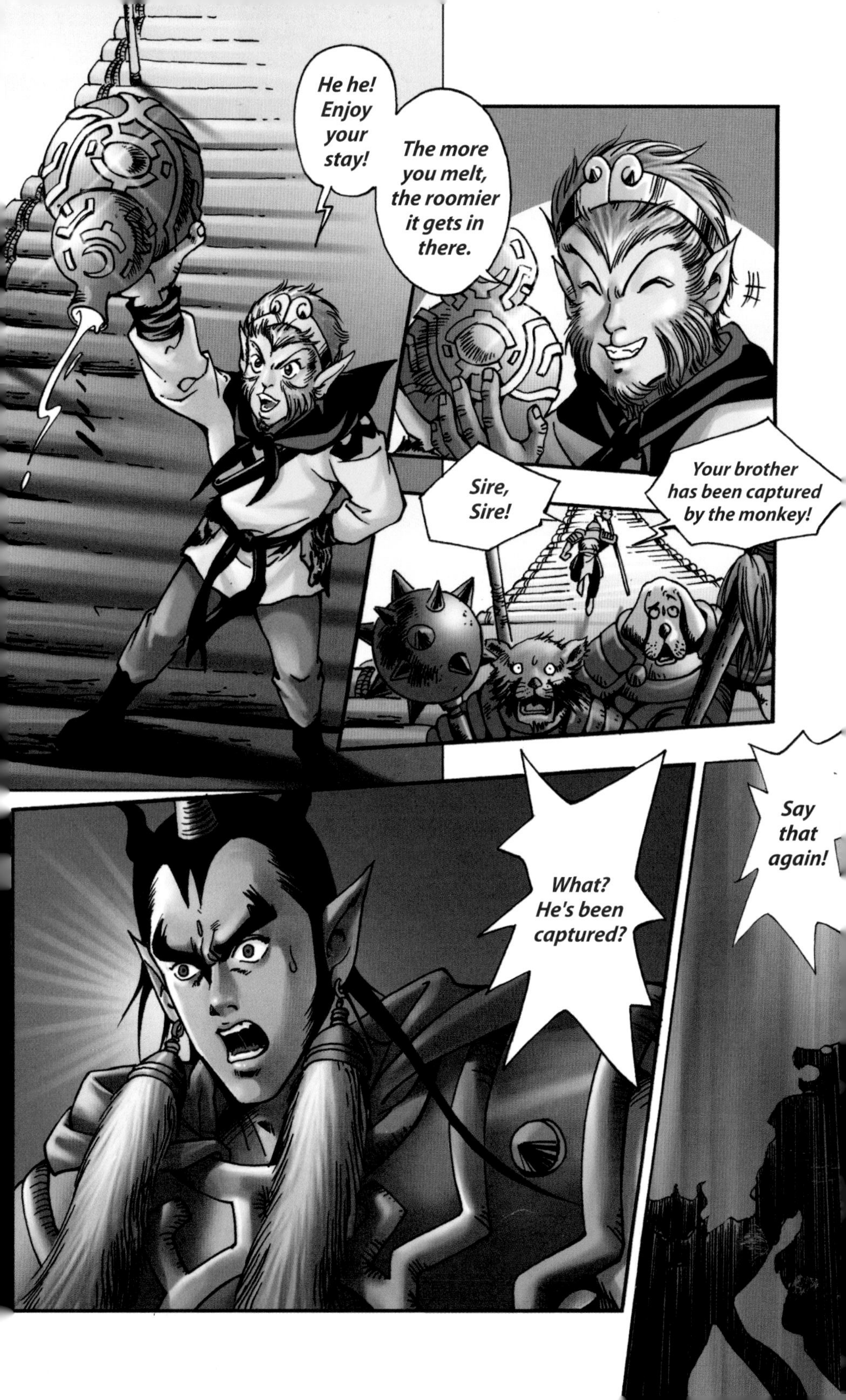
He he! Enjoy your stay!
The more you melt, the roomier it gets in there.
Sire, Sire!
Your brother has been captured by the monkey!
What? He's been captured?
Say that again!

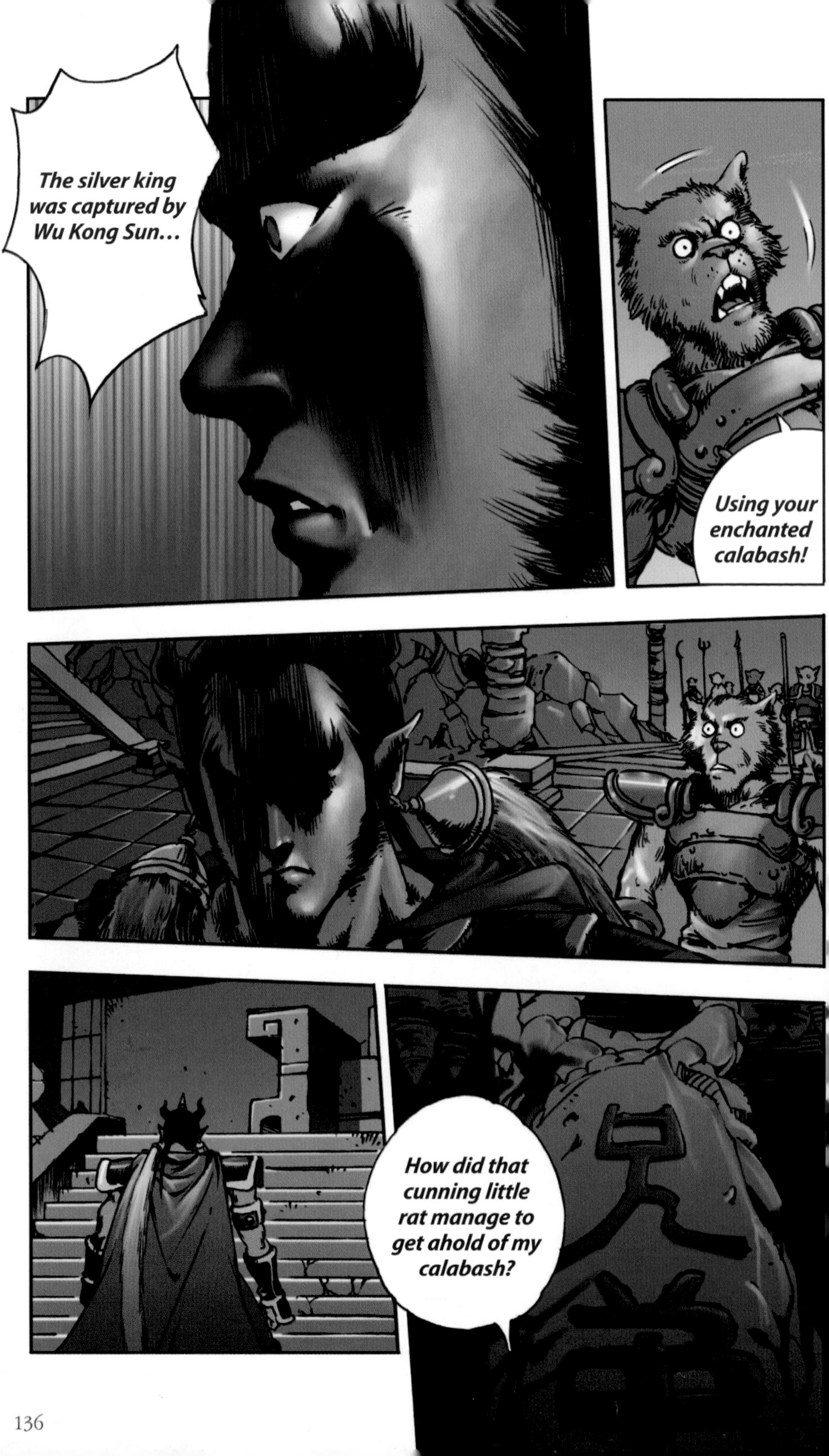
The silver king was captured by Wu Kong Sun…
Using your enchanted calabash!
How did that cunning little rat manage to get ahold of my calabash?

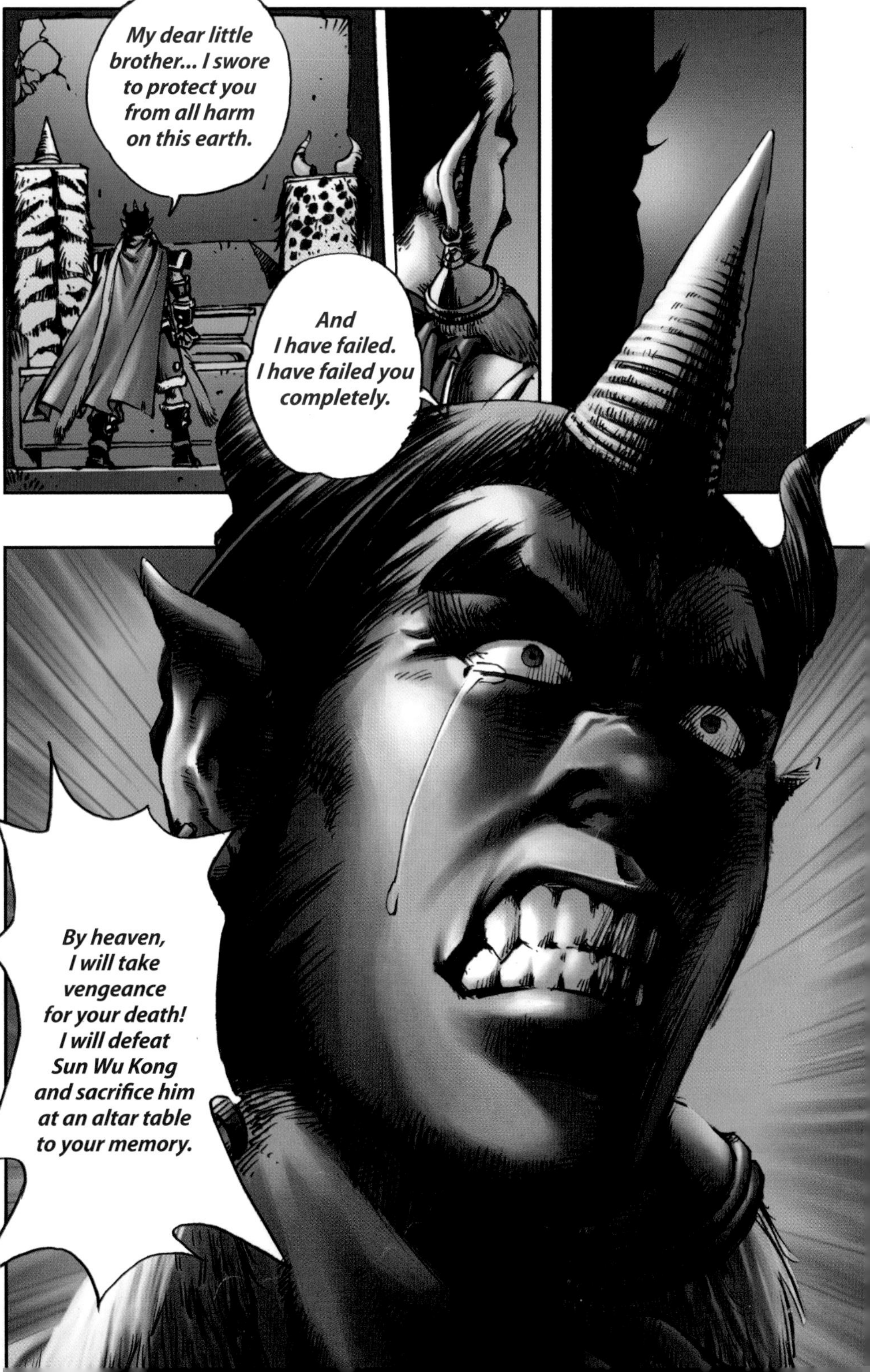
My dear little brother... I swore to protect you from all harm on this earth.
And I have failed. I have failed you completely.
By heaven, I will take vengeance for your death! I will defeat Sun Wu Kong and sacrifice him at an altar table to your memory.

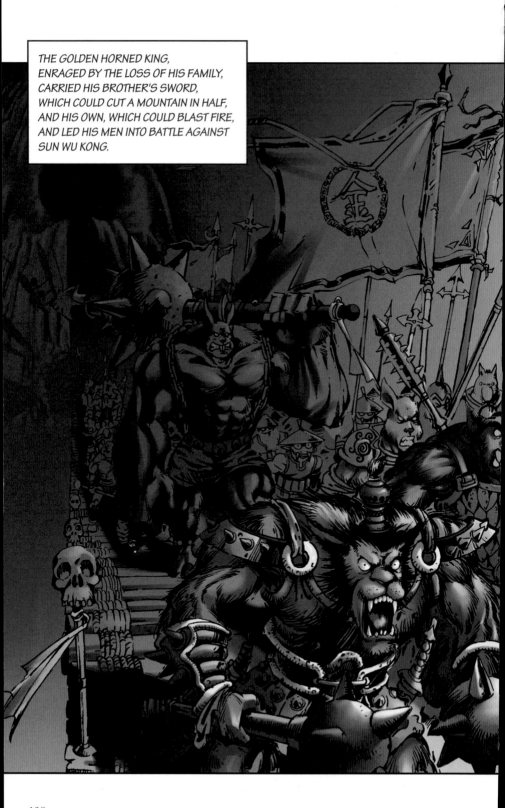

THE GOLDEN HORNED KING,
ENRAGED BY THE LOSS OF HIS FAMILY,
CARRIED HIS BROTHER'S SWORD,
WHICH COULD CUT A MOUNTAIN IN HALF,
AND HIS OWN, WHICH COULD BLAST FIRE,
AND LED HIS MEN INTO BATTLE AGAINST
SUN WU KONG.

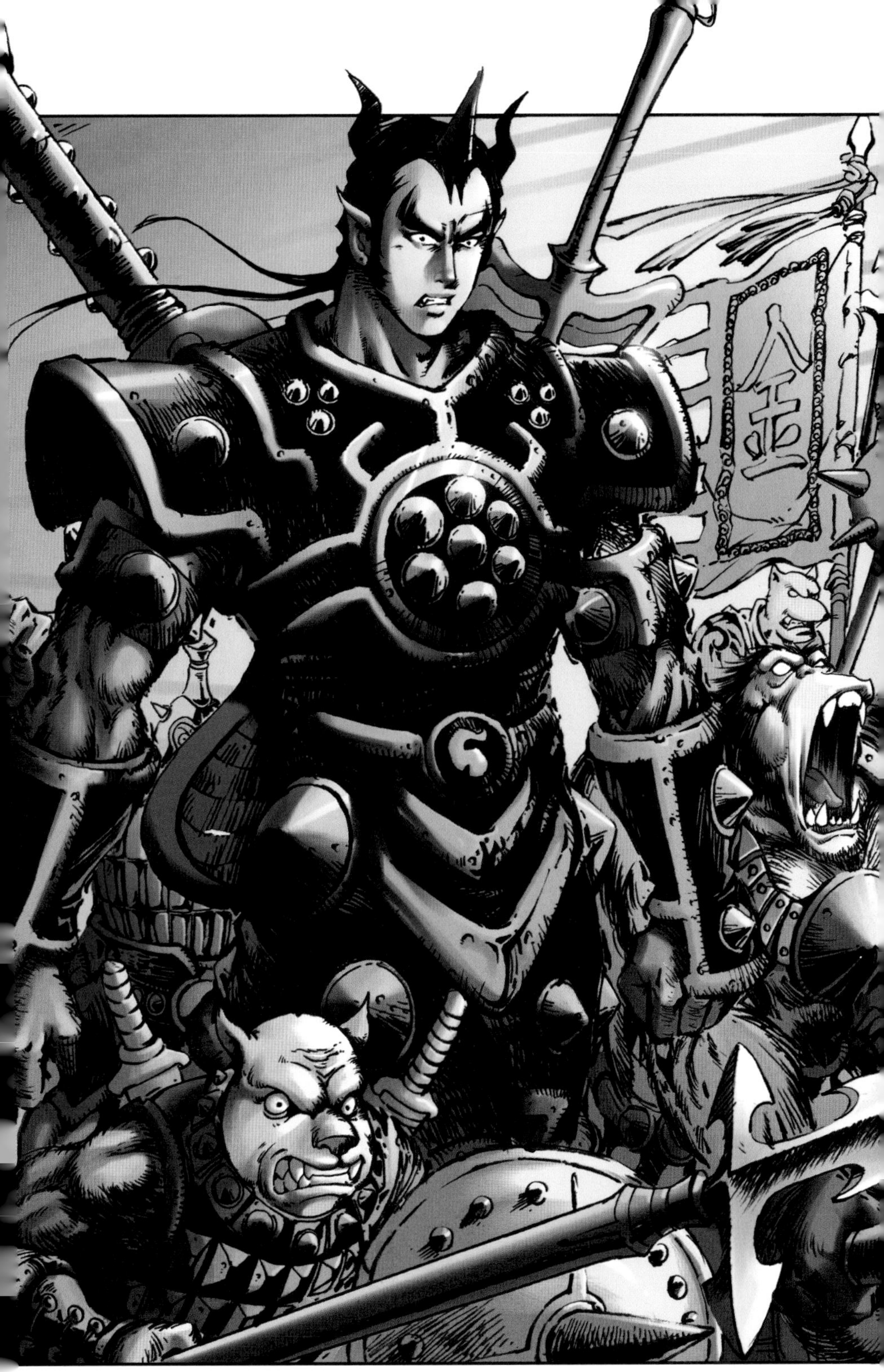
金

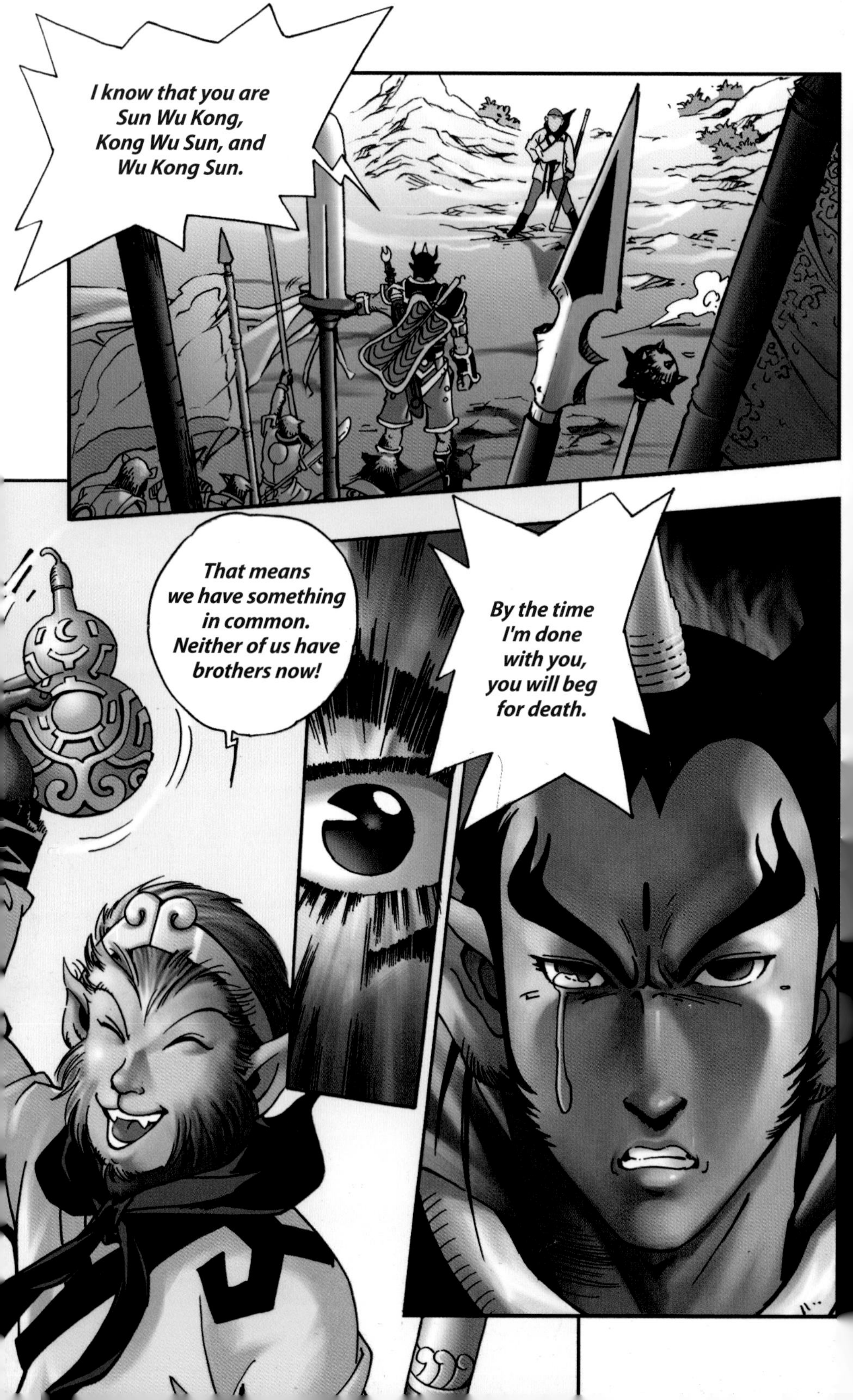
I know that you are Sun Wu Kong, Kong Wu Sun, and Wu Kong Sun.
That means we have something in common. Neither of us have brothers now!
By the time I'm done with you, you will beg for death.

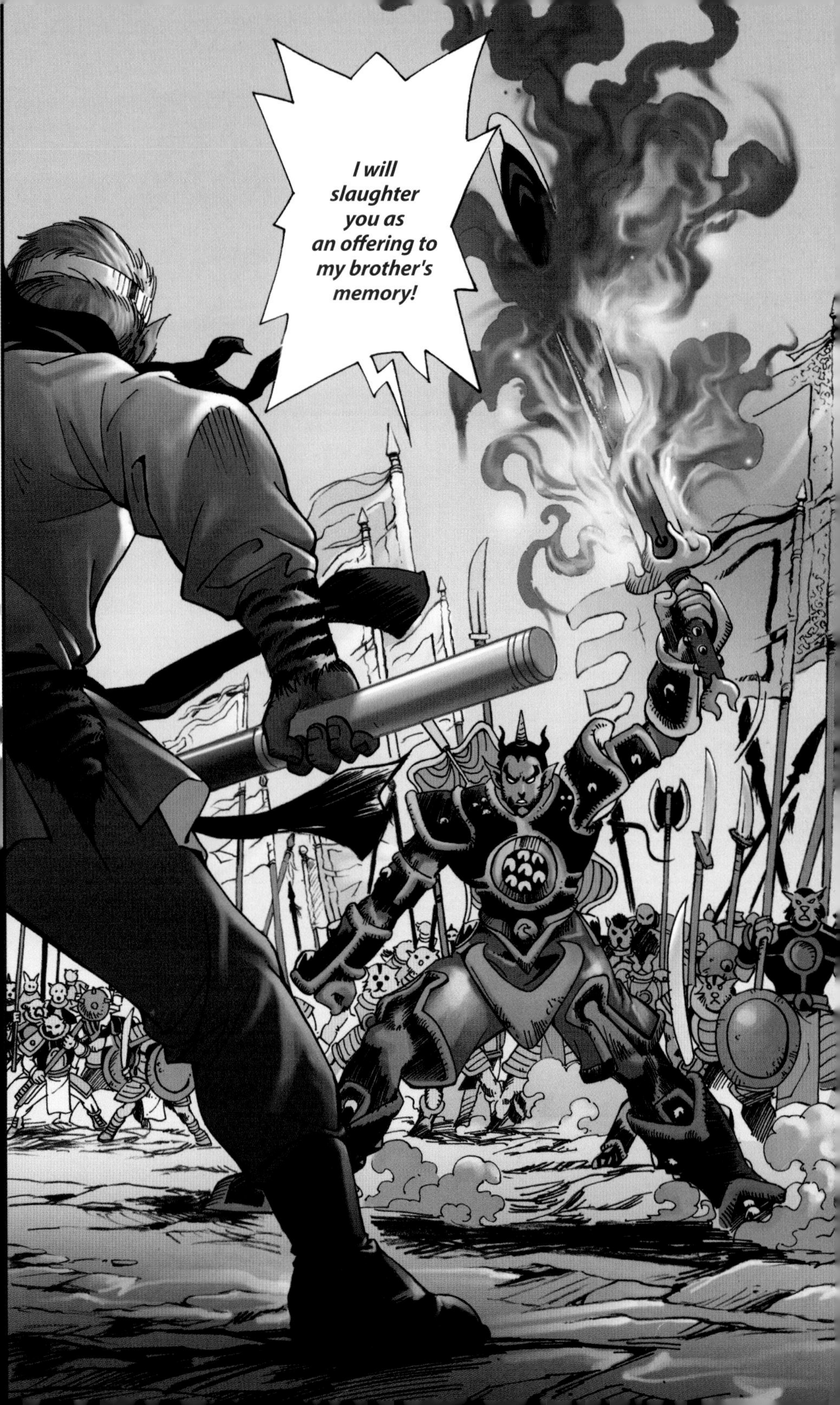
I will slaughter you as an offering to my brother's memory!

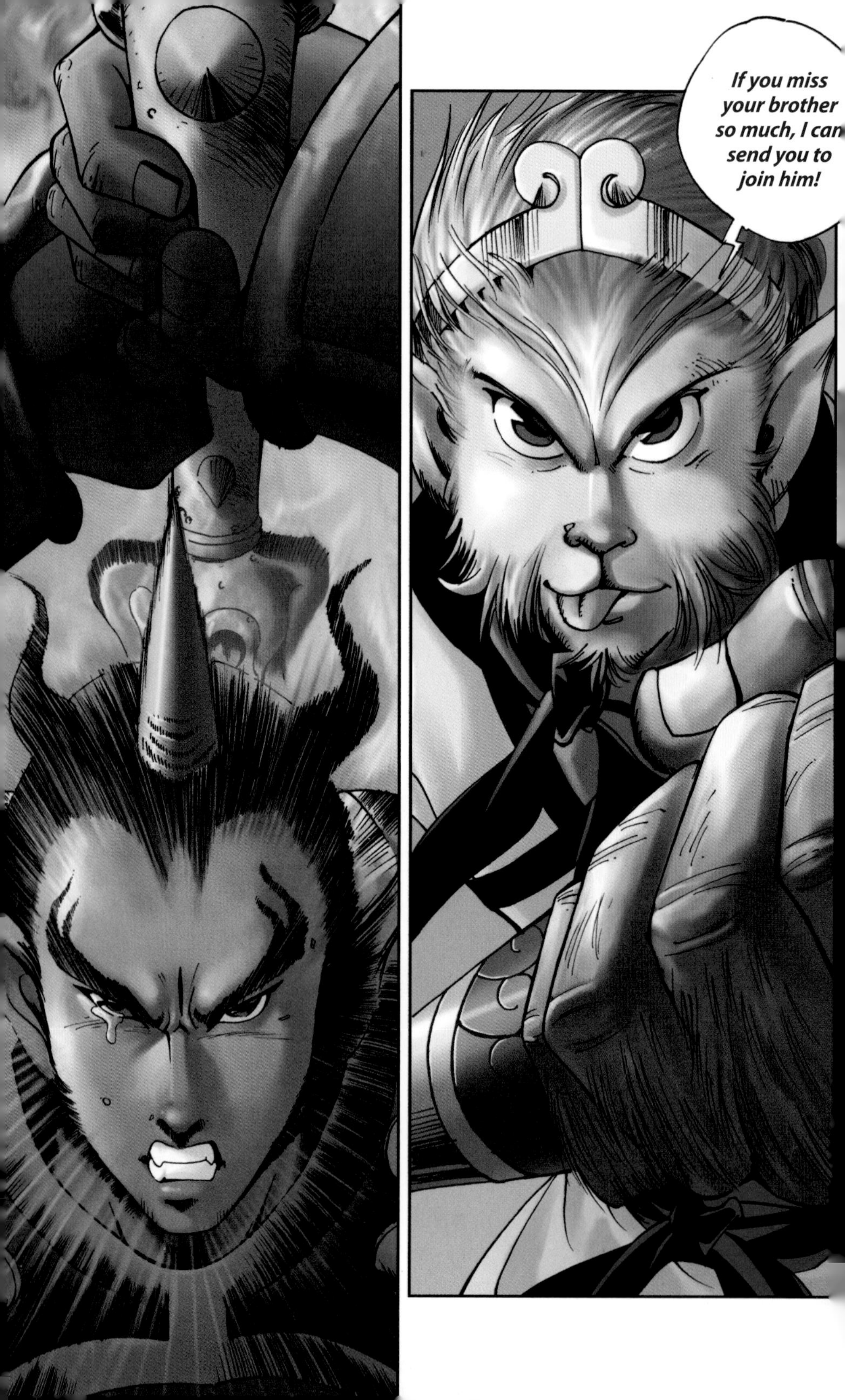
If you miss your brother so much, I can send you to join him!

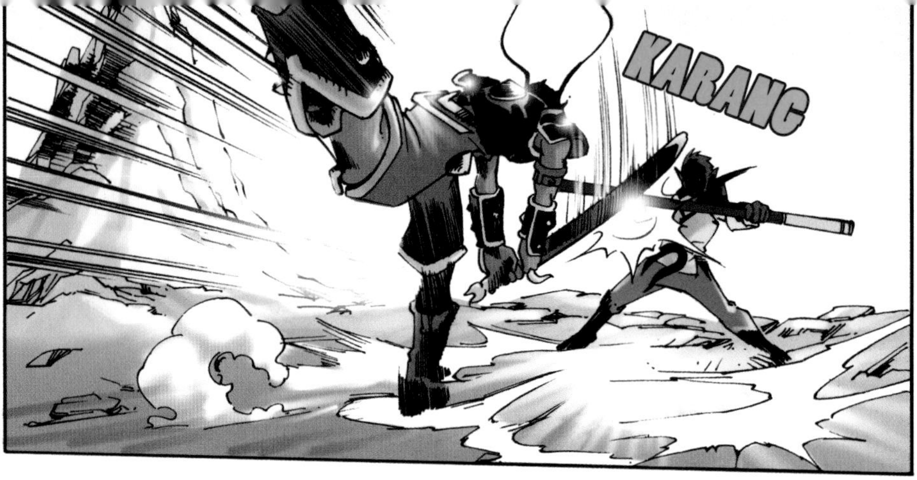
KARANG

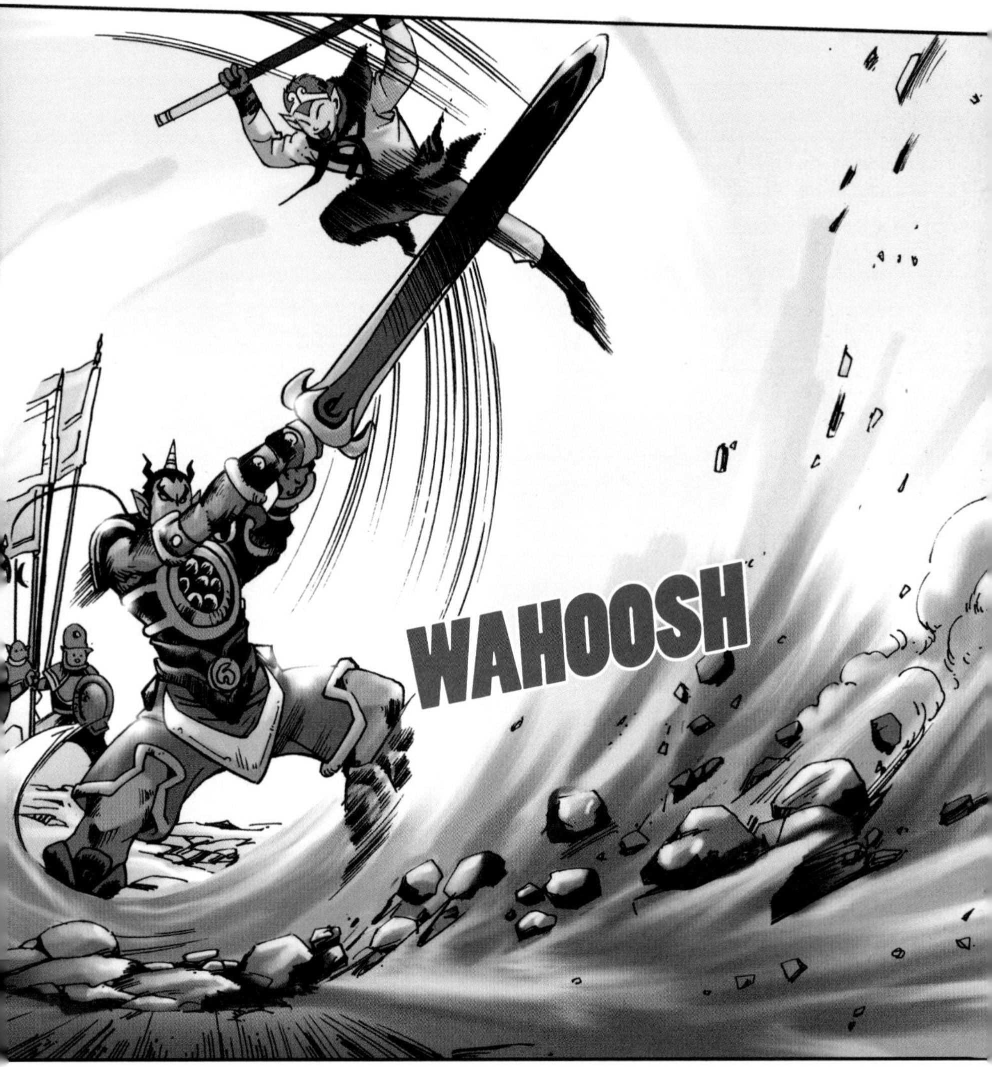
WAHOOSH

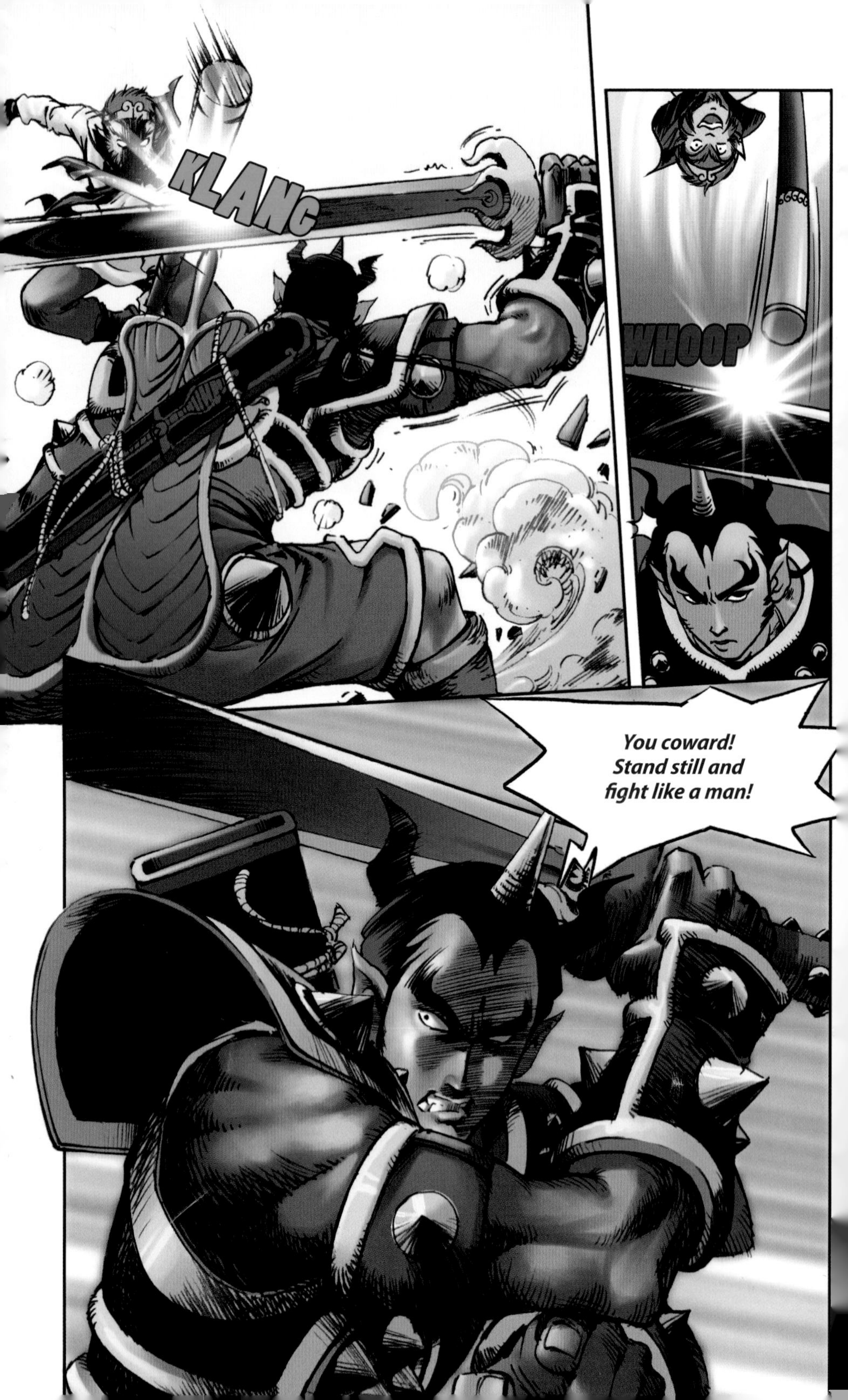
KLANG
WHOOP
You coward! Stand still and fight like a man!

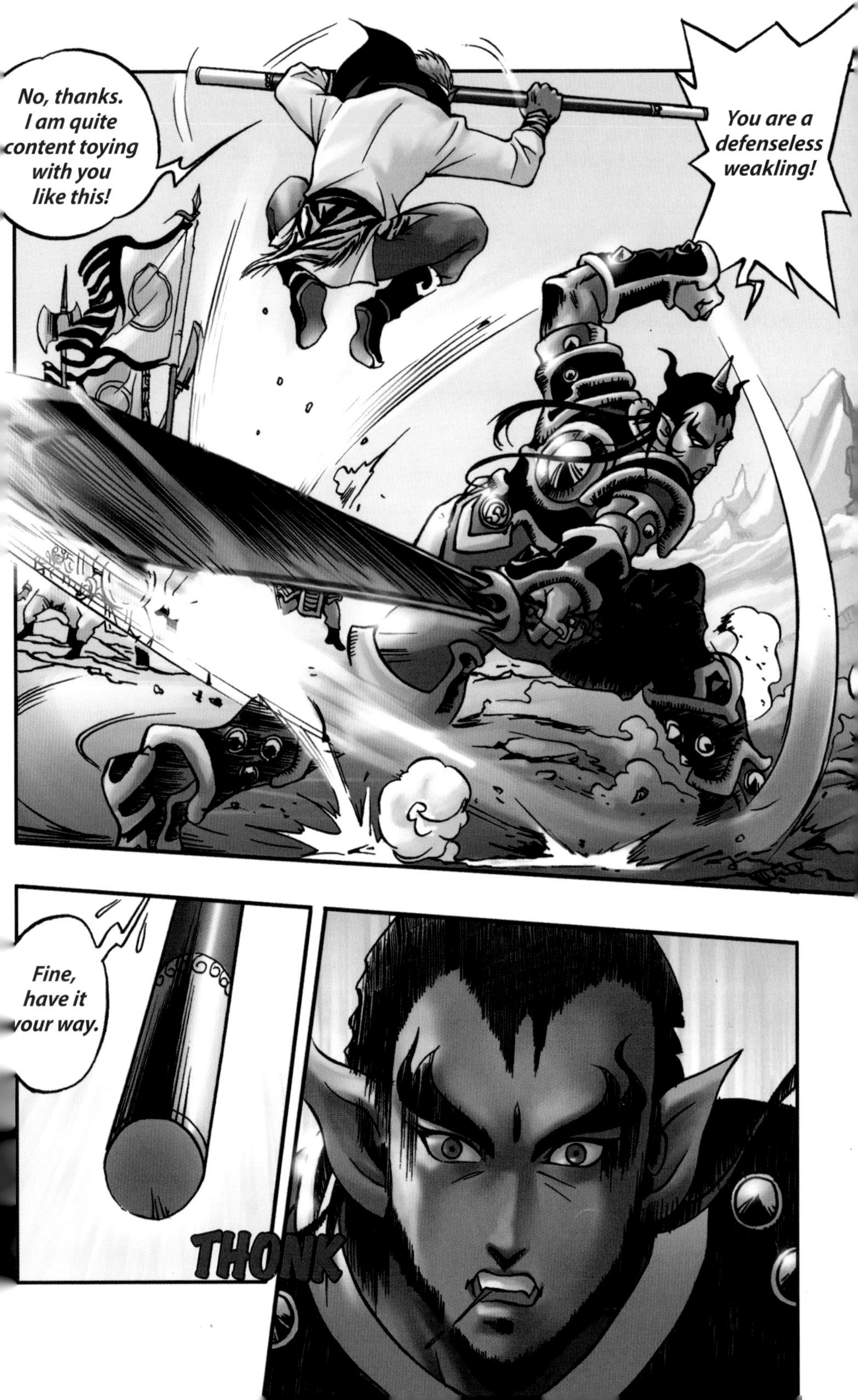

No, thanks. I am quite content toying with you like this!
You are a defenseless weakling!
Fine, have it your way.
THONK

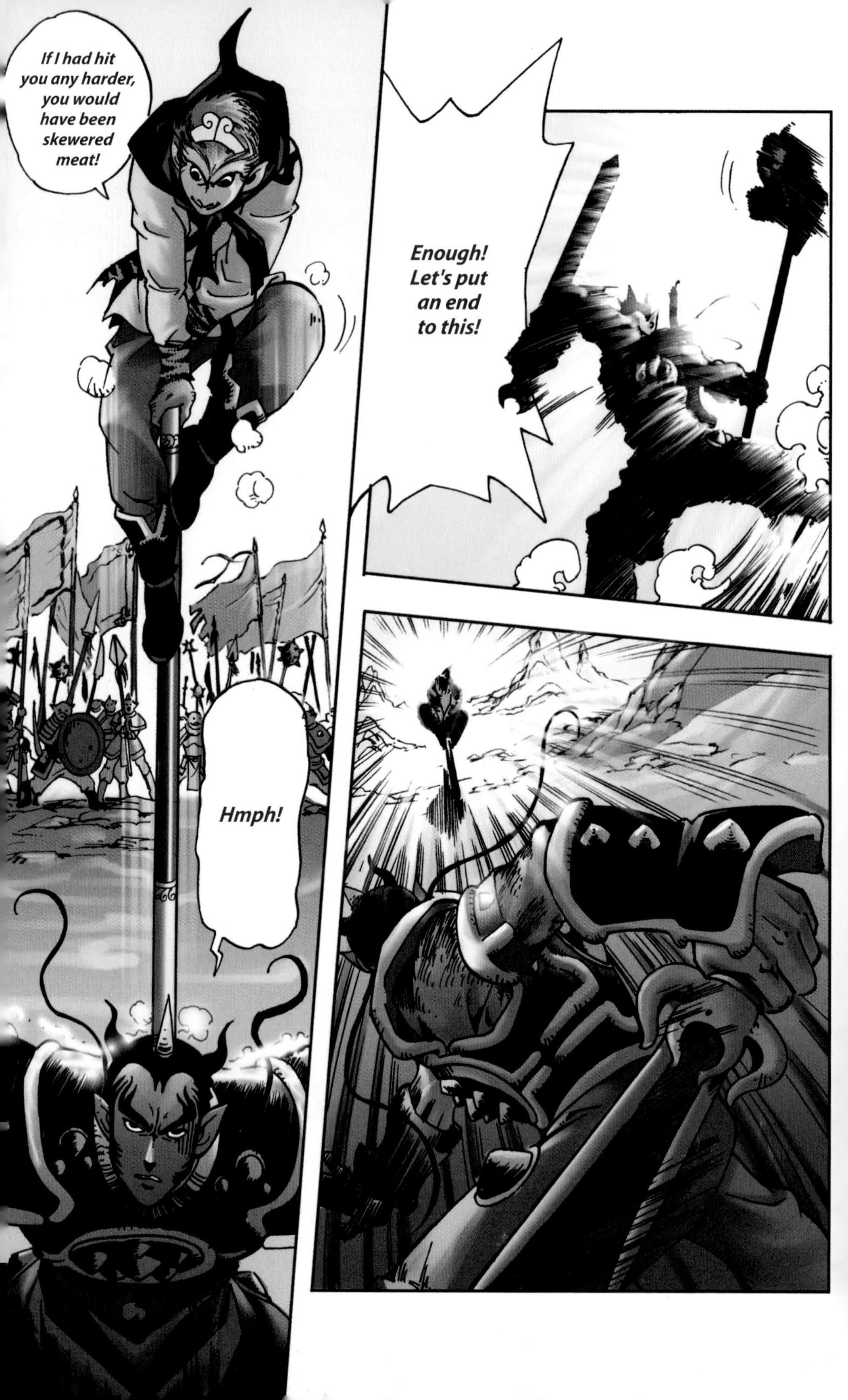
If I had hit you any harder, you would have been skewered meat!
Hmph!
Enough! Let's put an end to this!

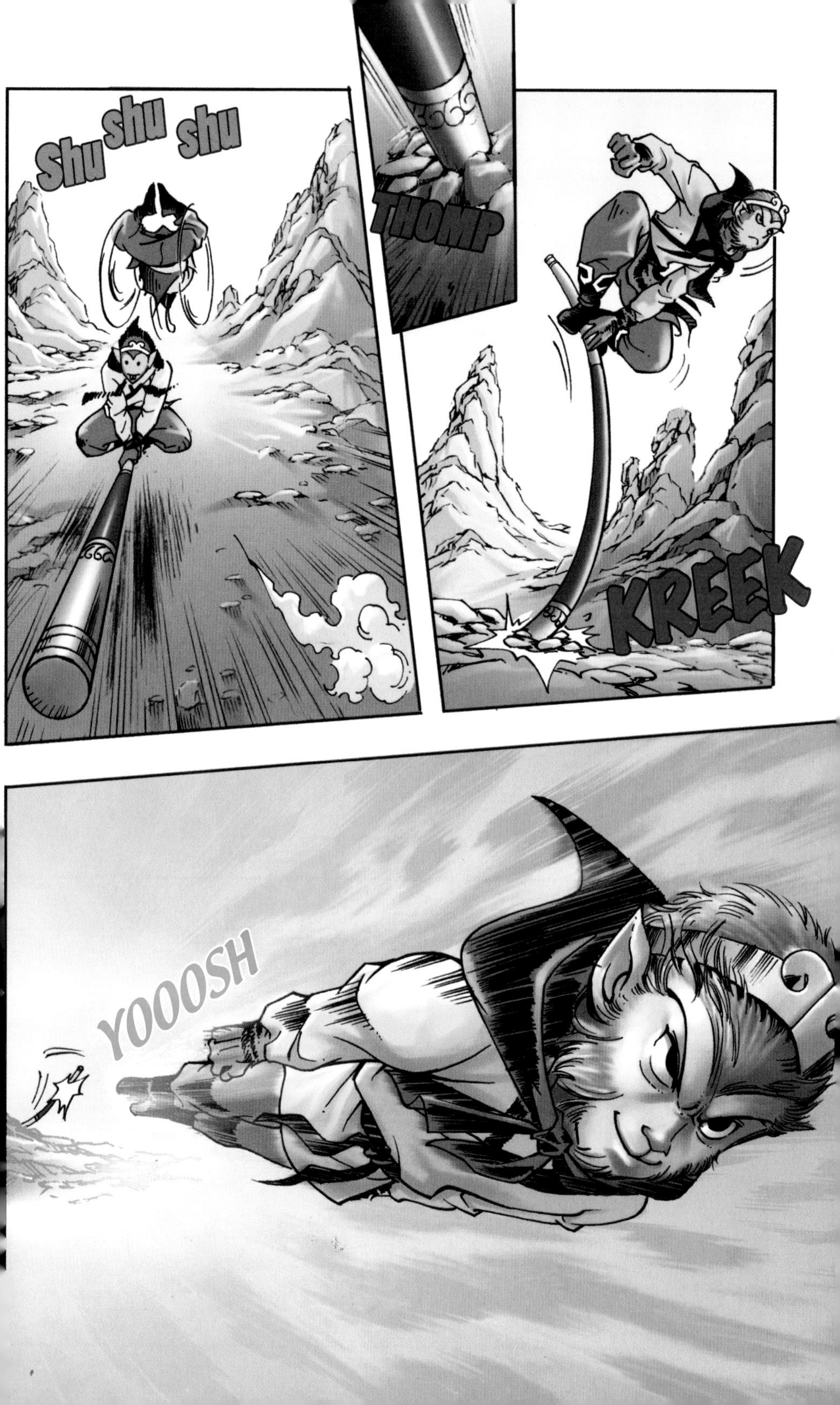
Shu shu shu
THOMP
KREEK
YOOOSH

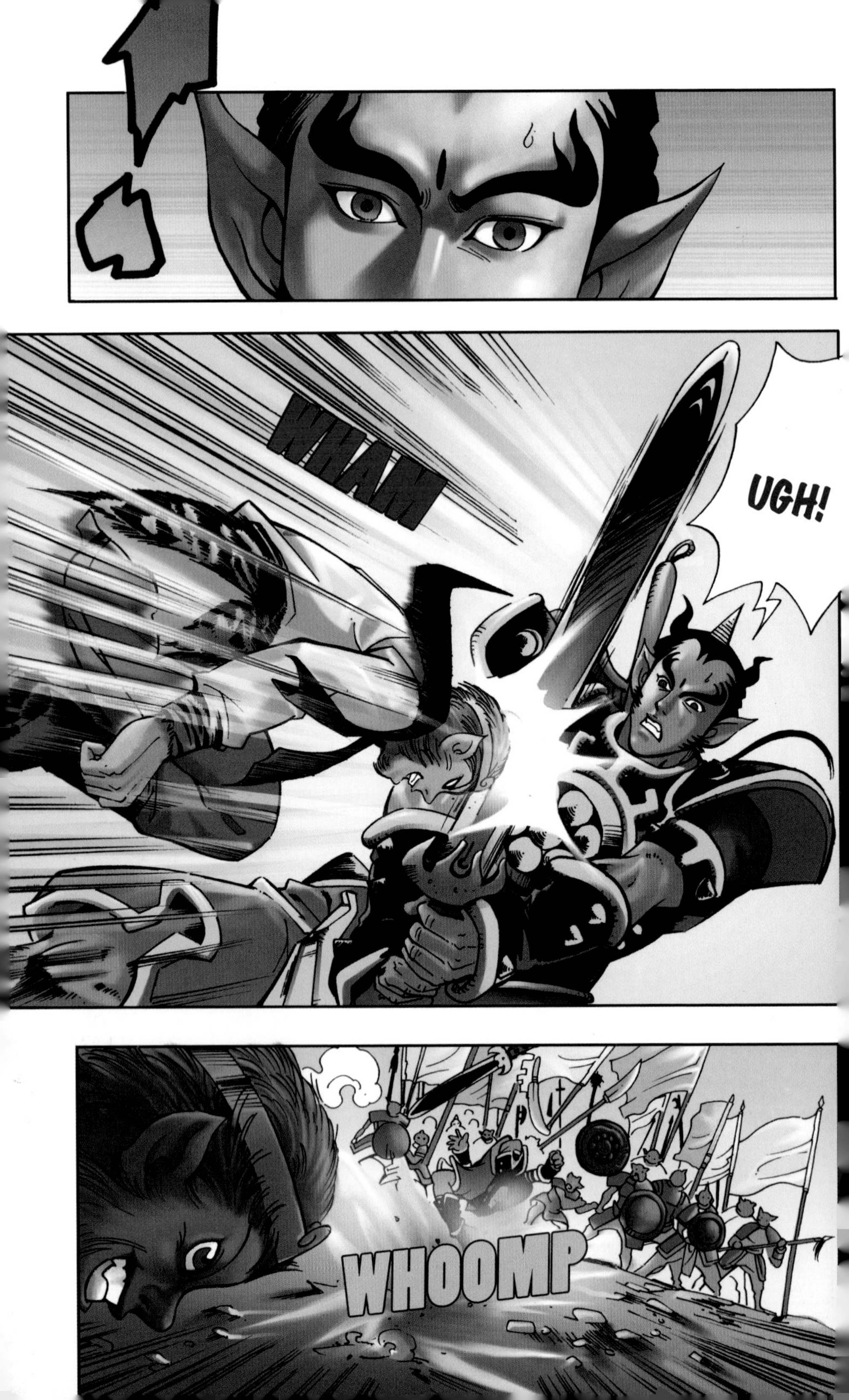
WHAM
UGH!
WHOOMP

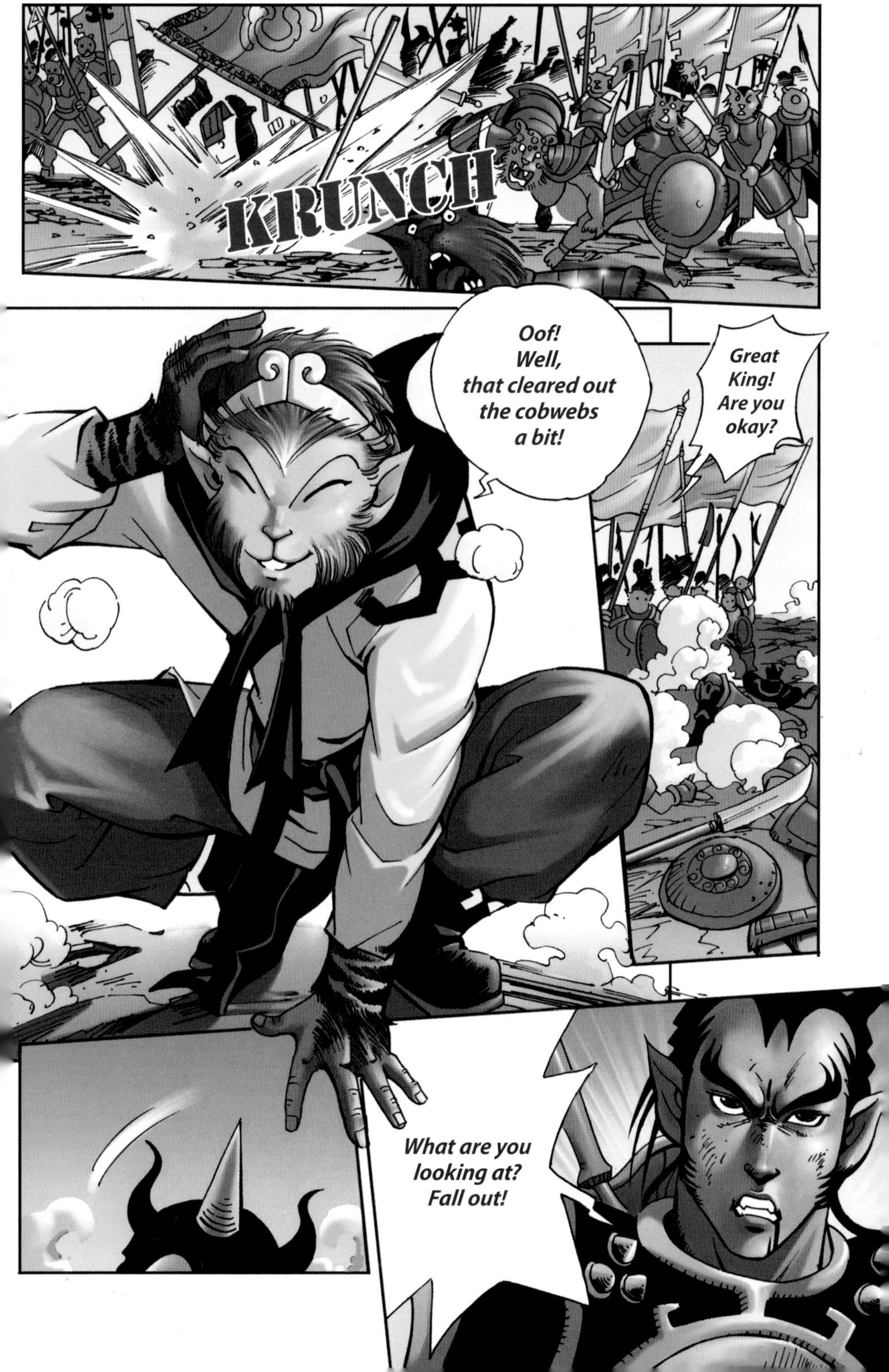
KRUNCH
Oof! Well, that cleared out the cobwebs a bit!
Great King! Are you okay?
What are you looking at? Fall out!

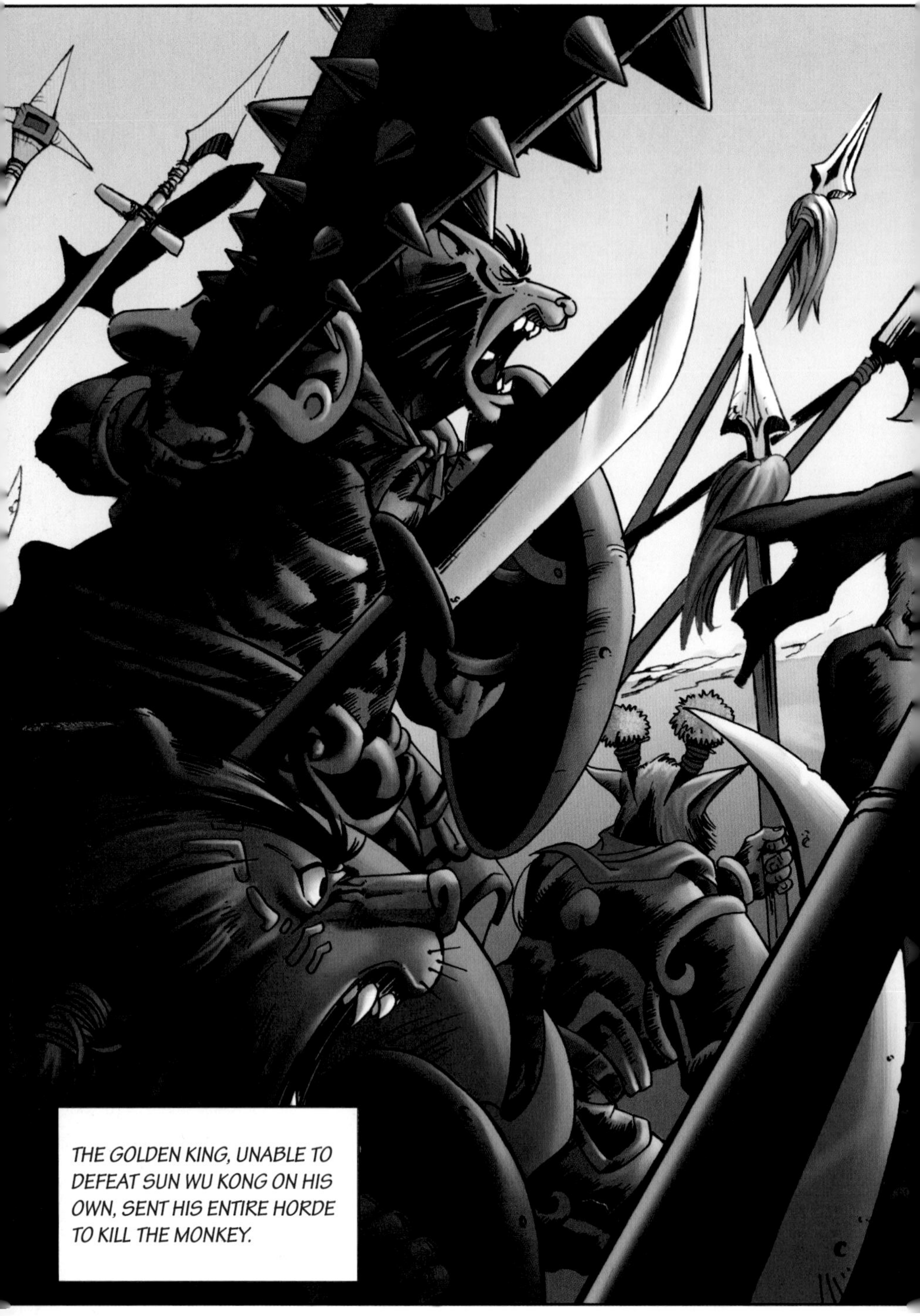
THE GOLDEN KING, UNABLE TO DEFEAT SUN WU KONG ON HIS OWN, SENT HIS ENTIRE HORDE TO KILL THE MONKEY.

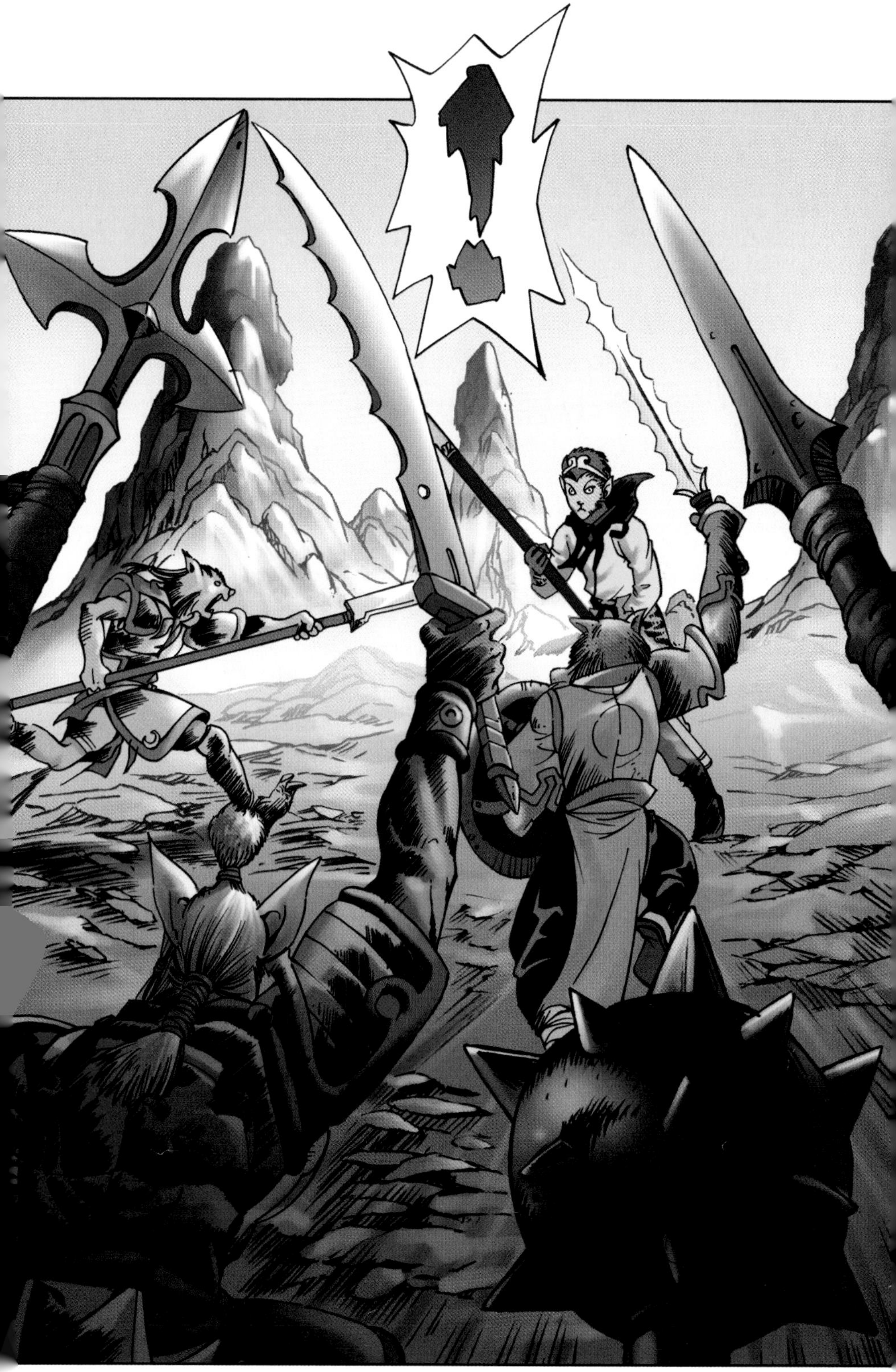
!

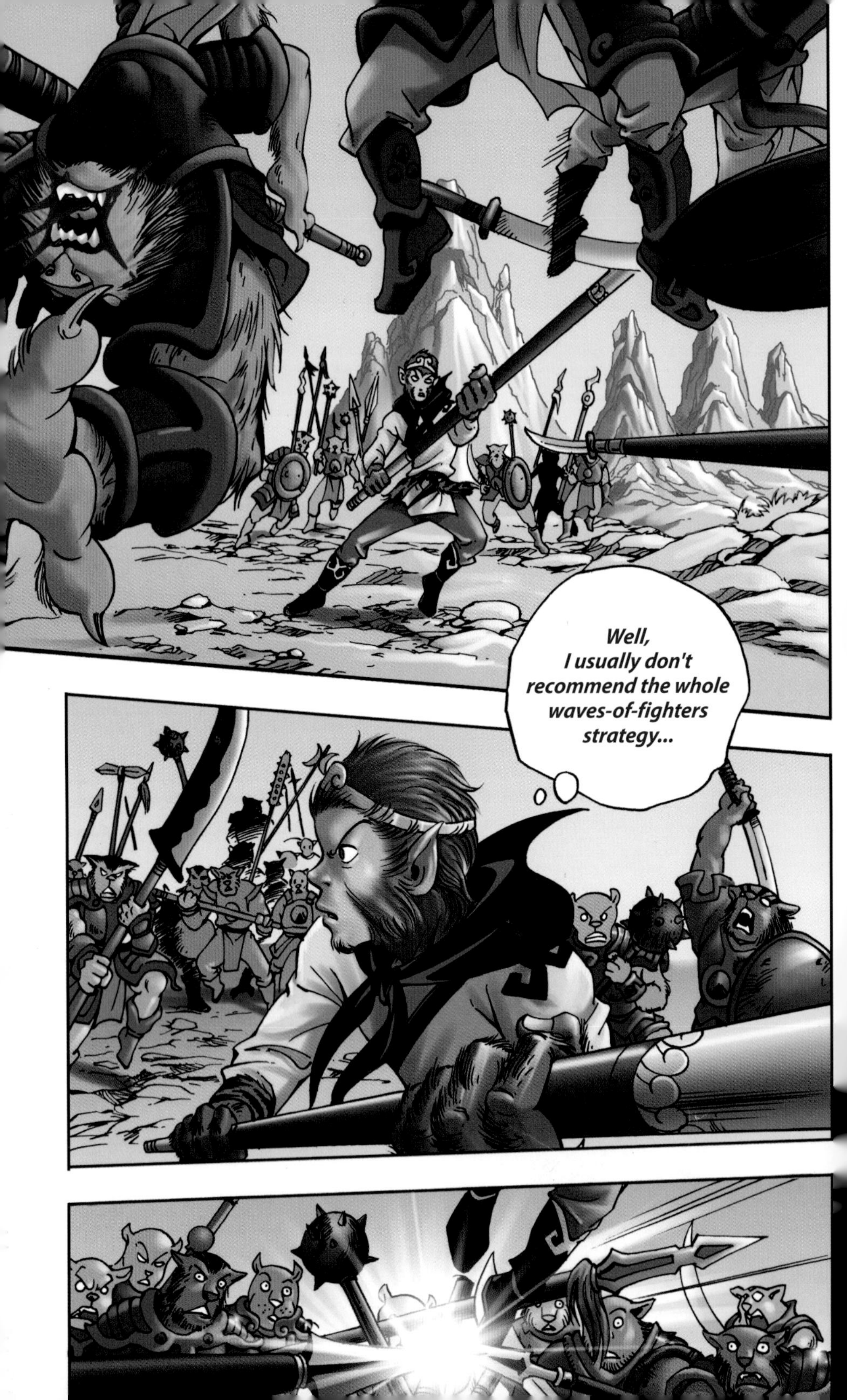
Well, I usually don't recommend the whole waves-of-fighters strategy...

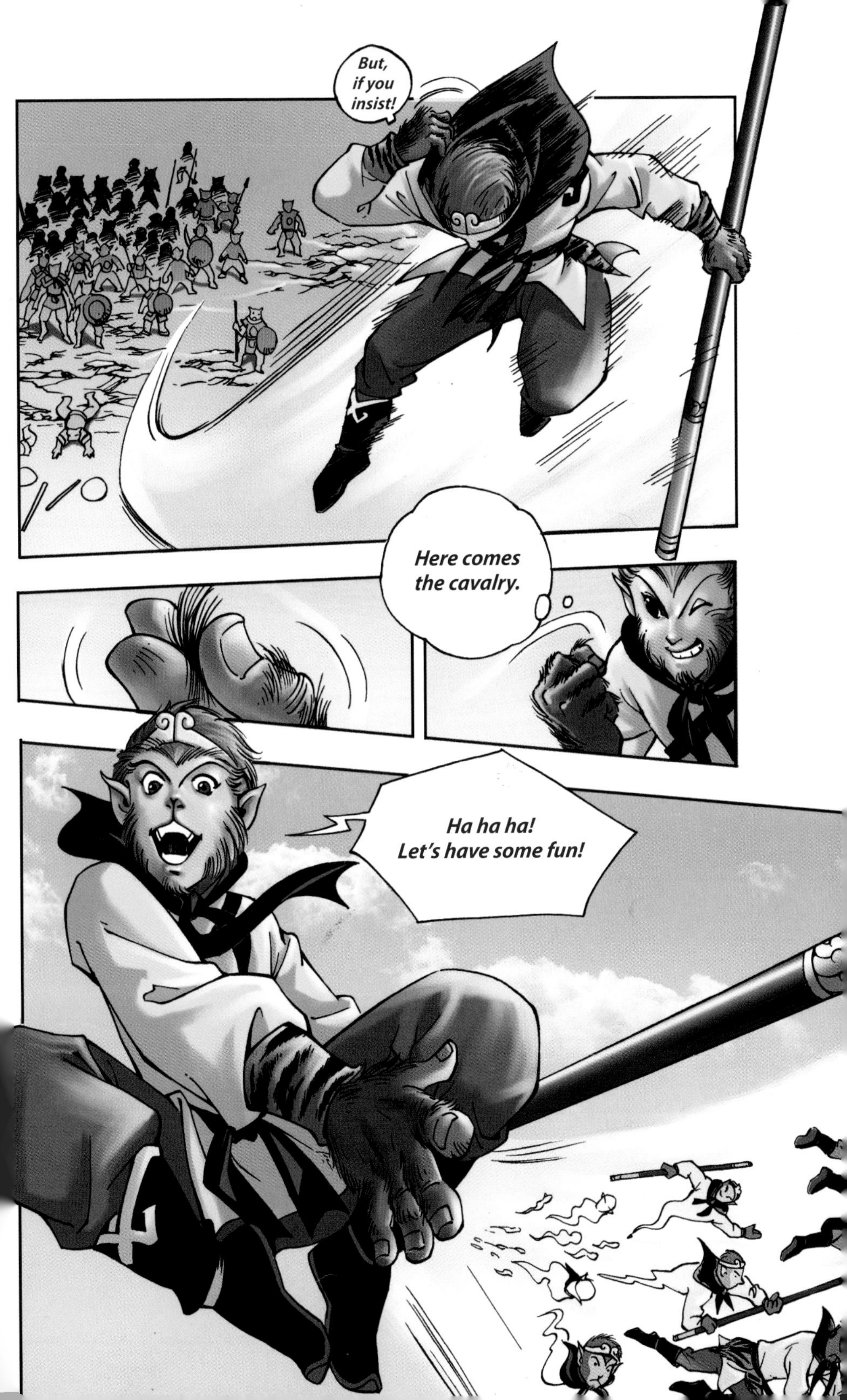
But, if you insist!
Here comes the cavalry.
Ha ha ha! Let's have some fun!

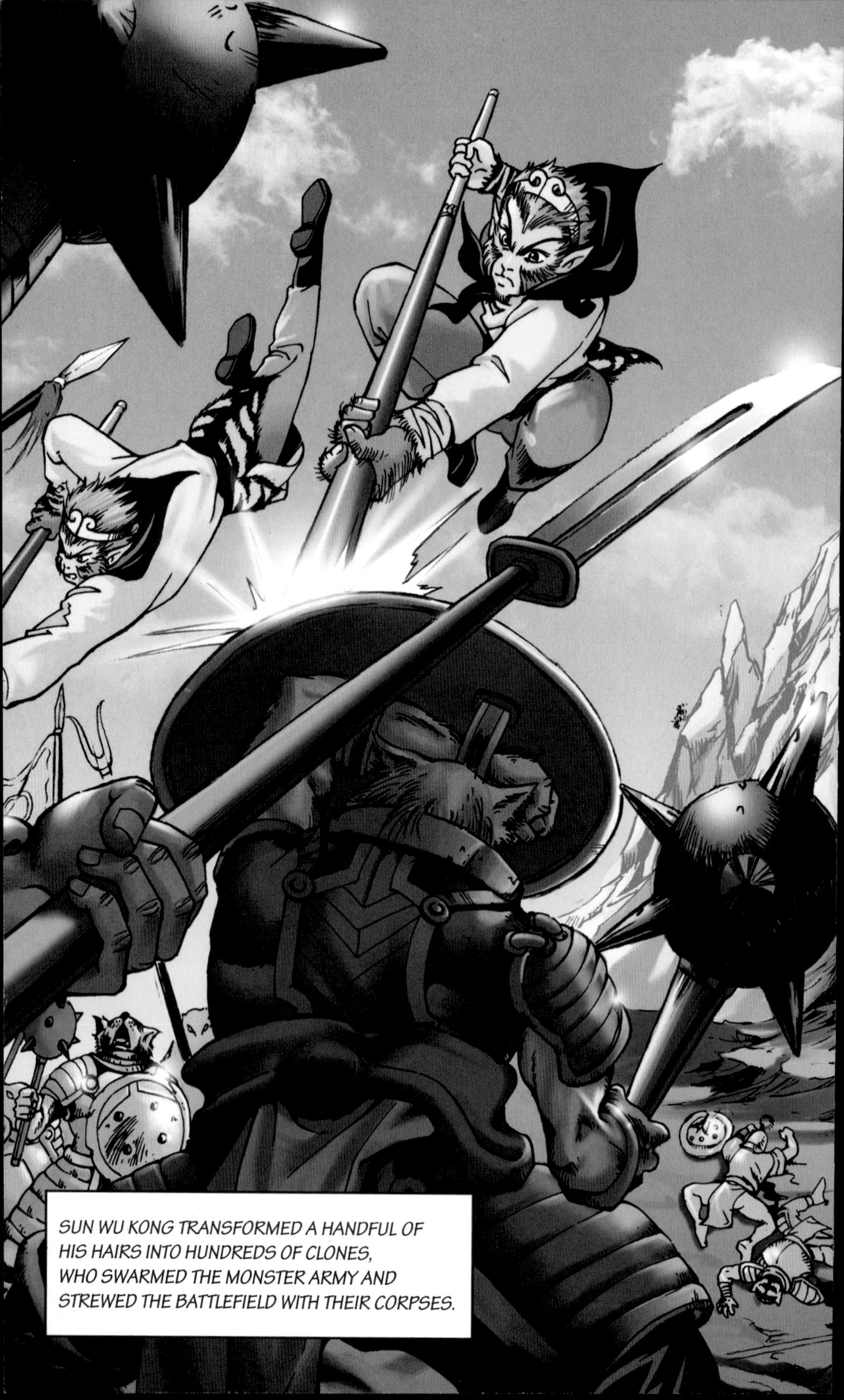
SUN WU KONG TRANSFORMED A HANDFUL OF HIS HAIRS INTO HUNDREDS OF CLONES, WHO SWARMED THE MONSTER ARMY AND STREWED THE BATTLEFIELD WITH THEIR CORPSES.

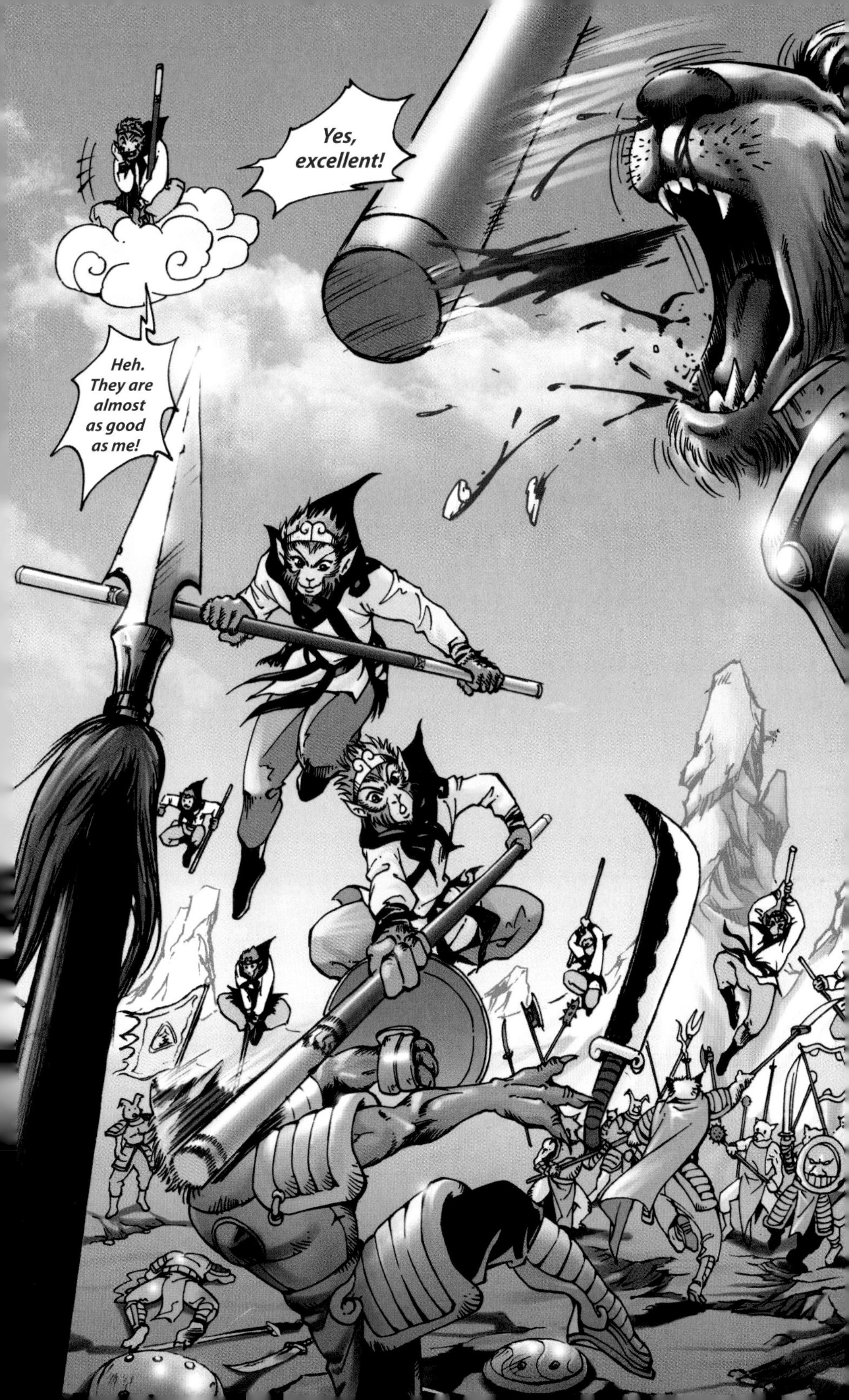
Yes, excellent!
Heh. They are almost as good as me!

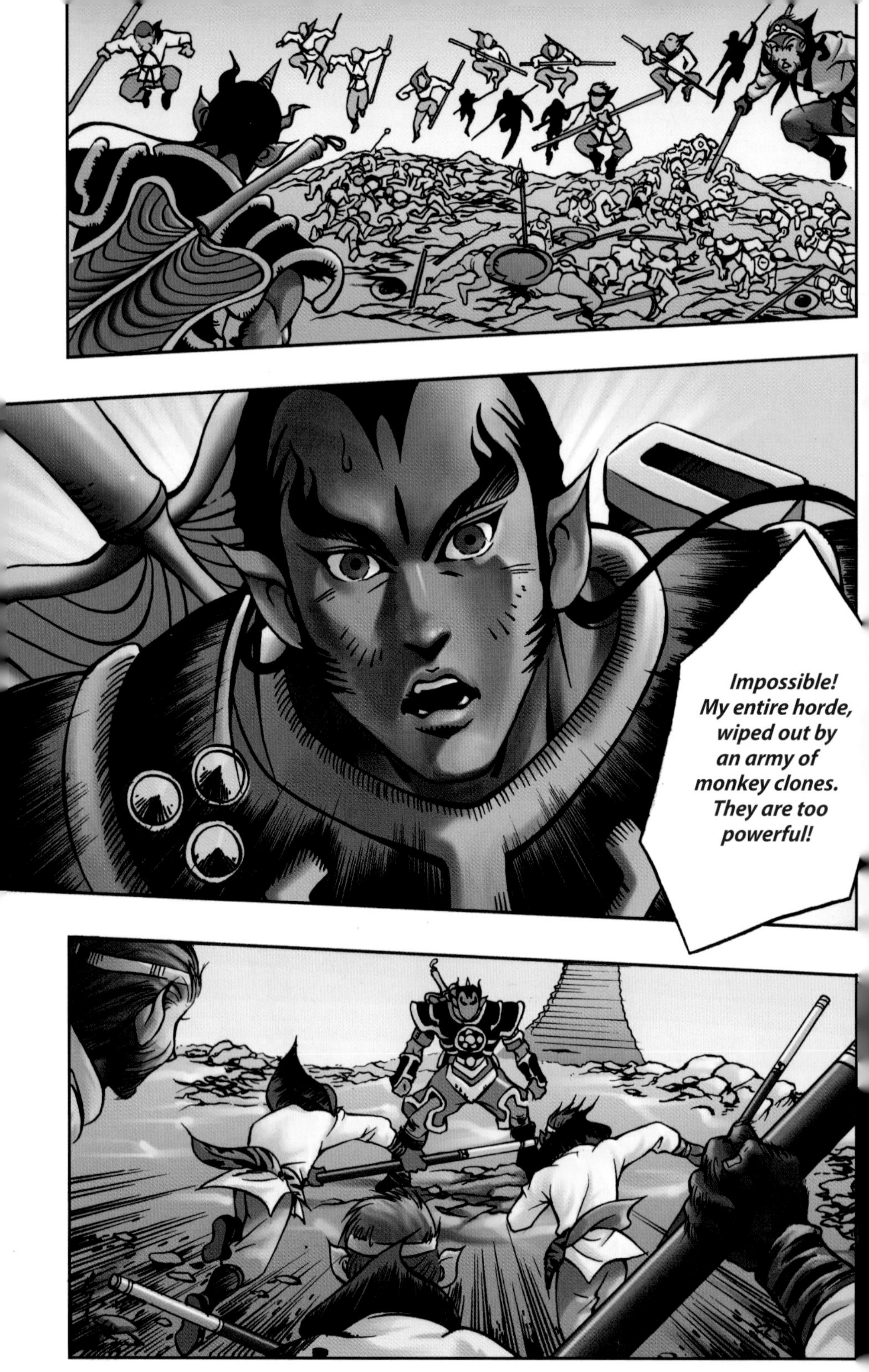
Impossible! My entire horde, wiped out by an army of monkey clones. They are too powerful!

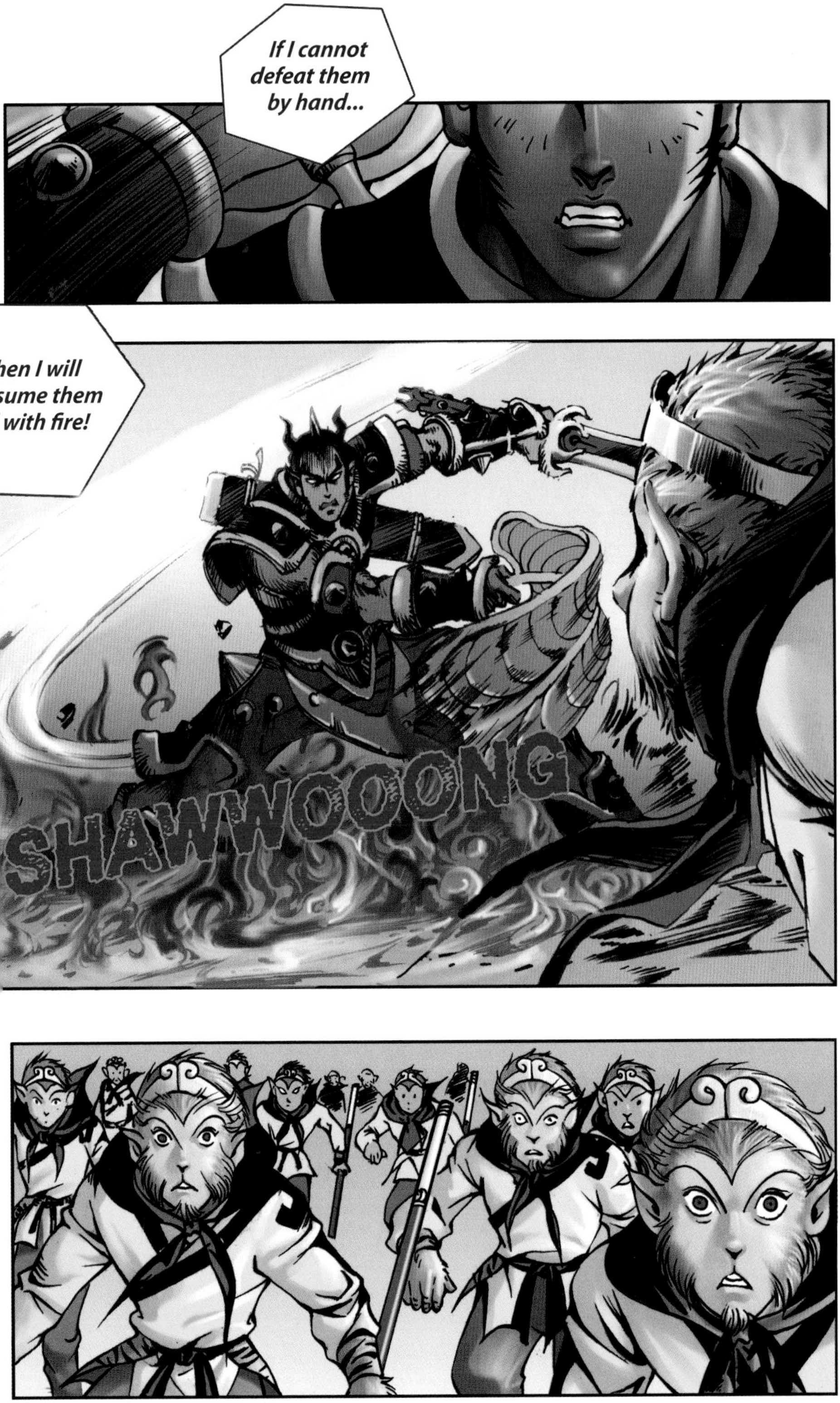
If I cannot defeat them by hand...
hen I will sume them with fire!
SHAWWOOONG

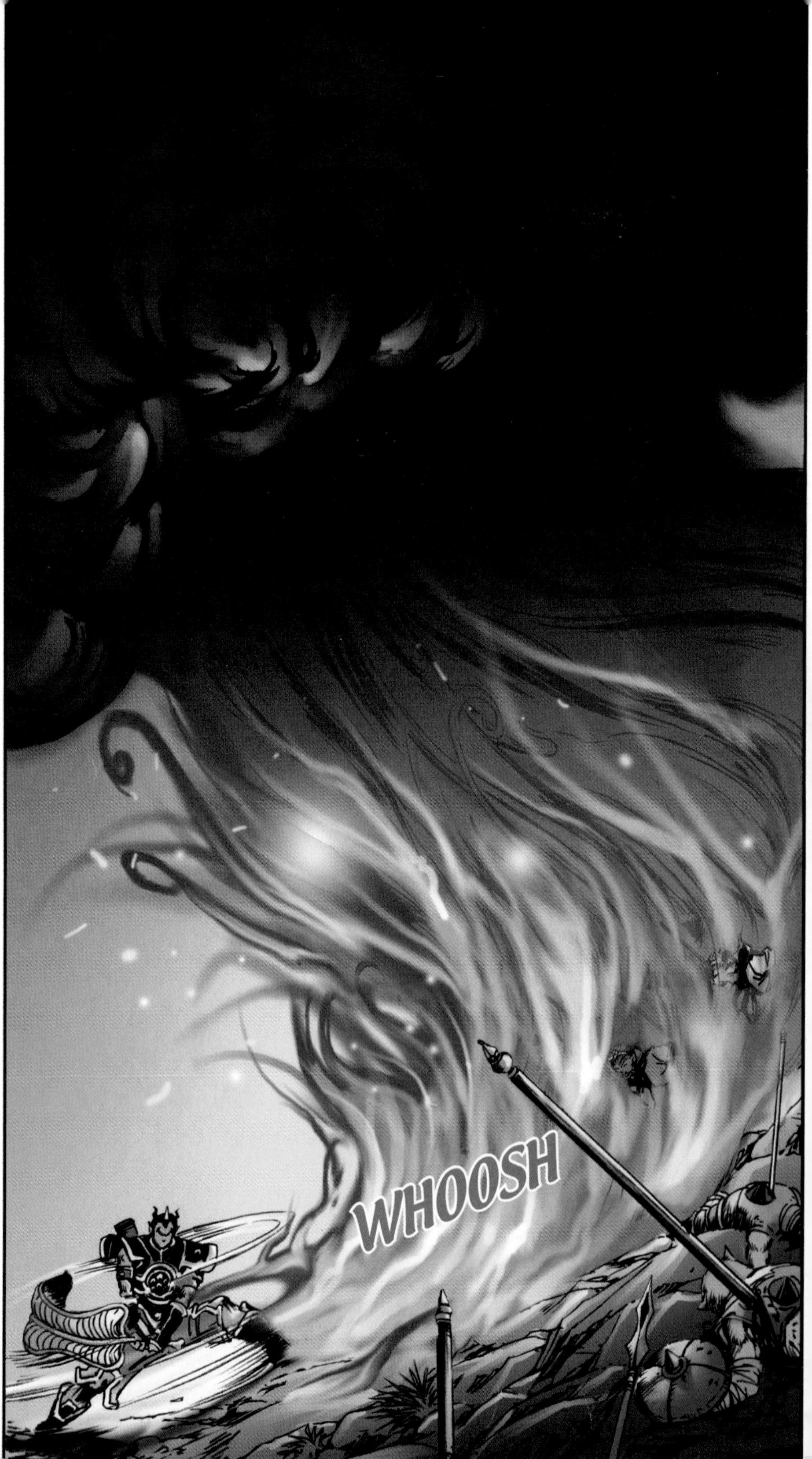
WHOOSH

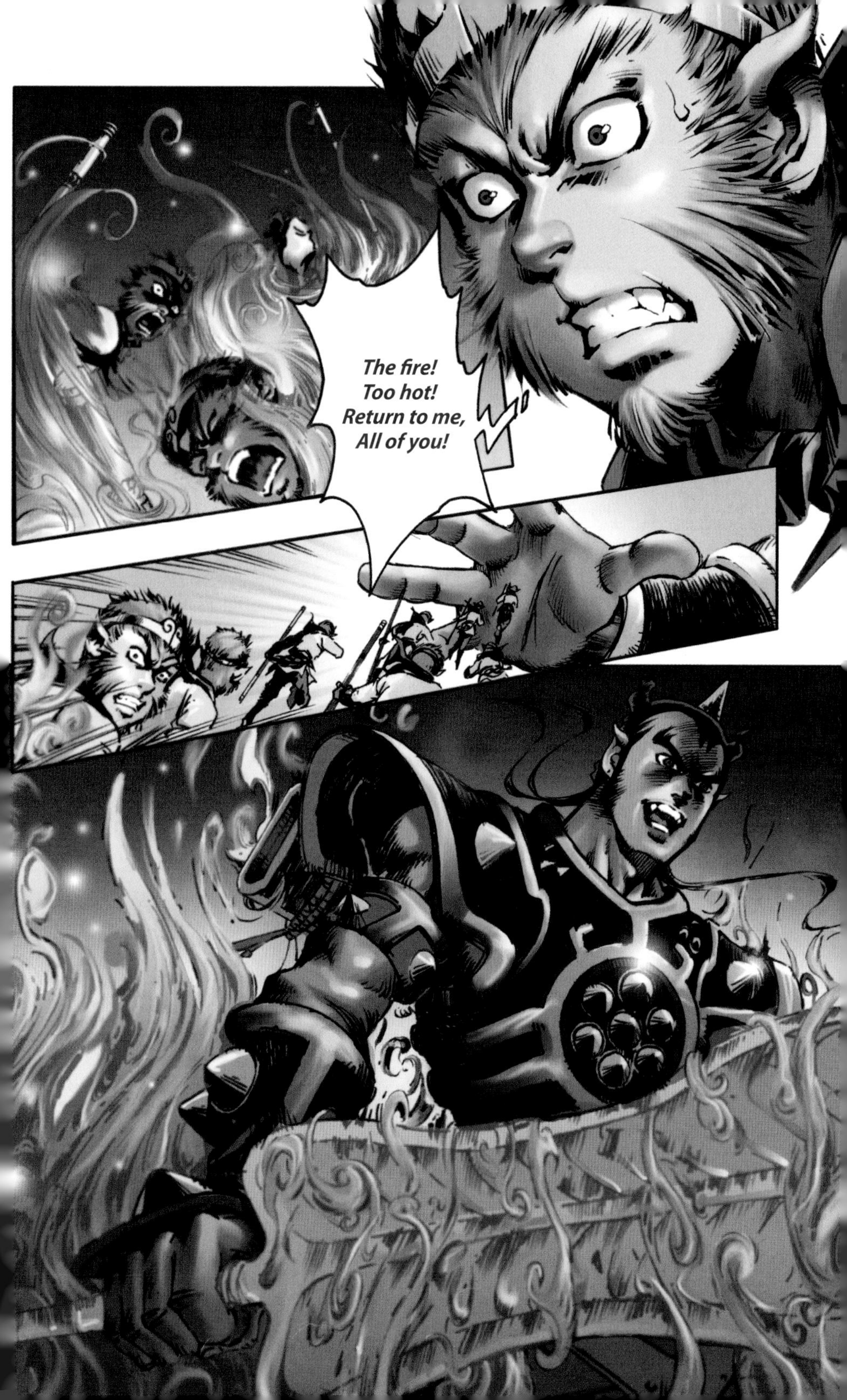
The fire! Too hot! Return to me, All of you!

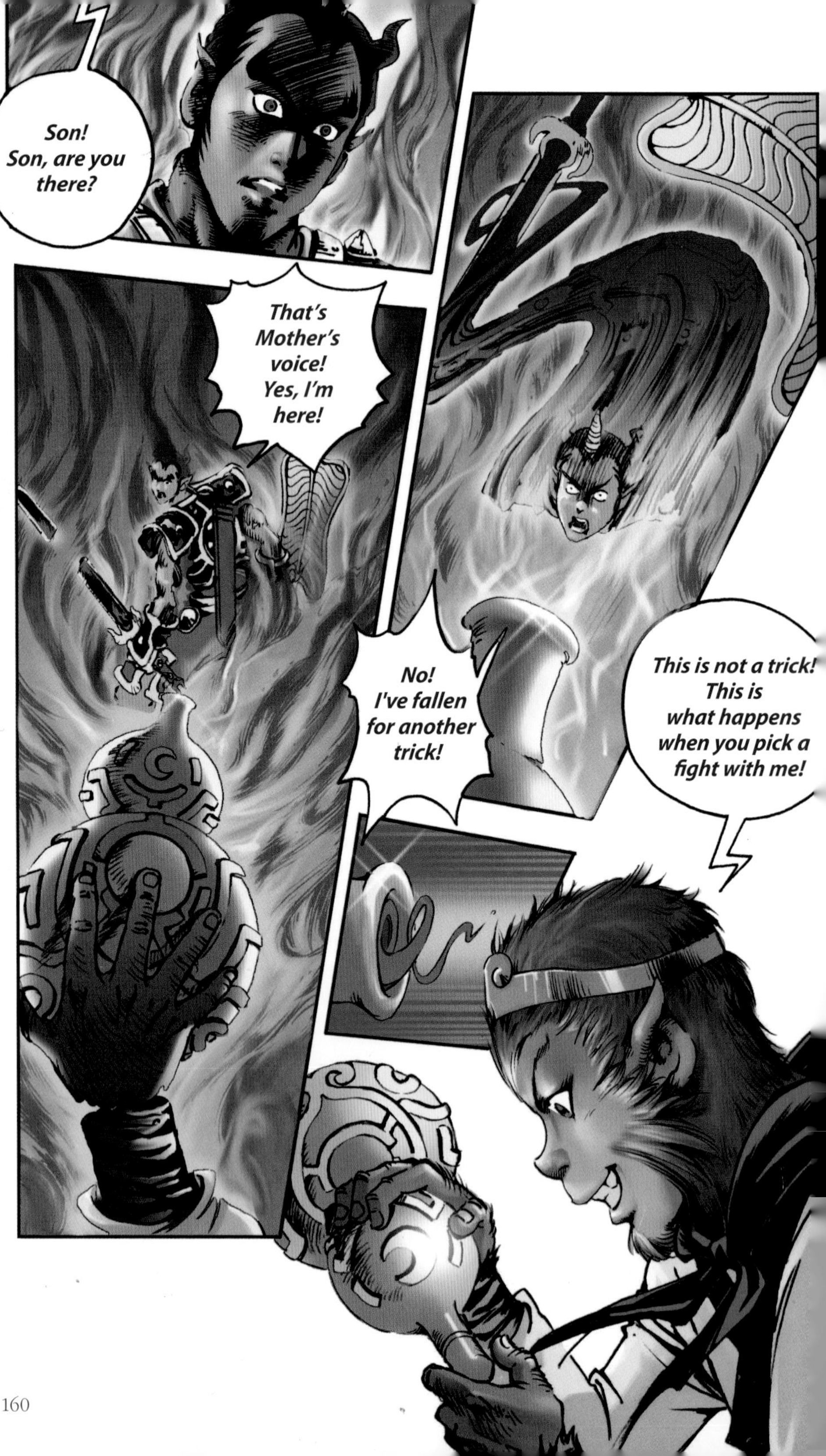
Son! Son, are you there?
That's Mother's voice! Yes, I'm here!
No! I've fallen for another trick!
This is not a trick! This is what happens when you pick a fight with me!

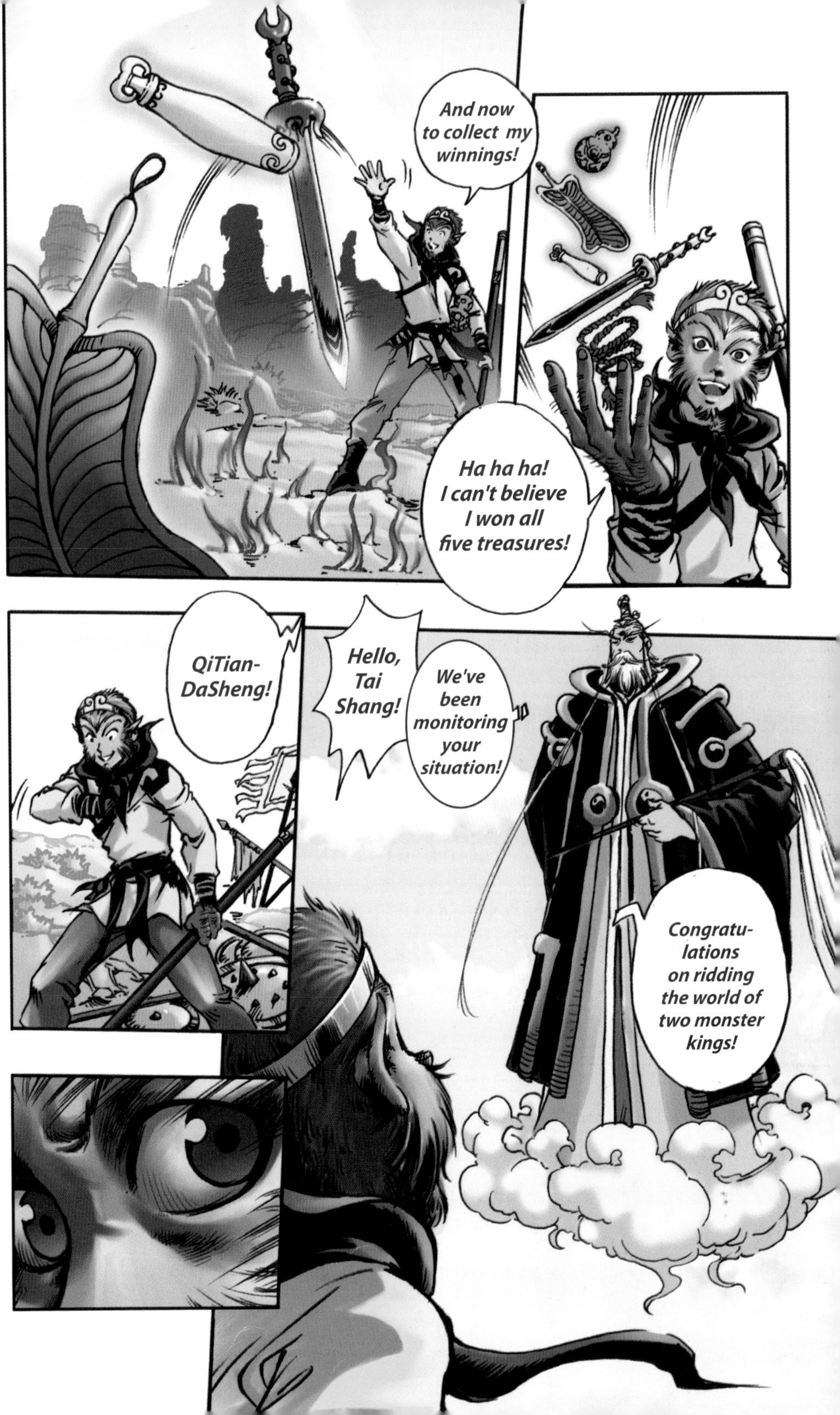
And now to collect my winnings!
Ha ha ha! I can't believe I won all five treasures!
QiTian-DaSheng!
Hello, Tai Shang!
We've been monitoring your situation!
Congratu-lations on ridding the world of two monster kings!

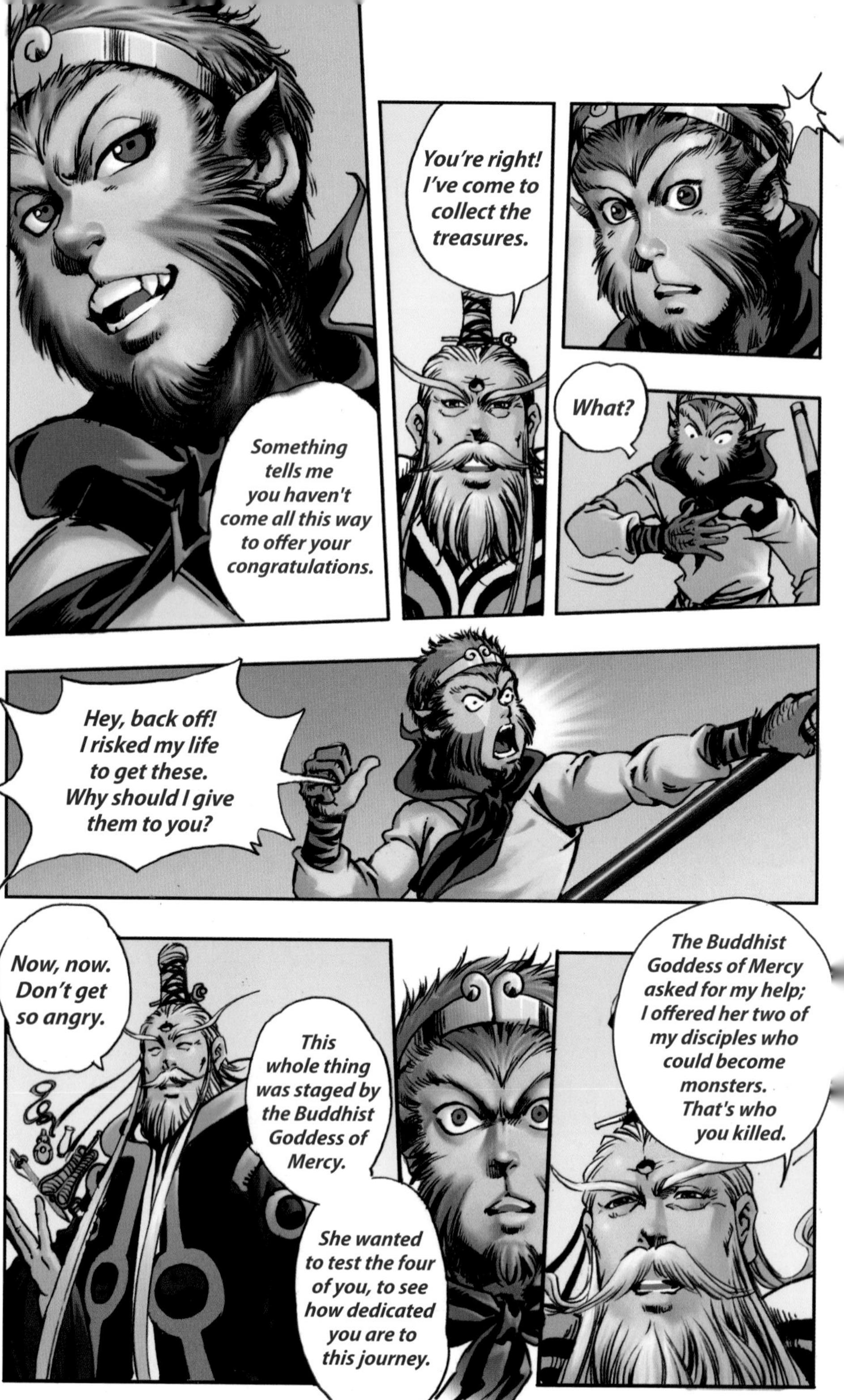
Something tells me you haven't come all this way to offer your congratulations.
You're right! I've come to collect the treasures.
What?
Hey, back off! I risked my life to get these. Why should I give them to you?
Now, now. Don't get so angry.
This whole thing was staged by the Buddhist Goddess of Mercy.
She wanted to test the four of you, to see how dedicated you are to this journey.
The Buddhist Goddess of Mercy asked for my help; I offered her two of my disciples who could become monsters. That's who you killed.

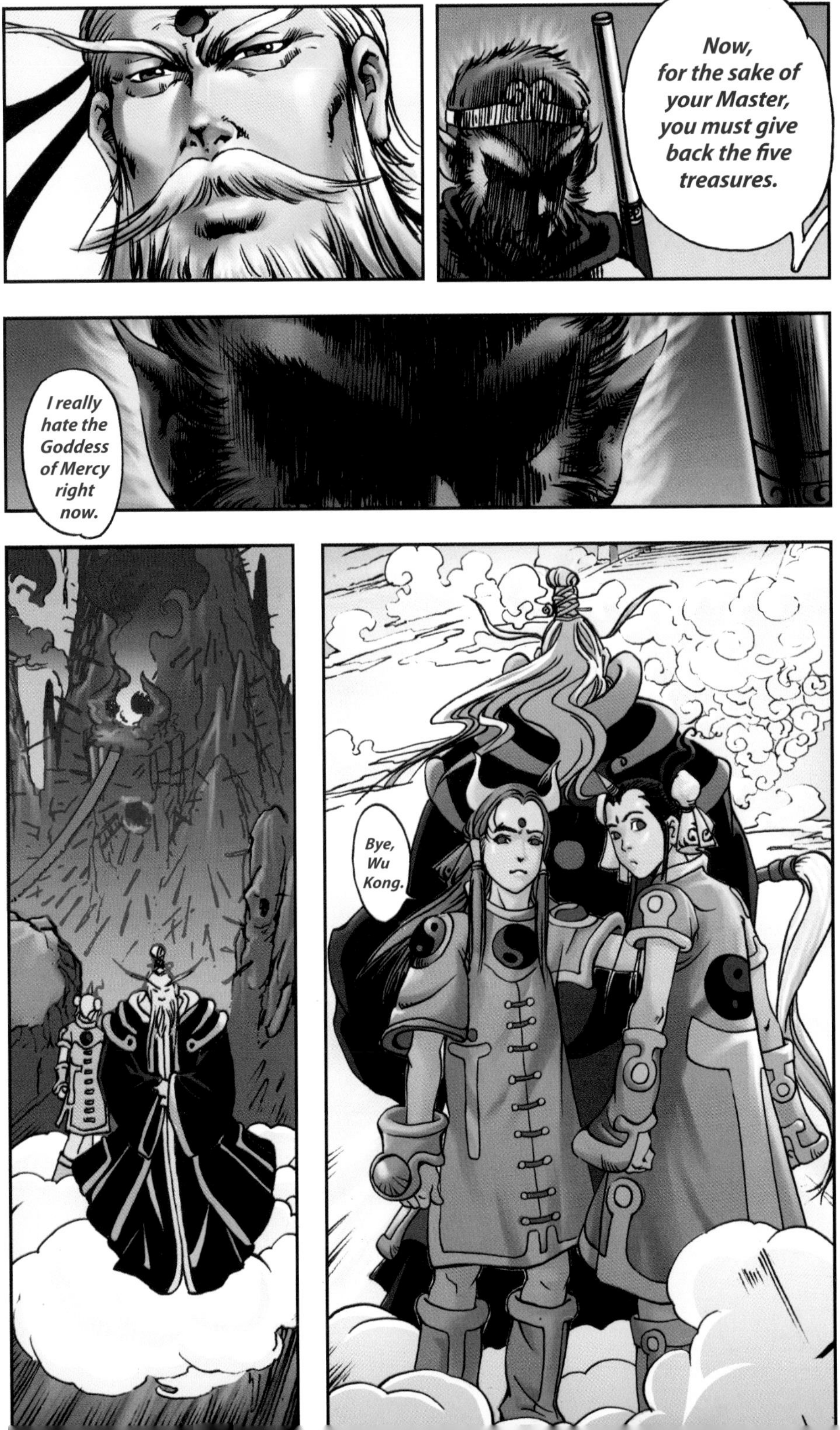
Now, for the sake of your Master, you must give back the five treasures.
I really hate the Goddess of Mercy right now.
Bye, Wu Kong.

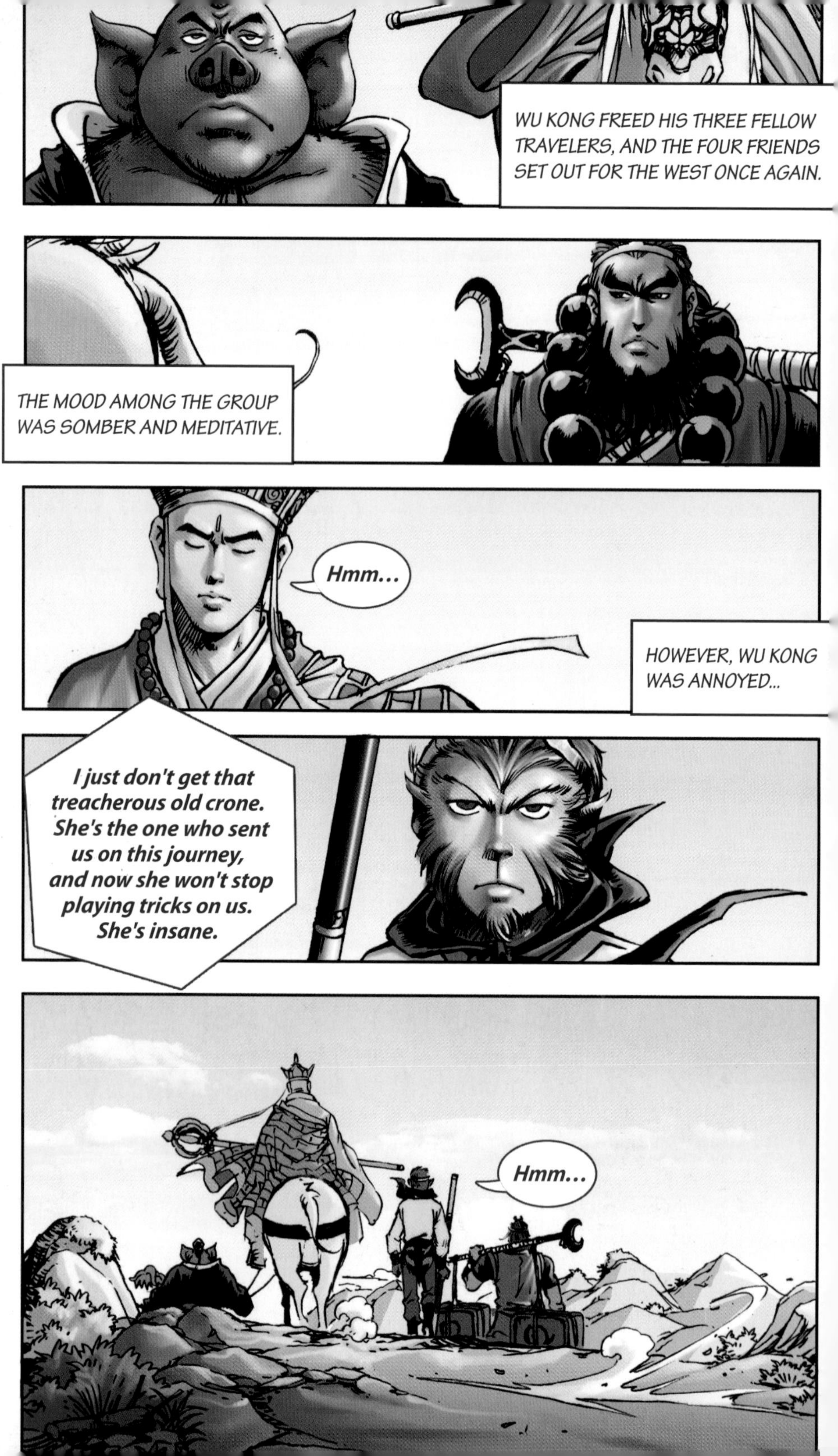
WU KONG FREED HIS THREE FELLOW TRAVELERS, AND THE FOUR FRIENDS SET OUT FOR THE WEST ONCE AGAIN.
THE MOOD AMONG THE GROUP WAS SOMBER AND MEDITATIVE.
Hmm...
HOWEVER, WU KONG WAS ANNOYED...
I just don't get that treacherous old crone. She's the one who sent us on this journey, and now she won't stop playing tricks on us. She's insane.
Hmm...

MONKEY KING

Appendix

—

TREASURES OF
THE MOUNTAIN KINGS

———

● *Having survived an encounter with the Yellow Robe Demon that nearly destroyed their fidelity, San Zang, Sun Wu Kong, Zhu Bajie, and Sha Wu Jing resume their journey to the West when they are approached by what appears to be a woodsman. The man warns the traveling companions that they are headed in the direction of Mount PingDing, dominion of two powerful monster kings who will kill them. He tells the group to return to where they came from; Zhu Bajie is quick to oblige. After delivering the hasty warning, the woodsman vanishes into thin air. Sun Wu Kong, sensing that the man was more than just a man, pursues him and discovers that the man was in fact the heavenly Guardian of Days, who merely wished to warn Wu Kong that they will be hunted by adversaries more powerful than any they have encountered thus far.*

Wu Kong heeds the warning, and quickly determines that the only way for them to survive is by ensuring that San Zang listens only to him, and not the foolish counsel of Zhu Bajie; after all, it was not long ago that Bajie's antagonism had encouraged San Zang to banish Wu Kong from the group. Wu Kong devises a plan by which he will ask Bajie to help him protect their master by going out on patrol to scout for monsters. Wu Kong predicts that Bajie will grow tired and fall asleep, only to return to the group and lie about having seen monsters.

When Wu Kong returns and asks Bajie to go on patrol, the pig agrees, and sure enough, within a short time of being on patrol he decides to take a nap. Wu Kong, who has been spying on Bajie in the disguise of a bird, attacks the pig's face, which wakes him up. Unable to sleep because of the vicious bird, Bajie makes up a story about seeing monsters and returns to San Zang. Wu Kong interrupts Bajie as he is telling the priest what he saw, and reveals that the pig is lying. San Zang reprimands Bajie, but urges Wu Kong to focus, for the moment, on facing the monsters of Mount PingDing. Bajie is sent out on patrol for a second time.

Meanwhile, in the caves beneath Mount PingDing, the Golden Horned King and his younger brother, the Silver Horned King, are awaiting San Zang's arrival. They have heard that eating San Zang's flesh will grant eternal life, so the Silver Horned King gathers his troops to patrol the mountain range and look for the priest. The first thing they discover is Bajie, still on patrol. He is quickly captured, but when king's men learn that the pig's flesh is not enchanted like the priest's, they are sent back out again.

This time, the silver king senses San Zang's presence and casts a spell to afflict the priest. To make his master feel better, Wu Kong clears a path through the rugged terrain. When this happens, the silver king sees Sun Wu Kong and, having heard of the monkey's power, decides not to attack outright. Instead, he orders his men to take cover and disguises himself as an injured guru who begs the group to help him. San Zang agrees, and Wu Kong, who can see that the guru is a monster in disguise, volunteers to carry the man on his back, in the hopes of carrying him out of sight and killing him. Before that can happen, though, the disguised monster king conjures three enormous mountains and buries Wu Kong beneath them. While the monkey struggles under the weight of the rock, his traveling companions are kidnapped.

San Zang and Wu Jing are brought to the lair of the two kings, who decide to throw an elaborate feast in which the priest will be the main course. First, though, they must capture Sun Wu Kong. The silver king dispatches two of his subjects, JingXi and LingLi, to retrieve the monkey. They are armed with two enchanted calabashes, which can be used to capture and melt a person.

In the mean time, Sun Wu Kong has been freed from under the three mountains by several guardian spirits, and is waiting in the disguise of a Taoist hermit when JingXi and LingLi arrive to retrieve him. They explain to him that they intend to capture Wu Kong by calling his name. When he answers, he will be sucked into the calabash and destroyed. The disguised Wu Kong hoodwinks the two henchmen into handing over their enchanted calabashes in exchange for a fake one that Wu Kong has. Wu Kong vanishes, leaving JingXi and LingLi to discover they've been conned.

Disguised as an insect, Wu Kong follows the pair back to the cave of Mount PingDing, where he learns that the two kings have invited their mother to the upcoming feast. Wu Kong then transforms into one of the messengers dispatched to bring her to the mountain and kills the other messengers. While bringing the mother to the feast, Wu Kong kills her and discovers that the mother is the notorious Nine-Tailed Fox Goblin. Wu Kong assumes her identity and joins the two kings for the feast. The kings take Wu Kong to visit the prisoners, and they are assessing their meal options when Bajie realizes that the old woman is Wu Kong in disguise. Wu Kong transforms back into himself and fights with the silver king, who subdues Wu Kong with the use of an enchanted golden rope. Although he is thrown in the dungeon with the others, Wu Kong quickly escapes and tries to pick a fight with the kings again. This time, in an attempt to defend himself against *the calabash he knows the kings will use against him, Wu Kong appears under the name Kong Wu Sun. The silver king challenges him to answer to the call of his name, and when the monkey does, he is sucked into the calabash. Unable to understand how this happened despite the different name, Wu Kong nonetheless escapes and steals the calabash he was just trapped in, switching it for a vase he has transfigured. He returns for a third time to confront the kings, this time under the name Wu Kong Sun and this time brandishing the enchanted calabash. When the silver king tries and fails to capture Wu Kong with the fake calabash, Wu Kong turns the tables and captures him.*

Enraged by the death of his family, the Golden Horned King leads his army into battle against Sun Wu Kong, who clones several hundreds of his hairs to fight the army. Wu Kong and his clones defeat the army, and Wu Kong captures the gold king in the enchanted calabash. His enemies defeated, Wu Kong is about to make off with all five of the enchanted treasures that the kings owned when Tai Shang appears and demands that Wu Kong return the treasures. It turns out that the monster kings are two of Tai Shang's disciples, chosen by the Buddhist Goddess of Mercy to become monsters in order to test Wu Kong and his friends on their journey. As the four friends continue on to the West, they are humble and introspective, but Sun Wu Kong is very angry with the Goddess...

A JOURNEY, NOT A DESTINATION

● *The Journey to the West depicts an odyssey undertaken by a monk of the Tang Dynasty and his three disciples, four unlikely companions who have been charged by the Buddhist Goddess of Mercy to travel to India and return with the sutras that will save humanity. Such an undertaking would be perilous by itself, but the Goddess of Mercy complicates matters by constantly introducing more obstacles and adversaries that cause the quartet to question the mission and one another. Why does she do this? When it is clear that this journey is extremely dangerous, why does the goddess further endanger the mission? The answer distinguishes Journey to the West from other comparable fables, and sheds light on the episodic nature of the story, which time and again fails to adhere to the tenets of the classic three-act structure.*

Many famous adventure stories center around a group of people seeking treasure. But unlike the heroes of similar works, the heroes of The Journey to the West do not seek a treasure that will make them materially wealthy, and recovering the treasure does not mean that the work will be done. Instead, the sacred sutras are a tool that, once brought back from the West by San Zang, will introduce people to a long and difficult path toward enlightenment. The sutras are a treasure that can only be measured in terms of spiritual wealth, and unlike the treasure of comparable works, their recovery will mark not so much an end as a beginning, and the heroes of the story will have their work cut out for them even once the journey is over.

In fact, the word "heroes," while appropriate for describing San Zang and his disciples, can be misleading if taken in the context of conventional heroism. In a traditional three-act story, a hero's shortcomings are revealed early on and vanquished by the story's end. But in Journey to the West, our heroes are continually falling victim to their weaknesses. San Zang is impatient and distrustful. Sun Wu Kong is vain and short-tempered. Zhu Bajie is gluttonous and selfish. Sha Wu Jing, while loyal, often refuses to come to the defense of his companions when there is an internal disagreement. The Goddess of Mercy recognizes in each of the four friends a tendency to fall into bad habits, so she continually introduces new obstacles to challenge the travelers in a number of different ways, and forces them to confront, if not necessarily overcome, their weaknesses. In doing this, the goddess is giving them an advanced education in what it will take to put the sutras into practice; she is teaching them about the true nature of life.

Ultimately, the repeated interferences by the Goddess of Mercy make The Journey to the West a story that is far more reflective of the real world. All too often, people overcome a certain weakness only to fall victim to it time and time again. The moral of the story is that life itself is a journey, and along the way there will be all kinds backward steps, even if you are a Buddhist priest or a monkey king. The key is to acknowledge weakness, and remember that the path to enlightenment is a continuous endeavor that requires constant attention and dedication.

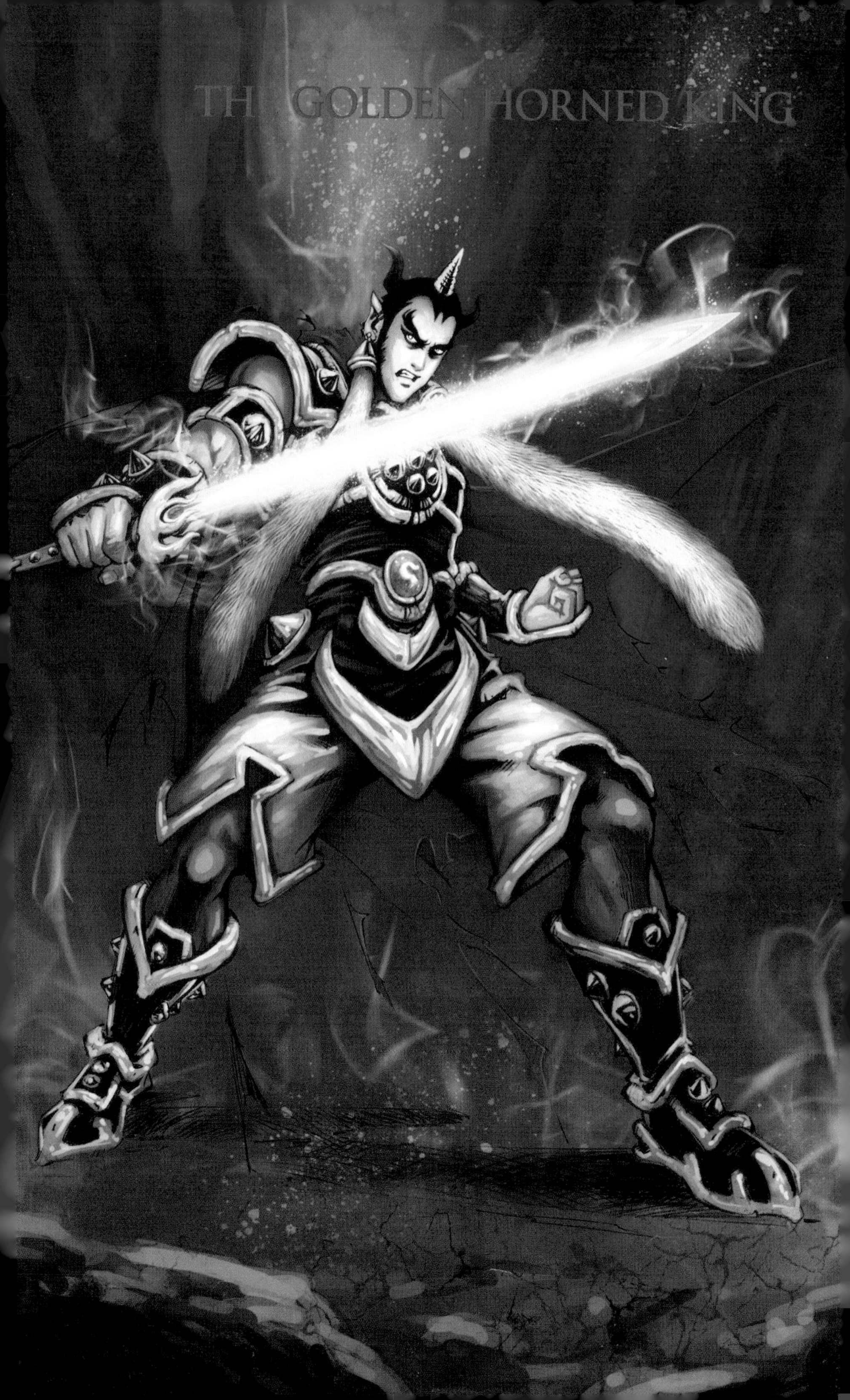
THE GOLDEN HORNED KING

Adventures from China MONKEY KING

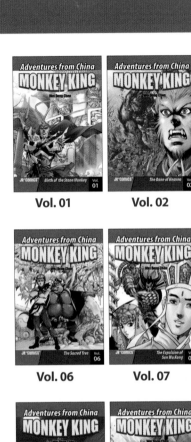

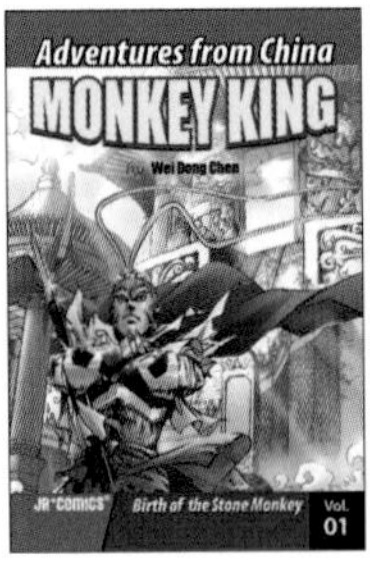
Adventures from China
MONKEY KING
Birth of the Stone Monkey
Vol. 01
Vol. 01

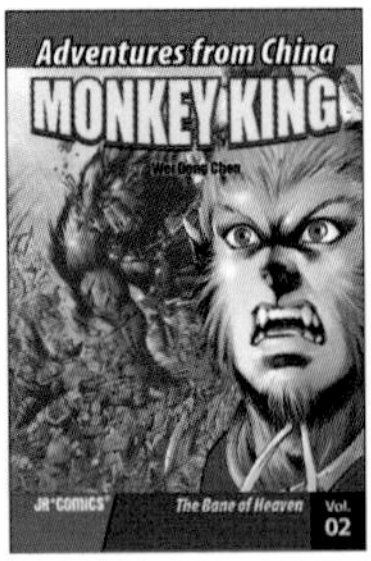
Adventures from China
MONKEY KING
The Bane of Heaven
Vol. 02
Vol. 02

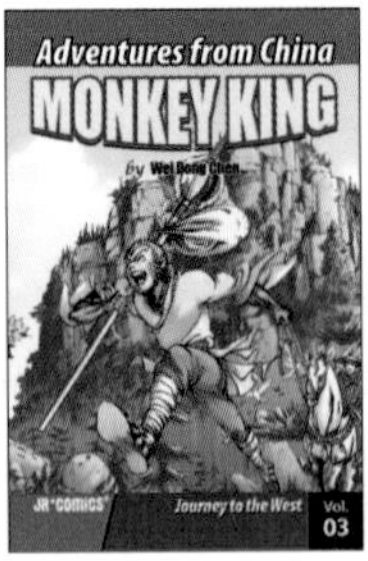
Adventures from China
MONKEY KING
Journey to the West
Vol. 03
Vol. 03

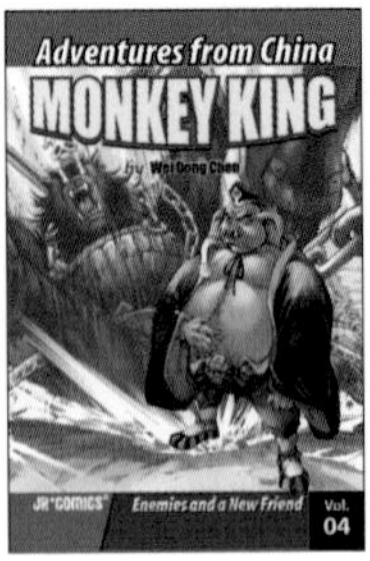
Adventures from China
MONKEY KING
Enemies and a New Friend
Vol. 04
Vol. 04

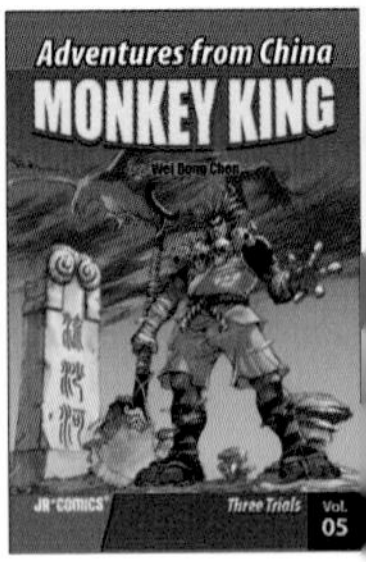
Adventures from China
MONKEY KING
Three Trials
Vol. 05
Vol. 05

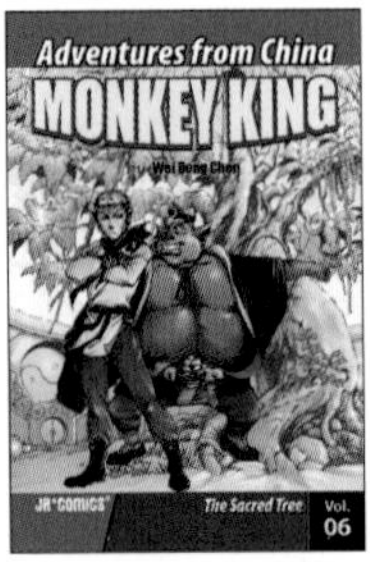
Adventures from China
MONKEY KING
The Sacred Tree
Vol. 06
Vol. 06

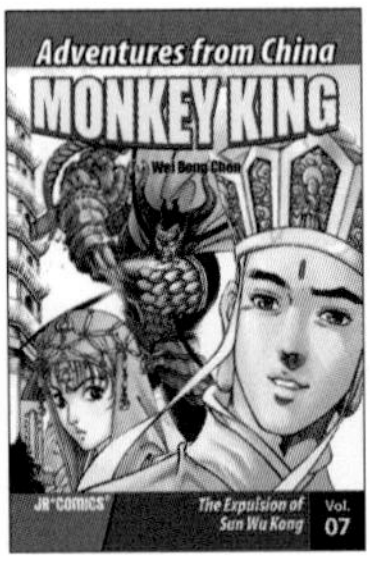
Adventures from China
MONKEY KING
The Expulsion of Sun Wu Kong
Vol. 07
Vol. 07

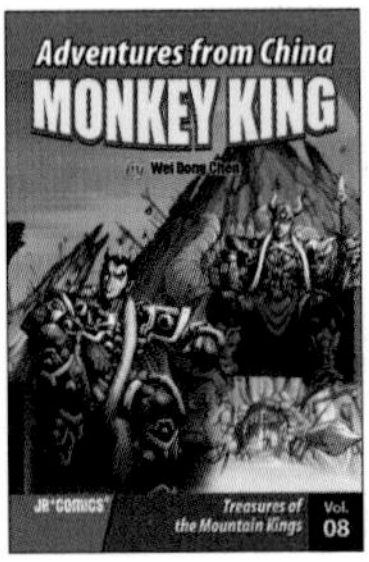
Adventures from China
MONKEY KING
Treasures of the Mountain Kings
Vol. 08
Vol. 08

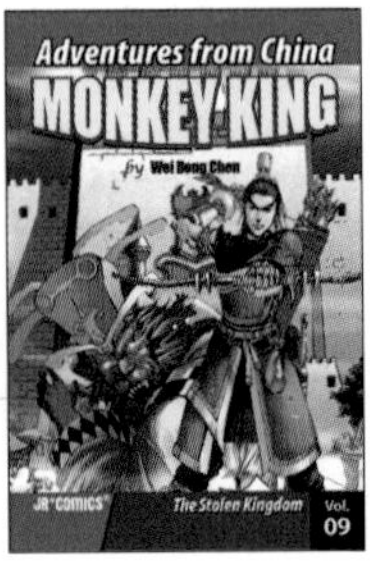
Adventures from China
MONKEY KING
The Stolen Kingdom
Vol. 09
Vol. 09

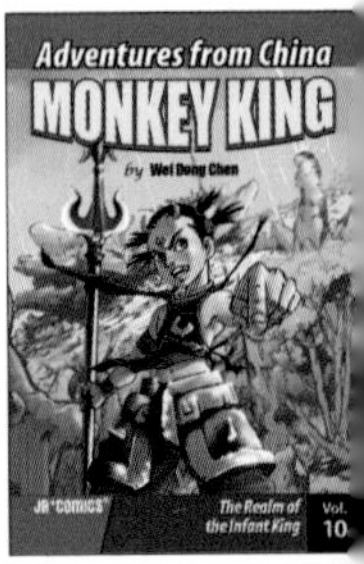
Adventures from China
MONKEY KING
The Realm of the Infant King
Vol. 10
Vol. 10

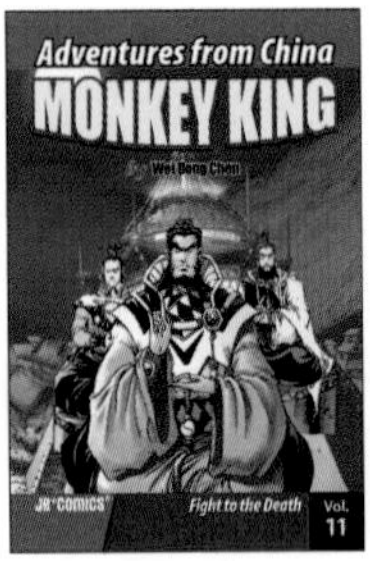
Adventures from China
MONKEY KING
Fight to the Death
Vol. 11
Vol. 11

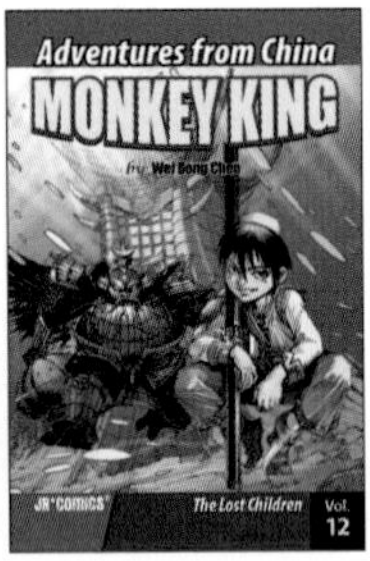
Adventures from China
MONKEY KING
The Lost Children
Vol. 12
Vol. 12

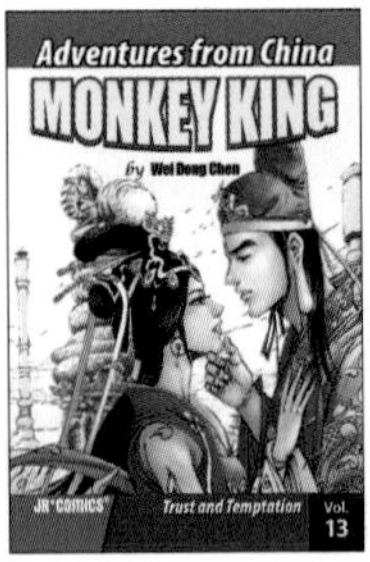
Adventures from China
MONKEY KING
Trust and Temptation
Vol. 13
Vol. 13

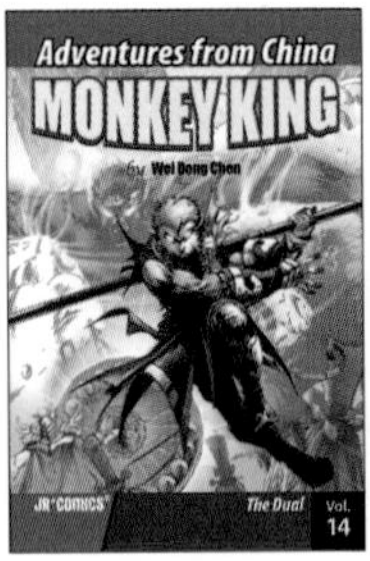
Adventures from China
MONKEY KING
The Dual
Vol. 14
Vol. 14

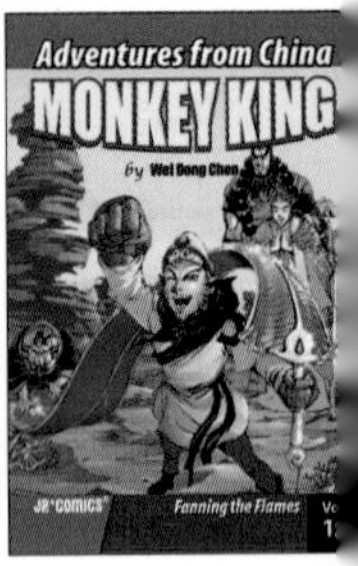
Adventures from China
MONKEY KING
Fanning the Flames
Vol. 15

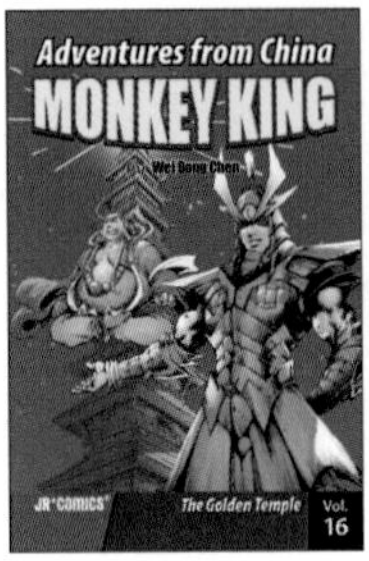
Adventures from China
MONKEY KING
The Golden Temple
Vol. 16
Vol. 16

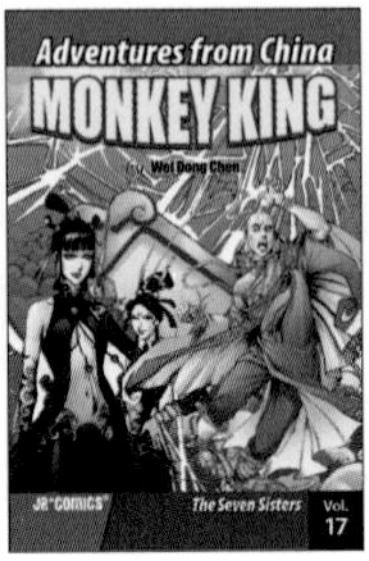
Adventures from China
MONKEY KING
The Seven Sisters
Vol. 17
Vol. 17

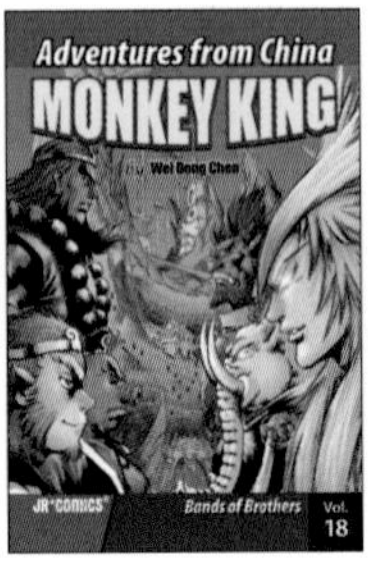
Adventures from China
MONKEY KING
Bands of Brothers
Vol. 18
Vol. 18

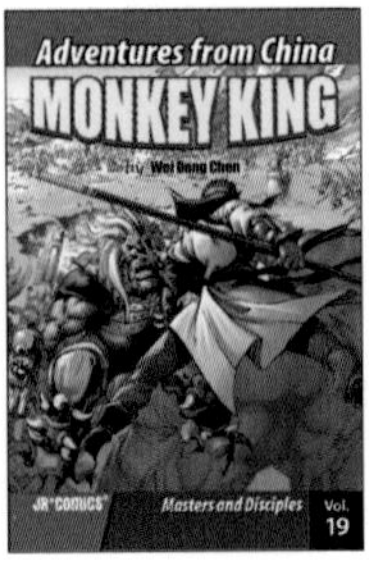
Adventures from China
MONKEY KING
Masters and Disciples
Vol. 19
Vol. 19

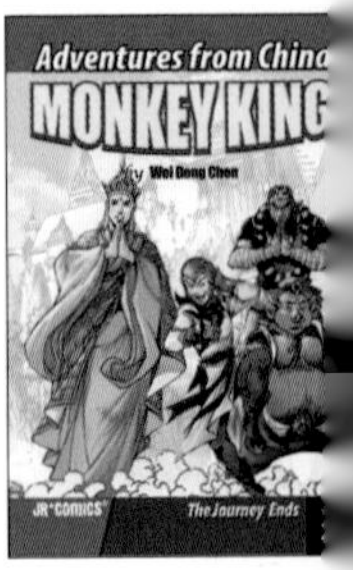
MONKEY KING
The Journey Ends
Vol. 20